THE
LEFT-HANDED
MARRIAGE

THE
LEFT-HANDED
MARRIAGE

Leigh Buchanan
Bienen

Ontario Review Press ✦ Princeton, NJ

Ontario Review Press
9 Honey Brook Drive
Princeton, NJ 08540

Distributed by W.W. Norton & Co., Inc.
500 Fifth Avenue
New York, NY 10110

Library of Congress Cataloging-in-Publication Data

Bienen, Leigh B.
    The left-handed marriage / Leigh Buchanan Bienen. — 1st ed.
        p. cm.
    ISBN 0-86538-102-X (alk. paper)
        I. Title.

PS3552.I35 L4 2001
813'.6—dc21

                                                            00-052415

First Edition

ACKNOWLEDGMENTS

Many of these stories first appeared, sometimes in earlier forms, in the following publications: "My Life as a West African Gray Parrot" and "He Was a Big Boy, Still Is" in *Ontario Review*; "To China" and "Technician" in *TriQuarterly*; "We Are All Africans" in *Mississippi Review*; "The First Secretary" in *Panache*; "My Mothers' Lovers" in *Descant*. "My Life as a West African Gray Parrot" was reprinted in *The O. Henry Awards*. "To China" was published in Chinese in *Chung Wai Literary Monthly*, translation by Yanbing Chen.

The author gratefully acknowledges the generous support of the MacDowell Colony, The Yaddo Corporation, and the Blue Mountain Center. Large parts of this volume were written during residencies at these places. The author also wishes to thank Northwestern University for its continuing support.

For Henry, and all our wonderful family,
who are my solace and inspiration, and with
gratitude for a life of reading and writing.

CONTENTS

THE
LEFT-HANDED
MARRIAGE

My Life as a
West African Gray Parrot

I

The dark, I am in the dark. They have put the green cloth over my cage. I am in the dark once again. I smell the acrid felt. I smell the green of transitions, the particles of dust in the warp of the fabric which remind me of forests and terror. I am in the dark. I shall never fly again. Even my masterful imitation of the electric pencil sharpener will not pierce the dark. My master and mistress are talking in the corridor. "That will shut it up," she says, knocking the aluminum pan against the porcelain sink and causing me, as she knows, pain.

My cage sits on a squat wooden table in a room facing the kitchen. The smell of roasting pig sickens me, although the odor of tomatoes and basil reminds me of my duty to God. My mistress does not recognize my powers. She calls from the kitchen, "What do you know, plucked chicken?" A visitor thoughtfully suggests the parrot might like the door shut while she sniffles her way through the cutting of onions. Worse, they leave open the water-closet door, shouting things to one another from within. The animal odors do not offend me, but my master sprays a poisonous antiseptic on the fixtures which irritates my sensitive nostrils and threatens my divine coloration. The red of my tail will fade in fumes of ammonia or chlorine.

Like blood, the color of my red tail has its own startling quality. This extraordinary color makes my red feathers magical. The red is a vivid crimson which glows from across the room. The red is the source of my power, my beauty, which I possess only briefly. The red is set off by its contrast to the pearl gray of my breast. The ivory white skin around my eyes, and the gunmetal gray of my chipped beak. The feathers on my back shade to light gray at the root, leaving a line of charcoal along the knife's edge of my wing feathers.

It is difficult to remember how beautiful I once was. The silken gray feathers falling over a young, full breast in layers as delicate as the tracery of a waterfall, each hue of gray, each smudge of crimson in subtle harmony with he rest. Now only the surprising crimson remains, the purest blue-red of my tail and the hints of the same crimson in my remaining wing feathers. Now to my mistress's distress I have plucked my breast almost clean. Pink dots appear where the oval pinfeathers were. Tiny blood flecks materialize from my pores like crimson teardrops, but not like the crimson of my tail. This urge to destroy myself and my unbearable beauty comes over me in spurts and impedes my progress. In a rush I grab five, six or seven feathers and pull them out in a flurry. The pain is delicious. The mistress shrieks at me from the kitchen when she catches me at it: "Stop picking, filthy bird." But she cannot separate me from myself. Only I possess the engine to destroy my own beauty.

My master and mistress purchased me because they had been told I could talk. The owner of the pet store, a fat Indian with one milky blind eye, pulled out my red tailfeathers and sold them one by one. He told my master and mistress I could talk, not because he believed it but because recently I had bitten his finger through to the knuckle. He believed a parrot's bite was a curse. This same fat Indian failed to mention the magical qualities which caused my feathers to be valued by those who bought and sold in windowless back rooms. My master and mistress praised my beauty with awe while the Indian, slumped in a small wooden chair in the back storeroom, wondered if he would catch a vile infection from my nasty bite.

The master and mistress proudly carried me home and installed me in a large cage on a table in the dining room, on top of a figured blue carpet and beside a tall window which let in the creamy winter light through white silk curtains. The cat came and curled up in a puddle of sunlight beneath my cage. At first the master and mistress fussed continually over my placement by the window. When the sun went down, at a remarkably early hour every afternoon, the master would jump up and pull the curtains shut. "The breeze will kill the bird," he shouted at his wife, as if she were not in the room. In reply she insisted that cold was no worry. She had seen pictures of parrots in the Jardin des Plantes shaking snowflakes off their wings. "But the draft, the draft, there must not be a draft," she shrieked. As the winter days shortened and became increasingly pale, this exchange was repeated. A small machine was installed in the dining room. Its angry red coils created a suffocating dryness which by itself almost catapulted me into my next incarnation. The heat radiating from those disagreeable wires bore no resemblance to the warmth of sunlight in my African jungle.

In those days a perch stood alongside my cage. On some afternoons, at the time when the winter light was strongest, my mistress would open the cage door allowing me to climb out onto the wooden perch, where I could stretch one wing then another slowly downward towards the floor. If the master was out, my mistress would sit down at the dining room table and recite speeches at me. The same sonorous words over and over. Her diction was beyond reproach on these occasions. Once she taped her voice and played it beside my cage for the entire day. I added to my repertoire the sibilant sounds of plastic across metal as the tape rewound itself on the white disc. Instead of her cultured tones I preferred the syncopated accents of the immigrant cleaning lady who muttered lilting obscenities as she scoured a shine into the inlaid tabletops in the living room.

During this early period I often whispered aloud, laughed, or simply whistled. The master and mistress were amazed when my laughter coincided with their amusement. They did not understand that laughter is a form of crying, that we laugh to keep our perception of the world from crumbling. My own laughter is a hollow chuckle, a sinister and frightening sound, recognizable as a laugh by its mirthlessness. When humans laugh they add wheezes and croaks to mask the sadness of laughter. My master and mistress do not yet understand that the highest form of communication is wordless, achieved by a glance upward or a bestial grunt, by the perception of a change in the rhythm of breathing, or by a blink of an eye, in my case the flicker of a brown membrane between lashless lids.

When visitors came into the dining room they used to remark, to the pleasure of my master and mistress: "Look! How it stares back at you." Meaning, they were surprised. My yellow eye pierced through whatever image they had manufactured of themselves, images of purpose and the aura of an imminent, important appointment which was constructed by a high, excited tone of voice. My yellow eyes can see behind a necklace of stones to the throb at the throat, behind thick tweed to the soft folds of the belly, to the dark roots of hair which has been falsely hennaed to a color which is a poor imitation of the red wings of the Amazonian parrot.

The guests were always amazed. At dinner advertising men and women in public relations were encouraged to speculate upon whether my mobile and bony throat (not yet exposed by picking) or my knobby, black tongue produced such extraordinary sounds. The mistress asked pensively: "Imagine how the bird speaks." The master replied with gravity: "The consonance between words and meaning is illusory."

At her urging they called in an expert in the field of Parrot Linguistics, a spectacled man who wore a Russian suit with wide, waving trousers. The mistress served him tea in a glass with a slice of lemon on the saucer. The man removed his thick glasses and examined the white papery skin surrounding my beak and nostrils. My beak was chipped, but he only commented, "I see nothing unusual about the beak or throat of this parrot."

"His tongue," my mistress urged, "look at his tongue. The bird has an exceptionally long and globular black tongue."

The expert had already donned his baggy jacket and removed his spectacles. "Yes," he said, "it is unusual for a bird to encompass such a wide range of laughter."

My imitations of the human voice exactly reproduced individual intonations. The precision of my imitation of the Polish servant rendered my mistress speechless with jealousy. Erroneously, the copywriters concluded mimicry was the source of my magic, and they congratulated my mistress on acquiring such a rare and amusing pet. In those early days of enthusiasm my mistress would wipe her finely manicured fingers upon a paper towel and scratch my skull, murmuring, "Now Polly, poor Polly, here Polly." In those days they both fed me tidbits from their table, corners of toast dripping with honey, a half-eaten peach with chunks of amber flesh still clinging to the pit, or the thigh bone of a chicken, a treat of which I remain inordinately fond. I would sidestep over, slide down the metal bars of my cage with my head lowered, and take the tidbit in one curled claw.

The mistress carefully saved all of my red feathers in those days, picking them out from the newspaper shreds with her long red fingernails. She put them in a box of tooled leather and closed the lid so that the incandescence of red would not startle a stranger who happened to walk into the room. Later they became so alienated from the source of my beauty, and so quarrelsome, they no longer took pleasure or strength from the color of my tailfeathers. They even forgot to lock my cage and sometimes carelessly left the door open after shaking a few seeds hastily into my dish. During the earlier phase they were proud to possess me. They purchased bird encyclopedias and left them open on the table turned to pages with pictures of parrots. The painted drawing of the yellow-headed Amazon intrigued me and greatly contributed to my education. Feathers of the palest lemon cascaded down from the top of the head ending in a ring of creamier yellow around the neck. The white cockatoos also inspired envy, especially for the flecks of fine pink and light yellow which tinged their wings. I admired their crests, feathers as a flag to the world, and the white back feathers which had the sheen of ancient silk. Another source of wonder were the many-hued black parrots from South America, so advanced in beauty they are rarely glimpsed even by their own kind.

Now when they stand beside my cage, my master and mistress only discuss the price I will fetch. "Is it eight hundred dollars?" he asks. "The last advertisement in the paper had one listed at eight hundred dollars." My mistress is greedier, but also more practical. "It will fetch more at an auction," she answers, "when people bid against each other in competition."

The refusal to acknowledge my sexual identity is a special humiliation. I laid an egg to announce my essentially female nature. Now that she hates and fears me, my mistress always refers to me in the impersonal third person. I have long since been moved away from the dining room, into a small dark room no bigger than a closet. The tiny unwashed window faces a bleak, blank wall of brick, and the door to a dark and dusty closet stands open behind my cage. The mistress uses my room for storage. The abandoned wire torso of a dress frame is a cage shaped in the outline of a woman. A broken vacuum cleaner lies coiled in permanent hibernation in one corner. Portraits of forgotten ancestors, who willed their property to other branches of the family, stand facing the wall. My cage is now cleaned only once a week. The room is too mean even to serve as an adequate storage facility.

The fat, neutered gray cat no longer likes to visit me because there is no rug on the floor and the room is unheated. She curls herself in front of the refrigerator, where a small warm exhaust is continuously expelled from the motor. We exchange remarks about the deplorable spiritual condition of our custodians. The striped gray cat and I together speculate upon whether or not the master and mistress will in their next incarnation understand the power of red, as distinct from the power of blood, the sole power which now strikes fear in their hearts. Both the master and mistress show a measurable anger when the tiny flecks of blood appear against my gray skin. My blood is either light pink or a droplet of burgundy, both distinct from the singing crimson of my tail. When my mistress concluded that the picking was going to continue she began to think of ways to get rid of me. But she would not consider letting me go at a loss.

II

It is difficult for me to remember the jungle, the sun in Africa, or my days in the dark pet shop owned by the blind-eyed Indian. My journey must be almost finished, for only the young command memories. In my native jungle parrots are caught by blindfolded boys who climb to the tree-tops and rob the nests of their chicks. The mothers swoop down, diving with their gray and white heads tucked under, as they shriek their protest. They will attack and tear the flesh as the bald chicks disappear into a knotted cloth held in the teeth of a boy who shimmies down the trunk as fast as he can. The parrots beat their red-flecked wings around the heads of the nest robbers, biting an ear, frantically flying from branch to branch as they accompany the marauders to the edge of the forest with high-pitched screams. The village boys are blindfolded because they believe they will be struck blind if they look into a parrot's nest. To these people we have long been recognized as magic birds, lucky birds, or birds which carry a curse. And now we are almost extinct.

With six other featherless shivering chicks who died within a week I was brought to a pet shop in the middle of the urban sprawl which constitutes a city outside the jungle. The owner placed me in a cage on top of a teetering pile of small cages. One contained a banded snake with a festering hole in his side, another held a monkey with a crippled arm. There were also green parrots and yellow ones from neighboring forests.

Eventually I became an ornament in the compound of a king, living in a gilded cage on a vast veranda shaded by a roof of woven rattan. Every evening a servant boy peeled me an enormous rainbow-colored mango. My cage was a tall cylinder, large enough to fly across and decorated with tin bells and wooden totems. Visitors came especially to admire me from a distance. They did not press their faces within inches of my nostrils, oppressing me with the odor of skin. They stood back to gaze at my feathers and offered me meat. Like worshippers, they came in formal dress. The women were wrapped in cloth of bright blue, and the men wore flowing gold-embroidered gowns which swayed and brushed the floor as they walked rapidly towards me across the veranda. Another parrot was resident in this royal household. She taught me bearing, demeanor and style. She had been the property of kings through three generations. She remembered kings who had been forgotten by their heirs and successors, and her beautiful piercing whistle caused all those within earshot to stop talking and listen to her call. When she was found dead at the bottom of her cage one morning they buried her with incense and incantations, mourning her loss with ancient, certain ceremonies.

The royal family also had a dog, a brown cur with an extraordinarily long and ugly hairless tail. The dog had to be locked inside the royal compound, or he would have been eaten by the many hungry people outside the walls. The cur was fat, and the urchins who roamed the mud streets in packs would have snatched him for roasting or stewing. The animal was so dispirited and envious of the esteem in which parrots were held that he spent hours lying beside our large golden cage discussing philosophy. The youngest daughter of the king occasionally came barefoot onto the veranda and held his head on her lap while she fed him morsels of goat.

Finally he became so fat and arthritic he could not climb the steps to the veranda. His view was that the vicissitudes of fate he suffered in this epoch were haphazard. In the next generation, he expressed this opinion while lying panting on the cool clay floor, it would be dogs with long tails, instead of birds with red feathers, who would be offered raw meat and worshipped for their wisdom. Who knows, he remarked with a supercilious snarl, whether or not the privileges you now enjoy because of your divine coloration will not be given to those with visible ears? He often called attention to his long, bald tail as if the tail by itself should have entitled him to all that he envied. On drowsy tropical afternoons my partner and I humored him by appearing to take these notions seriously.

III

It is true that when I strike I wound. I bit the finger of a small dirty boy to the bone when he poked a yardstick through the bars of my cage. His mother and my mistress were whispering in the kitchen, and they both ignored my shrieks of warning. The boy ran squawking in pain to his mother, and my embarrassed mistress banged the metal bars of my cage with a metal fork, shouting reproaches. The startled mother held her son to her breast and pressed a linen handkerchief of my master's to his limp finger. Furred tentacles of crimson stretched out along threads of cotton and silently eliminated the white between. The sniffling boy looked at me, where I was shivering in the farthest corner of my cage, and signalled his triumph.

I miss the treats, especially the blue-red marrow of chicken bones, which my mistress used to give me in an attempt to make me recite her name. In those days I used to climb upon the back of her hand. She held out her fist with the painted nails curled under, and I could feel her wince when I placed one gray claw and then the other against her skin. I uncoiled my talons to avoid cutting into the flesh of her hand and balanced myself by hooking onto the cage with my beak. She feared I would turn and strike for no reason, and her wrist would stiffen. At such times I was swept away by the sense of her as another living creature, myself at an earlier stage of development. This involuntary response filled me with sadness, for I thought of the generations and generations which remained before her, and I moved away from her hand and huddled on my perch, mourning as she soaped her hands at the kitchen sink. I no longer try to reach her, except with whistles and catcalls, for I know she has come to hate me. Sometimes I receive a reply. She will turn on the radio or rustle the newspaper in an answer.

If nothing else a cage has walls to climb. When my mistress enters the room I take my hooked beak and spill the seeds out of my plastic dish and onto the floor. I can spill almost all of my food in one angry gesture. My beak along the railings makes an insistent, drumming sound which never fails to evoke a click of annoyance from my mistress. When she leaves I slide down the bars and pick out sunflower seeds, the tiny grains of millet, and especially those very small twigs from among the shreds of newspaper. Sometimes my mistress and master discuss my fate in the corridor, using sign language. I can hear the faint rustle of sleeves as they gesture in the hallway. But I rarely listen. I am dreaming of my next life now. The cat curls up in front of the vent of the icebox. We plan together. She licks her paw, passes it over one ear, then her eye, softly.

I can still not resist music, especially the soprano tones. The high notes bring back memories of the sadness of being human. Until the music plays I can convince myself that I have reached a point where memories could no longer overcome me, a point where my feathers offer complete protection. But at the height of a melodic line I hide in the farthest corner of my cage, assaulted by emotions. The beauty of singing strikes home, into the depths of my parrot's heart. I relive my human life, the fears and promises of childhood, the exhilaration of striving, and the limited peace which settles in the breast on rare occasions. I surpass the highest notes with my own high-pitched shriek.

At first my mistress was delighted with these performances, calling the neighbors to witness. Later she shut the door when the radio played music, as if to keep me away from something. The music which I heard faintly from behind the closed door inspired me to dream, and when I sang I swooned, losing my footing on the perch, falling fluttering to the iron grate at the bottom of my cage. The music transported me back to the high trees of the rain forest where parrots flew from limb to limb high above the shrieking of monkeys, never leaving the shadowed protection of branches.

IV

The Attack. It came so startlingly that my screams of pain and fright escaped without thought. A large rat had crept from the alleyway, through the old crumbling walls of our city house, into a crawlspace in the closet of my dark room. The door of my cage had been carelessly left open. The gray beast with brown ferret eyes slithered his soft fat body up the table leg and into my cage. He stuck his black snout into my food, spilling the seeds, and proceeded to stalk me with a coldblooded ruthlessness born of generations of experience. In spite of his aged, spoiled softness, the beast struck swiftly, efficiently, with one bite after another, striking my wing, my leg, my throat, then pulling away from my reach. His rat snout twitched and the small dappled spots on his back quivered as he flattened himself to pounce once again at my neck, my throat. Shrieking, bleeding, I beat my wings helplessly against the inside of the cage. Feathers were everywhere. Blood splattered on the unclean walls from a bite on my chest, an open wound in my leg, and from a hole in my wing. In two bites he had pulled out all of my red tailfeathers. Aiming for the eye of the lumbering beast—in spite of his waddling gait, I could not place a fatal blow he was so insulated with fat—I bit the soft rubbery flesh of his nose. I dug my claws into the well-fed muscular shoulder until he turned his head and with bared buck teeth bit off one talon and a large part of the toe above it. Wounded, he went into retreat, his hairless tail threading its way around the door frame of the closet.

The attack must have been brief although my wounds were many. The vision of relentless, reasonless destruction remained: a fat waddling beast baring rodent teeth as he came to trap me in the corner of my cage. Hours later my mistress returned and found me shivering and barely alive, crouched on the bottom of my cage. At the sight of the blood, the scattered red and gray feathers, my mistress was distraught, especially when she realized her personal carelessness had exposed me to a danger which neither of us realized had been ever present.

For days and nights I was only aware of the electric light clicking on and off at intervals. My mistress, perhaps only regretting the loss of her financial investment, sat beside my cage and wept with a depth of feeling which kindled surprise even in my semiconscious state. Other visitors came and peered at me anxiously through the bars. Those who had marvelled at my feats of imitation came now to stand silently in front of my cage, disapprovingly clucking their tongues over the pity of it.

My bite wounds stopped bleeding almost immediately, but the shock to my spirit had been profound. Worse, a silent, raging infection daily gained upon me. Soon I could only rest my beak on the bottom rungs of my cage. Finally I could no longer stand. I simply crouched in a corner at the bottom of my cage and rested my head against the bars cursing the demon beast of destruction. I could no longer sing, speak or whistle. Every red feather was gone, and my wing and chest, where the feathers had been pulled out, were bare and covered with festering sores.

In the middle of the night my mistress took me to the veterinarian's hospital in the heart of the city, a large facility associated with an old and famous zoo. Although I could no longer raise my head, I felt no localized pain. A young man with a beard and a white coat picked me up in a towel, held me under a bright light, and put a stethoscope to my heart. With my last quantum of strength I flapped my mutilated wings in protest. Then the blessed darkness, my cage left on an antiseptic stainless-steel table, as the doctor switched off the bright light overhead behind him.

In the hospital it was impossible to distinguish night from day. The veterinarian in the white coat, his soft black eyes and his black beard made it difficult to determine his age, treated me with injections, ointments, and powerful medicines, monitoring my blood every few days. My leg was put in a splint and photographed. A milky white substance was applied to the open sores on my breast and wings. The veterinarian sat in front of my cage and talked softly to me as he wrote his day's reports in soft, smudgy pencil on a mimeographed form. When he looked up at me, so clinically, after scratching something on a paper attached to a clipboard, the vision of gray destruction was momentarily dispelled. Under his care I slowly began to regain my strength.

My mistress came to visit on occasion, although she hardly spoke or looked at me when she came. While I limped gingerly to the edge of the cage door, she would talk to the young girl whose function it was to inform the doctors of any unexpected events in the ward. In this large acrid room with concrete floors and row after row of cages, crises were frequent. Not all could be saved. My immediate neighbors were a white cat with cancer whose stomach had been shaved bare to expose a line of cross-stitches like teeth marks across her pale, pale pink skin, a dog whose back leg had been amputated so skillfully that if he stood in profile on his good side his silhouette looked whole, and a one-hundred-year-old yellow crested cockatoo whose anemia had been caused by a diet of nothing but sunflower seeds for over fifty years. She had been sent to the zoo for an evaluation by the heirs to an estate when she passed hands after the death of the old couple who bought her on their honeymoon in a pre-war London flea market.

During the latter part of my recuperation I was placed in a green-domed aviary in the zoo along with other tropical birds. The domed enclosure imitated the wild, which did not, I thought, properly prepare the displaced birds for spiritual progression through containment. Their instincts to fly, to be free, were inappropriately encouraged. Attitudes of confinement and limitation, required for passage onwards, were thwarted. In spite of my condition, I myself was overcome with a memory and desire for flight when I entered the dome, even though it had been years since I had been let out of my cage. The memory of flying overcame me with an exhilarating rush of recognition. To fly, to be free, to soar on a current of wind, seductive memories took over before I was able to re-establish the distance I had learned to impose at great cost to my spirit. The sunlight filtered through the green glass dome and through the imported foliage. I was unused to the soft, almost liquid light, unlike the dark chill of my room.

The tropical birds in the zoo immediately recognized that, unlike them, I had not been born in captivity. I was taken from the wild. Some had ancestors who were wild, but most, the exception being one all-black Amazonian parrot, were born in zoos, pet stores, or aviaries. They could not hope to compete with my heritage as the idol of kings. Two other members of my own species displayed themselves on a palm branch near the top of the green glass dome, showing that even in these circumstances they had learned to restrain from flight. One had a fine assortment of red flecks in the wing he stretched downward for my inspection.

I continued to hop away on my good leg, flap my wings and shriek at the touch of a human, but I knew I owed my resuscitation to the skill and expertise of the dark-eyed doctor. Those gentle educated fingers had deduced what was needed to make me well. His knowledge was the opposite of mine, gained measuring things outside of himself, mine the mastery of the mysteries within.

The creamy chill of winter passed into the shy green of spring. The doctor considered me well enough to go home. My mistress came and carefully listened to his instructions. The doctor never commented upon the cause of my injury, but upon arriving back in the apartment I saw the hole in the closet wall had been hastily covered over with a piece of plywood and a few nails.

After my stay in the hospital my mistress began covering my cage at night, perhaps because my laughter in the dark unnerved her, perhaps to protect her investment. Those occasional shrieks at midnight, attempts to discover if there were kindred spirits in the neighborhood, might have been frightening. One evening the mistress bustled into my small room with a large piece of green felt. It was an especially unusual occurrence because she rarely came close to my cage now, asking the master or even a casual visitor to sprinkle a few seeds into my dish. The first time she walked in with the cover she threw it without warning over my cage as I hissed and flapped my wings. Then she slammed the door shut.

My age, my great age weighs heavily upon me when the cover floats down over the cage for the night. The cover stills my voice, blocks out my vision of even this closet where I will be confined for the rest of my parrot life, unless I am rescued by a stroke of fortune or sold again. If another epoch is coming when parrots are worshipped and fed mangoes and red meat, I do not think I will live to see it. My fate will be to die in this tiny cage, surrounded by my own filth, without love, and reliant upon a natural enemy for conversation. The snow outside makes the wall behind my cage as chill as the marble of tombstones, and I long for the damp warmth of the jungle. What joy have I except the joy of my own whistle? Sometimes the city birds answer my imitations of their calls. Soon I shall be beyond the need to communicate, at a level where I recognize that the attempt to pass messages between living things is as foolish as words. In my next life I will live for five hundred years in a form which is incapable of development or destruction. Perhaps then the dog with his long tail will have assumed my position as teacher, scholar and despised pet, and the cat will be left to sleep undisturbed in the limbo of sunlight.

The master and mistress are huddled together in bed now, happy to know I am temporarily silenced. I hear the creak of the springs, a cough, the single click of the light switch, which I answer perfectly. I shut one yellow eye and wait for the morning.

To China

June 10, 1985
Hotel Okura, Tokyo

B. scheduled two days in Tokyo to pick up the materials for the production that we wouldn't be able to get in China. Extra electronic parts, duplicate sound equipment, fabrics. The flight was twelve hours. Narita is still the cleanest airport in the world. When we landed a high-pitched female voice on the loudspeaker asked very politely, again and again, for anyone with a rash or a skin ailment or cough or fever to report please to the quarantine authorities. Two years ago it was the symptoms for toxic shock.

I'm glad for the two-day layover. I am exhausted. If the commitment hadn't been made two years ago, I am not sure I would have come. I never quite recovered from the flu this spring, and I did hate to leave you. Did I say how much I love the little silver clock with the jumping fish on the top? Every time I change the time, which will be often in the next six weeks, I will think of you. It nestles in my hand very comfortably.

It is a great privilege to work with B. again, although he is as impossible as ever. On the twelve-hour flight he didn't stop talking for ten minutes. He talked all the way to San Francisco, straight through the two dreadful movies shown back to back, and up to the inedible American breakfast served just before landing. Finally, I started ordering brandy. Now I'm paying for it, by having to stay in the hotel room with a bad stomach. You've heard all the stories before, and so have I. The three wives. How each betrayed

him. Still, he is a genius. Then, after the wives, his work. Now the
critics just shower praise on him because of his past success. He
can't trust anyone to give him honest criticism. That's why he
organized this trip to China, or so he says. To touch an audience
again. To escape the incestuous theatrical world of New York. At
least I can be honest about his work. He's never been better. At
fifty-seven he's in full command of his powers and doing more
exciting things than anybody else in the business.

By the way, he knows you don't like him. He isn't stupid.
Besides, you can't dislike him. Did I ever tell you, I'm sure I did,
that when I first came to New York thirty years ago, he gave me my
first professional job. I was fresh out of the University of Chicago
and working in an advertising agency for the summer. That's what
bright-eyed young college graduates in the arts did in those days.
I still don't know what B. saw in me. We met at a party. Of course
I knew who he was. He already had his own company, although he
was only ten years older than I was. Anyway, he offered me a job.
Just like that. The job had a title, Assistant Producer. It turned out
there wasn't anybody to be assistant to, and he hadn't yet found a
way to pay me a salary. Never mind. I worked for him for the next
ten years, learned everything I knew from him. Those were
wonderful years, and I never left New York. But you know the
story of the break-up of the company. I wasn't the only one who got
out then.

I have never stayed at a more efficient hotel. At six in the
morning they bring you a cup of coffee in six minutes. And for Asia
it isn't a bad cup of coffee. Unfortunately they charge six US dollars
for it, but at least there is no tipping. And the people who serve
aren't menacing.

June 11, 1985
Hotel Okura

When we get to China, I shan't send letters. I'll just keep them with
my journal. That way I won't have to write it all down twice. You'll
have everything together at the end.

Today I woke up after sleeping three hours and couldn't tell
what time it was. It was daylight and raining outside, but
impossible to tell if it was morning or afternoon. Even your silver

clock was wrong because I forgot to set it. I went down to the Okura lobby where an enormous wall of clocks tells the time in every part of the world. I looked at that wall and realized I have been to most of those capitals. I remembered when I first saw you perform three years ago in Paris. Then we met. I came backstage to talk shop with the lighting designer.

Well, it was midnight in New York and eleven in the morning in Tokyo. There was no sign of any of our group. The only American in sight was explaining to the desk that he was not going to pay for any additional charges on his room bill.

I decided to do my back some good by going for a swim. Only twelve US dollars to go for a swim. Never mind, B.'s grant was picking up all the incidental expenses, although as usual he was complaining loudly about staying within budget.

The pool, which I found only after wandering up and down escalators and elevators from the hotel's new wing to the old wing, was almost empty. A Japanese man with goggles and fins sat at the edge. Several Japanese ladies were stretched out on the apron like sleek brown seals, although the pool was completely covered and there was no sun. They really are very beautiful, these Japanese women, whereas I find the men unattractive. I don't at all mind the short legs, even when they are slightly bowed. And their almondy skin and delicate bones are remarkable. All these ladies of leisure were in their thirties or forties, except one stooped woman with bruises on her legs who wasn't lying down. She looked about sixty.

When you swim in a Japanese pool, if you are a standard-sized American you scrape your toes along the bottom. Then there is an attendant who fiercely scrutinizes the Americans and all non-Japanese. All that foreign hair is suspicious in and of itself. The pool keeper made me remove my watch and also insisted I wear a ridiculous pink bathing cap. I thought he wanted me to remove the watch to protect the watch. Not at all. To protect the water. The same attendant actually made a very annoyed American girl remove her earrings. You would have got into an argument with him.

There was a long list of Don'ts printed in square, black letters on a board by the pool. Don't wear jewelry. Don't dive. Don't swim without a shower. Don't swim with a cold or a sore. No shoes. No bandaids. The attendant gave that scar on my chest a long look.

When I got back to the room it was deliciously cold. I fell asleep under three woolen blankets for the whole afternoon. The best sleep I've had in months. Now I must face the rest of the night wide awake with nothing good to read.

June 12, 1985
Okura

Little opportunity for tourism in Tokyo. We leave for China tonight. I did sneak off yesterday by myself for a few hours. I even remembered how to operate the subway from two years ago. When I sat down to rest in the middle of the Ginza, the busiest subway interchange, a young woman came and offered me a glass of water. Imagine that happening in New York! My destination was the Chinese painting hall at the Japanese National Museum. However they got them, those are some of the most moving paintings I have ever seen. Vast, serene landscapes and beatific mountains and trees. Dream landscapes, a rock, a jagged tree, the white moon. I don't even mind the spirit figures who look like eighteenth-century European angels in white gauze. We should do more of that. Otherwise, what's the use of living in New York.

Then in the afternoon B. insisted I go with him to the Meiji shrine. It turned out today was the beginning of some festival. The park, it has wide, tree-shaded paths like the Bois, was full of supplicants, mostly older women, on their way to say a special prayer. The massive central building was alive with bustling young apprentices in ceremonial dress—floor length white robes with thick sashes and long orange ties. Their hair too, held back with a smart orange tie and falling straight down the back. An officious young woman struck an enormous drum, bigger than she was, to call the prayer.

I was tired by the walk from the subway station, so I was happy just to sit on a bench and rest. I told B. I wanted to watch the ceremony. It was starting to drizzle. Of course B. wanted to cover every square inch of the park and revisit a small museum devoted to Meiji costumes, which I had forgotten. Fortunately the museum was closed.

All the way to the shrine—a heavy, dark wood structure which has burned down and been rebuilt several times over the centuries—the trees and bushes and shrubs arching over the walkway had white scraps of paper on their leaves and outer branches. At first I thought they were butterflies or blossoms, or some kind of Origami. But no, they were prayers. Little prayers written on bits of white paper and then tied to the trees or bushes near the shrine so that the message would go straight to heaven without interference, speeded along by all the praying nearby.

The temples and shrines all offer the services of prayer writers. They will inscribe your own personal prayers in ink with a fine hand or etch them with an electric burner on a small slab of pine. The prayer writers are young novices or old men, and they are doing a nice business. The prayers are hung on trees, or simply stacked on posts outside of the shrine. Many are in English and curiously specific. Please help me find a job as a teacher in six months. Let my son pass his qualifying exams. Protect my grandson who has travelled far across the seas to Fort Lee. Let me recover from the stomach operation I had in November. I was raised a Catholic, so I distrust all organized religion. My mother, who never left the small town in Illinois where I was born, would have understood everything at the Meiji shrine. She would have lined up to buy a prayer, along with the few other foreigners, and cheerfully paid the going rate, on the theory that her God, a generic kindly wise man, would never take seriously the petty distinctions between religions. Dying in the hospital, kept alive on machines to suffer, she never indicated to me she doubted. But I vowed, never again. I learned to hate the nuns and doctors who kept her alive. Buddhist, Christian, Shinto, to God they were all the same. In her book there were good people and bad people. I don't think I ever told you I too was raised and educated as a Catholic. By Jesuits, no less.

Shanghai
June 13

Last night when we arrived Shanghai had just been cooled by a ferocious thunderstorm. We were delayed three hours in Narita because of weather. The five official greeters who had been sent to welcome B. waited for hours, but they didn't complain. B. was treated like an ambassador. At the height of the tourist season the Shanghai airport had three jets in it. Your tiny Caribbean island would have boasted more planes parked in its tourist port. Two attendants with hand-held flashlights led us across the shining tarmac. Someone took care of the bags and customs, thank God, because it was all I could do to smile, bow and shake hands. We drove through the sleeping city—there is nothing to do in China past nine o'clock—in one of those Soviet-style cars with the little white ruffled curtains on the back windows. So the riffraff can't peer in. The good thing about arriving at that late hour was, thank God, no traffic. There is so much construction on the Shanghai airport road it regularly takes two hours to drive twenty miles.

The Chinese have a curious habit of driving at night without headlights. As if they were saving the electricity. The explanation offered is that the headlights blind the cyclists. One of the Chinese interpreters could see I found this answer highly amusing. He's about your age, twenty-five. Actually he's probably about ten years older, but he looks twenty-five to a Westerner. His English is excellent, and he has visited both New York and London. When he saw me struggling to pronounce his name, he said, just call me Tom. He's stocky for a Chinese, this Chinese Tom. Of course all Westerners look large and ungainly next to the slight Chinese. It's not just that we are taller (and usually obscenely fat by Asian standards) but Westerners, especially Americans, bounce around and occupy more than their share of the common space. At least this group of dancers and actors has some physical grace and beauty, so that you aren't ashamed to stand among them and be stared at. And some are wonderful to look at. Then, for the Chinese, there are these enormous black people!

Shanghai
June 14

The center of Shanghai is under a foot of water, the overspill from the recent typhoon. No one seems to be bothered by it. The Chinese roll up their plain gray trousers and wade down the street. They even ride their bicycles through it. People pull along children in tires. Men and women walk hand in hand down the middle of the street wearing the same huge black rubber boots. If I could find a way to do it, I'd send you a pair.

B. and the others will go to a welcoming banquet tonight. I crawled into bed to write to you, although I know the Chinese consider my non-appearance barbaric. In their Mao tunics the Chinese are as proper and formal as ever. They have put us in an old hotel in the former French concession, the Jinjiang. Everything for foreigners is still special. They shoo away the ordinary people at the hotel gate. No Chinese can come to your room, except official guides.

The place is under repair, which means the construction noise starts at seven in the morning and goes on until eight or nine at night. The hotel corridors are filled with white dust and broken boards. Supercilious workers in masks and overalls order you to a distant elevator. I will have to buy some of the cotton masks the workers affect. I had such a fit of coughing from the dust. In the meantime, the construction is yet one more excuse for poor service.

Another change from two years ago is that the clerks and the bellhops, if that's what they are, are all gussied up in a Chinese version of international hotel style. The men wear baggy jackets with ridiculous gold-braid epaulets. As if they were 18th-century French army officers. The cut is all wrong for the slim, narrow Asian bodies. The hostesses and waitresses wear the despised choengsam, slit up to the hip. But even this traditionally provocative garment is worn too big, no doubt out of some sort of compromise with the revolutionary ideology. I know you think I care too much about these things. But you'd laugh, too. It's worth going to the hotel dining room just to see the parade of today's politically correct costumes, as well as to experience the mis-management in the service and delivery of food.

The dining room is partitioned off with screens into a Western side and a Chinese side. Your pals who put safety pins through their cheeks and paste their hair into blue spikes could learn from these Chinese. I was shocked to see the hostesses wearing lipstick. As silly as much of the revolutionary ideology was, the turning away from that always seemed a step in the right direction.

June 15
Jinjiang Hotel

I am writing this in the lobby as I sit and rest while waiting for our official car to come and take me to the theater. Such a parade of personages. Tibetan monks in dark brown gowns, gaudy Hong Kong Chinese who even make the pastel clad Americans look drab and mild mannered, slithery Indians, lots of wary and unobtrusive German and English businessmen, stealing a march on us Americans. I enjoy being reminded that most Americans aren't New Yorkers. Yesterday I chatted with a woman who actually knew the small Illinois town where I was raised. The inevitable line outside of the airline ticket office. And always someone arguing about a bill.

Some will criticize me for not being completely frank. Only fools reveal everything. This is my fourth trip to China, and I haven't scratched the surface. Beware of people who want to tell you the story of their life, or tonight's drunken version. Like an old whore, Shanghai keeps her past to herself. Fifty years ago this city had the well-earned, international reputation of being a place where you could buy anything, from public officials to ten-year-old children. Drug addicts slept face up on the pavement, and beggars were everywhere. Just like New York. Now on the Shanghai streets at five in the morning little round-cheeked ladies, wearing white surgical masks and caps, sweep clean the street with twig brooms while the middle aged and old stand three deep on the sidewalk to do Tai Ji. I admire a culture which addresses bodily functions so simply, so efficiently. Finally, we make too much of a fuss about it all. Here, for example, the government just insists that everyone be cremated. The odorous night-soil cart, pulled by hand, quickly picks up and disposes of its cargo. You would expect a city of twelve million people and essentially no indoor plumbing to be a cesspool. But they get the night soil pots out, emptied and washed and put back before the bicycles and trams fill the streets. A letter will be delivered across Shanghai the same afternoon, for about a penny.

Which reminds me. You must. Must get your immigration status regularized. You aren't going to live with me forever. Incidentally, the lease to the apartment is in the top right-hand drawer of my desk, if anyone asks you. I know you think that immigration lawyer is going to do it all for you, but I'm not so confident. So far he has only taken our money. Every year at tax time you hide like a fugitive. It isn't worth it.

Luckily for you, this lecture is terminating because Chinese Tom and the Ministry car are here.

June 16
Jinjiang Hotel, Room 4357

A little stronger than yesterday. I can no longer recover from these flights in a single day. Worked all day today from eight in the morning until seven at night. B. going full blast. He was annoyed when I insisted upon an hour's break. Got a huge amount accomplished under trying circumstances. Chinese Tom is a great help. His last job was with an American film crew, so we seem like quite reasonable people by comparison.

Did I tell you I love the clock? It's right here by my bed.

June 17
Jinjiang

The rest of the dancers and actors arrive in three weeks. Our hosts have been assuring us that everything we requested six months ago would be here, but there are many, many omissions. The lumber is the wrong grade and quality. And none of that special kind of strong sheer silk which was promised. Something about a flood in the south. Five hundred yards of the wrong green, instead. Even the stage itself is a problem. The last company was a circus, and the stage was destroyed. B. will never let his dancers perform on it, and I don't blame him.

Thank God the Chinese have conceded to the Japanese on the question of air conditioning. My room is delightfully chilly. I am even enjoying a cup of piping hot green tea. Outside it is a steam bath.

Chinese Tom has decided I am his personal responsibility. He is also very good with B., who falls into sputtering fits of rage about three times a day, rendering all Chinese speechless. I have told Tom the best thing is just to go hide until it is over, and then return and pretend like nothing has happened. Yesterday, since it was Sunday and we weren't working, Tom insisted upon taking me to the Jade Buddha Temple. Although I had seen it on my last visit, I was glad I went back. It was much changed. The temple was full of old monks, all identically dressed. They sat in rows, flipping over the pages of religious books with a wooden stick. At first I couldn't figure out what they were doing, since they were clearly not reading the books.

It was to keep the mold out by exposing each page to the air. All the while they were being supervised by a stern young monk who insisted the visitors be quiet and remove their shoes. The temple had real Chinese worshippers too, kneeling in front of those grinning, ugly porcelain statues with the little aprons.

That so many monks should be occupied with preserving their religious artifacts was entirely new. Two years ago I saw some young people playing badminton in the courtyard of one of the most sacred Buddhist shrines. Another surprise, there was a fine traditional calligrapher in the temple gift shop. I bought you a present. A calligraph of a beautiful and wholly romantic T'ang poem, written seven hundred years before Europe thought it invented Romance.

Tonight I didn't feel like sitting in the dining room, despite the educational value. So Tom brought me an orange. Just what I wanted. I wonder where he got it.

June 18

I'd forgotten how hairless the Chinese are. People on the street stare at my goatee. The men in the open T-shirts have nothing on their chests and very little on their faces. The Shanghai shirt is a brightly colored undershirt with big round arm holes. For China it is a stylish garment, especially in contrast to the steely gray and blue pants worn by everyone. I hear the American tourists asking for those shirts in the foreign exchange shops. The Chinese pretend they don't understand. All the workmen on the road and in the open trucks wear them. Bright green, bright pink, maroon, bluest of blue. Everyone works in groups, and always extra people just standing around. So you see the bright shirts together. Then rubber tire sandals or plastic flipflops with lots of muscular leg showing. In the summer the customary garb is shorts, ridiculously baggy shorts, tied up with a rope or a belt. You'd be amused at the legs. You're always complaining that in America we hide the most beautiful parts of ourselves, our legs. In China in the summer, bare legs are everywhere. And they don't look like American legs, nor are they very beautiful. Wiry, thinner, bowed, more muscular. Often scarred. And with that curious sexual neutrality which is characteristic of the new Chinese persona. And hairless.

When you come to Shanghai you realize there are over a billion Chinese and twelve million of them, it seems like more, live in this city. Everywhere there are people. Old people, young people, on the streets, in the houses, standing outside of the old wooden factories and smoking while they wait to get off shift. I've been told there is no Chinese word for being alone which has favorable connotations. All the Chinese words for being alone imply loneliness, desertion or sadness.

Yesterday on Nanking Road, B. pointed to a long narrow window above one of those hole-in-the wall noodle shops. A dozen pair of feet, soles facing out, toes up, were neatly lined up in a row on the ledge of a window opened onto the street. The sight was hilarious, in spite of the fact that it was just tired workers renting a mat to lie down upon for a few hours in the middle of the day. How like B. to catch it. I would have missed it altogether. My eyes were on the traffic.

Today I tried to explain to Chinese Tom the phrase, You can't get there from here. He smiled and nodded at the end of the explanation, but I don't think he understood. We had been talking about Americans being individualistic. In China, he said, it is a virtue to submerge your individuality. They call it eating from the common bowl. Surely not a virtue in America. In America we try to grab or break the common bowl.

Remember, you're just one, just one pair of feet. Tonight mine are killing me, and it seems of vast importance what is happening to every toe, even if each one is only a minuscule fraction of the ten times one billion toes wriggling in this mysterious and fascinating country. In your case, I hope all ten toes are dancing.

June 19

The days here are hotter than New York in August. We're at the theater all day. At least it's dark and relatively cool backstage because the ceilings are high. I manage all right if I can lie down in the middle of the day. My stomach has been a problem. I did better with the Japanese diet, even though raw fish is not easy to digest. As long as I can eat some plain rice in the evening, I'm all right. The Ministry of Culture installed two Western style toilets in the theater. It won't be enough for nineteen dancers. But for now B.

and I have one to ourselves. I notice Chinese Tom and some of our hosts sneak in there when they can.

Last night we were taken to a production of La Boheme at a famous conservatory which was shut down during the cultural revolution. The performance was surprisingly good, although I thought they were too deferential to the available recordings from the West. The voices were lovely. It was sung in Chinese, with the Chinese libretto projected vertically at the side of the stage. The Chinese singers, especially Mimi, had transformed themselves into Europeans for the occasion. They had even built up their faces with putty so they would have real big noses. The Mimi sung with great delicacy and beauty. The Chinese Rudolfo was also affecting, in spite of a large and ugly chin and masses of shiny black Chinese hair sticking straight out from his head. Incidentally, all the Chinese men past forty dye their hair. The results are very good.

I asked Chinese Tom if he could understand the libretto. After all it's a tonal language, and the technical problems of fitting a four tone language onto a melodic line are not trivial. He admitted he only got half of what was sung. But then, our singers in New York enunciate so poorly, we don't get much more, do we? It was a rare and lovely performance, even if the house was a little ramshackle. The electricity, the excitement, just crackled out from the audience. Only four performances. This one was jammed with all sorts of people crowded onto wooden benches. One old man jumped from his seat every time Mimi was in difficulty, and as you know that's for most of the opera. His companion would pull him down by his jacket, and the people next to him would laugh behind their hands. The old man was so wrapped up in the performance he could not sit still when Mimi fell to the ground or was in distress. When she finally expired, he spread his hands over his face and wept and wept. Some of our country people take these stories literally, Chinese Tom said. But I wasn't laughing at him, country bumpkin or not. I wanted to cry myself. I hope our company gets half of that response.

On the way back in the car Tom told me more about himself. He was sent to the countryside during the cultural revolution. But only for a few years, I think he said five. Only a few years? I was better off than many of my comrades, he said. Especially since I had been a student of foreign language and literature at the University. His father knew someone who arranged for him to be sent to a relatively peaceful province, where at least he was left alone. He met his wife there. She is a doctor of traditional medicine, as they call it. She was pulled out of medical school and sent to take care of pigs. Later they let her go back. Tom showed me a patch of discolored skin on his shoulders, permanent dark lines, like lash marks. From carrying heavy buckets of water on a pole ten miles every day.

I suspect this is leading up to his asking me to help him come to America. On some sort of a fellowship. Well, I don't mind doing what I can.

June 21

Last night there was another formal banquet at a new hotel now being touted as having the best food in Shanghai. The building was indistinguishable from any new high rise building in the United States or Paris. It even had a fake waterfall in the lobby, and a woman in a Western evening gown playing cocktail music on a piano. At these banquets the food is truly a work of art, to look at as well as to eat. Meanwhile the ordinary people keep cycling by on the street outside, until they fall down dead from overwork or government mismanagement.

The convention at these banquets is that the host does all of the talking, and everyone else sits and listens and eats. However, B. used the opportunity to demand additional supplies, including lumber, an additional assistant, and the use of an international phone line for several hours a day. All such requests had been refused before, and our Chinese hosts were somewhat startled to see them surfacing again. They had planned to exchange friendly toasts and pledges of future cooperation over Mao Tai, an absurdly strong drink consumed in great quantities at banquets, although you don't see people falling down drunk on the streets at night the way you do in Tokyo. I did no more than raise the tiny glass to my lips letting a few drops of liquor burn my tongue with every toast.

It was all calculated, of course, B.'s apparently uncontrolled loss of temper, followed by demands which had not been met before. I've seen B. pull this trick fifty times before. It works everywhere, Yugoslavia, Rome, Russia, even New York. First, he pretends to be puzzled, to honestly not understand why whoever it is won't give him what he wants. Then he progresses to the all-out attack. Accusations of betrayal, the broken promises, the personal perfidy. Shouting, arms waving. This time he even knocked over a glass. Then, threats. The rest of the company will be cabled and told to cancel. The threat must be credible. The Chinese stared, first at him and then at each other. Our two principal hosts retired briefly. They were joined by the official greeter, the one who everyone assumes is the government informant. The result seems to be that we'll have the phone line, at least, tomorrow, and they're working on the lumber.

In the car on the way back to the Jinjiang, I congratulated B. He was exhausted. These are performances, and they take it out of him. We start tomorrow at ten in the morning instead of eight.

June 23
Jinjiang

Look, you are better off not having come. Really, I would have loved your company. But everything considered, it was better you stayed. There was nothing for you to do here. Who knows, this audition might have turned out to be what we have been waiting for. It's a cliché, but after years of listening to stories about people's careers, I'm convinced that happenstance, chance, and luck do change your life. Look at me. I met B. at a party and worked for him for the next ten years. I owe everything to him.

By the way, if you need cash, there is some in the top drawer of my desk. Top right drawer. Take whatever you need. The bank books are there too, along with various insurance policies.

June 24, 4357

I can't write much today. I fainted at the theater. It was mortifying. B. stopped everybody in the middle of what they were doing. He wanted to come back to the hotel with me. I finally persuaded B. that Chinese Tom would be better able to assist me. When we got back to the room the air conditioning was barely working. I lay down, having some difficulty breathing, and I think I even scared Tom. I asked him to get me some oxygen. It isn't like America where you can just go to the corner pharmacy and buy yourself a can of oxygen. When Tom came back with the oxygen he was very quiet. He had been gone about two hours, and I thought he'd never return. If I could have used the telephone, I would have called for help myself, although there are no telephone books in this country, and I wouldn't have known who to call. Tom wouldn't tell me where he got the oxygen. He must have had to do something he didn't want to do.

June 25
Room 4357, Jinjiang

Really, it's a national disgrace that we are so bad at languages. I meet scores of Chinese who read and write and speak English fluently. We cannot manage the simplest greeting in Chinese, let alone read a street sign. Take Tom, for example. He reads and writes English and French. He started studying English at age eight. He is an artist, of course. Probably he begged for this assignment. You never can tell when contact with a foreigner, especially a man of B.'s international reputation, will result in the offer of a fellowship abroad, or an invitation to an international festival. At the same time, a job such as this always carries a risk here. The winds of politics may change. You could be sent to take care of pigs for far less than having an association with a visiting American theater company. But he can learn so much, just from watching B. at work. I still go to rehearsals. What is he going to do today, to get the best, the newest, the freshest approach out of every single member of the company, including me. And he never disappoints me. Whatever you say about him, and I do say it all, he is a great artist.

My friend Tom has been highly trained in Chinese traditional painting, like so many of their young people. And very gifted. He dashes off the stylized paintings of horses, trees and birds and says with great contempt that what he paints in five minutes will sell in the tourist shop for a hundred US dollars. The government gives him five, and he's glad to have it.

Yesterday I tried to tell him that the stand of bamboo he did for a backdrop was not wholly without artistic interest or merit. He just shrugged. He has an unrealistic view of how wonderful it is to be an artist in the West. Don't despise fluency, I said. I don't think he understood. I told him I knew artists who agonized for months, or even years to produce a pea of little value. He wasn't listening. He's like you. Because he can do something easily, gracefully, he thinks anybody could do it. But they can't. Most people can't do anything, let alone do anything well or beautifully. Can't do anything worth other people paying attention to.

June 27
4357

These past few days I have stayed in the room. B. came. He really has been very attentive. Remember that the next time you're going to make rude remarks about him. He sat by the bed and held my hand and offered me all of the antibiotics and pain killers in his personal drugstore. I laughed which made me start coughing again. But I'm not in pain, I said. Still, it was comforting to know the stuff was there. The hospital for foreigners is supposed to be pretty good, he said. They give you a choice of Chinese style or Western style medicine, just like the two sides of the dining room. I don't want to go there. I took some of the herbal medicine Tom brought me yesterday. It must be a very strong decongestant with some kind of stimulant in it. I have felt better for several hours. I even washed up. You take this horse pill, it has the consistency of a Tootsie Roll, but it does not taste like chocolate. Then you must follow it with about two quarts of boiling hot water. That's probably what does the good. What I really wanted after that disgusting pill was an American Scotch with a huge pitcher of good old-fashioned American ice water.

So that he would stop pressing me to drink more hot water, I got Chinese Tom to tell me more of the story of his life. His father and mother were separated and sent off to the North to labor camps during what he refers to as the recent troubled times. Because they were teachers. He and his sister and brother were at first left alone in the city. At thirteen he was the oldest, with the responsibility for taking care of the younger ones. An uncle lived in a nearby town. But we were all right, he said. We had enough to eat and a place. The mother didn't survive the camp. The lack of bitterness expressed by the tellers of such tales is astounding. So many have suffered so needlessly. Yet there seems to be a collective agreement, that it's a waste of time to be bitter. Or perhaps this is

just the face that is put on for Americans. In normal times, if there
have ever been normal times, he would have studied to be a dancer
or an actor. Painting came later as a second choice, because it was
less political. He never thought he would be an administrator in
the Ministry for Cultural Affairs, but it turned out all right, he says.
Many opportunities. His wife runs a clinic for herbal medicine in
Shanghai. At least when our doctors are trained we don't send
them off to clean pig troughs. Although we allow our young
people to kill themselves in many stupid ways.

Tom keeps asking me, what am I writing in the notebook. I tell
him it is a letter to a friend. And a diary of my journey. My
impressions. He can see it takes lots of time, and that I always try to
write something even when I am very tired or don't feel well.
Someone I miss very much, I tell him.

June 29
4357

I am feeling a lot better, although still weak. Tom brought me some
soup and rice gruel and some dumplings. I ate a little rice gruel. He
also brought me more medicine from his wife's hospital and another
canister of oxygen, which I am saving for the night. There is certainly
nothing to lose from trying the traditional Chinese medicine. Tom
boils up these leaves and sticks and powders in a big pot and makes
a kind of foul smelling soup out of it. You must drink the liquid and
inhale the fumes. It certainly takes your mind off your symptoms.

Both B. and Tom want me to go to the foreigner's hospital, but I
am comfortable in the room as long as Tom doesn't mind bringing
me food.

Last night the television news showed a sunrise from one of
the favorite Chinese vacation spots, the Yellow Mountains. A
landscape from the ancient paintings. Some fifty people were
crowded onto a small rocky precipice, waiting for the ribbons of
color. When the round, red sun rose from behind the jagged, inky
peaks, people jumped up and down and cheered and clapped.

This morning at six I woke up feeling completely well. As if
nothing was the matter. I am sitting at the hotel window and
watching the thousands of people pour through the streets on their
way to work. Streams of bicycles, buses crawling along with

people hanging on their sides, people just walking, in blues and grays, with white shirts, occasionally a green or bright pink streak of a work shirt wheeling past.

June 30

He has not been strong enough to get out of bed for two days. There will be a party at the United States Embassy for their national day in a few days time. He has been talking about resting up to go to that party. All of the Americans came to visit and talked a lot about that party. When they left he turned his face to the wall and asked me to go and get him more oxygen. This time it took me four hours. I had to go and beg it again from my wife's sister-in-law at the city hospital. She said this was absolutely the last time she would give me any. I have told her a little bit about him. If someone is that sick, she said, he should be in the hospital where we can properly take care of him. Do you want to bring shame to the country? But he doesn't want to go. When I returned he was very bad again, and all the oxygen was gone. I called the desk to change the sheets, but it took them a very long time and he was shivering. I wrapped him in a blanket and we sat on the sofa together. I promised to bring him some of our black hair dye tomorrow. He drank a little tea with herbs and felt stronger. I will stay in the room with him now.

July 1

Suddenly he had the idea he should go home, be sent back to New York. He woke up and insisted that we go down to the airline reservation office to book the ticket. Then he wanted me to cable New York for the money, in case they wouldn't allow him to use his ordinary ticket. I told him the Chinese airline would not allow him to fly. He was too sick. He insisted I call the office of the American airline in this hotel. The American airline said that if he came to the airport or to the hotel reservation office, they would book him on a flight out if there was an opening. But they also told me there were no openings on flights out of Shanghai. All flights for the next two months had waiting lists. Still, he made me help him get dressed so that we could go down to the airline office at the hotel. He thought if he went he would persuade them, that they had just told me the flights were booked because I am Chinese. It took an hour to get him dressed, with many rests and sitting down in between. This used up almost half of the new tin of oxygen, which I advised him was not wise because the evening was coming and I could not get any more. He leaned on my arm the whole way, coughing as soon as he got into the hallway. At the airline desk, he had to sit down because he was coughing so much. The agent said without question he was too sick to fly. She wouldn't book him on a flight even if there were any openings. When he stopped coughing he asked her how much money she wanted for a ticket. He said he had cash. Look, he said, holding up a white business card. You can call my doctor in New York. He'll tell you it's all right for me to fly. The agent didn't even answer. Then he started to cry. Finally after another hour I got him back to the room. We must have closely missed a visit from the Director. There was a note on the door. Probably they thought he was feeling better if he had gone out of the room. Then he fell asleep with the last of the oxygen, but making a very heavy sound.

July 3

As soon as he awakened he insisted I go to the Embassy to ask for a particular man. I went just as he instructed, but all the Americans were preparing for the big party for their national day. There was a guard in uniform with a rifle at the gate. He would not let me inside. I said that I had an important message for one of the diplomats. At last an American who was not a soldier came. I couldn't persuade him to come to the hotel. The person to whom the letter was addressed was away from the city. He'll have to come himself, the American diplomat said. I didn't like that man.

July 4

When he woke up he asked for something. His medicine? His diary? The small clock by the bed? There was a dull beaded necklace in the pocket of the suitcase. He wanted that. He wrapped it around his wrist. Then he wanted the clock. He held the clock and the necklace, and when I helped him to a sitting position, he seemed to sleep peacefully. Although he was talking, it was in a peaceful, quiet way with his eyes shut. I was afraid to leave him. I thought later to try one more time to get another tin of oxygen from my wife's sister-in-law.

Just as I was about to leave, the Director arrived. He was very agitated. Some of the other Americans from the group were with him. They were all very upset and angry. They had just come from the Embassy party. I explained that I had tried to deliver a letter to the Embassy, but the soldier sent me away. The Director demanded the letter from me, but I had left it there. The Director insisted I call an ambulance to take him to the foreigner's hospital. I answered that he said over and over he didn't want to go there. Do you want him to die right here, the Director said. After some time when the ambulance had not yet arrived, the Director and I carried him down to the lobby. I don't think he knew we were taking him to the hospital. He woke up and smiled at the Director. He thought the Director had got him on a flight to America.

At the hospital the doctor in charge of the foreign patients immediately gave him some oxygen. I explained that he was here with a famous American dance company. At ten when I went back he was resting in the middle of an ordinary ward with clean sheets, although no air conditioning. He had the feeding tube in his arm with the western medicine in it. A young nurse was sitting beside him waiting to give him oxygen when he needed it. We just have to wait for the western medicine to take hold, the doctor said.

July 7
Reuters

There are unconfirmed reports that the Chinese government is considering quarantine procedures and the testing of certain incoming tourists after the unexpected death of a visiting American who was a member of an official United States arts delegation. The body of the 47-year-old New Yorker, who died in a Shanghai hospital last night, was immediately cremated. Several members of the American dance troupe returned precipitously to the United States. There is discussion in high government circles about introducing testing for some tourists or delegations.

The Circus Comes
to Kampala

An afternoon performance best suited everyone. And on the day, at three-thirty Johanna piled Maisie and John into the back of the Volkswagon. She was hot. Did anyone with any sense go out in the middle of the afternoon, she asked herself with a British sense of reproach. In 1963, Americans in Uganda still felt the authority of the British. Just an hour before the Toro kitchen girl, Ursula, had confronted Johanna, almost accusing her, it seemed—her large and beautiful eyes shedding so many tears—as she said that her sister had given birth to a dead child. A message had been brought by hand by a very small, thin boy. Johanna embraced Ursula awkwardly. "But," she asked herself as she held the sobbing woman, "What can I do?" The thought that she was late, that the children were fighting in the steamy car, and that people might be waiting for her took the edge off her sympathy. Knowing it was the wrong gesture, Johanna gave Ursula the rest of the day off and told her to go upcountry to her sister.

Philip was supposed to be waiting for his family at his office. But the prim African secretary at the Institute lay down his newspaper when Johanna came in and announced that Philip had left in a hurry several hours ago. With the Administrator, the secretary said. He probably thinks he's telling tales, Johanna noted. As she walked back to the car, Johanna was annoyed. She didn't like to drive through town with the children. Just being on the road was dangerous. Somewhere in the scenic distance there was a rumbling. The sky was clear, but here that didn't preclude thunder. Or it could be drums. Or guns. Sometimes in the middle of the night Johanna lay awake and listened to the drums talking across the darkness. Then, when she was alone and awake, it seemed that if she could understand those messages she would learn something important.

She found the children sitting quietly in the back seat. "We'll just have to go on without him," Johanna announced to their sulky faces in the rearview mirror. "He can find his own way and meet us later." And for the thousandth time she felt an irrational annoyance at this country where communication was difficult, where you couldn't reach into every corner with a prying telephone. But her friend Mary Lou who was also bringing her child would be late. Ever since she married an African, she had adopted an African sense of time, which was one reason why Philip disapproved of her. And for a moment Johanna felt as if everyone were bound to disappoint her.

The tent was set up in a meadow which served sometimes as a market place, or a parking lot, and occasionally sporting contests were held there. A hired African took tickets at a gate which didn't pretend to fence in the circus or its audience. The peanut vendors lined up and squatted on their haunches, stretching out their hungry hands to a dawdler, hoping he might turn into a customer. The children were excited and ran ahead, unmindful of the fact that unchained wild animals might be about. Johanna tried to remember circuses she had been to as a child. Who had taken her? Her mother? She would have liked them. Johanna's memories were of indoor places. Here the bright sunshine and the fresh outdoor smells pervaded everything. The afternoon sun glared but it gave an atmosphere of brightness and freedom, too. The tent was patched in places and threadbare. And inside it was dark to the point of mystery. It was a gypsy circus. With an air of festivity swarthy middle-aged women and dwarf-like dark men hurried to and fro, carrying armloads of costumes, or lugging between them an awkward prop. On the side, cardboard booths served as dressing rooms. Behind the dressing rooms, when the hill sloped down, the turkey vultures picked over garbage which had been tossed onto the grass. Lions and tigers lounged in their decorated cages which stood on colored wheels above the ground. And tied with a piece of string to a tent stake was a large, overheated grizzly bear wearing a starched ruff. The sweat ran into his eyes, and he panted in the heat. Johanna laughed. He looked just like she felt.

Maisie had made friends with a clown in a T-shirt. Perhaps he was a Macedonian. He was painting a red bulb on his nose. Although he was dressed only in his underwear he sat stiff and formally before the piece of mirror propped up before his eyes. His dark socks were stretched taut by elastic garters.

"Good afternoon, sir," John said. And the clown turned his huge painted mouth up into a smile and winked to a friend smoking a cigarette on a camp cot.

"A gentleman, I see," the clown said to Johanna. And she smiled back and watched him skillfully paint his smile up into the corners of his face. His partner, a thin clown, watched through eyes which already had their red lines drawn in. He refused to be engaged in conversation. Maybe the beefy one did the feeling for the two, Johanna thought, and she led the children on.

The barker, an American, of course, was leaning over a young Indian girl, trying to persuade her to sell Coca-Cola during the performance. The teenager, who must just now have strolled in off the street, was listening. She held her skinny hands together and fixed her eyes on the entrance gate. A gypsy woman approached. The child was sent away.

"We never have enough people," the gypsy explained to Johanna. She laughed gayly and nodded to the manager. "He picks them too young." She looked at Johanna. "Have you seen our Rosalind?"

"That tent doesn't look very steady," Johanna remarked to the barker.

"You must be thinking of the Minneapolis 1940 disaster with Barnum and Bailey." The barker went on to say, "They never lived that one down."

"No, I hadn't heard of that," Johanna replied. "I just think this tent doesn't look too steady. And she had the feeling that the barker had had something to do with the Minneapolis disaster. "The roof is blowing," she said in the voice she used to correct her recently acquired servants. And she wiggled the nearest tent stake with her foot. "See?"

The barker raised his thick chin. And his eyeballs, which were red, too, bulged. "I know my business, lady. This is a good show. You'll like Rosa's act."

Johanna nodded as if she believed him. But his rudeness had made her homesick. Johanna was bored with the exotic politenesses of foreigners. Where were the honest insults? Maisie had slipped her hand. "Daddy?" Johanna heard her call. And she looked up to see Philip walking towards her. He was hurrying. And his white shirt was sticking to his soft white skin.

"There's been a revolt," he said importantly. "An insurrection of the police guards. The airport is closed down. The main roads out of town are blocked. Even the hospital is under guard, they say." He was holding Maisie by her bottom as if she were a leafy green tree growing out of a round basket. "That's why I was late," he said.

"Why?" Johanna asked. "This lost territories business? Maybe that's why Ursula left."

"Could be." Philip placed Maisie on the ground with a sigh. "You're too heavy, darling, for this heat," he said. He looked around automatically for his son and smiled at him. "The Prime Minister made a speech. But someone said there isn't too much to worry about. At least not immediately."

Johanna caught sight of her friend Mary Lou. She might still have been in Atlanta. A thin flowered dress only made her legs look barer. And her long blond hair fell down her back—Johanna allowed herself an extravagant metaphor—like so many unfulfilled wishes. She had that air of nervous agitation which is partly cultivated for the flush it brings to the cheeks. Or so Johanna often thought about Southern women. Unfeigned, however, was the annoyance with which she half dragged and half carried Amina, her beautiful half-African son, by one thin-skinned arm. At two his beautiful face already had a characteristic pout.

"We couldn't get the car out," she apologized. "Adegwa had parked it way up on the hill. The baby wanted her bottle and the nurse couldn't give it to her." She stood in between Philip and Johanna with her shoulders haunched slightly forward. "And Adegwa said everything I did was wrong."

Johanna paused. "Have you heard the news?" she asked.

"You mean about the demonstration," Mary Lou said, making a face. "You know how things are here. I passed by the Parliament

on my way. There were a few policemen standing out in front."
She looked up to the faded tent top where meaningless colored
flags waved. Inside, the town children were already clamboring
on the bleachers. "Just enough to send the servants running back
to the countryside. The policemen had their straw shields out."
Mary Lou laughed. "And I heard that the minister who arranged
the riot got a tear gas bomb in his face." And she threw back her
head with an abandonment which made her hair appear even
longer. Mary Lou caught Johanna's eye. "They always come
back," Mary Lou continued. "The radio and newspapers love to
dramatize these things. You've only been here a few months.
You'll get used to it."

"You're probably right not to worry," Philip commented.
"Adegwa can tell us what happened."

Maisie lay her head against Johanna. The cat cages were rolled
inside. And the clowns, barely recognizable in their polka-dot
suits, skipped through the tent slit. The lions stretched, yawned
and stood up as the cages bumped over ruts in the ground.

"Come on, Daddy," John said. His voice whined a little. And
Philip got the better of an urge to correct him. "They'll start
without us."

"It makes me nervous when the airports are shut down,"
Johanna said to no one in particular.

"It isn't as though it hasn't happened before," Philip felt called
upon to say.

"It's another empty gesture," Mary Lou added. "That's always
the way, here"

Outside the tropical sky had been bright, but inside Johanna felt
as if it were a rainy day. The ring was flimsy—two-by-fours laid
end to end. Folding chairs stood at its very edge. The lions were
pacing restlessly now. And from an old scratchy phonograph
record came suspenseful melodies, of twenty years ago. Johanna
strained forward to see. Maisie was restrained from climbing up on
the back of her folding chair. Philip sat back and looked around, as
if he expected nothing. Mary Lou wrapped her skirt around her
legs and placed her feet on the chair in front of her, an improper
way for a woman to sit by African standards.

A short man wearing a red costume and holding a whip took
the position of center stage. He placed three-legged stools at

intervals and glanced at the caged animals as he did so. For a lion tamer he was too short and too fat for the bold costume. With a reluctant air he pulled back the lock to the cage and let the gate crash open. A lion growled. The keeper placed a stool for him to jump down upon. First came the scruffy small lion. Philip yawned and turned his eyes towards the exit. Next a beautifully marked tiger poured himself out into the ring. He was a well-appointed beast, who would have been magnificent except that his stomach dragged along the ground. Finally two maneless young males descended into the ring and sprang to their chairs after pawing at the whip. The lion tamer was fully occupied now. Johanna forgot his seediness. The cats climbed on and off their stools. And the old male rolled over once onto his back and yawned at the audience. The tiger with the sagging belly produced what Johanna thought was an impressive roar, displaying oddly spaced, pathetic teeth.

Philip whispered, "There's nothing here we haven't seen before."

Maisie had her thumb stuck in her mouth. Her eyes became full of remembered nightmares when the tiger roared. Johanna's mind was wandering. The tiger had her sympathy. After having a baby she often felt as if her insides were dragging along the ground in just that way. Getting up and going to work in the afternoon. That's all this was to the tiger. The incense. The music. He saw through all of that. And who was that pudgy clown poking at him with the whip. And across the dimly lit, sawdust space between them Johanna smiled at that tiger.

The American barker, who now wore an outdated purple costume, was trying to hurry things along. The lion tamer was puffing a little. The red coat was too tight. The beasts were refusing to go back to their cages. The tiger sat stupidly on the floor, and Johanna hoped he wouldn't disgrace himself. The barker turned up the clanging music. The martial, monotonous rhythms only seemed to drag things out more. The Indian boys in the bleachers started to catcall. Finally the scruffy lion placed one and then the other paw on the step. Then he hauled his whole body inside his cage. The maneless lions followed. Even the tiger fell in line. The cages were rolled away, and Johanna watched the cats curl safely back into their corners, going back to sleep.

"The lions are back in their cages," Maisie announced correctly.

"It's sad," Mary Lou said. "These beasts are rejects from some-where. They should be turned out to pasture. It's cruel."

"At least they're leading useful lives," Johanna replied.

In the wings stood a costumed man and his partner. They whispered to one another while they waited for the barker to put on their music. The man was dressed as an American cowboy in a hat, chaps, bolero and ankle-high boots decorated with red patterns. His partner or wife wore one of those costumes designed to display thighs and the flesh of her middle. But all that suggestive nudity emphasized superfluous fat rather than voluptuous curves. Was that Rosa? The barker blew into the microphone, startling everyone, and announced Annie Oakley and Buffalo Bill. Mary Lou and Johanna clapped. In the upper bleachers where the Indian families sat, a teenager booed. Someone else laughed.

A well-dressed couple from the American embassy turned around in their first-class seats and smiled. Isn't it all too funny for words, their wrinkled noses asked. I don't think I can understand it, Johanna answered back with her eyes.

Buffalo Bill was a Will Rogers kind of cowboy—tall and lanky with straggly hair which might have had brambles in it. His face was not American. He didn't have American teeth. They were yellow and stumpy and he looked not lean, but undernourished. No, Johanna would have bet anything he wasn't an American. Some kind of nondescript postwar Eastern European. How they all loved the Wild West mythology, she thought. Buffalo Bill was shooting randomly into the air and walking with strides of decision and purpose around the ring. His friend Annie Oakley followed him a few steps behind, simpering, and making curtsies to the audience.

"What's going on here?" Philip asked. And there did seem to be little purpose to the act. Johanna wondered what was happening at the demonstration. Philip really should have been there. She regretted having dragged him off. Away from his real work. But the regret only made her angry at him for letting her do it.

John's smile was rapturous. He wrapped his arms around Johanna's neck. Living abroad made even imitation American seem attractive. The wild animals had frightened the children, but this was something they could believe in. Amina stood on his mother's lap. In his excitement he kicked her belly. Mary Lou slapped him on the legs. He started to cry but stopped himself.

Maisie, who was standing beside him, reached up and touched him on the knee.

Johanna found her mind wandering. Her gaze was on the ceiling. She set her teeth, and fixed her attention again on the center ring. Hopeless. Annie Oakley's smile was painted on. She waved festooned banners in the air while that insipid Buffalo Bill shot down balloons. She was too old for the act, and her staged pride seemed to be a joke shared with the audience. Philip was staring into the first-row seats, trying to identify someone who looked important. What, Johanna thought, if there really was something to be worried about? What if all this melodramatic rioting were an honest-to-god revolution? And she had a ridiculous image of the hot baked streets of the city being colored red from one ill-defined curb to the other. I've never even seen a dead body before. Of course it'd be an African. What silly things we think of, Johanna said in reproach to herself. Philip smiled at Johanna who was twisting her fingers in their Maisie's curls. What if all our lives really were in danger? What if I were killed, she asked herself. It would all be his fault. And her fingers swimming in Maisie's soft hair stopped. No, it couldn't be.

Buffalo Bill was now shooting at rings and flowers tossed in the air by Miss Oakley. When he hit the target (which was by no means every time) she showed a widely spaced pair of front teeth to the audience. Her lips closed over those teeth when the music started.

"He doesn't look like he's ever seen a real cowboy," Philip said. "I bet if he'd open his mouth he'd speak German."

"Have you?" Johanna asked. "Seen a real cowboy, I mean."

"Bulgarian," Mary Lou said. "I'll bet he's Bulgarian. And she's a Turk. She's darker."

The well-dressed people in the first rows were getting restless. The children liked all the shooting, but the fat old Hindu women in the back row were beginning to rummage for those red nuts which made them look as if they had been drinking blood. Finally at a signal from the barker a tall wooden contraption mounted on roller skates was rolled into the ring. Festoons hung from its sides and the whole construction had an air of family gaiety about it. A garish gold star with thickly colored-in lines radiating from its center had been tacked to the top. It was shaped like a coffin lid turned up on end. As on a model's mirror, light bulbs ringed the edge. On the surface black lines of a female figure were crudely outlined with the name Rosalind written in glittery gold beneath.

The barker turned off the phonograph. Annie Oakley raised her arms over her head, pointing and gesturing once again. On a small table against a background of mothy velvet, whose color might once have been midnight blue, waited an odd and varied collection of knives and swords. Some pieces had antique designs. Some were new and and had the dull, efficient sheen of stainless steel. There seemed to be no order to the collection. But in that stuffy tent and against the dark and shabby background the cutlery gleamed like a live thing. Philip turned his attention away from the audience and to the ring.

Johanna kept her eyes fixed upon Annie Oakley. Cautiously the woman stepped up onto the platform. She leaned her body against the table. The black lines outlined a position for her arms, and indicated where to put her legs which showed gooseflesh above the black and white cowboy boots. Johanna now saw that the crude gold star even served some function. It demarcated the place for her head.

"That poor woman," Johanna cried out. "He'll surely miss."

"He's a jerk, all right," Mary Lou agreed, and she giggled.

Buffalo Bill might have heard her. He glanced up at the audience as he chose his first weapon, a cutlass with an engraved handle. Drum music came from the platform. Annie Oakley exposed her gapped teeth once more to the audience. Johanna saw her shuffling her feet on the small footspace. To think of that woman going through this act twice a day made Johanna's heart shudder. What a way to earn a living. Shouldn't she have stayed in one of those rocky Yugoslav cities? In America at least, anyone who could read and write and was slightly more than imbecilic could earn a living behind a desk. But a more subtle line of work seems to have been the fate chosen for the woman on the platform. And Johanna couldn't decide whether she was fortunate or unfortunate as a result.

If her skin was flabby the pattern made by the shiny steel was clean. Almost Grecian. And beautiful. Two dots for the neck. The audience clapped as each knife imbedded itself in the wood with a resounding thwack. Then, the waist was precisely delineated. Her outstretched arms were nailed down with threads of air. But he was such a cowboy, Johanna thought. Such an incompetent. Next her legs were fastened by knives which were thrown to pinpoint the fleshy thighs. Annie Oakley was no longer smiling. Johanna wished it were over. Philip sat forward. His forehead was lumpy with anticipation. Mary Lou watched every motion with a sarcastic smile. At last the final knife, a short jewelled sword was delivered. Buffalo Bill stepped back and opened his arms to the audience. Annie radiated his success. The banal martial music started again. Annie leapt away from the platform with the freedom of youth, leaving the knives behind to tell the story.

Johanna clapped. She was laughing. "Thank goodness," she said. "I never thought they would make it."

"Amateurs," Philip said, and he turned away. The spectacle was not worth his attention.

"I'm glad that's over," Mary Lou said in her sarcastic way. "All those near misses."

Johanna watched Annie Oakley and Buffalo Bill carry their props off stage. Mary Lou was staring at a dot of evening sky which peeked through the frayed ceiling. She didn't clap the performers off stage. She lifted her blonde shoulders and the bones showed softly. The children were getting restless. Two bicycle riders turned circles on themselves, round and round, weaving arabesques in the center. "Aren't those our friends the clowns?" Philip asked. John climbed down from his chair and into the empty seat in front of them. Certainly the thin and the fat clown were nowhere to be seen.

"They're probably short on staff," Philip explained to no one in particular. "They can't take everyone along. Too many air fares. Like moving a whole town." He smiled at Mary Lou. "Besides, it's an additional form of suspense."

A spangled lady came in, rolling hoops. A ribboned poodle, a city dog, jumped through them. Johanna thought she recognized the soft fat legs of Annie Oakley, but she couldn't be sure. Was this Rosa? It seemed the announcer was taking a rest. The poodle at least was a new character on the scene.

Mary Lou was feeding Amina peanuts. She bit through the salty husks with her teeth and one by one placed the nuts in the child's mouth. He chewed slowly and deliberately and opened his mouth for another when he was finished. "You are silly," Mary Lou said. She turned to Johanna. "You know he'll never eat anything at home. Then he is hungry all day. Just a bowl of cornflakes in the morning and then nothing for the rest of the day."

It seemed to Johanna that it was becoming darker inside. Late, too. But night could not have arrived yet. She listened for rain and heard a distant rumble which might have been thunder. The several light bulbs dangling down from the holely ceiling reminded her of hotel rooms where she had slept overnight as a child. The bare light bulbs made that mood as close as yesterday, but the circumstances, the years surrounding those rooms, were lost in a blurry haze. Outside there were loud noises. Perhaps they were already firing in the streets. And a shiver ran down Johanna's spine. The circus was running faster now. The second-rate character of the performance seemed less important. And the badly matched two-by-fours, the patchy tent, and all that was there seemed to be speaking. Like the drums pounding their secret messages in the middle of the night. And as she lay awake in the African darkness, listening to the others sleeping all around her, Johanna had the feeling those drums were talking about her.

A snake charmer was performing. Pythons ringed her arms and writhed down her back. They wrapped themselves decisively around her waist. The snake charmer also looked Eastern European, with thick black hair. She must be Rosa. As with her sisters, too much of her badly preserved body was exhibited. Her suggestive costume looked like the clown's idea of a bathing suit. The snakes' tongues silently flicked in and out. Were their fangs drawn, Johanna wondered. Or did snakes carry poison in their tongues? Their black button eyes were bright, as with ambition.

Mary Lou grabbed Johanna's arm. "I read in the local newspaper," she said confidentially, "this woman is a fraud. All the cobras she's handling are harmless. An English woman who has a snake farm outside of town challenged her." Mary Lou laughed. "Can you imagine," she said. "This old Kenya settler is enraged because some third-rate circus comes to town with a fake snake charmer?"

Johanna agreed it was ludicrous. She remembered that pythons had no venom. They choked their victims to death. It was a pretty risky profession after all.

The biggest snake, a blue-green reticulated python, had wrapped itself around its mistress's legs. The barker held the microphone to his lips to give the illusion of a whisper. The snakes were all out of the box. Crawling all over each other and making curved trails in the sawdust. Johanna was frightened to the point of nausea. She lifted her feet off the floor. One small plank was all that separated the audience from the snakes. Any enterprising python or cobra could slither over that.

"Let's get out of here," she said to Philip. "Anything could happen here. They don't have the right equipment."

Sweat shone on the snake charmer like grease on a channel swimmer's body. Mary Lou watched with her lips parted. Johanna hunched forward in her chair and eyed the exit. The woman picked up the snakes with her bare hands. Two and three at a time. They resembled in her hands bunches of cut-off hair, or the entrails of a sacrificed animal. She slid the wriggling handfuls into boxes, shut the tops down on them, and locked them up. Her own slithery skin reflected the same gleam shining from the snakes' scales. She picked up a last long serpent by the tail, smiled at the audience, and watched as the snake curled himself into a marvelous arabesque.

"Don't be such a sissy," Philip said to Johanna. But he too squirmed until the last lid was clamped down. Maisie started to cry. She hid her face in her mother's neck and tears dropped inside Johanna's dress. Mary Lou's dusty son stood up straight and tall. Like Mary Lou his face registered no emotion, only a sheen of indifference.

Men started carrying off the snake-filled boxes, four-handed, like pirates hauling treasure chests. The middle-aged snake charmer stood in the center of the ring and bowed an elegant, low, and sweeping tribute to her own performance and to the audience privileged to watch. Her red satin suit showed dark continents of sweat, and her frizzy hair flew away from her face fantastically. Johanna clapped and clapped. For a moment the spangled costume was believable.

The clowns returned dressed as high wire artists. They rode bicycles across the tightrope, balancing a long trembling pole. Maisie couldn't believe they were the same men she had seen undressed outside.

"Why do you fill the child's head with such nonsense," Philip said crossly. Johanna turned away.

"What I've heard has been vague," Mary Lou said. "The army barracks are under siege. The airport has been closed down."

Philip picked up John and placed him on his lap. "The Prime Minister has threatened to put the King in jail," he said as if he had good evidence for the fact. "But no one knows the straight story. Even the students didn't know, and they usually lead the rioting."

Mary Lou interrupted. "I'm sure it is all exaggerated," she said. "There are only about one hundred men in the army post here. What are they going to do? Arrest everyone. There aren't enough policemen. And besides if everyone of importance was put in jail they couldn't pay themselves." She laughed at her own view.

"You can't dismiss it all that easily," Philip said. "Even if there are only one hundred men it's the most important barracks. Even if by our standards," he coughed, "it's not much of an army. When an army revolts it's an event of political importance." He pulled in his chin as if he were lecturing. "Maybe it's even a revolution," he said with a wide-eyed gaze. "I should be there for the record."

Johanna had turned her attention back to the ring. "What's going on now?"

The barker was arranging something. Like a surgeon, he placed his hands under a sheet and adjusted something covered up. Then he stood back. What was unveiled was a long, hospital-like table with a slot down its center. Inside the slot was a low sword blade, lying lengthwise, like the rudder of an overturned boat. Beside the table, on a skimpy platform was a large and evil-looking rock.

"This is something," Philip complained. "I didn't remember that the circus was so sadistic. Like a torture chamber."

"This may be a different tradition," Johanna said. "It all still looks homemade," Mary Lou interjected.

Buffalo Bill touched the blade with his finger. He sliced a piece of paper in half. Now he was wearing a leopard costume. Johanna thought that he was a little old for it. This time his woman was dark-haired and with too much red, red lipstick on her mouth. Was it Annie Oakley in a wig? Her costume showed a strip of luminous material down the back. A giant might have picked her up by that bright strap. The bared back itself was fleshy and strong, for all the indentation of the waist. There was something mystical about the crazy-looking woman, Johanna thought, and fear had something to do with it. Stiffly she lay down on the table.

"It is some kind of Yoga," Mary Lou said. "You know how the Hindus make themselves insensitive to pain."

"Isn't she the one who was with the pythons?" Johanna asked. She felt confused and it was important to know if any real distinctions could be made here. "It makes me nervous," she added, and she shifted her feet back and forth in the sawdust as though she were preparing to move somewhere. "What is it all for? It seems very stupid to me."

Mary Lou agreed. "Why did we come?" she asked.

Philip reached out and grabbed his wife by the soft part of her upper arm. He said to Mary Lou, "She takes these things seriously. As if these shoddy cheap tricks still had some meaning. Worse than the kids." Maisie had her thumb in her mouth. Philip pulled her up on his lap. "Don't be frightened, baby," he said. And he held her hand in his own.

No visible change was registered on the snake charmer's face when the barker placed the heavy stone on her bare belly. The stone, he announced after wiping his forehead with a hand-kerchief, would be hammered until it was broken in two.

"It's a silly trick," Philip said. "It's perverse. I don't believe the knife is sharp after all. And probably that isn't even a real stone, just some papier-mâché imitation."

Mary Lou's eyes were fixed and wide on the center action. She clasped Amina tightly as though he were a hostage on her lap. The child squirmed, cruelly, trying to get away. Johanna gripped her chair. "Isn't it awful?" she said in a whisper. And she looked down into the sawdust, as if counting the specks of color and light would relieve her of the obligation to look further. Philip started to speak to her. She found John's hand to hold. "Don't interrupt," she said crossly to Philip, anticipating that he would make fun of her. "The barker asked us especially to be quiet."

Philip laughed. He turned to Mary Lou. "She really believes it. At her age. Isn't that silly?"

"What a pain you can be," Johanna replied crossly. Johanna couldn't watch. But she listened with all of her attention. The sound of blows came as if from far away, like pain experienced at the end of a long hospital corridor. She stole a close-lipped look.

The woman's teeth were clenched behind the outline of a smile. Those gapped teeth were not amusing now. They just made her look more vulnerable. It continued. Nothing changed. Johanna was almost praying. The audience was ensnared and for the first time completely quiet.

"It must be a trick," Philip whispered to the others. Johanna made no contradiction. Then she heard clapping. Over?

Buffalo Bill was holding the mallet over his head and grinning. The barker had his hat on. And Annie Oakley no longer wore that tight-lipped expression. Her mouth had sagged. The stone had broken. They had done it. Or so it seemed. The barker conducted and encouraged the applause, like a man scooping up dreams by the armful. But Annie's eyes were not open. Buffalo Bill bent over his partner. Annie's eyes remained shut.

"Why doesn't she get up?" Johanna asked.

"Something's wrong," Philip said with that masculine sense of rectitude. And he walked the few steps which separated them from the ring.

The barker was frowning. He stared at the tent opening and turned the music up. Perhaps the next act could be hurried along. Philip spoke to the leopard man. The entertainer shook his head, either in negative reply or because he didn't understand the question. From her place in the audience Johanna watched as Philip lovingly raised the woman's head and supported her against his body. The sword blade she had been lying on was bloody. And a raw cut had appeared alongside that strip of fluorescent cloth down her back.

"You take the kids," Johanna said to Mary Lou, giving her no chance to object. And she went into the ring with Philip. The embassy woman whispered in her husband's ear and nodded at Johanna's action.

The crowd was sullen. They hadn't paid to witness bloody mistakes. The barker was trying to repair illusions. He turned up the music. The clowns came, prodding ahead of them the uncomfortable looking bear in a starched green ruff.

"I think she should go to the hospital," Johanna said to Philip. Buffalo Bill seemed incapable of acting. The barker tapped the sawdusty floor with his baton. "That would be the best," he said in his flat Midwestern voice.

Philip was still trying unsuccessfully to arouse the woman. Johanna turned and asked Buffalo Bill directly what had happened. But he only threw up his hands and looked at her. His brown liquid eyes streamed sad and helpless tears over the sagging middle-aged cheeks. I'm too old to start life over again, those eyes seemed to say, and I don't understand what I did wrong.

"Come on," Johanna said. And she pulled at Philip's arm. "There's no point in staying here." And she took off her light raincoat, covered the woman, and between them they half-led, half-carried her away. In the car Johanna held the snake charmer's head in her lap. The eyes were open now, but cloudy and vague like those of a sick animal. Mechanically Johanna smoothed back the coarse hair. With her own motherly body she braced the woman against the bumps in the road. "There, there," she said consolingly, still not sure if the woman understood English.

It was dark now, really dark, and Philip tried to squeeze more light out of the headlights. "How's she doing?" he asked into the back seat. The streets were empty as if the city were waiting for something. There was no overt sign of revolution. At the corner they stopped beside a wagonful of policemen who were laughing and shouting on their way through the darkness. They're probably drunk, like the politicians, Johanna mused. Occasionally the car lights gleamed off the shiny body of a pedestrian. Or a bicycle, like a pinwheel from the depths, would careen dangerously close to the car's body.

"You have to be careful," Philip said. "If you hit one of these guys, you're finished. You'd just have to run for it. The crowd would tear any foreigner apart without bothering to find out who's at fault."

Johanna remembered that some friend back home had given them that advice. She couldn't remember the occasion.

"That was probably an exaggeration," she said. "People love the horror stories." The woman lolled her head over on Johanna's knee as if in agreement. Johanna wiped a line of drool from the patient's mouth. As she did so she suppressed a wave of regurgitated spittle in her own throat.

From every floor of the hospital fluorescent light streamed out into the night. The building was a beacon in the darkness, beckoning to passersby like a roadside show. Along the corridors of tropical diseases and accidents of bad care and wrong decisions, lay the promise of help. Philip drove down the concrete ramp leading to the Emergency entrance with an engineer's precision. A policeman stopped them at the gate.

"Why are you stopping me," Philip asked in his abrupt way. "I have a sick woman here." And he counted on his color to bluff him through.

The policeman replied with equal anger that he had a job to do, as best he could. But he let them in with a scowl for a scold. "They're soldiers inside," he said in a final aside.

The waiting room was crowded. And there did seem to be some sort of official gathering near the rear. Old men waited, leaning on their canes, and pregnant women held limp children in their arms. A young man cried softly into his hands off to one side. The benches were arranged in rows like church pews. At the head where the preacher would have stood a worried Indian in a token white jacket copied information into a schoolbook. Sighing, he wrote down the familiar complaints. His diagnosis varied little. "Malaria" for any symptom of fever. And "Dysentery" for stomach trouble. Simple starvation was the only cure for digestive disorders. And he told the patients not to bother the doctor about them. The doctors walked importantly to and fro between a series of alcoves behind the large, overcrowded waiting room. With maddening slowness the patients in the first rows were directed one by one beyond. But the people in the waiting room could see nothing of what went on up ahead. A woman in a sari with a stethoscope around her neck motioned to Johanna to come forward. And together they put the woman on the bed. Johanna sat down beside her charge on a small aluminum chair. From where she sat she faced, on the other side of the corridor, a pair of pink-soled black feet which had fallen hopelessly apart in unconsciousness. Policemen guarded some cubicles, and Johanna assumed that meant that someone important was lying there.

The Indian doctor put her dusky ear to the circus lady's chest. She peered suspiciously at the cuts on her back and asked, but not as if she expected an answer, "How did she get that?"

"She seems so dazed," Johanna said anxiously. "Sleepy, almost passed out. What do you think the matter is?" She hoped for an answer from the middle-aged woman, who had a large and hairy wart on her nose. But the doctor was impatient to get on to the next patient. There was no time for explanations. She shrugged her shoulders and tucked the end of her sari into her waist. "You'd better send her upstairs," she said. "What happened?"

"Oh," Johanna hurried to explain. "It's such a funny story. Not amusing." She wanted to correct that impression. But the Indian woman seemed to have already lost interest.

"She's probably in a state of shock," the doctor said. And she walked out.

The matter-of-fact tone of her reply quelled Johanna's desire to explain. But why not be reassuring, Johanna thought. After all, it cost nothing.

Philip found them. He reached for the actress's tired fingers and she responded with a weak, flirtatious smile. "She looks better," he remarked to Johanna.

"We have to take her upstairs," Johanna replied gloomily. "To have her committed. They can't do anything for her here."

An African orderly came and stood by the bed. And taking one end of the heavy aluminum table together they swung the bed, woman and all, out into the corridor. The waiting patients still stared into an abyss of their own complaints and pain.

The elevator faced onto an outside corridor where everything was refreshed by a continuous breeze. Far down the hill cars passed peacefully. Johanna listened for the distant sound of drums or gunshots. The policeman standing guard in the hallway was dozing on his feet. The orderly in his starched green suit seemed no more than twelve years old, and he pressed the button with a child's love of mechanical action. On the fifth floor the African sister helped Johanna roll the patient onto a clean white bed. The ward was empty except for an old, old Indian lady who turned away at the sound of newcomers and coughed disagreeably into the yellow wall. Johanna realized that the ward was empty because it was private. The public wards, free to many, were filled to capacity. The nurse handed Johanna a muslin gown out of the drawer. "Perhaps she'll be more comfortable in this," she suggested, and she smiled. The beautiful young woman in her starched uniform which so smartly outlined her waist pulled over the screen, brought in a thermometer, and filled the water jug with tepid water. Her cap set off her round black cheeks to perfection. Such self-confident prettiness must in itself urge the patients back to life. But what does she think of it all? Johanna could not imagine, although the nurse's snappy walk told her something of what she thought about herself.

Philip was waiting in the hall. The circus lady seemed to have gone to sleep now. And Johanna sighed and stared at her dozing body. When the nurse returned a pair of long-handled, curlicued scissors were swinging from her waist. And in her hand was a clipboard with a badly smudged mimeographed sheet attached to it. Johanna asked when the doctor was due. The nurse gave no answer. And in the stillness of the late afternoon Johanna's thoughts turned back. Were the children all right? Mary Lou had probably taken them to her place. Under different circumstances Philip might have objected—he considered Mary Lou a bad influence. But they'd be all right there, Johanna was prepared to remind him. Mary Lou had worked in nursery schools in England, where she'd met that handsome African economist who was her peculiar fate. But apparently they could not get free to love one another. And now Mary Lou was left with her children and her contempt for this continent for company.

The doctor had come. He had a streaky gray moustache and that air of specialized knowledge so characteristic of the profession. What medicine could he know? Philip was trying to explain. The doctor lifted the woman's hand, held it in his own, and stared at the ceiling. In the pale hospital gown the woman's garish face seemed even more overburdened and tired. Her heavy eyebrows had blurred. Her lips parted and showed again the widely spaced, uncared for teeth. The doctor looked too at the cuts where the blood had dried in random patterns. "How do you feel?" he asked enunciating every word. "Your back isn't too bad. Just some nasty cuts. No stitches are needed." He took her hand in his confident worn fingers. "I'd take her home," he said to Philip, "and let her rest." Philip still wanted to explain. Home was that communal tent. Where were the words to express that indefinable sense of disaster which they had momentarily shared. The barker had played upon it. It was tied up with the unfathomable political events, the worn and dilapidated circus, and the amateurishness of the actors. They had all expected someone to get hurt. The old Indian ladies in the back row probably looked forward to it and had come out for no other reason. The Americans in the first-class seats cringed in pleasant anticipation. And the African children stood in the doorways silent and wide-eyed, waiting, because they had nothing better to do but steal a glimpse of the show. Philip wanted to tell the doctor that he didn't know the woman's name. Had he thought himself some kind of gallant knight when he offered to drive her to the hospital? Or was it his wife's idea? Probably something silly like that. Johanna always wanted to get into the act. Would the doctor care? Poor Buffalo Bill. Those had been real tears in his eyes. Philip watched as the doctor put the woman's hand back on the crocheted quilt. He looked at his watch. They're just interested in getting it over with. To pack you off one way or another. They're probably relieved when the patient dies, he thought, and panic made his heart beat faster. But the brown eyes of the doctor with the freckled lids were puzzled, not reproving. And his middle-aged shoulders had been worn into a slope. Philip blushed and recalled how hard most of the doctors worked in this hospital. And for their efforts they usually got a severe case of one of those incurable tropical diseases their Western constitutions had no strength to resist.

"Let her stay the night, then," he said. "Get a good night's rest and return tomorrow."

"She's probably in shock," Johanna commented idly. The woman was no longer watching. She had nothing but her face, to identify her, with half its make-up rubbed off. And Philip made up a name for her when the nurse with the glittering scissors wrote on the badly printed forms. Maybe at least she would get a good night's sleep in the clean institutional bed.

"We'll stop by the circus and tell them she's all right," he said. As if that would settle something. "He's probably worried."

Johanna hung back guiltily. She felt as if she were abandoning a newborn child. From the corridor she waved goodbye to the unresponsive body. For all they knew the poor thing couldn't even understand English.

Philip took his wife by the hand. They sank to the ground floor in the bed-sized elevator and walked through the still crowded emergency room and out into a night as warm and as dark as a stranger's breath—to locate the car, pick up their children, and find their way home. The next day they left town.

The Left-Handed
Marriage

"In describing Nuer concepts of time we may distinguish between those that are mainly reflections of their relations to environment, which we called ecological time, and those that are reflections of their relations to one another in the social structure which we call structural time.... The larger periods of time are almost entirely structural, because the events they relate to are changes in the relationship of social groups.... A man's structural future is likewise already fixed and ordered into different periods, so that the total changes in status a boy will undergo in his ordained passage through the social system, if he lives long enough, can be foreseen. Structural time appears to an individual passing through the social system to be entirely progressive, but, as we shall see, in a sense this is an illusion...." E. E. Evans-Pritchard, The Nuer

Jackson S. Michaels wondered in recent years why so much of his life aroused in him only a feeling of weariness, or boredom. He had few complaints. As a young corporate lawyer in the early eighties, by the luck of the times he made more money than he could ever spend, and he still enjoyed his international corporate practice and a good reputation. He was bewildered when successful men his age retired, or left the field. Sometimes they said they wanted to spend more time with their families, but Jackson never believed it. These were men pursued by wild animals who barely noticed the wives and offspring running to keep up with them.

Jackson was grateful to be more happily married than most. His wife Marjory was slim, clever and independent. Marjory said that there were two types of people in the world. Those who made things happen for them, and those who let circumstances or chance determine their lives. He was mostly faithful to her, certainly more faithful than the majority of the married men he knew in New York. Marjory made few demands of him, and he was the father of eleven-year-old twin girls, Josephine and Marianne, who called up his strongest feelings in surprising ways. Twins! As soon as they were born they took over his wife's complete attention, and were her entire preoccupation for years. Now it seemed as if the period of diapers and highchairs, emotional concentration, and little shoes and jars of baby food had passed. Jackson was old enough to count his blessings, to be thankful for everything which had, he admitted it, come his way rather easily. And he was young enough, forty-four, to expect more. Not that everything he had couldn't disappear in a moment, he had seen that, too. Still, Jackson knew that for men in most parts of the world it was enough to be able to put food on the table, to know your wife and children were taken care of, and to do work which was respected.

His fiftieth-floor window faced Central Park. The pattern of roads circled below him like the marked paths on a game board. A reticulated taxi was threading its way through bare tree branches, past the smooth gray backs of rocks, massive as elephants. It was March and beneath the soot which coated everything with a film of urban slime, Jackson detected hints of green beginning to appear on trees, in the mud, and on the spindly bursts of bushes. His partner, Smathers, talked on at the head of the mahogany conference table while Jackson catalogued the signals of spring far beneath him. The balance sheets blurred. The drumbeat of the figures was familiar, in any event. The money was multiplying, and the plan, it was his plan, was for the client to take over a competitor's enterprise which was starved for cash, creating new positive balances.

When had he begun to be bored? The trip last winter, the African expanses, had been a distraction, but a temporary one. It only made him hungrier for a real change. Perhaps that was why Marjory's proposal appealed to him. Jackson's externals, his profession, his education, his looks, his expensive clothes and neatly barbered hairline suggested a dedication to convention, or at least the status quo, but Jackson adhered to no such allegiance.

It was one of the secrets of Jackson's success that at any given moment, when he perceived it to be advantageous, he was willing to abandon an entrenched position, thus throwing off his opponents. He cared nothing for consistency. He was secure in his work environment. His bold moves in acquisitions had bankrolled the firm for years, and allowed it to dominate its corner of the market. No one was going to challenge his authority, at least not in the immediate future. There was no other person, except his present wife Marjory, whose opinion mattered to him.

As he progressed up the social and economic ladder, Jackson had effortlessly assimilated the unwritten codes: that eccentricity, even cruelty and perversity, were ,tolerated as long as they did not demand public acknowledgment; that charm and affability greased all gears, and that a person with a respected position who appeared to be playing by the rules could get away with almost anything—theft, adultery, fraud, or even bigamy.

Smathers buried his papers in his briefcase and locked it. Jackson liked Smathers enormously, and he was one of the few people at the firm Marjory could stand. When Smathers' wife was dying last year, Marjory came in several times just to have lunch with him and let him talk. He hoped Smathers wasn't annoyed by his dreamy lack of attention. As soon as Jackson realized that Smathers needed only his agreement on the final figures, Jackson slipped away mentally. He appreciated that his presence was ceremonially required when a decision was made committing such a large amount of money. Much of his professional life these days, it seemed, was spent waiting for someone to finish a ritual display. Jackson closed the heavy glass door—it was cleverly designed to be opaque in the center, where a face and body would be framed— behind Smathers, locked his desk drawers, and put on his new spring hat which had a jaunty quail feather in its band.

No, Jackson had no one else to consider. His father had been dead for more than twenty years. His mother lived in an expensive nursing home more than a thousand miles away. Jackson's first task as an adult was to provide for her after she had a stroke. When Jackson thought of her it was to recreate her in scenes from his childhood, since she was now a remnant of the person he loved as a child. She didn't remember the twins and often she wasn't sure who her son was when he routed himself to pay her a visit on his way elsewhere.

He had no brothers and sisters. In all the years of preparatory school, college, and law school Jackson made no friends whom he considered family. Marjory's parents were both dead, and she hadn't communicated with her older brother since he had borrowed a substantial sum of money from Jackson who didn't have much at the time. No, he thought, there really was no one who would make any trouble, or even care, about their marriage.

Yesterday had been much like today, meetings, dollars. He'd worked mechanically through the numbers for the buy through lunch. As he walked through the canyons of steel and concrete to the train station, Jackson felt the deteriorating city infrastructure lowering relentlessly down upon him, massive and metal, a torturer's rack. In the morning commuter's dark departure he had chosen a sock with a hole, and his feet hurt as if he had been walking barefoot all day on sun-baked clay. Then when Jackson sat down in the club car, finally, when he had been looking forward to an hour alone with the evening sports news, he was buttonholed by a former associate, Fitch, whom he hadn't seen for five years at least and barely recognized. As soon as Fitch started talking though Jackson recalled all too well the way his eyes slid from side to side in his face during bursts of self-derogatory banter, although now the high forehead was topped by a crop of kinky hair. An Afro toupee? A permanent wave to hide his baldness?

Although he asked after the family, Jackson knew Fitch only wanted to know how much money he was making. At one point Jackson even thought Fitch was going to screw up his courage to ask directly, or perhaps put the bite on him. Jackson remembered, when Fitch departed the firm with some bitterness before being denied a partnership, he called Jackson for several months afterwards, as if such fateful circumstances could be reversed, or Jackson, who was thought to be a rising star, could change the community view of him. But if Fitch was remembering that, he thought better of reminding Jackson of it. Instead he recounted with more specifics than Jackson cared to hear about the story of his wives, his spoiled children wasting their time and his money in boarding schools, and his sexual encounters with younger women, fueled by mail-order videos and artificial substances, legal and illegal. These girls didn't grow up like our wives did, Fitch said confidentially. He added in a stage whisper, You don't even have to pay for it.

When the conductor limped through the car to announce his town, Jackson felt as if he could fill in the details himself. Fortunately Fitch was going one stop farther, and Jackson hurried off the train without the pretense of being glad for this reunion. Jackson was happy to be alone in his old station car, with its holes in the floorboards and rusted chrome trim. The door made a heavy steel sound against the leafy suburban silence, as the train lumbered off down the tracks, swaying slightly from side to side on its way to the state capitol.

The twins, Josephine and Marianne, were standing beneath the huge, thoughtful sycamore on their front lawn. The tree had lived longer than Jackson would. Its mute, solitary presence was a steadfast, if somewhat disapproving, reminder of the fruit and shade trees which used to keep it company before the development happened. The white house with its graceful front porch had once rested on thirty acres with an orchard, and now the sycamore seemed outsized on what had been turned into a suburbanized plot of an acre, surrounded by a checkerboard of split-levels. As usual the twins were waiting for him, wearing fuzzy slippers and long flowered flannel gowns, jumping up and down to keep warm in the damp spring evening. Jackson scolded them for coming too close, as he steered the car into the garage.

When he reached the house, Marjory was watching the twins with the storm door ajar. She was tall, almost six feet, the same height as Jackson. Her hair was short, with bits of gray she refused to dye streaked through the black. Before doing some acting, she had been a model, and from habit or training, she still moved with the graceful authority of a lioness. I know you're looking at me, her open stride announced. Standing at the entrance of the handsome old-fashioned house, it had been inherited from Marjory's parents, she held the door open and smiled, as the twins scooted under her arm. Yes, there was no denying it, Jackson thought as he picked up Josephine. One or two green feathers were sprouting on the forsythia and green down appeared on the muddy surface where the lawn would soon reappear.

After supper when the twins were in bed Marjory and Jackson had gone as usual to drink their coffee in the den, where a fire was lit. A fine zebra skin, a trophy from last year's journey, was stretched out on the wall behind the sofa. Jackson was idly trying to remember something he wanted to tell Marjory, something they had to do, such as renew their passports, only that wasn't it. As he licked his spoon with the dividend of crusty melted sugar from the bottom of the cup, Jackson noticed Marjory also was eager to speak. Her chin was set purposefully, the lower teeth lined up straight with the upper ones. She was straining forward from the room's most comfortable chair, a deep green satin relic once belonging to her parents.

"Jackson?" It sounded as if his name were being called by the teacher from the front of a long-gone classroom. "Jackson?" That definite snap to the last syllable. Her tone said, pay attention. "It's time you had a second wife."

Jackson undid the laces of his shoes. The shoes were a quarter size too small. He took off his socks and put his city-weary feet on top of the African drum beside the chair and stretched his toes.

"There are laws against that," he said. "Besides, I am not unhappy."

Marjory was not finished. "I'm not young any longer." Jackson thought she looked ten years younger than her forty years, a girl taken unawares by biological aging, as if the wrinkles and sags were happening to someone else. Her legs and arms were slim and freckled. The necklace of lines around her neck seemed to be an error, contradicted by her long, swinging stride. "I can't have any more children."

This was true. After they recovered from the shock of having twins, they both wanted more children. When they were first married they had guarded their life without children. But once the twins were here, they both hoped for a son after a suitable interval.

This isn't enough of a family, Marjory said. They had been trying for six years now, and there was no sign of new life, although Marjory believed she had suffered at least two spontaneous miscarriages.

Neither Jackson nor Marjory discussed this directly. Both were unwilling to subject the other to the scrutiny of tests or probing by doctors. But the fact, this discouraging prospect of no new members of the family, no additional extensions of themselves into the future, cast a pall.

"The structure is all wrong," Marjory said. "We could raise twenty children, and we are only four."

The four-square character of their activities troubled her. Four at the square kitchen table, four seats in the car, two and two in line at the movies. Even their relish in each other's bodies, partly spontaneous, partly encouraged by the possibility of conception, diminished and was replaced by a soul-killing determination to procreate. There were weeks when they slept apart in the same bed.

Jackson was delighted with his twin daughters, but although he never admitted it in public, and certainly not in front of Marjory, he did desire a son. More than once he had secretly thought of adopting a boy, an orphan, or the child of unfortunates. So many children were consigned to a blighted life. His mind idly turned to the oddity of his never trying to change her mind about adoption, as he listened to the proposal.

"Broken homes are barbaric." She was staring into the empty fireplace. "For the children, for everyone."

More often than not, Jackson and Marjory had noticed, the partners ended up in a marriage similar to the first, simply worn down by the carnage. He let her continue.

"The civilized answer is a second wife. A younger woman. Someone who can give you a son, help raise the girls, and…be more interesting to you."

Jackson counted up the nights he had spent in town this month. Seven? Nothing unusual. Still, Marjory was no fool. She knew what he was feeling, and he never tried to dissemble. Wasn't she right about this? Wasn't that just what he would like?

"I suppose you have somebody in mind?" Jackson pointed one toe at her, as if he were floating on his back in a big warm pool. He smoothed the hair down on the back of his neck. His bare feet were pale and bony, and strands of black hairs curled over his instep like spiders.

Marjory answered him without irony. Her tone was straightforward, as if she was telling him where they were meeting for dinner. That was it! Smathers wanted Marjory to find an evening when they could have dinner with his daughter, Iris. She was still at loose ends after her mother's death, and Smathers hoped talking to Marjory might help her focus on college.

"As a matter of fact," Marjory answered, prim as a missionary, "I do have a girl in mind."

Jackson waited dreamily for her to continue. He couldn't imagine who it would be.

Marjory stood up, and as she reached down for Jackson's cup their fingers touched. She must have been mulling this over for weeks, he realized. Jackson's day-end lethargy, his boredom, vanished. Even his feet no longer ached. He had no intention of giving away his instinctive reaction: that Marjory had lost her way somehow. Still, he had heard of more bizarre family arrangements. The occasion demanded rising. Jackson stood up, and leaned towards her, as if to embrace her, and then he stepped back quickly, as his bare feet touched the cold floor. He had been all set to stay in his chair and finish the evening paper, as the fire burned down, just as usual.

"Can't you guess?" Marjory was pleased with herself.

Jackson shook his head. He hadn't the faintest idea.

"Angela."

"Angela?"

"The children like her. It would be a good opportunity for her." The spoons sounded against the cups as she walked. "Besides," Marjory's voice trailed down the staircase from the kitchen over the sounds of running water. "She's very pretty."

Last winter Jackson had spent one month in Kenya negotiating a complicated agreement for the firm's largest client. It was one of those assignments which cannot be avoided for the firm's largest client: setting up an international environmental foundation in Africa for the chairman's son to run. No one else in the firm was free, or wanted to be away around the holidays. Jackson actually welcomed the idea of doing something entirely different. To his surprise Marjory had wanted to come with him. The twins went to stay with a teacher from their school who needed the money. It was the first time that Marjory had been outside of America and the first time they had been away together for a long time.

Jackson had toured Europe as a student, years ago, and his work regularly took him for short trips in and out of international airports. Travel was no novelty for him, merely a calendar change which scrambled the body's rhythms, with occasional severe inconveniences, and snatches of beauty and terror. Marjory had always been scared of flying. Although she prided herself on being a logical, reasonable person, the family planned vacations somewhere accessible by car. Jackson thought she would change her mind about coming to Africa, but she was adamant, consulting several doctors about drugs to anesthetize her for a day and a half of flying.

For that month in Africa Marjory and Jackson lived like newlyweds, curling against one another in the tropical mornings, breakfasting on papaya and dark, viscous coffee on the sunny verandah. In Kenya no one scheduled business meetings before ten or eleven in the morning. For the first time in years Jackson was not rushing through the dark to make the commuter train. Since they knew no one else, they talked, to each other, about things other than the logistics of their lives, and the imagined future of the children. They agreed, they didn't deserve any of their good fortune, or this luxury, but it was delicious nonetheless. And Africa was deeply engaging.

Jackson's schedule was his own, and his purpose, to establish an anonymous charitable organization which would eventually transfer large amounts of money from a family foundation into the local economy, required subtlety. It especially required tact in dealing with the many government officials, who were harder to see than the vanishing wild life in the parks. The hint of a large transfer of hard currency in the future held a strong attraction to African politicians in the present who saw their own tenure as short-lived and fragile. Jackson was driven over hundreds of miles of bumpy gravel roads in a Mercedes by a garrulous Sikh, to inspect ramshackle buildings which were called factories. These were really shacks with an extension cord run out to an illegal power source, where he interviewed locals in charge of isolated rural conservation projects. Most of the time at the end of the dusty journey there was nobody in charge, or even to be found at the destination, although the roads may have been teeming with people walking.

Marjory accompanied him at the beginning. She wanted to see the North, where there was civil unrest near the Somali border, and they were told it wasn't safe for her to go unaccompanied.

There, women were rarely seen on the street, although they were the ones at the back of the lean-to factories, running the sewing machines, weaving the cloth from sacks of lumpy wool. If they saw Jackson, they ran away quickly, hiding their faces and giggling, although in Kenya the Muslim rules were not as strictly enforced as elsewhere. They weren't going to be publicly flogged because Jackson had caught sight of them or because they wore white socks. No one was stoned in the street there for adultery. Still many women went out shrouded from head to toe in Islam's black garb, in a *buibui*, dusted with the red clay of the village ground. Jackson and Marjory caught sight of them from time to time hurrying from one doorway to another.

After hours of driving across a parched countryside sometimes they came to concrete villages empty of everyone except skinny children, about the same age as the twins, who chased after the car, waving and laughing, and sometimes throwing stones. Their destination was usually just another village, one just a little bigger than the twenty or thirty they had just spun through. There Jackson had desultory conversations with polite clerks who fiercely apologized and said that the Officer would be in tomorrow, or next week, or next month, when they had driven five hours because they had been told that someone in authority, someone capable of making a decision or with information, would be here today.

Sometimes Jackson would find someone and he would be given suspiciously new government regulations to put in his briefcase. Well, how the country ran its government wasn't his problem. If he could create a legal entity which operated in the country yet existed free of the government, that was enough. Upcountry they slept in heavy tents on a raised wooden platform, a canvas house with flaps for windows and doors, semi-permanent accommodations left in place for big game hunters, the occasional team of international health workers, or lonely environmentalists. In the middle of the night they heard the footfalls of passing animals. One morning they found their car with a large dent in the door from a passing rhinoceros. These huge armored beasts had poor vision and high levels of aggression, often charging strange inanimate objects and injuring themselves. In the far Northern desert, children were stark silhouettes against the treeless horizon, leaning on sticks taller than themselves, their job to watch over a few sharp-shouldered cows. In the first week they crisscrossed most of the country.

Later when Marjory found herself alone during the day in Nairobi, she occupied herself by visiting the nearby wildlife parks. Nairobi Park was only a half hour away, on the apron of the city. Marjory could hire a car or drive herself for an afternoon, always catching sight of giraffe, lions, and wildebeest, and some segment of the endlessly repeating cycle: chase, kill, procreation, the watchful defense against predators, the carcasses of the young and the very old left in blood-caked grass by a satiated hyena. Zebras and gazelle grazed at the alert, raising their heads and quickly looking over their withers for danger, herds of hundreds, once they had been thousands, always on the move. Marjory liked best the living theater of the female lions curled around their cubs, those fuzzy, playful creatures who would grow up to be killers with no enemies except man. Or the elephants crossing the road with their young in a stately procession to water. From time to time, she would see in the distance the lone bull standing in the high grass, exiled from the herd of mothers and babies.

During the first days Marjory wished she had brought the twins, missing them terribly. Then she made friends with an English woman, named Isabel, who ran a women's cooperative near the hotel. Together they hired a car and driver and went to village craft factories in the densely populated areas surrounding Nairobi. Isabel came to Kenya when she married Abu, a Kenyan African who had been sent for his education to Oxford two decades ago. Abu eventually left the university without getting a British degree, returning to Nairobi where he took over his father's tire business. The newly married pair repatriated to live permanently in Kenya, over the futile objections of her family.

Abu's family called his marriage to this European a left-handed marriage, a liaison with an unsuitable partner, a union which would be grudgingly acknowledged if it produced children, but never really accepted by his family or the community. Because Abu was educated, everyone expected he would have a future in politics, all the more reason why a foreign wife was not desirable, but events beyond his control took over and his family's hopes for his political future were not realized. Abu did, however, become a successful businessman, and all of his many relatives in the villages and the city had televisions and cars.

During the course of the past fifteen years Isabel had almost single-handedly revived dormant handicrafts, including the production of traditional bark cloth and stenciled cotton. Isabel printed her own original designs on cloth as well, encouraged local painters and sculptors, sponsored an African art gallery, and sold all of these goods to tourists, all at a considerable profit for the women's cooperative she founded. After some years, Isabel told Marjory, her husband had taken a second, and then a third wife, the last one younger than their first child, a daughter. Isabel had married an African in his twenties who seemed to embrace everything European, including his English wife's idea of a monogamous marriage.

"At first I thought it was pressure from the traditional elders, that he couldn't shake the structure," she told Marjory. "I thought he couldn't disentangle himself from his family. That they insisted. And it wasn't his idea."

This seemed strange to Marjory. Which part wasn't his idea?

"But, no," Isabel continued. "He said, the tradition freed him."

Marjory wondered what he meant by that.

When Isabel had lived in Kenya long enough for her family in England to have given up on her return, Isabel concluded that her husband had never renounced polygamy, that he had always planned to take another wife. And while he had not exactly lied to her, certainly not when he said he loved her, he didn't exactly tell her the truth either. For example, Isabel told Marjory, Abu never told her himself about his most recent young wife. Isabel learned about her from her sister-in-law. In fact when Abu first went to England to the university, he already had a child by a girl in his village. There was little Isabel could do about that situation when she found out about it upon her arrival, especially since she loved her husband and had no desire to return to live in England. As the years went by, Abu's family continued to regard her as an interloper, although now they liked her and even depended upon her. Nonetheless, when the couple's beautiful, light-skinned daughter reached puberty, Isabel sent her to an expensive English boarding school on a legacy from the grandparents, gave up the battle for her son, and moved into the city, opening the handicrafts shop down the street from Marjory's hotel. She now lived in the apartment on the second floor above it. There was a gold-skinned young Indian who ran the shop during the day, and Marjory suspected he was more than an employee. The building belonged to one of Abu's uncles.

On their drives through a countryside carpeted with huts and people, with children everywhere, chasing the cars, or sitting on their haunches and waiting, the two women became friends. Isabel was a bit older, and better educated, but they found a kinship. The geographical distance between their experiences made it easier for both to speak freely about their lives. In their chauffeured car the two Europeans passed African women walking single file down the road carrying long branches for firewood balanced on their heads. Romantic in the morning fog, if you forgot that the long branches and twigs denuded what little was left of what had once been a large forest surrounding the city of Nairobi, where the Mau Mau hid during the fight for Independence.

Isabel took Marjory to the tin-roofed sheds, no more than three walls of dirt-splattered concrete, where the soft tree bark was wetted down and hammered into the traditional red cloth, where children glued beads onto the handles of traditional fly whisks favored by African heads of state, bought in airports by tourists and soon relegated to attics and yard sales. Rattan baskets in their hotel room became filled with bark-cloth applique, Isabel's bold hand-printed designs, raffia mats, the tippy round tin tea pots used by everyone everywhere, and an Indian hammock. All this joined the antelope-skinned drum and a zebra skin piled next to several large, gaudy ornamental neck rings, traditional to the Masai.

"Don't you see," Marjory said passionately to Jackson, after hours of bumping along muddy roads listening to Isabel. "It's the structure. The structure of their lives. No matter what kind of new business, or occupations people have. That will never change."

Jackson, who was finally making headway on the project to establish the environmental foundation, was startled when he returned at the end of the day and saw all the accumulated stuff. But he only asked how they would get it all home.

Then, Marjory discovered the ethnography museum. It was open pitifully few hours, in keeping with the lackluster displays of dusty pottery shards of unknown origin and chipped obsidian passed off as hand axes. Was this the only surviving record of a race of great warriors whose descendants now seemed to only want to own a car? Bones from the Olduvai Gorge pushed the age of man back thousands of years before Europe could claim human settlements. Where were the relics of those civilizations? Were these stubborn traditional practices all that remained?

Marjory took up residence in the chilly library established in the museum and then abandoned by lonely colonists. There, sitting in a huge square wooden chair on a threadbare cushion, an African exaggeration of Western comfort, she drank smoky English tea and reimagined the lives of the settlers. She read the memoirs of the British, whose elegant writing preserved their astonishment at coming upon the vast lands and herds, thousands of animals dotting the landscape as far as the eye could see, their wonderment at the inexhaustible sunshine and warmth, and the sharp realization that they never ever wanted to return to stony England. Marjory devoured the library's random collection of anthropological musings on Africa: Evans-Pritchard, Turnbull, Green, Stanley, Huxley, and Bohannon. These astute observers and writers of chronicles, some of them British colonial officers in the field, shared a duality with the British settlers, whom they typically despised. They watched themselves and their native subjects, the ostensible subject, creating detailed kinship charts, describing circumcision rites and ethnographic hierarchies, often while meting out punishments and rewards, executing rebels and arming soldiers, as administrators of the British colonial regime.

The settlers adapted. Their identity was set by the date when they left England. A strata of British society was lifted whole from pre- and post-World War I Britain and placed down in Kenya where it continued as if subsequent events in Europe and the rest of the world never took place. The colonists found England unrecognizable when they went home, and later the Crown's grant of independence to the former African colonies was a personal betrayal. Their communion with the breathtaking, treacherous land, so empty of civilization, their love for wild animals, and their condescending intimacy towards the Africans with whom they lived and worked hardened into a common political intransigence, irrespective of class origins. There was a yahoo similarity to their experiences, recounted with rapture for a readership at home. The confrontations with savage beasts were Biblical. The natives were exotic, handsome when young, cunning and also endowed with primordial wisdom. Encounters with them as soldiers, huntsmen, or servants were narrated with an air of enchantment at the settler's own cleverness and self-love, which wafted undiminished from the fragile, discolored pages of the volumes in the abandoned library.

Marjory became fascinated by the traditional customs and lineages, as seen through the foreigner's prism, relationships laid out with such seriousness on the page in ink-drawn schema: a chief's family tree, the descendants of polygamous marriages, age and sex grade rituals, the reported meaning of patterns of scarification. The British settlers were in love with the cattle people, the Nuer and especially the Masai, who plastered themselves with red ochre and spent their lives standing among their beloved cattle, whose milk and blood were their only subsistence. It was said there were more than a hundred words in these languages to describe a heifer, allowing the speaker to capture her individual beauty.

Jackson was pleased, and amused, that his wife, never an intellectual, should spend days reading thick anthropological tomes. He had the highest regard for her intelligence. At seventeen, in a typically headstrong way, Marjory had disappointed her father, an urbane and sophisticated doctor, by refusing to go to college. She aspired to be an actress and ended up as a successful model. After high school she presented her father with an acceptance letter from a well-known acting school in New York and announced that she had saved enough for the first six months, and would support herself in New York for the rest of the year, which she did.

That was when Jackson met her: she was working as a model in the afternoon and going to acting classes in the morning. The modeling jobs were so much more lucrative than any possibilities in the theater Marjory gave up the training. Marjory's father was relieved when she married Jackson, who was establishing himself in a recognized profession and a few years older. Although until his death it remained a sadness that his only child was ignorant of history, art and literature, and unacquainted with the basic tenets of science. At their wedding Marjory's father all but apologized to Jackson because she had no college degree.

Still he was disproportionately proud of her successful career in New York before marriage.

Jackson and Marjory were living at the Norfolk Hotel, long a favorite place for settlers coming in from the farm. Marjory could see scars from their drunken revelries in the dark paneling in the bar, taste their strong thirst as she drank their drinks, shandies and whiskey. Masai beggars sold curios on the sidewalk outside the hotel. Isabel maintained that they still sold women and children in the villages.

Jackson noticed that the men he dealt with—they were mostly his age or younger—rarely commented upon the past, or his Western demand for the formality of law. The papers he negotiated created an abstraction, a foundation, a legal entity in an American system which had a presence, if not an existence, in Africa. Perhaps they regarded his concern with documents as a cultural marker, an allegiance to tradition akin to the striated scars still visible on their own round cheeks.

Unlike Marjory, Jackson was not strongly affected by Africa. He found the traditional culture mildly interesting, the landscape and the people occasionally beautiful, and the society he dealt with, represented by government officials and lawyers, replete with contradictions. Mainly the cultural differences were a hindrance, a challenge to what he wanted to accomplish. When his cream-colored Mercedes splashed mud on the skirts of the women bent over by loads of firewood, he was genuinely sorry. In fact, he seemed to take more notice of it than the Africans sitting beside him. The Nairobi vegetation, its eucalyptus trees and bougainvillea, reminded Jackson of San Francisco, another pretty place where he felt a stranger. With African businessmen and politicians he was reserved, curious but respectful, flaring his nostrils slightly when he entered the room. That the people whose corrals he could see on the far hillside cut their cheeks to the bone for beauty and used cows for currency aroused in Jackson no more than acknowledgment. He considered the condition of the people crowding everywhere around him to be hopeless, if he thought about them at all. He found Marjory's enthusiasm for the cultural divide touching, if difficult to take seriously. And at that point they were still hoping she would soon be pregnant. In the meantime it was good she had found a way to distract herself.

One part of Africa did affect Jackson strongly. The beggars. Their twisted bodies and rheumy eyes, the stumps of amputated limbs wrapped with bandages dirty enough to have come from World War I. Jackson had heard that fathers deliberately blinded their children so they might beg more successfully. The amputees sat with kneeless legs splayed across a wife's stained skirt, or they hobbled with the support of a tree branch. Their open appeal for pity and cash, and the fact that the three-legged beggars were escorted by children, or were children themselves, raised in Jackson a sickened rage, whether these were victims of their families, a cruel religion, some civil strife, or accident.

He could not bring himself to put pennies in their greasy caps or small pink palms, even when his pockets were uncomfortably weighed down with large copper coins, another relic of the colonial era. It was a scam, a racket, then, ashamed, he reminded himself that the beggars were accepted by this society where there were few salaried jobs, even for the able-bodied. The beggars even had a function in the religion, to remind the healthy of their good fate. But Jackson never got used to them. He would cross the street or walk a block out of his way to avoid stepping over their crutches. Their condition was something he could do nothing about, he preferred to think about things he could do something about, on the other side of the street, and avoid the pleas of the suffering.

One day Jackson returned unexpectedly to their hotel room and found Marjory curtained behind a flowing black *buibui*, the black full-length garment covering the entire length of the body and face, with only a net window for the eyes, the garment which Muslim women were required to wear in public, if they were allowed out at all. The tall figure robed in shiny black was only a Halloween witch. The broad-shouldered American physique, that confidence of carriage, was unmistakable. She had been staring at herself in the smoky mirror opposite the bed when Jackson arrived back unexpectedly early. The flimsy black cloth, a nun's habit in a Muslim mode, fell in floating tiers from the top of her head and then her shoulders, hiding the geometry of limbs, the curve of the female body, the age and shape and identity of the woman. This black garment was worn every day by Muslim women, symbolically a permanent consignment to mourning for the fact of being born a woman, a prison from which there was no escape.

Marjory stood still as if waiting for the click of a camera behind the mirror's dark glass. Then she caught Jackson's eye in the glass and lifted the veil. In a moment the yards and yards of shiny black silk billowed into a soft heap on the ochre carpet. She was his recognizable American wife again, pulling closed the green velvet drapes, locking the door, pulling down his trousers, and laughing at his surprise as she ran her fingers over his ribs and down his back, her body a white shadow now in the darkened room, the garment at the foot of the bed a blood-dark pool on the sand-colored carpet.

Late into the night, as Marjory snored gently beside him, Jackson lay awake thinking about her proposal. The window was open and he could hear the breathing of the branches of the ancient sycamore. Jackson remembered the urgent sound of the tropical rain beating against the tent roof on their upcountry trips, a spirit crying to come inside. Then the drumming thunder rolling across the vast landscape, leaving as the rain's remnants a few puddles blown onto the wooden floor. In America the distant bleating of a truck, the jagged soprano line of breaking glass, or the rolling of steel wheels across a metal track as a garage door closed behind the rump of a car.

Angela Rogers, the twins' high school babysitter was, Jackson had to admit, a judicious choice. Her father, a handsome Korean War veteran with an artificial leg, had been a fixture in the community, propped against the counter of Perfect Day, the town's luxury dry cleaning establishment, for years. And then one day he simply disappeared. Her mother, Polly Rogers, had thereafter raised the girl alone, and was a sly, chattering woman with hair the metallic color of rusty water. After advertising her husband's disappearance in the local paper, Mrs. Rogers rented out the upstairs bedrooms in her sprawling Victorian house in town, which was walking distance from the train station. When Angela grew to be handsome, with an uncanny resemblance to her long-gone father, people were surprised they remembered the incident of the advertisement.

Angela's cheeks were shaded with blond fuzz, and her legs looked as if she had been running across sand even in winter. She covered the ground swiftly, with her nose pointed straight ahead, like a knobby-kneed cheetah. She acted as if she knew where she was going. Her shapely green eyes, one a little above the other, were asymmetric in her placid, round face, the kind of flaw which might have made another a great beauty. Angela's nose and chin were too large, but the total effect created by her open demeanor, tawny hair, and sleek youthfulness, was more than pleasing. In June, with luck, she would graduate from the local high school, in spite of flunking advanced algebra and avoiding biology or any kind of science for the third year in a row. She was brilliant as a 1920s flapper, the lead in the senior class play. Not only had she learned all of her lines, and looked exactly of the period in her skimpy beaded dress, but her persona on stage perfectly transposed the far from empty-headed charm of the Noel Coward heroine to the present audience.

From under the blinds Jackson could sense the dawn's approach. This was the genius of Marjory's suggestion: he'd be doing a good deed. The cycle was all too familiar. One season the beautiful young girls were tossing their manes and prancing down Main Street under the eyes of the current cohort of football players. In two or three winters, with blotchy complexions and bruise-colored circles under their eyes they were pushing a stroller in the supermarket and counting their coupons, the football players having long since retreated to bars. Jackson could at least help Angela preserve her youth. If she married him she would have a better life.

In the dark, a cough from down the hall. Jackson tiptoed along the shadowed path of carpet. A year ago he had installed an elaborate burglar alarm system, but the hair still stood up on his neck at an unexpected noise. Both girls were sleeping. Josephine's arm dangled over the edge of the bed, her palm upward. Marianne was jackknifed on top of her wrinkled sheet, the blankets wadded like a stone beneath her shell-shaped feet. Jackson straightened her legs, tucked the nightdress beneath her knees, and billowed the comforter over her. The gas furnace belched and turned over in the basement. Even asleep their expressions were similar, but not identical, childhood played in two different keys. Josephine was strong with her chin dimpled like Marjory's. Marianne was gentler, her mouth softer. Their two combs and brushes, the twin dressers with the ruffled gingham skirts, were all reassuring to Jackson in the striped light coming through the blinds. The branches of the sycamore rustled, as if sending him a message. Why not, after all? He was free. He answered to no one. Who would care?

Jackson padded down to the living room, checked the windows and tried the front door, taking care not to set the alarm off against himself. The smell of last night's fire reminded him of Africa. Jackson looked down the curving street at the suburban houses, some fenced, others hidden behind the shrubs. The backyards rolled down the slope of the former orchard, forming an undulating checkerboard of suburban preoccupations, here a bright swing set, there a sandbox and a wading pool, a basketball court, or a greenhouse. At least his house wasn't part of that predictable, rectilinear pattern. When he came upstairs, Marjory turned over to the rustle of crisp linen and leaves. Jackson kissed her ear, where the damp curls were streaked dark with sweat.

Together they worked out the calendar. Otherwise he could technically be guilty of adultery, or polygamy, or perhaps even statutory rape. Adjustments needed to be made for the laws and native customs of New Jersey. At first Marjory suggested that since no one would prosecute—after all she would never charge him with bigamy—Jackson should simply ignore the formalities of law and marry Angela and simply declare that he was divorced. This is what traditional Muslim husbands did. The town officials were filing clerks. No one ever checked the rolls. People lied regularly on the application form about prior marriages, or even put down false names. But Jackson was not willing to do that. After all they did know people in the town. There would have to be a proper, legal divorce. Or else anyone who didn't like him, or had a grudge, someone like Fitch, could threaten blackmail. Jackson wasn't ready to be put in that vulnerable a position, even if the goal was in fact to create a polygamous unit—the older wife with one set of children and a younger wife with another set of children, and the husband the master of both houses.

No, some deference had to be paid to American legalities. Jackson would divorce Marjory and settle upon her sufficient property to generate a generous income into the indefinite future. Marjory would continue to live in the Shady Tree Lane house. It was inherited from her parents and in her name already. Jackson would make the traditional arrangement when he married Angela. He would establish her in another residence, in another part of town, far, but not too far, from Marjory and his first children. After all the new wife and the older one, after the passage of time, sometimes became friends, and allies, even in America. This slight rearrangement of the typical pattern of divorce and remarriage, a commonplace among their social and economic group, would generate little more than a passing acknowledgment among their community. Jackson's mother would be told about the divorce, as a matter of respect for her former primacy in his affection; the fact, the rearrangement of a social reality which might once have deeply affected her, would mean nothing to her now and be displaced, or forgotten, in a moment.

As the father and still head of the household, Jackson would come and go in his old house, having access to the children of his first wife, the twins, and to Marjory, who would remain his number one wife. Who would know this arrangement was a little different? Most husbands regularly saw the children from their former family. Lots of husbands still slept with their first wives after a divorce. After all, this plan was only a preemptive strike, an inoculation against the ravages of the American divorce, harmful to children, devastating to the fabric of family which bound together communities.

Marjory thought it advisable not to explain the entire plan to Angela. Jackson agreed. Particularly, he did not want anything to cloud her frank and open nature. Why complicate matters by filling her head with ideas she wouldn't understand? What did abstractions about African polygamy, or hunger and faraway ethnic traditions have to do with Angela, or New Jersey, or with being the wife of a rich and successful New York lawyer? With the proper handling, Jackson hoped, an affectionate relationship would grow between the two women, who were both intimately connected to him, and among all of his children.

Angela was sweet tempered, and not stupid. She could learn a lot from Marjory, if Marjory would take her under her wing. Only her family circumstances limited her. Except for trips to the city clubs with adventurous friends, she had never been out of New Jersey. Jackson hoped the young girl, with her energy and eagerness, would pull Marjory back from the shoreline of depression. Who knows, perhaps, when the oddity of it wore off, they could all take family vacations together in the south of France. The divorce, not the marriage, would be the formality, the legality, merely a meaningless ritual required by society. Jackson did not anticipate any personal trauma for himself. He was keeping everything he had before, and just adding a new dimension, a new person, to the roster of his sexual partners, this time with a few extra trappings. No reason for the children to be upset. The interchangeability of parents, waking up to strangers in the house, was a commonplace among their schoolmates. Many children hardly knew whom they would find at the breakfast table in the morning.

As the plans unfurled Jackson began to feel an awed admiration for his wife, whom he now thought of as his number one wife. True, she had not anticipated all of the logistics, but the originality of the plan, its boldness were entirely hers. Jackson was only taking it upon himself to enact it, to see to the implementation. Matters of minor disagreement were negotiated out, just as in the world of the market place. If only all of his relations were as positive and amicable, with an outcome pleasing to all parties.

Take the matter of the actual getting of the divorce, for example. Jackson's first inclination had been to insist upon a regular, in-state no-fault divorce. But the mandatory waiting period foreclosed taking his second wife in June, as soon as Angela graduated from high school. Creating an indeterminate period when she would have to work, or in some way occupy herself, a hiatus of uprooted independence, would be risky. A quick Mexican divorce recommended itself. The property could be transferred and rearranged separately. And somehow a sleazy, foreign proceeding was more in keeping with their conception of the paper quality of the act. Jackson put a red circle around the last weekend in April and wrote "Juarez!" in the margin of the kitchen calendar by the telephone.

Mrs. Polly Rogers, the two sides of her frayed orange cardigan wrapped over her round chest, shuffled towards her kitchen at the back of the house, plugged in the kettle, and hobbled back to her chair facing the front door. Polly Rogers walked unevenly, at a tilt, rather from inactivity than infirmity. If the occasion required she could scuttle across the floor with a startling alacrity, as those tenants who sought to evade her at the beginning of the month discovered. The radio was playing sweetly serenading strings. Polly Rogers thought the classical station was the right backdrop for a conversation with Mrs. Marjory Jackson. Polly Rogers liked to wear orange. It matched her hair which, when it was wrapped into a topknot on her head, made her resemble, she thought, a favorite subject of Toulouse Lautrec. Polly Rogers had never been to France, and for all she knew women in Paris still dressed like that.

The roomers' mail lay in an abject pile on a long oak table. Once it had been a real library table, once the living room had been more than a pass-through where Polly Rogers sat waiting in a faded blue chair for the roomers at the beginning of every month. The hall beneath the stairs tunneled to the kitchen, and an oval mirror allowed Pally Rogers to simultaneously watch the front door and the back entrance without rising from her velvet cushion.

Polly Rogers was conscious of her rounded orange shoulders in reflection as her fingers sorted out the letters for Thompson, Quigley, Pepper, and Rogers. Only Mr. Thompson, he was addressed on envelopes as Duncan P. Thompson III, ever received real mail with a stamp and handwriting. For the second time this month Mr. Thompson had received a mailing postmarked Chicago. Polly Rogers pinched the thick envelope between her fingers, held it to her nose and sniffed. It seemed to be a letter. The postman delivered the other two roomers, Miss Quigley and Mr. Pepper, circulars with muddy addresses which could have been for anyone. The existence of Joseph X. Bell did not seem to be acknowledged by the postal authorities. Polly Rogers suspected he was on the lam from the law, or his creditors, hiding behind an alias at the top of the staircase, in the bedroom with the dormer window over the unused garage, the most cramped and least desirable room in the house, except for Angela's domain in the attic.

There was a thick envelope for Angela as well, from St. Louis, Missouri. Polly Rogers held it up to the tinted light coming through the ornamental glass of the front door. She considered slipping a fingernail under the half-open flap, changed her mind, and licking the envelope pressed it shut instead. It was probably worthless coupons. Angela accused her mother of opening her mail, but actually Polly Rogers rarely did. She had decided it wasn't worth it. Angela was always sending away for free trinkets, chances which turned out to be nothing more than opportunities to spend money. Who would Angela know in St. Louis?

Out of habit Polly Rogers scanned the table for her former husband's curiously feminine, sloppy hand. He favored a fool's indiscriminate felt pen, with a ribbon-like flourish on the downward stroke. An apology, an explanation, even an unbeliev- able one, an excuse, would have been welcome. But Polly Rogers never saw her own name in that loopy, fey writing emerge from the sad, melting pile on the hall table. The man's getaway was complete. Polly Rogers scanned everything else, the envelopes inscribed to *occupant*, the supermarket flyers, hoping for a personal message between the return envelope and the form letter. Today she diligently read all solicitations, sighing at the exhortations and exclamation points, as she waited for Marjory Jackson to arrive on her doorstep.

It was usually Mister Jackson who picked up Angela and brought her home. Marjory just made the appointments, typically calling precisely at 9:00 am. Polly Rogers hoped that Marjory was not coming to tell her something unpleasant. The girl was occasionally excitable, even difficult, and that rosebud mouth could erupt with startling obscenities. Had Angela been caught sneaking her boyfriend Craig in through the back door after the grownups left? Craig drove a souped-up and lowered seventies car, painted white with red flames down the sides, which rarely approached unheard. Or had the child been caught sneaking sweet liqueurs from the liquor cabinet? Polly Rogers hoped it wasn't anything worse. Angela had been involved in a flurry of minor shoplifting incidents last year. On the telephone Marjory Jackson sounded cheerful, even excited, not hesitant or reproachful, but there was certainly something on her mind. She wanted to talk to Polly Rogers about Angela.

There, the kettle was singing, and the doorbell ringing. The family terrier lifted his gray-haired nose and broke the anti- cipation with a feeble protest. Through the colored glass Polly Rogers could see the distorted bobbing head of Marjory, unused to waiting on doorsteps, peering from one side to the other, to find a piece of clear glass. Polly righted her red topknot, pulled her sweater closed, and sprung open the door. Her limp was accentuated as she retreated from the threshold.

That night Marjory reenacted the interview with Polly Rogers for Jackson. A subtle negotiator, Marjory had drawn Polly Rogers into reiterating her tale of abandonment and economic woe. Unlike others who quickly became nervous when Polly Rogers turned on her story of financial marginality, of the heroism required to live by her wits without the support of a husband, Marjory encouraged her to relate details of personal economic sacrifice for Angela, only for Angela. Misfortune, bad luck, and malevolence, on the part of the System, her husband and unknown conspirators, including his former employer Perfect Day Cleaners, who never told her he borrowed against his pay check and her credit card before skipping town, was all orchestrated against the background of a Beethoven trio.

The house needed a new roof. And the mortgage! After thirty years, Polly Rogers was still paying mostly interest because she had to keep reborrowing for infusions of cash. Polly Rogers sighed, pulled an orange thread, unraveling a few more stitches from the waist of her sweater. And the roomers! Even if she raised the rent a few dollars—the strings heehawed in the background—what good would a few extra dollars a month do? Polly Rogers sensed Marjory's visit had something to do with money. Marjory was so very sympathetic: honest working people couldn't make ends meet these days, while lazy, greedy people in New York City literally picked up gold pieces from the floor.

Perhaps Angela could help, Marjory suggested. Polly Rogers put on a furrowed brow, genuinely puzzled. Angela would probably clear out her clothes and music and escape to New York as soon as she graduated. Her two best friends were already squeezed into a closet-sized apartment above a bank in the East Village. They might be held up at gun point just walking into their own front door. The roommates took turns sleeping in the one bed, since one worked as a bartender all night. One of them had just come home to have an abortion. The bass hummed its disapproval. Marjory nodded and was silent. Children try their parents, especially these days. The viola took the theme to a higher register. Marjory was solicitous. Perhaps Angela could be dissuaded from this impetuous path. Fresh water was added to the pot. Marjory too was concerned for Angela's welfare. As a mother she understood the difficulties Polly Rogers faced, raising the girl alone in today's dangerous world with little money and no family to help her. And look how well the girl had turned out, all things considered.

Both Jackson and I have been watching Angela, Marjory said.
She is basically a good, hard-working girl. We've never been
displeased with her. She's fond of the twins, reliable for a young
person, and always helpful. She needs to think of her future. Now
introducing a new theme in a disturbing, darker mode. We'd like
her to be part of our family, more permanently. Marjory paused.
No, not as a servant. But with appropriate compensation, even a
settlement for her family. There were some unusual formalities.

Polly Rogers thought Marjory was going to offer to employ
Angela and then send her away for some sort of training. Angela
had such poor grades in high school it wasn't clear she could
matriculate in any school except a remedial program at a
community college, the kind of school so desperate for funds they
accepted anyone who was a resident. Polly Rogers protested,
trapped by her own eloquence: Well, it wasn't really as bad as that.
Polly Rogers knew the time remaining to exercise influence on
Angela was rapidly diminishing, as was the girl's external worth.
After a few years of urban self-abuse, she would be spoiled goods.
Perhaps she had exaggerated. Her orange bosom expanded, as
rounded as the breast of a robin in a cartoon. After all she did own
the house, even if it was mortgaged. Because the house was so near
to the train station, there never had been any trouble keeping the
rooms filled, even if the rent didn't always appear on time. She
could raise the rent five dollars a week next year, and even rent out
Angela's attic room.

Oh, but Marjory knew that keeping one's head above water was
perilous. Polly Rogers was a saint to carry on under such hardships.
So cunningly were all the harmonies played. The gray-nosed terrier
stretched out a paw in his dream of chasing a rabbit. Angela would
soon be legally independent of her mother and everyone else.
Marjory would like to help her to pay back her mother for all of those
years of sacrifice, and keep the girl on a steady path at the same time.
You see, here Marjory modestly looked in her lap, Jackson and I are
getting a divorce, and we could use her help for a while. Marjory
didn't contradict the impression given that the reason for the
divorce was too personal to be mentioned.

Polly's astonishment allowed Marjory to continue without
interruption. Had the girl been foolish enough to sleep with
Marjory's husband?

What was marriage and divorce these days? Nothing. A formality. Marjory said Angela could live with Jackson, with us, help raise the children.

That must be it, Polly Rogers concluded. The bastard seduced her, or perhaps the other way around.

In a few years the children will be gone, Marjory continued. We'll make it worth her while. The twins need someone cheerful, and good tempered, but an American. It must be someone from their own culture. It's important that they like her, and they do. Marjory hesitated. Five or six years, and perhaps a child, and Marjory and Jackson would pay her a wage, a good salary, and then for her to go to college, anywhere she wanted to go. Angela would be in her early twenties, still a young woman, still with her life in front of her. Why not?

A child? Polly Rogers thought she heard correctly. It was a strange proposal. At least they weren't running a pornography ring, or selling girls into prostitution. She didn't think Angela would go for it. Polly Rogers suspected Angela had already had at least one abortion. She certainly was no virgin, and might not be able to conceive a child. But Polly Rogers expressed none of these reservations. The girl had no interest in college now, nor had she ever talked of getting a job.

Then, Marjory astutely observed, she doesn't have any other plans, does she? And we would settle some capital on her right away, although she wouldn't be able to spend it immediately.

Polly Rogers could see the attraction of that for Angela. Her current boyfriend's future was bagging groceries at the supermarket.

Marjory was confident that Angela's practical side would win out, once she understood the sizable monetary aspect. At her age she would never be able to earn or save as much in so few years. Marjory knew Polly Rogers only wanted what was best for her daughter. Marjory suggested that paying off Polly Rogers' mortgage might be part of the bargain. Then Marjory wondered if she had gone too far.

With a rattle and a squeak the front door was pulled open. A damp cloud of March air rolled into the living room. Mr. Thompson, a damp and rumpled figure of a man of an indeterminate age past fifty, bounded into their midst, the wind at his back. He nodded his red chin toward the ladies and hung his coat with its dripping hem and his sodden hat on the outstretched arms of the wooden coat tree. Shaking the raindrops out of his hair, he sidled towards the pile of mail.

Habit saved Polly Rogers from a spontaneous response she might have regretted later. "Oh, Duncan, there's a letter for you from Chicago," Polly Rogers chirped. He nodded as if to thank her, and under his sidelong glance, the ladies bade each other farewell, promising to talk further, as the music rose to a thin mournful climax.

Jackson's response was instinctive. He had a strong, visceral distrust of people on the wrong side of luck. He certainly did not want to be in a contractual relationship with anyone like Polly Rogers. It was not her economic marginality, but the way she used it which made Jackson nervous. He didn't negotiate with desperate parties, they couldn't be trusted. Nonetheless Jackson appreciated what Marjory had accomplished. Polly Rogers had not rejected the plan out of hand. Jackson himself would have been too direct, too businesslike, too impatient, not willing to listen sympathetically to the old tale of how the world had done her wrong. He would have turned the negotiation into a transaction.

"I don't think she'll give us any trouble," Marjory said over her shoulder, climbing the stairs in front of Jackson.

A month later, after returning from a Saturday dinner in New York with Smathers and his daughter, Jackson drove Angela home. The late hour, the dark and dampness of the Spring night, were conducive to suggestion, Jackson hoped. Angela was chewing gum, and wearing shorts and sandals with no sweater or jacket. She rubbed her ankles together, like a cricket, and flagged her toes. Her cheeks were glowing. Jackson had spent the dinner trapped in awkward, monosyllabic exchanges with Smathers while Marjory talked to the daughter. Then he threaded the car through a hypnotic river of blurry headlights on the turnpike. Now, on the quiet country street Angela was disconcertingly alive, as fresh as an African sunrise. Four cream-laden courses and two bottles of wine weighed Jackson down somewhere in his middle, and he was leaden and earthbound beside her. Her pencil case and school book rested lightly on her bare thighs, the brown paper cover written over heavily with repetitions of her initials, and her name, in thick, shaded block letters, and another name surrounded by colored, solipsistic spirals, smoke from the smoldering embers of her heart. She seemed to be quivering and alert, for a breathing moment inside his car, in the night, in her clothes, in his life.

Jackson felt imprisoned by his indigestion and his custom-made suit, which held him in the grip of a boa constrictor. He suffered a hundred traveling twinges and disconcerting rumbles in his interior, and his feet were hobbled in thin, pointed Italian shoes he had foolishly bought while killing time in an Italian airport. That a new moon was being chased by silver clouds made Jackson feel even older. At least he had taken the station jalopy, with its leaks and rattles, its floor littered with weeks' worth of scraps and bits, instead of the antiseptic bubble of the Cadillac, a dirigible floating along the highway.

"Angela," Jackson began. If he hadn't been punching the worn gear shift into reverse, he would have looked at her soulfully.

Angela interrupted him. "Oh, yes, Sir," she said. The "Sir" was not promising. "Mrs. Jackson said you wanted to speak to me about something, about a job."

That deferential tone would be another thing to work on, Jackson resolved. Nor was it a good sign that she called Marjory, Mrs. Jackson. This was a person who was going to be an intimate member of the family, who was going to share his bed and board. His heart sank when he realized she had never called him by his first name.

"Please call me Sonny," he said. No one in his life had ever called him Sonny, but he had always liked the name.

Her smile was wide, friendly, but posed, as if for the yearbook portrait. Usually Angela was at ease with her physical self, although tonight she was worried she might be pregnant. "OK," she said, but she couldn't say the name. "I know I need to save some money. For school." School seemed to be the last thing on her mind.

Jackson turned off the paved street and decided to head down a gravel road, a maintenance track next to the golf course. He would park by the long third hole, where he inconsistently drove his ball over the little green pond which was usually surrounded by a flock of geese. The turnaround there should be pretty in the starlight, although the moon had momentarily skidded behind the clouds. Too late Jackson realized his error. Darkened cars loomed on either side of the track. His bouncing headlights, like a police searchlight, floated over the shadowed mounds resting in the roadside brush. Engines turned over in his wake; cars with their lights off were slinking away behind him, reversing down the dirt track.

What had Marjory told her? "School? I thought you hated school?"

Hadn't there been a murder here a few years ago? Dimly Jackson recalled anecdotes of muggings and small-time drug deals. Didn't the police warn women to stay away from the golf course at night? He swerved to avoid a dark car crawling towards him at a slant with one set of wheels on the grass, and reassured himself that such events were no doubt infrequent in their town. Perhaps she thought he was going to offer her a job. Well, it was a kind of job, wasn't it?

Angela's school book slipped off her lap and onto the floor, among the shards of discarded coffee containers. Jackson's headlights washed over a garish red and white car which Jackson had noticed on his own quiet street earlier in the month. Hadn't that been Angela in the front seat next to its driver? Angela's head was down, her hands groping for her book and the spilled colored pencils.

"Not regular school," Angela said, her voice muffled by her legs. "To study to be an airline stewardess. Or a model." She set the irrelevant book on her lap and came up with several paper containers crumpled into a ball. A strong but oddly mixed collection of scents mingled with the scratchy odor of moldy upholstery.

Jackson's headlights picked up a circle of whitewashed benches around the silhouette of a large dark tree. He stepped out of the car and quickly examined the terrain to be sure there were no holes or branches in the way. Angela rolled down her window and sunk down into the creaking springs, still holding the sticky wad of garbage. Jackson stood alone in the moonlight and waited. The road flattened out and presented a clear patch to turn around in.

Angela showed no sign of moving. "I'm sorry about your family, about you and your wife breaking up," she said through the window, as if announcing the fact to him. That wasn't how Jackson thought about it.

Surprised, Jackson abandoned his plan for a romantic approach under the stars and climbed back in the driver's seat. Slamming the door behind himself, he wrestled the car into reverse. "Oh," he said. "It's all right. It's probably for the best." Had Marjory told her? Jackson's arm was flung over the back of the passenger seat, as he maneuvered the car backwards towards the tree with the chalky necklace. Not getting stuck here in the mud was more important than an opportunity for an embrace.

Angela's head was tucked into her lap. She moved closer to him. "Mrs. Jackson, wasn't she a model?" She had assumed a schoolgirl voice, filled with awe, with expectation. Perhaps Marjory had told her the plan. "She must have been awesome."

They were turned around now. Jackson's headlights quickly skimmed over the hoods and front seats of cars parked in the underbrush. A few honks of protest were sounded, now that they realized he wasn't a cop. Double shapes bobbed up in the windshield and then disappeared.

Jackson hesitated a moment. "Angela?" He had no idea what she was thinking or what Polly Rogers or Marjory might have told her, or what was going to come out of his own mouth. "I want you to be my wife. To marry me and become a member of the family." It was better to make the proposal without the contrived endearments. "I'll take care of you. It needn't be torture, or even forever. Just for a few years. And the remuneration would be substantial. Your mother is not opposed."

Cruising through the empty main street of town, they passed the sleeping stores, the darkened movie marquee, the community notice board plastered with staples. The old car was spinning along, enjoying a run through the dark now that it was awake.

Jackson didn't expect her to understand. Did she know remuneration meant cash, even if it was some time in the future. "Think about it," he said. "Marjory can't have any more children, and we both want a son."

Probably he should have lied and said he had fallen madly in love with her, that he couldn't resist her young seductive body. She could have understood that, the all too familiar tale of the middle-aged American male, deserting his life partner for the enchantment of youth, seeing how many women he could bag after the separation.

Angela's ready answer, the crispness of her reply, frightened him. "It's a deal," she said. "For four years." There was no hesitation in her response, or doubt in her tone. "Then I'll go away to school." It was as if she were consigning herself to a period of indentured servitude.

"What about a child," Jackson asked, sensing this was the moment to push for a commitment. "We'll help you get into college."

"That's good," Angela said. "But just one. And you pay for me to go to school after." Now she looked at him. "And take care of it then."

Jackson's breath escaped as if he had received a sudden blow to the diaphragm. He had not expected such ready agreement. Would it be matched by fact? "Yes, yes. We...or rather the family, will raise the child. Even if it is a girl."

She was pushing the contractual nature of the arrangements farther than he had dared. So, this was how serial polygamy was implemented. If Angela had any personal affection for Jackson, it was not apparent. But she must not find him totally repulsive. That she was so bold to dispose of her own life, her own body, startled him. That she could be so calculating about giving up a child was chilling. The young were indeed radical, foreigners. Suddenly, as if overcome by a surprising grief Jackson wondered whether he could learn to live with a stranger, especially one with a cold heart. To explain who he was all over again, to undress in front of someone who did not know or care who he was.

In front of the Rogers' house Angela waited with her hand on the door handle. Did she think he was going to kiss her? The downstairs of the house was dark; on the second story a single lamp was burning. One of the roomers was reading, or perhaps writing a letter.

Of course, Jackson reached for his wallet. He hadn't paid for the baby sitting. Embarrassed he gave her ten dollars extra.

"Think some more about it." He was afraid she had made up her mind too impulsively. "Don't be too casual. Four years can be a long time."

Angela's legs flashed in the car headlights. She took the slanted wooden steps two at a time and waved a hand at him from behind her back. Jackson waited until he saw her light appear in the attic.

Mr. Thompson III coughed as she passed his door. From the second-floor bathroom came a steamy, perfumed cloud. Angela tossed her school book, pencil case and wallet onto a pile of dirty laundry and fell face down diagonally across her unmade bed, laughing and hiccoughing. No wonder she looked so fresh. Angela had spent the previous two hours experimenting with everything in Marjory's bathroom cabinet: astringents, greasy night creams, stimulants, eye liners, relaxers, liquids and lotions had been rubbed on, scrutinized, and scrubbed off, one after the other. Her cheeks were still burning. She had tried to put everything back so that Marjory would not notice the intrusion. If Jackson hadn't been so preoccupied he would have smelled it on her.

Polly Rogers, her limp very evident, and out of breath from the last flight of stairs, nudged open Angela's door. She leaned over the brass bedstead and held out her hand for the cash. If she didn't take the money, it would be gone the next day. Polly thought that the girl set her baby sitting fees too low for the rich families on the other side of town. Angela held back the extra ten dollars.

Angela made a face. "Mr. Jackson said you knew all about it." She sat up on the bed.

Polly thought Angela's face was blotchy from crying. She twisted the tie of her bathrobe around her hand. "You don't have to do anything you don't want to," she said. "We can get along without them."

Angela was sitting cross-legged, pulling her shirt over her head. "It's OK," she said. "At least I'll get out of here." She eyed her mother through the round neck of her black T-shirt, looking for a moment like a nun with her face ringed in black cloth. "And you agreed anyway. Didn't you?" Her voice was low, and her mother made no response. "You might have warned me." The girl in her was no longer apparent, having been replaced by the practical spirit of a middle-aged person of indeterminate sex. "But it's OK. Actually it sounds like a pretty good deal."

Polly slipped out without waiting for more.

On the first Sunday in May Jackson left Marjory to reseed the front lawn while he went out to look at real estate. From their tree house in the sycamore the twins watched Mrs. Abbott, the agent, pull into the driveway in her dark green sporty jeep. "Who is that?" whispered Marianne, wiping peanut butter onto her sweatshirt. A loose-leaf notebook, listing the homes for sale, lay open on the front seat of the car. She peered through the windshield at Jackson's traditional house, whose faults were masked by its charm in the Spring morning. "Let me know when you want to move this one," she said.

"It's not for sale," Jackson said testily, as he slipped into the back seat. Jackson was engrossed in a complex and secretive takeover, a raid on a neighboring business, and what he wanted to do now was to be at home planning his strategy for next week, not looking at real estate.

At their first stop the owner of the cottage, Mr. Grayson, must have been waiting for them behind the front door which sprung open as they reached the front steps. The thin wooden walls so close to the soggy stream promised a winter of coughing. Still, the cottage did have the charm of weakly watermarked stationery. A sweet, no-nonsense fireplace was flanked by two chimney seats which the twins might like. The boxy living room had slender windows facing the unprepossessing brook. The incessant sound of running water might be reassuring, or maddening. Perhaps Jackson was still feeling queasy from last week's trip to Mexico. The bathroom was disproportionately huge and light, sporting new brass fixtures and a footed tub. Someone imagined himself dreaming there, but the poorly fitting window sash suggested bathing in the winter would be bracing, at the very least.

Jackson had put his wedding ring in his pocket where it rattled disconcertingly against his house key. The last time he had taken it off was when he had a scan at the hospital. The trio parted as heartily as drinking companions on the steps. At a roadside rest spot overlooking water, Mrs. Abbott opened the listing book on an iron picnic table riveted to a concrete slab. They went over the offerings while three generations of an Indian family at the next table, all dressed in identical purple windbreakers, solemnly unloaded box after plastic-covered box of their fragrant lunch.

Their second stop was a white frame colonial in a new section of town which Jackson found to be a poor imitation of the Shady Tree Lane house. With a closed mind Jackson listened to Mrs. Abbott check off the features: "Air conditioning, forced air, double wiring, a new water heater, and a new furnace.... " In every room Jackson recalculated his estimate of the age of the woman, the previous owner, who was showing the house: hair dark at the roots, muscular legs in baggy shorts, but bony at the hips, so that her thighs did not touch. Divorced? His current transitional state encouraged such speculations. Jackson was amazed at how many women contacted him when the word was out about the divorce.

"Didn't you say ten-thirty," the woman asked Mrs. Abbott, implying she might have changed clothes for the occasion.

In the car Jackson asked, "What about an apartment?"

The town zoning allowed only a few multiple dwellings. Next door to a shopping center, a mile from Polly Rogers' house on the main street, they stood before a massive steel frame, an apartment complex under construction. One section had all four walls up, and a muddy hole had been dug for the second.

On Sunday morning the building site was deserted. Across the street stood a church shaped in a hexagon. Over its entrance hung an abstract sculpture of clustered crucifixes, many crosses of different sizes and thicknesses, piled into a jumble and suspended from an iron chain. Organ music and the singing of a choir wafted across the empty street, blessing the morning.

Jackson walked among the steel girders and peered into the encrusted mouth of a cement mixer. Steel reinforcements, like outstretched fingers, reached up to the sky. The roof was yet to come. Mrs. Abbott, in white pumps, tiptoed behind Jackson on the two-by-fours laid at angles across the mud, reading from the brochure: "Rent: five hundred...approximately. A very small deposit." She waved her hand. "Living, dining el, kitchenette. Nothing to keep. Two bedrooms, fifteen by twelve each. Good sized," she added amicably.

Jackson was beginning to appreciate the agent's skill. The idea of moving into a place no one else had lived in was appealing. The building sat square to the street. At the back there was a parking lot, and the remains of a grove of trees, a remembrance of the town's rural past. Jackson remembered the little grove of trees as a place where mothers brought toddlers to throw bread at the ducks on their way to the supermarket. The ducks were probably still there.

A stick-figure woman and a man so tall he might have been on stilts, stood side by side next to a square for a window, in the crass commercial representation of his future home. The bedroom would face onto the parking lot. The remaining trees might muffle the sounds of the busy four-lane street when he and Angela went to sleep at night. There would not be neighbors, although someone would live across the hall.

"Leaves a lot to the imagination," Mrs. Abbott said. "You can decorate from scratch. A clean slate. Occupancy, June first."

The church was expelling its congregation. Ladies in hats and the men with crossed arms stood in groups of two and three along the four-lane street. The larger children scuffed the soles of their Sunday shoes, while the younger ones wrapped themselves around their parents' knees, silently pulling towards home, until an impatient mother or father uncoiled them or stamped a foot. Organ music continued to rain upon them all, even on the unrepentant Jackson and the businesslike Mrs. Abbott. Mrs. Abbott removed her white shoes, balanced in her stockinged feet on a two-by-four, and offered Jackson a paper towel and a spray bottle of windshield cleaner for his own shoes. Heads at the edge of the herd of worshipers looked at them and then turned aside, as if they were sinners caught naked in the act.

It would be easy even for Angela, who had no housekeeping skills, to keep. She wouldn't need a car, a definite plus. Her friends, even her mother, could easily visit. Parking in the supermarket lot next door was ample. There was no land, home in the usual sense, or yard, nothing to fight over with neighbors, no neighbors. Like the stick figures in the advertising brochure, only the essential characteristics of a home or furniture would be needed. No neighbors who had watched you come and go for ten years and thought they knew who you were. Jackson told Mrs. Abbott to prepare the papers.

When she dropped him off at Shady Tree Lane, Mrs. Abbott reminded him, "If you ever put this one on the market..."

Back home the coffee table was littered with travel books and schedules. It was not usual that the breakfast dishes were piled in the sink, and their bed unmade. Where was Marjory? They often went back to bed on Sunday, followed by the twins, who came in with their books under their arms. But today, he had work to catch up on and there was no sign of any of them. Jackson hoped they would soon all come home to find him upstairs.

Jackson's divorce came through on schedule with the help of a Mexican lawyer the firm found for him. The three days of sunshine in Mexico cleared up an infection that had been clogging his sinuses. Jackson had not intended to move out of the Shady Tree Lane house, after all it was his home. Since the divorce was only a formality, a legalism, why should he? He was astonished when Marjory, in tears, insisted he leave. The twins expected it, she said, now that they were divorced. They knew what divorce was from their friends. With much grumbling and complaining he carried out some clothes, but he wouldn't let Marjory box up his books and belongings and put them in storage. His fishing gear, his skis, his high school sports trophies, and his outdoor boots maintained their position in a corner of the basement.

"I'm sorry, I'm really sorry," Marjory said, as he packed up his clothes, as if for a short trip. And he believed her. It was less clear what she was sorry about.

During the week Jackson moved into the city. His firm kept an apartment for out-of-town business people, and Jackson took a furnished sublet in the same building. It was small but it had a view of the park and was within walking distance of his midtown office. Jackson was surprised that many of the people he knew only casually from the train had heard he was divorced. He didn't miss the commute, or seeing those familiar faces, people he cared nothing about, every day. At first on weekends he slept at the Sunrise Motel and spent hours on the golf course and at the movies, something he hadn't done for years, with Angela on Saturday and with the twins on Sunday. At least they could all talk about the movie.

During these few weeks Jackson and Angela always had dinner together out on Friday and Saturday evenings, at an overpriced country inn or restaurant. The food was uniformly mediocre, and the atmosphere pretentious, but Angela who was not used to being taken to such places didn't care. She noticed little beyond the interior decorations and the head waiter. Marjory had taken her to buy a trousseau and she wore her new, expensive clothes with obvious pleasure. Mostly they talked about arrangements for the wedding. Jackson had little interest in the details, or the formalities themselves, all of which seemed to preoccupy Angela, but he was pleased Angela seemed engaged in plans where he played a central role. On Sunday nights for these few weeks she went home to her girl's bedroom in her mother's house, to get a good night's rest before school the next day. She seemed to agree it was important that she graduate from high school.

Jackson hated the Sunrise Motel. The windows were permanently curtained, and the television offered only pornography or bloodshed. He detested instant coffee, even if it was free. He missed his children, and it was distasteful to bring Angela there. He liked to comment on items in the morning paper and know Marjory was listening. The truth was, he missed her. On week nights he wanted to watch the play of expression on his daughters' solemn or hilarious faces, when they talked about whatever concerned them that day.

Angela's appearances at the motel were brief and functional. In a rare moment of intimacy she told Jackson that after their engagement, she wore a large diamond engagement ring, her sort of high school boyfriend, Craig, had grown a beard, and then dropped out of school and left town. "He looked ridiculous with that beard," she said with some vehemence. Jackson wanted to ask if this was the young man driving the white car with red flames on its side, but he didn't. He held her in his arms and felt her tears wet his bare chest. Age and experience served Jackson well in those moments. They soon started going to New York for weekends, which was much more satisfactory to all concerned.

The wedding was planned for the middle of June. The financial arrangements with Marjory and Polly Rogers were settled. Jackson assumed the mortgage on the Rogers' house, and quitclaimed to Marjory his marital interest in the Shady Lane house. Both residences needed repairs, and Jackson paid for those as well. Jackson's financial situation, thanks to his practice and the market, remained strong, and these obligations were no burden. By contrast, the apartment was refreshingly new, cleanly painted all white, and miraculously completed on time. In its few small rooms the furniture was simple and functional.

Angela wanted to be married in a church. Polly Rogers commented that she had not set foot in a sacred place since her first communion. Jackson did not object. Church meant nothing to him.

They picked a pretty Presbyterian church with a white steeple in the next small town. The closing of one leg of the commuter line had forced the parish to sell its organ and make do with a donated upright piano. Nevertheless, the church kept going, hired a young minister right out of the seminary, and began taking in business as it came along.

Tom, the new minister, was blonde and extraordinarily handsome, with hair the color of corn silk falling in a cowlick over his forehead. His arms and upper body might have belonged to an underwear model, and his personality was magnetic. Still the thought that this startling young man would counsel him was ludicrous. Angela kept her eyes demurely down and barely spoke during their initial meeting. Jackson's view of ministers, especially Presbyterians, derived from nineteenth-century novels, images of dimly lit rectories and talking to old ladies regarding the building fund. Jackson wasn't used to thinking of ministers working out at the gym, or having a business plan. Weren't they supposed to be taking care of the poor?

Tom looked at them with such naked curiosity that Jackson was momentarily tempted to speak openly to him, to reveal the entire plan. Somehow he thought Tom would understand. But the temptation passed, and Jackson was freed from Tom's alert glance, as frank as a proposition in a bar. Jackson put his right hand over the white indent on his wedding ring finger and said he hoped the marriage would be a new beginning, mentioning that there were twin daughters from a previous marriage. Jackson reassured the minister he could afford two households and wrote a check to the church well above the expected amount. Tom hesitated, as if wanting to ask more, about the divorce or the twins, or Jackson's own spiritual condition. Then he simply slipped the folded check into his breast pocket. The church offered special counseling for families in disruption, he said, and out of the corner of his eye Jackson noticed a flicker of interest pass across Angela's serene face.

In the car Angela talked about her dress, which was white and satin and required several fittings. She like to think of herself dressed in it, at the shop, in the mirror, and eventually in photographs. Marjory and Jackson had eloped, and Marjory never had a wedding dress. The twins became unpredictable. Josephine was blotchy with tears when Jackson moved out, and Marianne refused to speak to him and hid under the bed. But they both had wanted to be bridesmaids. When Jackson called home from the city to speak to them, Marjory was businesslike: They had gone to bed. Jackson thought they would have liked to have heard about the lace and satin trimmings on the dress.

When Jackson visited Marianne and Josephine, Marjory retired to the kitchen. While he was talking to his children in the living room, a place where he never used to sit with them, Marjory whispered into the telephone. People whom Jackson had never heard of cropped up in her conversation and were referred to uncharacteristically with endearments. She began wearing flamboyantly fashionable clothes and makeup, which she had not done for decades. She refused to say anything about her plans, answering abruptly or even rudely, that it was of no concern to him. He noticed that she had started to darken her hair. Angela was often at her mother's. They were closer now than they had ever been before. Jackson was looking forward to being married again.

There were four of them at the ceremony: the bride and groom, Polly Rogers, and Marjory, who, Jackson was surprised to see, still wore her old wedding ring. Angela had thought the twins might like to carry her train or be flower girls, but Marjory vetoed that.

Tom read the vows radiantly, and delivered a short speech on the sanctity of the institution, its permanency in the eyes of the Lord. He stared at Jackson throughout. Polly wept. Angela smiled and was as beautiful as any bride in a magazine. With her hair pulled away from her peach-colored face, she looked grown up. Jackson lifted the veil, kissed her cheek, and intercepted Marjory's stony appraisal over Angela's white-satin shoulder. A schoolteacher who had been a substitute teacher for the twins played a Schubert march on the upright. Polly Rogers wiped her eyes. Marjory pecked the bride on both cheeks and kissed Jackson rather sadly, he thought. She said she only wanted his happiness, words which put fear back in his heart. Three new red suitcases were piled in the back seat of a rented sports car.

A few weeks later on a Sunday when the children had gone to a birthday party and Jackson found Marjory unexpectedly alone, he reminded Marjory of the original terms of their arrangement. He said that, as far as he was concerned, they were still married. She would always be his first wife, his most important wife. When they finished making love, she cried and said she couldn't sleep with him again. Jackson had no reply. They had been married eighteen years on that day.

As the summer went on, once in a great while Marjory still prepared food for him, listened to him talk about the power struggles at work, or inquired after Angela. The house looked different. Things were missing. She said she couldn't stand any of this anymore, with an expansive gesture which included the kitchen, where they were quietly drinking coffee, the rest of the Shady Tree Lane house and him. Next the twins told him Marjory was looking for a job, which surprised Jackson since she had no financial reason to work. Jackson continued to deposit the support payments in what used to be their joint account, and padded the stipend with extra money. He still wanted to take care of her. At the beginning of the marriage Marjory occasionally bought Angela clothes and coached her on the etiquette of business dinners: never contradict or speak over a man and wear expensive, sexy clothes and perfume. During this time Angela became fiercely jealous, and asked minute, obsessive questions about what Jackson did when he visited his old home.

Towards the end of that muggy New Jersey summer, as he came to pick up the twins Jackson found a medical van parked in the driveway of the Shady Tree Lane house. And on the street an open moving van being loaded with living room furniture he recognized as his own. The neighbors on both sides were busy weeding their front gardens, with a good view of the comings and goings. Jackson walked through the front door and heard the twins in the backyard. A figure clothed from head to toe in black passed along the upstairs hallway now bare of books. Anger clouded his vision at the sight of his departing furniture. His king-sized mattress was being maneuvered around a newel post, only the feet in sneakers and the fingers of the moving men visible behind it, so that the bed seemed to be sidestepping by itself down the stairs on its own four feet. From behind the mattress came a cheerful warning to Jackson. Apparently they could sense his hostile approach behind the mattress blind.

Jackson flattened himself against the wall, holding his breath and his temper. A slide projector and screen had been set up in the dining room. The souvenirs, the African drum, some of Isabel's prints, the Masai collars were piled into a cardboard box. An envelope of airline tickets lay on the top of the pile. The whir of the projector fan was a calming white noise against the bang and clatter of the stampeding family furniture. On the screen a tusked elephant, ears flapping in anger, was heading down a dirt road straight for Jackson. The Nairobi Game Park, on a quiet afternoon last year, one of his best pictures.

All the decorations, the little boxes, the pictures and the lamps had been stripped from the walls. A set of graceful, hand-carved end tables lay on their backs on green pads with their legs in the air. The chairs were lined against the wall, as in a funeral parlor. The drapes were down, and the untamed New Jersey humidity filled the corners of the empty boxes of rooms, reminding Jackson of the suffocating rain forest. They never did get around to air-conditioning the place.

Upstairs Marjory was talking to herself. From beneath the wings of the buibui she displayed a bandaged hand. "I scalded myself making tea...in that African pot," she explained to Jackson, to the kids carrying furniture. "I was preparing...I planned to be out of here by now..." She frowned. "I didn't want you to have to see this." What didn't she want him to see? Her costume, the moving furniture, the mess? "I am about to. I am supposed to...give a lecture at the library—about women, about Africa."

Jackson sat down on one of the chairs against the wall, as if he were in a government office waiting room. "Was I supposed to come and find everything just gone? Did you think you could leave without me finding out about it?"

Jackson thought she looked ecstatic, in an elated, elevated state. He sat and watched the raid continue.

Marjory winced. "I am gone," she said. "There is nothing you can do about that. And the twins are coming with me."

Marjory had taken a job, teaching in a Kenyan school. A school sponsored by an American labor union and Presbyterian missionaries. The school wasn't far from where Jackson had set up the foundation in northern Kenya.

"To teach what?" Jackson was incredulous. "What can you hope to teach anyone? Especially them?"

"Oh," her confidence was brittle and wafer thin. She pulled back her silken sleeve to look at her watch and winced. The watch was a new one with a cartoon face and a bright green band. Jackson wondered what happened to the platinum one he had given her for their fifteenth anniversary. "You know. Reading. Writing. English. The usual." She came down to his level. "How to navigate through the American immigration system. How to type, if they have a typewriter. We have orientation and training in Atlanta first." She looked at Jackson. "At least it isn't someone else's idea … of what I should do."

Her face was still masked with pain, as she prepared to walk out. "You were right," she said. "If that means anything. I didn't keep my end of the bargain." She paused and then smiled. "So what are you going to do? Have me flogged in public? Cut my hands off?" The corners of the tickets in her hand were as sharp as arrows. For the first time in their relationship Jackson wanted to strike her.

"But everything went exactly as you planned," Jackson protested. "Only better. You were right. I'm very happy."

"At least the twins can live with me," Jackson said, rising to the occasion.

"I doubt if Angela would like that," Marjory replied, her attention now turned to putting together her belongings. "Anyway, they're excited about seeing Africa. You can fly them home as often as you like."

"But you don't know anyone there." Jackson wanted to cry out against all of this disorder, these new splintering plans.

"The church provides everything," Marjory said, her tone asking how he could think she had not thought of that. "It will be fine. All the other teachers are from abroad, too. Most of the others are Europeans, or American college kids. They have to make arrangements for the foreigners." Marjory signed the movers' receipt, clipped to a dark brown board dappled with drops of sweat. "At least I'll be doing something for someone else." She sniffed and wiped her nose on the back of the bandaged hand and then gave Jackson a surprisingly passionate kiss on the mouth before going out the door.

Jackson lay in the hammock in the backyard with the twins.

"Guess where we're going?" Marianne asked, triumphant.

"I know. I know. Africa."

In the car on the way out Jackson leaned on the steering wheel and watched the moving truck pull away. Large parts of his life had been lived in that bed, at that table, and within those four walls.

It was September and still over ninety degrees outside. Angela was knitting something out of bright red wool. Jackson sat opposite with the Sunday paper in the boxy living room and wondered if she was making something for him. Marjory had called from Kenya, full of cheer and details about their journey. Josephine had a cold, but otherwise all was well. The new job, the communal living, the training, learning Swahili, it was all exciting, the people wonderful. The twins were having a great time. Jackson was darkly suspicious. She had a young lover. She said little about herself, but the twins promised to write regularly. Their voices were impatient. Isabel met them at the airport. To get them through the private customs officials, without the bribes, Marjory said, laughing. She was sending a blurry Polaroid of the one-room school and the dormitory with the tin roof where the three of them would share one room.

Angela was talking. Jackson listened with half an ear. Polly Rogers had been over yesterday. Polly was complaining about her new roof on the Washington Road house. Angela had gone out for some cold cuts and run into Mrs. Abbott in the supermarket parking lot. Mrs. Abbott mentioned that several attractive, large homes were on the market, including the Shady Tree Lane house.

"I put a bid on it," Jackson said. "Anonymously." He sensed that if Marjory knew it was his bid, she would turn it down.

Angela clapped her hands. "And guess what," she said. "Mr. Thompson proposed. To my mother!" Angela said she told Polly Rogers that Mr. Thompson was just after her money now that she had some. Mr. Thompson had girlfriends all over the country, Angela had told Jackson earlier with disapproval. That mousy little man had girlfriends all over the country? Jackson now believed any couplings were possible.

"And you should have seen mother today. She did look sharp."

Jackson thought Angela had let her own appearance deteriorate. She had gotten a bit pudgy from all of the eating in restaurants. Still, he was glad to hear her be so enthusiastic about her mother.

"She was wearing a new suit. Blue, very pretty with her red hair. And those treatments have really helped her back. She hardly limps." Angela changed her needles from one hand to the other. "I love that house," she said. "She's crazy to get rid of it."

Jackson was scheming as to when he could go and visit the twins, under the guise of checking up on his other African projects. He suspected that Angela mislaid or forgot to give him some of the letters and cards from the twins. He would feel better if he could actually see where they were all living. If he moved into the Shady Tree Lane house, the twins could have their old room back.

All through college and into their twenties, the twins remained very close. They asked but were never told the reason for their parents' divorce. They always felt they had been lied to about it. The experience in Kenya turned out to better than even Marjory had hoped. The other teachers were Swedes and Norwegians of indeterminate age, and idealistic Americans in their twenties. Four of the young Americans and a Swede, who used to be a minister, lived together in the compound on school grounds. They treated the twins like younger sisters. Later the twins appreciated what it meant to be picked up and out of their suburban American environment, to be recreated as foreigners in Africa. As a white foreigner it was impossible to escape standing out in a crowd of Africans.

The twins started a small afternoon nursery school in the church for the children of staff and villagers, scraping together toys and books from donations. Their status as Americans gave them other responsibilities beyond their age. The children worshiped them, and stroked their hair. When Jackson visited them, he was impressed by their poise, how quickly they had grown up. They didn't miss home very much, they said. They became used to being special people, people who commanded attention, people who had something of value to learn or teach, or give away, even if it was only their language.

Marjory died in Africa after an automobile crash, followed by tardy and inept emergency care. One of the many unlicenced drivers on the Kenyan roads slid headlong into their car as it was making its law-abiding way down the muddy road. She was with Isabel at the time, who lost a leg as a result of the accident. The twins were home visiting Jackson, looking at colleges. Jackson didn't even hear about the accident until after Marjory had died.

After that Jackson's fear and antipathy to Africa coalesced, and he refused to let the twins return, even to bring back their clothes or few belongings, or to say goodbye to friends. They cried and comforted each other, but for years they felt that their mother's death was unreal. Only Angela was unmoved. She said she felt she had never known Marjory. Jackson hired a courier to bring home Marjory's ashes—she had been cremated without his permission—and their few school books and the family's possessions, which did not include any of Marjory's jewelry, not even her watch.

For that year before college the twins did live once again in the Shady Tree Lane house, redecorated in French country style as a weekend place. Angela complained the house wasn't big enough for all of them, especially with the baby.

The twins suspected that Jackson never told them the whole story, and for years after their mother died they spent hours speculating on the scenario which ended up sending them to Africa. He probably had an affair with Angela when she was their baby sitter, they decided, and was too embarrassed to admit it. Jackson and Angela divorced when the twins were just about to graduate from college. Angela's son Tyrone, six at the time of the divorce and fourteen years younger than the twins, was raised alternatively by Angela in Los Angeles, and then by Jackson's third wife, Louise, a practical and kind person who grew into the maternal role.

When Tyrone lived in the Shady Tree Lane house, Angela would turn up on short notice to visit. She was still very pretty, but distant, although often tearful at their partings, calling herself their stepmother, which she never was. She never had any other children, although she married several times. Josephine and Marianne never felt they knew Tyrone, or that he was their brother. They remembered him as an exceptionally beautiful child with hair startlingly pale, the color of corn silk.

After college both Marianne and Josephine longed to return to Africa, a place whose imaginative importance expanded as it receded in memory. After much effort, they succeeded selling themselves as experienced African hands and became summer volunteers on an environmental project in Northern Kenya. For two months in the desert they taught fuel conservation techniques to young women in black robes and veils. En route in Nairobi for a few days, they tried to locate Isabel. They were told by the African woman in charge of the crafts cooperative that Isabel had gone back to England.

After Chekhov

Seaside resorts, even when they are in a decline, have an unreasonable, festival atmosphere about them, and in 1959 Anita Sarah Delmar made plans to stay all of July at the Grande Hotel on the Boardwalk of Atlantic City. Photographs of her grandmother, smiling from within coils of a fur boa, which had been taken on the same boardwalk fifty years ago, came to mind. To go someplace where her grandmother had been, instead of the currently fashionable ocean beaches, appealed to her present desultory mood. And for a most reasonable sum Mrs. Delmar was given two very large adjoining rooms overlooking the boardwalk and handsomely decorated with Hollywood-style blond furniture and crystal chandeliers. Colonel Delmar—the title survived from active service in the Philippines in the last war—had to be in Formosa this month. And why was it they had never bought a summer place? When they last thought about it they had a quarrel. Mrs. Delmar said she wouldn't go to a place where Jews weren't allowed. Then there were those summer excursions of Colonel Delmar's. Somehow the building project—they had gone so far as to telephone an architect—never got started. And, as a result, instead of sitting on a suburban lawn Anita Delmar was sitting on the sand squinting at her son as he poured bucket after bucket of ocean into a tiny dent in the beach.

Bathers in slow motion walked by carrying balloon-like loads, chairs, balls and umbrellas. The beach was not crowded, but a steady flow of strollers passed overhead to the rhythm of the boardwalk music. One peculiarity of the resort crowd stood out. The young girls and boys tried to look old and sophisticated, while the middle-aged men and women paraded in candy cane stripes and pastel colors. Four sailors in shining white suits walked by, laughing with their arms linked. And one or two old men could always be found sitting on the benches which faced the sea.

Mrs. Delmar was thirty-five, but she sprinkled her conversation with up-to-date slang and took a youthful, loose-jointed stance which fooled people. It amused her that the lifeguards called her "Ma'am." And she almost didn't care that the summer dandies who patrolled the water's edge in pairs hardly troubled to look her figure up and down. She decorated Eric's castle with mussel shells and ice cream sticks, waded in the water, and took long afternoon naps in the shaded hotel room. At eight o'clock she dined alone in a huge nearly empty hall lit by crystal chandeliers, and as she ate she read about strikes and a distant war in the evening paper from the city.

Nine years ago when she met Colonel Delmar Anita was working as a secretary to a well-known Broadway talent scout and getting over a broken college romance. Like many pretty girls, she had done some acting in college. Anita could sing and dance well enough to be in the front line of the chorus in the campus musicals, and she loved everything about the theater. Her job was hard work, low paying, and fun. Famous actresses and producers were always stomping through the office in the middle of a crisis. And Anita was given free tickets to Broadway openings for herself and her equally impecunious friends at the Barbizon Hotel for Women. At one of those openings she happened to be seated next to an older man in uniform.

Colonel Delmar was a handsome, deceptive forty. Then, as now, his dominant physical feature was a shining bald skull with a fringe of shaved stubble around the edges. With characteristic resourcefulness Colonel Delmar had managed to turn what for most people would have been a liability into a distinction. He kept his head an even shade of brown, and the skin on top always looked freshly oiled, like a piece of fine teak or walnut. His bearing was impressive, especially since he almost always wore his uniform. It was a time when military men were proud to wear their uniforms in civilian society. He seemed wonderfully knowledgeable, serious and stable, so unlike her other frivolous young friends. Colonel Delmar knew the answers to everything, and his whirlwind courtship was as carefully planned as a maneuver through an enemy mine field.

After nine years of marriage Anita was still pleasantly surprised when he came into a room, removed his hat—he owned many beautiful ones in shades of tan and gray—and bent down the well-oiled prehistoric skull to offer his cheek in greeting. Sometimes when he slept she ran her fingers along the back of his neck and felt the bristles there.

When they met, Colonel Delmar's wife had just divorced him and gone to San Francisco after a miscarriage. He told Anita all about it the first night they met, when he eagerly took her off for dinner in a tiny French restaurant in the Village. Anita felt such simple sympathy for the man's confessed loneliness she forgot her own disappointments of the heart. Within three months she had promised to marry him and make things right. At the news Anita's father, a retired doctor, called his broker and settled some mineral stocks in her name. Her mother, who had been living in a nursing home since a stroke three years earlier, never took cognizance of the event. The wedding was small, almost to the point of apology, and for Anita it remained colored with surprise at how well the groom and his father-in-law hit it off. The band, a trio of college friends, and the fact that the embroidery on the bodice of her dress itched were Anita's memories of her wedding. For the rest, there was a feeling of propriety, of hurry, and the impression that people were waving goodbye from behind a transparent pane.

Three months after the wedding the bride admitted to herself there was nothing pathetic about this busy, square-shouldered man. His business, which he had been disinclined to say much about during the courtship, turned out to be selling guns and tanks to the highest bidder. This business, which he entered by chance after being in scrap iron, had made him a small fortune. Anita also learned, in that incidental way in which wives learn important things about their husbands, that sometime in the last few years he had suffered a mild heart attack.

It bothered Anita to be rich. She had never known anyone who was rich, that is, rich enough not to consider a long time before buying a new coat. Her memories of her father were of late, slow lectures on the virtues of saving money. The truth was she also missed her job. Anita was proud of having worked for a living, and she felt contempt more than envy for the women who seemed to want nothing more than to occupy themselves with the disposal of another's income. Also she detected a certain authoritarian tone which the earners took towards the spenders. Anita knew Colonel Delmar would never let her go back to work, and she never even raised the question. He fooled me with his uniform, Anita said to herself later when she remembered their informal courtship. Somehow she saw less and less of her working friends. One moved to California, another married and went to live in Connecticut. And her former boss had long since hired another secretary so that she just felt replaced when she went by the office.

Still, things could have been worse. True, Colonel Delmar did only as he pleased, provided that caused no immediate embarrassment. He relied upon no one for trust or affection. Secretly, Anita discovered, he regarded his failed first marriage as an accident which might have happened to anyone. His pretty, new wife seemed to be a more appropriate outcome. When Eric was born he was happy, but slightly puzzled. As if he wasn't sure the biological process in any way involved him.

For Anita the birth of her son was the most surprising and wonderful thing that had ever happened. In a single stroke that sense of displacement, of detachment, which had coated her life like a film was wiped away in a single excruciating stroke. Everything— the routine chores and the luxuries—was rendered sensible. And if this euphoria, too delicate to be happiness, did not last neither did her youthful purposelessness return. Outwardly her life became no more interesting, but she no longer looked for it to be transformed. There was a curious lack of congruence between the way she perceived her life, an outsider's impression of it, and the fact of it. She had no second face behind her public face. But if the future seemed too straight ahead, the blur of a busy present papered over the faulty perspective. Anita cropped her hair, shortened her skirts, and always had Eric trotting at her heels. The years of Eric's early childhood passed painlessly, and now he was five, almost ready for school. Everything seemed fine until this past spring when Anita's best friend, an older, well-travelled woman named Sophie, died after a short but horrible battle with cancer.

Sophie had also come to New York as a young stagestruck girl just out of college, and like Anita she had married a wealthy older man. Together they went to the theater, exchanged novels, and laughed over long lunches at the Algonquin. When Sophie became ill, it was as if Anita herself had suffered a mortal wound. Even the company of her darling Eric was no consolation. Then the fact of it. Her only friend's incomprehensible suffering, the helpless submission at the hands of the paid caretakers, her wandering, freed mind which no longer found it necessary to distinguish between this day, last year, and moments in her Minnesota childhood—all of this burdened Anita like a shameful secret. And aside from Anita the only one who cared was Sophie's longtime maid who sniffled into a handkerchief as she wandered through the silent apartment in slippers. Anita sat in Sophie's beautiful white bedroom and stared past the blue curtains at a man mowing circles in the lawn and wondered. The incongruity between her own random days and the musical stateliness in which death approached her comrade was unacceptable. The discrepancy was so basic Anita felt it would be ill-bred to mention it. Like talking about bowels or dentistry at the dinner table. Towards the end when Sophie only ate crushed ice, Anita could hardly sit at her own dinner table and watch Colonel Delmar masticate his steak.

The Colonel was impatient with his wife's moods and silences. And the day Anita remarked that Sophie confused her with the nurse, he asked why she went if her friend no longer knew her. Why indeed, Anita asked herself. It was true Sophie often did not know Anita was in the room. Anita supposed she went to accustom herself to the lesson being given from the bed. Those arms which rested on the puffed quilt like bones in cotton belonged ten months ago to her round and laughing friend. A kind of camaraderie grew up between all the regulars at the hospital. The old man who dozed in front of the TV and waited for his wife to die three doors down. The stout woman with the red curls who walked up and down the scrubbed corridors leaning on a cane. The teenager who came and held her father's hand for an hour every afternoon and then slipped away, outside for all the world like all the other freckled and gum-chewing teenagers scampering home for supper. These well people visiting the domain of the dying formed a short-lived but special kind of friendship.

Eric's nurse had gone back to Norway for the summer. After the long and exhausting bout with Sophie's illness, Anita welcomed the excuse to take the child to the shore by herself. After all, next year he would be in school. It was one of the last times they would have together without having to worry about outsiders. Eric stood and let the water dig holes behind his heels. Anita held his hand and watched the water run up, fill the moat around his castle, and fall back. They walked to the pier and looked for sea urchins which might have been stranded behind the tarry poles. Then back and Anita sat once more on the sand and listened to the ocean's voice. The big ships on the horizon moved so slowly across the gray line between sea and sky that Anita had decided they were painted there. Then when she forgot to look she discovered they had inched closer to a distant spit of land which seemed elongated for the interception.

As Anita read to the child in the afternoon she had a sense of being taken back to when he was a baby, when their body rhythms had been exactly synchronized. Anita now strained her eyes reading the tiny blurred print on games and toys. Eric invariably chose things too complicated for his age—models requiring tweezers, glue, and saintly patience. Then they quarreled, like brother and sister, when the toy didn't come together as magically as the statements on the box had promised. Sometimes Eric kicked the box onto the floor when his mother couldn't get it right. Then he fell sulkily asleep and wriggled out of her apologetic embrace. Anita would smile to herself during her bath and think about what a passionate child he was as she dressed for dinner in the light of the doorway.

Downstairs the fat drummer whisked-whisked the samba beat, and nobody danced on the square of polished wood in the center of the dining room. In between courses Anita timed the beaky headwaiter on his trips to the kitchen and speculated on how many men were required to hang the twenty-foot drapes which masked the view of the ocean. Tuesdays and Thursdays she filled the inside and both flaps of an air letter to Formosa and heard her message flutter to the bottom of a shiny brass box standing at attention by the hotel registrar.

At the beginning of her second week Anita noticed a familiar looking woman walking with a cane up and down the boardwalk. A white toy poodle bounced along beside the lady. Later that afternoon Anita heard the poodle's high yapping bark from inside a Bingo parlor. The next afternoon when Anita was paying her bill—she preferred to pay by the week—the poodle's cold wet nose touched her ankles. Anita patted the silly puff of fur on the dog's skull. The older woman pulled the poodle up short, peered back at Anita from behind smudged lenses, and asked after her friend in the hospital. Of course they had met in the waiting room when Sophie was dying.

That same evening the older woman, whose name was Mrs. Deitrich, made her uneven way across to Anita's table and asked if she might sit down. Mrs. Deitrich wiped her lips with her handkerchief periodically as she was eating. She confessed, as if it were her own fault, that her husband's sister in 6B had had a second stroke and died a month ago. She nodded when Anita said that Sophie too had not walked out of the blue and white room overlooking the garden. Over the soup Mrs. Deitrich catalogued the weeping relatives at the funeral. Her husband had been dead for two decades. Then the mortician's work and the selection of the grave site (a power struggle between two factions in the family) were all reported. Mrs. Deitrich didn't pause until she had herself dosed with sedatives and asleep on the night of the funeral. Frequently mentioned in the narrative was her only son who had just taken a new job in a New York advertising firm. Mrs. Deitrich spooned the last of her ice cream puddle into her mouth. If only his father were alive to see it, she sighed and swallowed. Anita gathered there had been some difficulties in the boy finding a job. Anita found the old lady comically tyrannical, but she told her something about Sophie's sickness and appreciated her listener's silent attention punctuated by the clicking together of her front teeth at climactic moments. Somewhere in the telling it became unimportant that Mrs. Deitrich was a domineering old woman and not her friend. For all her exaggerated responses, despite the fact that she talked too much, the eccentric old lady seemed to understand. The next evening in tacit exchange Anita listened to a rambling account of the heartbreak (Mrs. Deitrich's) attending George's recent broken engagement and the tortures the poor boy suffered at the hands of a spoiled, selfish fiancée. According to his mother women were always throwing themselves at George. Later that night as Anita lay in bed kept awake by the coffee she wasn't used to drinking, she tried to think of some place to hide in the huge empty dining room. The next evening Anita had cold turkey sandwiches sent up and played Go Fish with Eric as they ate.

That weekend Anita noticed the new arrival on the beach—a young blond man with no suntan, rather unhealthy looking, with an effeminate face and limp curly hair. He didn't look almost thirty. When he whistled the familiar white poodle trotted up to him. Usually he was smoking a cigar, and the cigar seemed to require an extraordinary amount of attention, for he was often bending to light it against the sea breeze or standing up primly and knocking an ash off on the boardwalk railing. Yes, there was something ridiculous about him, Anita thought. She had expected a person rather more dashing to be the hero of Mrs. Deitrich's melodramatic tales. When the dog trotted up to her, Anita patted its tiny white head, as fragile as an egg-shell head, and introduced herself as an acquaintance of his mother's. George tucked the dog under his arm, held out his hand and smiled at Anita as if he knew all of her most intimate secrets.

George and Anita sat together on the beach in the mornings, while the old lady rested in her room. Eric built castle after castle at the water's edge and was surprised anew each morning to find nothing left of yesterday's work. Anita sat on a slung striped beach chair with her face hidden under a large white hat. She always covered her legs and arms in the sun. George equally pale and terrified of the sun sat cross-legged on a towel beside her. He had a small white scar on his cheek, and it became whiter and more noticeable as he became sunburned. The poodle cantered back and forth between his master and the water and never tired of yapping at the waves. Anita wriggled her toes into the sand, leaned on her knees, and watched the horizon. George talked almost all of the time. He had a slight catch in his voice, an intake of breath before each sentence which made the listener pay close attention.

He told Anita amusing stories about his friends. He described how much he hated the army and how his mother bribed a local officer to have him spend basic training in New Jersey. He was less than ten years younger than Anita, but it felt like a generation. He was cynical about his quite ordinary job in the large advertising firm, where he was paid little to do little. It was clear to Anita he was going nowhere. But he had no intention of staying there. He was, he said, not really a businessman, but a writer. They walked along the Boardwalk at night when the velvet sky was decorated with stars while Eric slept the deep sleep of the sunburned.

One day before lunch the four of them, George, Anita, Eric and the poodle, walked twice along the Boardwalk and then went on the merry-go-round. Eric kneeled on Anita's lap, grasped her around the neck, and exhaled in her ear at high speed. Then they rode the bumper cars and Eric jumped up and down on her legs. George tied the poodle to a post where he howled miserably. Sometimes they ate sticky sweet snow cones which dripped sugary purple water. Anita liked to listen to him. His voice was rapid and eager. Like a child who couldn't wait to tell. His job, his girls, his friends—she knew about all of them now too—the famous silly people he looked up to, why he couldn't live on his salary, his mother, all were the subject of minute examination. What he said, what she did, what he wore, how she looked, who said what and meant something else. And he did make her laugh. The facts, the impressions, what did or might have happened—in short the fabric of his life—was laid out like a blanket at her feet. As if her scrutiny were necessary to the flow of his existence. Falsely, Anita felt a part of it all. She wanted to tell George he'd done the right thing not to marry that stubborn rich girl who wouldn't consider living without a maid. It was hard to make no reply to the sarcastic, desperate eruptions occasioned by his mother's interferences in his romances. It was clear the old lady had stifled the engagement with her family arrangements and spying.

With one eye on Eric, who was jumping the waves and egging on the barking poodle, Anita listened to George repeat word for word an argument he had had with his mother the previous evening. She nodded at what he said, her reply, and their eventual stalemated silence. Throughout the dialogue, George emphatically hit his knee with his palm. His chest and face were covered with thick white cream. He looked ridiculous, like a clown with a face full of whipped cream. Anita couldn't see his eyes behind the dark glasses, but she knew he was watching her. The mask-like effect, which was added to by a grotesque plastic nose guard he had attached to his glasses, accentuated the bitterness in his voice. How much alike we are, thought Anita, and she dug her toes into the hot sand and rested her chin upon her knees as she listened to him.

Eric's feet slapped on the sand as he darted to and from the wave's tongue. The toy poodle gave up the game and lay next to George with puffed forelegs stretched out, dripping saliva onto the sand. Anita reached out and put her hand on George's greasy arm, holding it still. Soon it will be me spending the mornings indoors, Anita thought. And she wondered if Eric would be as ironic and attentive as George.

Far down by the pier the beach bulldozer turned yesterday's trash under the sand leaving a fish-bone track. Sometimes the gray shadow of a whale could be seen in the clear blue water. The gulls swooped down for tidbits from the wake, and Anita listened to their circling calls. George's voice droned in her ear until she heard only its rhythmic alteration of anger, impatience, and love. Eric had wandered down toward the pier, and the poodle followed. The noise of the heavy motor of the bulldozer mingled with the gull's high-pitched cries and the gentle music of waves breaking. Eric's legs scissored and caught the sun's shine. It all might have gone on forever. When George tilted forward on one palm and kissed the sandy point of her shoulder, Anita jumped up as if she had been touched by a ghost.

She stared at his white, greasy face, his bright teeth and lovely blond hair. If he hadn't been covered with goo she might have slapped him. Instead Anita stood up abruptly, fetched Eric and led him by the hand back to the boardwalk. The poodle, his tail wagging, started to follow. Anita hissed at him and stamped her foot in front of his nose. The dog turned down his tail and bounced off. Eric's feet flapped in his untied sandals. George turned on his square of towel and faced the ocean. The panting poodle came and lay down with its feet pointed towards the sea.

After lunch Anita lay down on the twin bed in Eric's room with the shutters blotting out the bright afternoon and tried to sleep. A knock, so light as to sound like a scratching, came on the door to her room. She tiptoed barefoot to answer it, ushered George inside, and pulled shut the inner door between the two rooms. Her face was long, and her hair which was tucked underneath a bright snood in the morning stood away from her face distractedly. George thought she looked peculiar, or ill. He had come planning to make a perfunctory apology, and he had expected a tepid reception. His face was clean, and he wore a tie, probably he had

just left from having lunch with his mother in the dining room.
Now he walked wearily over to the window and peered through
the small crack between the heavy wooden shutters. The sand on
the carpet squeaked against his shoes and set Anita's teeth on edge.
The white mark on his cheek was clearly accentuated as a scar.
Anita pulled back the light cotton spread and sat down on the bed.
She did not look at his face. From the next room they could hear the
faint whistle of Eric's snoring.

They were whispering. "Don't cry. There's nothing to cry
about." The whole incident had been blown way out of proportion,
George had said in his eager, breathless way.

And that was the signal for the tears to spill over and down
Anita's face and onto the fresh white sheet. "Isn't your mother
waiting downstairs?" Anita asked, as she searched her pockets for
a handkerchief and then took the folded white one held out in
George's folded hand. He sat down heavily beside her, draping his
jacket over the ladder-backed chair facing the blond vanity table.

The next morning, still sniffling and blowing her nose into
George's now sodden handkerchief, Anita crammed the beach
clothes, dirty and clean alike, into her suitcase, bought a two pound
box of salt water taffy for the doorman, and hustled Eric onto the
early morning train for New York. Eric sulked in the corner of the
carriage and refused to sit on her lap. So Anita watched the
landscape click by in the dirty window frame—scrub sand, to
suburb, to cityscape in a progression which seemed as inevitable as
age. New York was cool and empty. The apartment was strangely
silent without the maids or the Colonel. Anita wrote a letter with
lies in it to her husband and told herself she had done the right
thing to leave. It would all be as good as forgotten, except that in
her hasty departure she had left her diamond wristwatch, an
anniversary present from the Colonel, on the bathroom sink in the
hotel room.

The nursemaid was still away, so Anita and Eric lived on sandwiches and cokes from the corner drugstore and went to the
deserted park in the hot afternoons. If he's smart Anita said to
herself as she held Eric's hand at the light, he won't even call. July
melted into August without incident except that Anita began to
have difficulty buttoning her clothes. No more cokes and ice cream
cones, she vowed. Colonel Delmar returned from Formosa with

his skull more beautifully burnished than ever, carrying in his pocket a coral necklace for his wife, and for the boy a scale model of a US Navy warship. The watch was insured, he said when Anita got up the courage to tell him.

Colonel Delmar seemed engaged, healthy and as serious as ever. The trip, in which he had armed a whole fleet of fishing boats, had opened his eyes to what kind of help was really needed out there, he remarked the first evening they went out for dinner. At another dinner when the conversation took a similar turn, someone suggested that Colonel Delmar set up a kind of information center. Another expedition might be useful. And within two weeks six or seven men expressed an interest in taking part. The group would be self-financed and yet composed of people who had skills. In the afternoon Anita could hear her husband's hearty voice remembering himself to people—buddies from his service days, former business associates, and even friends of his first wife. His statements, the phrases, his very intonation became so familiar that Anita felt she could have given the pitch herself. Colonel Delmar came to meals with a forgetful expression, as if he were rehearsing the tone he would use on the next call.

Meanwhile Anita seemed to be occupied with what she customarily did this time of year. She took Eric to and from his new school, exchanged courtesies with acquaintances over the telephone, where no one could see her face, and made excuses not to go to luncheons downtown. She took taxis everywhere. When it began to feel wintry, she called for her fur coat to be brought out of storage. When Eric's first grade teacher asked him to bring in something for the class, she spent two afternoons with him putting together the model of the battleship brought back by the Colonel. She thought of going to visit her father in Massachusetts, but the old man would have been confused by her arrival and she didn't want to explain. Besides Anita suspected he'd somehow become involved in this Formosa expedition, and she didn't want to know about it.

Skirts were short that season. And Anita was conscious to the point of embarrassment of knees and thighs and flesh. The bare-legged girls on Park Avenue who walked their large hounds so conspicuously made her blush. She scolded the maid unfairly and sent Eric, his chin held high in defiance, to his room for the smallest trifle. In mixed company she took to sighing and making cynical remarks about "men" and "love." And if Colonel Delmar were standing near he would stop what he was saying, twitch his nose, as if he smelled something sharp, and make an uncharacteristic ironic comment. And at those moments Anita thought he looked for all the world like someone's lost rabbit, with his small twitching nose, his smooth, round head, and his small dark, defenseless eyes. When the steam hissed up in the radiators early in the morning, and Anita awoke with her nose and mouth and lungs dry, she didn't think she would make it through the season.

Worse, she was spending time with people she cared nothing about. People like that awful Mrs. Rose, the wife of one of the Colonel's business partners. "You know," Mrs. Rose had remarked one recent afternoon. "You ought to see a psychiatrist." The two women were standing side by side before a wall-sized mirror at the dressmaker's. The assistant tapped Anita on the waist, and she stepped around a quarter turn. "You seem depressed. Not yourself," Mrs. Rose had the nerve to continue. And she lifted up her skirt a half inch to see if the hem was the right length. Anita held out her arm stiffly from her side while the assistant pinned a dart. "Everyone has noticed it. As your friend I thought I should be the one to tell you."

Anita stared back into the flat surface of the looking glass. The mirror was so clear everything seemed magnified. "You've changed your hair again, Marie," she answered. "Do you still go to the same fellow. The one you liked so much?"

Mrs. Rose pivoted half way around and turned her back to their twin reflections. In the taxi the two women were silent. The afternoon traffic crawled through midtown, and they progressed by inches.

"I think you were right about the red," Mrs. Rose finally said at a stoplight. "It's just a little too tomato-ey for my skin." And when she stepped down Mrs. Rose turned and waved as if she were sending her dearest relation off on a long ocean voyage.

It's disgusting, Anita said to herself as she overtipped the cabbie. She was angry that this woman whom she regarded as trivial and stupid should have noticed her unhappiness. Maybe it's true, Anita thought as she stepped onto the department store escalator, that the exciting part of my life is over. And she watched the impassive, well-powdered faces going down in the opposite direction beside her. They probably all feel like I do, she told herself, restless and frustrated. But what's to be done about it? And the time before her marriage, a time in fact full of worries, doubts and misgivings, now appeared as carefree and happy. Now, she thought, her life was merely processional, and she would do anything to get out of step.

Anita settled herself on a high-backed stool and waited for the clerk to notice her. After all, who of her friends would she call contented? The clerk slid open the drawers silently and spread out in front of Anita ruffled garments as light as clouds. Anita took off her gloves and stretched one flowered item over her fist. The silky material kissed her hand. She counted off her friends and acquaintances. Mrs. C.—the clerk laid out a creation of black silk with black ribbon—was too hysterical. Besides she was a hypocrite and slept with her chauffeur. Anita had often caught her in foolish, needless lies. Mrs. J.? Anita waved away a box of white slips the clerk had started to open. Her veneer of well-bred nonchalance was so satin-smooth it was impossible to know if anything was behind it. The white slips were replaced by another box containing matching garments of red and white polka dots. At least Mrs. S. had some life. Pale blue bows peeked out from the corners. But Anita had seen Mrs. S. slap her teenage daughter across the face. And since then Anita had never been able to look at Mrs. S. without superimposing on her face that same expression of determined, witless anger. The clouds of nylon and bubbles of lace piled up beside Anita's elbow. Silkiness tumbled out of bright boxes. The tissue paper rustled as if it were telling a secret. The garments were as soft as a cool, creamed hand. The clerk tapped her thick black sales book with her pencil. And Anita, freeing herself from the gauzy materials billowing beside her, pushed away the pile of merchandise, slid off her high perch, and hurried away.

In the elevator twenty people pressed against one another and stared at the ceiling. A dozen different scents mingled to form an odorous cloud in the enclosed car. The little group expired in a single breath at the street floor as they dispersed like so many molecules of gas escaping into the atmosphere. The elevator operator stuck her head around the door, snapped her gum, and grinned at her friend in the twin uniform two brass doors down. But not to me, Anita said to herself. I never thought it would happen to me.

Outside the snow was falling and the streets were soft and dark. The homebound crowd pressed Anita forward. In front of her a sea of covered heads zigzagged ahead. Anita felt she would be delivered from the lock step of this jostling crowd only by finding George Deitrich, loving him, and changing her life. The cars passed as quiet gray shadows at the corners. No taxi showed its beacon. The store dummies were skiing on soap snow, and plastic children grinned at a painted snowman. Eric would never understand. Anita turned the corner to an almost deserted residential avenue. A gray-haired lady held a small dog on a leash, and the dog's nose was in the air smelling winter as Anita walked by. A woman with a bent head passed Anita by and a whiff of chicken and onions floated up from her shopping bag. A blond boy in a blue school uniform came up silently from behind and startled Anita by standing close to her at the light. So I've turned into a frivolous, idle woman who falls in love with young men, Anita thought, as she watched the boy's blue serge back recede down the street. When she arrived home her feet hurt, her fur coat sagged and smelled, and her shoes had disintegrated. Only her fox hat had shed the snow. Anita could hardly sit through dinner and listen to Colonel Delmar's voice.

A few weeks later when Anita was selling tickets to a theater benefit, a revival of *The Sea Gull* for one of Colonel Delmar's charities, she found the excuse for calling Mrs. Deitrich. The old lady said nothing after Anita introduced herself, then she sneezed loudly directly into the telephone and declined. She no longer went out in the evening by herself, Mrs. Deitrich said. Anita stuttered as she thanked the old lady. She terminated the conversation before being sure she had been remembered. Had George told his mother about their afternoon in the shuttered hotel room. In the background a man had been talking. Perhaps it was only the radio. The address fixed itself in Anita's mind, and she found reasons to steer herself in the direction of the apartment.

The building was a prewar gray stone structure, and its awning-covered entrance had been laid out with geometric primness. It was grand, even elegant. In the middle of the city a tiny patch of grass grew right in front of the doorway. This little lawn was surrounded by a miniature iron fence with knee-high spikes. Men carrying briefcases and women with large packages paraded in and out of the lobby and hurriedly greeted the liveried doorman. Anita watched from a booth at the corner drugstore across the street and thought, probably a hundred people live in that building. How to find an excuse to go inside? A dog sniffed at her ankle, and Anita looked up to see a frail looking old man smiling down at her from the other end of a terrier's leash. Not that way. She hurried to the counter and paid her bill and walked away rapidly. It was too early to go home. She remembered seeing a gold and jeweled watch, with a ruby-eyed mermaid curled around its face, in a Fifth Avenue jewelry store last week. The watch bore an uncanny resemblance to the one she had lost in Atlantic City, the one Colonel Delmar claimed to have had custom-made for her in Hong Kong. Anita hailed a cab and took herself to the jeweler's window.

At six o'clock a greenish haze, like a watered wash, hung in between the skyscrapers. Lights were winking on and off. The buses were crammed with standing people, riding home from work. In the jewelry store window the wares were lit up behind a thick prism of bulletproof glass. The stones were shining like eyes. A man stood in front of one of the corner windows, not the one where Anita had seen the watch. The sag of his shoulders was familiar, and above his collar were the limp blond curls. He was wearing a soft blue scarf which was unevenly tucked into his coat and expensive gloves the color of a gull's breast. Anita went and stood behind him. The diamonds on their black velvet trays glittered—stars in a velvet night. George was staring at the stones and smiling. Why should it be this rather silly young man who was looking and looking at that expensive jewelry, as if he would like to lift it. The jewels twinkled back at him, eternally flirting. Anita heard the heavy click of the light changing behind her, then a horn prodded a taxi forward. A man hurrying home to supper swayed against Anita and buckled her knees with his briefcase. Anita had forgotten how much she remembered about him.

"Annie," George said, splashing her with snowy slush as he turned around. And he took her gloved hand in his and patted it again and again, all the while frowning and blinking his eyes as if something were flashing on and off in his brain. They ducked into a nearby lobby. The people standing and waiting in wool hats and rubber boots stared at them as the revolving door pushed more slush onto the already wet and dirty floor. Men held newspapers over their heads as they hurried outside at the sight of a cab. Then if unsuccessful, they came in and sharply blew their noses in handfuls of handkerchief. Anita saw them all with great vividness as she stood, open-mouthed, listening joyfully to George's voice once more. The older men were like stuffed generals in their expensive, tailored suits. And the slimmer, younger ones, the trainees and junior assistants, were the rank and file in off-the-rack uniforms. The secretaries could have been stewardesses in their dark slim skirts and white blouses. A great unnamed army was disbanding its ranks until the morning. Anita turned her back while George wrote a phone number on a scrap of paper from his wallet. He stuck the piece of paper in her coat pocket and kissed her forehead. Anita put her hands over her eyes. The man standing next to the cigar counter peered out into the dark street and made no sign. Anita turned down a marble corridor to where she thought there might be a ladies' room just as a familiar looking man entered wearing a foreign-looking green uniform. Snowflakes glistened in his black moustache. George clipped on a pair of red earmuffs and circled through the revolving door, disappearing into the darkness.

Colonel Delmar's plans to bring a small number of volunteers to Formosa were becoming complicated. He was negotiating with several government agencies and private suppliers. And each day a special delivery letter, with an embossed seal on the envelope, arrived. Colonel Delmar was spending most days at home talking on the telephone, while his vice president took care of his company. The small room off the living room had been turned into a study and was covered with pale green maps with crosses marked in ink. And an electric typewriter he had just bought himself chattered in the background. The men going with him were like himself: rich, past middle age, and veterans from the last war.

Anita's life was now wholly given over to winter. In the morning it was dark when she helped Eric dress for school. And it was night at five o'clock when she came home, sometimes directly from George's dark-curtained bedroom. The family had planned a two-week Caribbean cruise during the school holidays, but Colonel Delmar abruptly cancelled the plans and went to Ft. Bragg instead. Anita and Eric ate Christmas dinner by themselves at the Waldorf and enjoyed it. In the evening Anita came home bundled up in her fur coat. Her cheeks were red and blotchy from love-making and pinched from the cold. If he was not there, she would go into Colonel Delmar's study and feel the light silk camouflage materials the expedition was stockpiling. She stared at the enlarged photographs of the jungle and picked up the huge rubber boots bought for the swamps. On New Year's Eve when Colonel Delmar called from Texas at midnight to announce the completion of all arrangements, Anita and Eric were asleep.

Anita had another concern. Before he left she wanted Colonel Delmar to take out an insurance policy on her life. Colonel Delmar at first refused to take her suggestion seriously. Then, when she persisted at breakfast, where he was most receptive to new ideas, he was puzzled. She even dug up some statistics implying that women who were insured lived longer than women who carried no insurance. He finally agreed. And at the same time, without telling his wife, he tried to reinsure his own life at a higher value. Anita took her policy to a lawyer no one knew and willed the death benefit to George Deitrich.

Then, the telephone calls stopped. Colonel Delmar went out one morning and did not come back for two days. Anita didn't think him the type to get into accidents, so she didn't call the police. Instead she waited and put off anyone who asked for him. When he came back he said his doctor had refused to allow him to take the trip. His heart condition was serious. The insurance company as a consequence would not increase his policy or guarantee to underwrite the expedition. They could not go forward without insurance. Colonel Delmar admitted that his first reaction was to go anyway. But what if something really did happen, he asked Anita. No, he would make the arrangements for the expedition and make himself useful at this end. Then he'd make a trip in July by himself again. No one seemed to raise any objection to that. When he finished Anita knew he never wanted the subject discussed again.

Anita was alone more than ever. George spent the evenings with his mother. Eric went to sleep. Even the Norwegian nurse seemed to have somewhere to go. Anita wandered from room to room in the dark house, unable to sleep. It was as if the entire house, chair by sofa by table, item by item, had to be put to sleep with the touch of her hand before Anita herself could close her eyes. The drapes, the footstools, the flowers and the bed itself had to have their eyes closed before Anita could lose consciousness.

Anita never slept for more than a few hours at a time, and the only place she rested peacefully was on the twin bed in Eric's room. His even breathing was soporific, and if she tuned her breath to his she could drift off to that gentle, rocking rhythm. Sometimes Eric turned over, opened his eyes, and smiled at her. Then an hour or two later she sat up afraid and tiptoed back into her own room. Although he slept in his own room, Colonel Delmar didn't approve of her falling asleep in Eric's room. Anita suspected that the Norwegian girl told Colonel Delmar when she fell asleep in Eric's room.

Anita Sarah Delmar made a reservation for the entire month of July at the Grande Hotel on the Boardwalk in Atlantic City. The resort no longer seemed a quaint place where her grandmother had been photographed in a wicker chair. Anita wondered if that arch lady, flirting with her across the generations, had stolen kisses beneath the pier and held hands with a stranger as the waves licked her toes. When Anita told Colonel Delmar that she was going back this year, he looked up from his maps and suggested that perhaps he would join her for a week in August. Anita picked up a khaki undershirt from the pile on the bed and put it in the suitcase. Colonel Delmar frowned, refolded the shirt, smoothed the front flat, and put it back on the bed. He told her the insurance company sent a check for her watch and promised to buy another one in July.

Anita was pleased to find the hotel unchanged from last summer and that the desk clerk—already beet-red and peeling—remembered her name. The management gave her the same rooms as last year, with the little balcony looking out onto the ocean, the heavily shuttered windows, and the blond Hollywood furniture. The first night Eric curled up in his bed facing the window as if he were home, but Anita stared at the white ceiling and glass chandelier in the shadows. Tears, she knew, had become an addiction. Now, and this was a comfort, the gentle sound of the ocean drowned out her own weeping. She wept into her deliciously clean pillow because her life seemed upside down, and after weeping she felt relieved enough to go on living that life. She wept because she was afraid of the dark and of being alone, and because she was afraid no one loved her. Then she cried because she wasn't with George and she loved him. But he did love her, she knew that. Sometimes her daydreams of happiness were turned into nightmares.

Anita was wakened by Eric breathing on her face. He stood beside the bed already dressed in his swimming trunks and with a bucket and a shovel in one hand. The sun was blazing. As soon as Anita was dressed, they hurried to the beach, carrying towels and sun cream. Everything except the sea itself was bone dry. The hawkers croaked from their boardwalk stalls. And as they walked by, a fat waitress resting on her doughy arms clicked her tongue at Eric. Four sailors were hanging over the boardwalk railing and making lewd remarks about a sunbathing teenager. And a vendor waved a fistful of straw hats in front of Anita's face while walking backwards directly in front of her path. The ocean stretched on and on under the brilliant sun. The same stout ladies walked with their dogs, and their sleek husbands peeked from behind sunglasses at the young girls' bikinis. Teenagers patrolled the beach in pairs. Nothing had changed, after all. Anita put out her towel, stretched her legs, and watched Eric start his castle. Everything will be all right when George gets here, she told herself.

When Anita let herself into his room the next night, it seemed years since their last meeting. The wrinkles around her eyes changed into smiling lines of joy. "Look," she said taking his hand and leading him to the window. She had worn his favorite blue dress. "Isn't it beautiful?" And she pointed to the old-fashioned room, the view of the ocean from the shadows, the salt-smelling air and the vast, starry sky.

George was silent. He was thinner, more handsome and blonder than last year. His lower lip stuck out in a pouty expression Anita recognized. The white scar was prominent. She held his face in her two hands. And he smiled in spite of himself and kissed her. His mother hadn't believed the story he had invented to explain his going away. He had never gone on vacation by himself. She threatened to come down to Atlantic City and see what was going on. He would have to leave earlier than they planned. She had made sly insinuations, insulting him. They parted without saying goodbye. She might even turn up here, for all he knew. In short, everything, even for this brief time, was confused and spoiled.

Anita sat down by the window. The lines in her face were once more wrinkles. It was low tide and when the breeze disappeared the ocean gave off a sour smell. Anita waved in the direction of the telephone. Neither of them had eaten dinner. Things were too hopeless for tears. She foresaw a time when all this would no longer be worth the gigantic effort.

George sat on the side of the bed and cracked his knuckles. Anita helped him out of his jacket and persuaded him to take a shower. She ordered cold sandwiches and a bottle of wine from room service. George remembered that he hadn't told her the last, the latest thing. It was absurd, ridiculous. His voice cracked as he laughed, and that made Anita laugh. They seemed close to something. And for the one thousandth time Anita went over the alternatives. They were as unsatisfactory as they had been yesterday, as impossible as they would be tomorrow. Everything of importance they could do nothing about. Who they were, their positions in life, what they wanted, and more and more...

After this Anita's life would return to what, after all, had been its more characteristic pattern. This too was foreseeable. Breakfast and the items in the morning newspaper with Colonel Delmar. Coral necklaces, silk gowns and summer cruises. Cards in the afternoon with an interchangeable set of women not too different from herself. And this, now the consuming thing, the only important thing, would sink and disappear as if it had never existed. This amiable, chattering young man, cracking his knuckles, with his blond hair flopping over his forehead, a young man who was worrying himself to no point, would go out from her life, marry somebody else, and swim away from her. He too would find it incomprehensible that his life had been centered in this darkened bedroom. The end was as predetermined as the beginning.

Anita sat beside George on the bed. She took his hand in both of hers. The room clerk knocked and set down the tray with two wine glasses and a bucket full of ice with a bottle of wine in it. George went to pay and found he'd left his cash at home in his anger. Anita paid the clerk and waved him away. George started to apologize, but she put her fingers on his lips. That soft white flesh which had surprised her when she first laid eyes on him last year was familiar now, dear to her. George looked his age, Anita now thought. He was disappointed for her, Anita knew, and miserable at having quarreled with his mother. The old lady probably knew everything, Anita realized. And nothing could be done about that either. And she sat and stroked the back of his hand where some fine blond hairs grew and pulled open his fist. She traced the lines on his palm. Already she was scheming to put off the old lady, to sidetrack Colonel Delmar's vacation plan, and somehow to steal some other precious bit of time for the two of them. How to reach the next island of imagined happiness? To cheat their fate, for a deluded moment at least. This would be ecstasy, if only for the moment before the next wave of mistakes and circumstances washed up its deposit of pink broken shells, foam and seaweed curly as hair.

We Are All Africans

W. slid from a dream of glaciers to the gloom of a square, concrete-walled room. In the distance he heard the buzz of a small plane. The drone came closer, shifted down a register, and then was switched off. It might have been early morning or late afternoon. Little light came through the single, barred window opening onto flowers. And little light came from the corridor. Nor did W. hear any rustling of straw or creaking of bamboo from the living room. The big room with its painted gourds and bright pieces of cloth scotch-taped to the walls must have been empty.

The room where W. lay had been forgotten by the rest of the house. One wall opened onto the corridor connecting the kitchen with the dining room. The wall was only waist high, with a wire grating on the upper half. Sometimes a servant did the ironing there. Now W. lay on an army cot within the slick orange folds of his sleeping bag. His hiking knapsack, propped up in the corner on two squat metal legs, kept him company. Above W.'s body, connecting window and grating, a blue plastic clothesline had been hung. It sagged in the middle. But aside from that afterthought, the concrete was unrelieved. There was not a table or a closet, a ledge or a shelf, to break the progress of the crude planes.

W. had no idea how long he had been asleep. Vines and bushes, all brightly colored, cut off the bright tropical sun. Evening and morning were indistinguishable blurs. Even the blazing midday was filtered out and weakened. W. had lost count since the four days on the mountain.

The grate cast a ribbed shadow on the cream wall. That wheezing, labored sound was his breathing. W. shivered inside his sleeping bag. He wanted to rise, but his lungs wouldn't support that. He remembered the shadows of disease he'd seen photographs of in medical texts. But his indisposition was only that, a temporary thing. Back at sea level, he'd be breathing again normally. This sickness, this altitude paralysis, was a common thing. Especially in the tropics.

W.'s head lay on a pillow of dirty laundry. And when he glanced to either side he saw the curious dark boundary which had been painted up above the floor, like the water line on a small boat. The sea-green of the floor rose about a foot and made a border at ankle height with the cream walls. The plaster was cracked in several places, and tiny landslides of dust trickled down the wall.

There was something sticklike about the way his legs lay under the single layer of the sleeping bag. Were they the fault? The head and shoulders of Ellen Moore, the mistress of the house, floated down the corridor. She stopped for a minute on the other side of the closed door. The top half of the door to W.'s room was grating too, so that the servants could not be private there. So handy having this built-in cage for him, almost custom-made for his needs. Ellen's arms were full of vegetables and fruits. Then she was blown past him and down to the kitchen. Joe would be along soon, she called over her shoulder. Joe would be coming home soon and would come in and see W. The smell of oranges, the tart green oranges that grew on the mountainside, and the sweet perfume of mangoes, drifted into W.'s room. The sour taste of unwashed linen and phlegm was camouflaged for a moment. W. had wanted to climb that mountain more than he had ever wanted anything. Perhaps his attitude, not his body, had been wrong?

Ellen and Joe Moore had been living near Arusha for two years. Joe gave technical advice to a coffee cooperative. Ellen had opened a shop which sold local handicrafts: Masai beads, placemats and coasters out of barkcloth, the tiny carved animals the tourists were so fond of. Without her glasses or her large leather handbag, Ellie would have been taken for a prosperous African. She wore the long skirts cut out of the traditional fabric and sandals. Joe too might have been mistaken for an African. He dressed in the shirts of national cloth and baggy trousers. But something about the way he held himself, his walk—he'd played basketball in college—denied it. Perhaps it was only his habit of stuffing his hands into his pockets and making a fist.

The Moores planned to settle in Africa. But, they had confided in W., after two years their applications for citizenship had not yet been acted upon. The three of them had been sitting on the verandah off the living room and talking, before W. left to go up the mountain. The warm evening and the beer they were drinking made everything feel damp. And as the evening wore on they were clammy and cold. Joe made witty remarks at the expense of his fellow bureaucrats. Behind them the lizards scuttled between the raffia mats which were hung up on the white stucco wall, which had been left with ripples in it. Thick globs of plaster made waves over which the lizards ran. W. didn't ask too many questions. The ingenious local furniture, made of twigs and branches, had been softened with pillows. Some of Ellen's ladies had embroidered the pillows with daffodils and roses. That the Moores did not plan to come home, whatever the bureaucrats decreed, was evident. And in the candled African darkness no explanations seemed to be required. W. volunteered that he too thought of coming out when he finished medical school. Perhaps for one of those two or three year terms in the tropical disease hospital. The Moores nodded. After all, who were they to tell him not to come?

Now for all his real pain and discomfort, W. knew that he was not going to die, not now at twenty-seven years of age. He'd have a second chance, a third or fourth. He'd live to laugh at his own obituary. W.'s pain, although it absorbed him completely at this moment, was not going to be fatal. In the empty room he examined it with a lover's attention. It was not mortal. The altitude had tricked him; it was what had made him empty his insides onto the mountainside. His lungs had been stretched by the thin air. He suffered delusions. His steps had faltered. He hadn't made it to the top. But, W. reassured himself, his constitution was basically all right. Those years of vitamins and exercise would tell in the long run. Even after three days without food—W. pinched his own arm—there was plenty of flesh left. But his fingers couldn't hold onto it for more than a second. The guide who had led him down, who had forced him to go down, he was at least partly responsible.

Down the hall W. heard the tinny clatter of utensils, of plastic and aluminum. The cook's shoulders in their white uniform floated down the corridor. The future citizens were feeding. And although W.'s lungs were rattling and his throat was thick, he smelled onions frying. The Moores must be whispering or not talking, W. thought in surprise. His empty stomach turned over then he drifted off again.

When W. awoke, a round, dark, mature face bore down upon his own. Two flat fingers pulled down his eyelids. Then a brown ear fanned out on his chest. The patient thought that a novel touch and tucked it away for his own repertoire. The stethoscope took root in the head—the ears were remarkably like W.'s own, small, delicate, and tucked into the skull. Then the cold metal cone bounced up and down over the ailing area. Fingers pinched his wrist. A smile opened the face above, silently as if from a scalpel. W. saw the bleached hairs on his arm stand up against the chill touch of the doctor.

The Moores watched from the doorway. W. lay on the sagging cot unable to raise his head. The Moores leaned against the wall side by side. The round-faced doctor knelt on one knee next to W.'s bed in the posture of a prince. W.'s blood sample made a fine red globe on his fingertip, in defiance of the weakness he felt in his bones. Then it was smeared blue between two pieces of glass. His companions, they didn't help him. If he'd been with his own kind, it would have made a difference, wouldn't it?

The doctor diagnosed altitude sickness, extreme exhaustion, heart palpitations, and overexposure to the environment. Leave the man alone. The Moores thought he should be flown home immediately. He had his ticket. And they were not his family. His condition seemed precarious. He looked worse than he was, the doctor answered. The fact that he couldn't talk, that his breathing was labored, made it all seem more serious. Actually, there was little to worry about.

The khaki knapsack was stretched by sharp corners and long edges. Bulky objects strained against the material. The outside pockets stood open; and the top was pulled tight. A sweater rolled in a ball, squares of stale, speckled chocolate, and triangular tins of fish plumped out the center. Towards the bottom lay a pair of sneakers he had ruined in the ocean, two argyle socks a girl had knit for him in history lectures, and some maps tied up with a rubber band. A battery-operated razor fitted in its own leather case. Slipped down the side, in a lemon-colored oilskin packet, was W.'s passport, his open return ticket, and three thick packs of unsigned checks. Deep in the center a Japanese camera buried its long nose. W. had never been caught with it around his neck. The film, boxes and boxes of it, lay scattered through the rest of his belongings. A school notebook, its wire spine uncoiling, sat conspicuously on top. A quarter of the pages were filled with observations, written in a small hand, and W. had used a highly abbreviated, annotated style. W.'s leather walking shorts, a souvenir from last year's hiking trip to Germany, stood also without support and faced the wall.

The climb up the mountain was the climax of W.'s four-month walking holiday in Africa. He had arranged to visit with his friends from America, the Moores, before and after the ascent. He had left some of his bulkier belongings behind in their spare room. They were friends, or rather acquaintances, from university days. The Moores had stood in the doorway in bathrobes and waved him off into the early morning. W. jumped into the back of the Land Rover with an easy conscience. He looked forward to sharing his adventures with his compatriots when he returned—triumphant from the ascent.

The first day was spent weaving through the mountain foothills. Going up all the time, the car drove through deeply populated slopes green with coffee and banana trees. Large family houses with straw roofs were hidden in the greenery and invisible from the road. Women with baskets and bottles on their heads, men on bicycles, and children of all ages lined the roadway on both sides. The children waved and ran to keep up with them. The women smiled, or some turned their faces away. The mountaintop, crested with snow, was invisible, unimaginable even, from the foothills here below.

There were five in the party when they set off. W., the African guide, a middle-aged German couple, and the driver who spoke some English. W. had hoped to fall in with people more like himself. Or, really, he preferred to be alone. Neither the German, Professor Steinmetz, nor his wife, spoke good English, although Steinmetz seemed to understood W.'s exchanges with the guide. W. had passed a graduate exam in German, but when he grasped Herr Steinmetz's hand in the freezing dawn, all he could remember was: please, good evening, and Bahnhof. The guide seemed to know more words than W. Still, Steinmetz insisted upon speaking to the African slowly and brokenly, enunciating syllable by syllable until the words were not recognizable.

In the early afternoon they came to the end of the dirt road. It simply stopped, arbitrarily, and a footpath led away from its ending. The car turned around, and they began walking. The area was still thickly populated. The women with loads on their heads passed the mountaineers. And they turned their heads to stare at the hiking party as they disappeared into the leafy walls on either side of the path. Then the thick greenery began to thin out. They approached the mountain meadows, rolling, scrubby fields where it was impossible to grow anything. The people who lived in the foothills had a name for these fields: the devil's skirt.

The walking was hypnotizing. W. had trouble keeping up. The others seemed to go ahead without visible effort. W. sullenly brought up the rear. Even at eight thousand feet he could feel his reflexes slowing down. W. asked the guide how long it would be until they stopped. The guide answered, it would be forty minutes; but W. couldn't add that onto what his watch, an elaborate machine which had the date and a compass on it, said. He hesitated over each step, deciding with painful care where to put his foot.

When the party finally stopped in the late afternoon, W. was senseless with exhaustion. He sat inside the crude mountain hut while Professor Steinmetz and his wife admired the scenery below. They spoke excitedly, and W. had difficulty reminding himself that there might be something to get excited about. At six o'clock the peak cleared for a few minutes. In answer to their shouts W. came and stood outside to stare at the dazzling, melting glacier. It looked no closer now that it had last night from the Moores' garden. W. found it difficult to grasp that the day of mindless walking had any connection with the proud peak above his head. After a few minutes he was dizzy and bored with looking at it. W. returned inside while the Steinmetzs remained shivering outside until the quickly falling dark made the peak invisible.

During the night, they had all crawled into their sleeping bags immediately after eating. W. felt as if he were smothering in a cotton cloud. His lungs were weighted down and soggy, despite the sharp cold. At the same time he was drained of strength by the silent, inconclusive struggle for breath. His body was licked with sweat, and the chill air settled into the damp pockets of his flesh.

The altitude had set up a hum in his ears, and his vision blurred off to the side.

When he closed his eyes, W. drifted into a dream of cold climbing. He was floating to the top, his feet bleeding and bound. His nose and eyes were running, and a small crowd was somehow watching it all from down the slope. The clerk at the tourist agency in the capital, the Moores, a student he had eaten with at a youth hostel, the stewardess on his plane out—what lovely, fine hands she had—and the driver who had carried them off to the end of the road, they were all watching his ascent. The mountain received him on its table top, supine, majestic, like a royal lover. And he, the climber, had become expanded, inflated, large enough to lie down across the miles of flat ice.

Just before dawn a stream of German from Frau Steinmetz's sleeping bag awakened W. Her tone was authoritative, demanding, then as if taking another part, she whispered an answer and was silent. But W. could not return to his dream position. As he closed his eyes, hoping to meet again those encouraging figures coming down the hillside, he noticed the guide, sitting with his feet pulled under his chin and staring into the darkness.

In the morning, they rose before dawn. Frau Steinmetz directed a volley of German at her husband as she changed her underwear inside the sleeping bag. Professor Steinmetz propped himself up on one elbow to listen, but he offered no response. At a pause in the narrative he leapfrogged out of bed and into his trousers and disappeared outside the hut. The guide was putting out the food. W. admired the woman's healthy, pink lungs. Already before the day's climbing had started W. felt unequal to walking. It took all his strength to deposit his breakfast in a steaming, tan puddle outside the cabin door.

The second day they walked across the saddle between the two peaks. The rocky earth was covered with coarse, spongy moss. The clouds cut off the world below and sometimes the mountain peaks as well. The land was etched with crevices. The thick, primitive growth was difficult to walk on. And when it sprang up against his swollen feet, W. felt as if he were treading on a live thing. He remained preoccupied with his physical state. The vomiting didn't recur, but his head was lighter than the thin air. His feet, they had become the most important part of his body, turned and crumpled beneath him, like the paper legs of a cut-out doll. It became increasingly difficult to keep up with Frau Steinmetz's steady, rocking hips. The others were always a few lengths ahead, and they had to stop periodically and wait. When W. caught up, they were ready to start walking once again. Frau Steinmetz and her husband kept up a steady conversation. The guide said nothing; he kept his mouth closed around a small pipe. W., who had always been a great talker, was incapable of speaking. He tasted blood, or was it only salt, in his mouth and on his tongue.

In the afternoon the glacier loomed above them steadily. W. fixed his eyes on it when he stopped. He remembered being told that the ice cap was melting and would be gone in fifty years. The moss had given way to rock as they climbed higher. For the last few hours W. had to stop every fifteen minutes and wheeze and pant. He coughed and spit onto the toes of his boots. The others waited with obvious impatience. Once Steinmetz walked back for him. He lay a leaden, scholarly arm on W.'s shoulders and spoke soothingly into his helpless ear. If only I could understand his advice, W. thought swimmingly. But he could only think of his breathing and his feet. After a few minutes Professor Steinmetz went to wait with the others farther up the hill.

That night W.'s head felt close to bursting. He couldn't eat. When the others slept his empty stomach and his draft-filled head prevented him from escaping. When he lay down on the cold mud floor of the hut, his legs and feet throbbed. Here up above the clouds there had not even been the drama of the mountain's nightly visitation. Professor Steinmetz was snoring. His wife sighed. W. closed his eyes. With his eyes shut he saw the peak repeated everywhere, and he assaulted it in a hundred different ways. In a plane he circled around the crater. Then like an eagle, he rose effortlessly on strong cold gusts of wind. He climbed hand over hand up a rope which had been lowered from the cloudless sky. A golden funicular carried him up the steep slope.

The third morning W. awoke feeling weaker than ever. He attempted eating with unfavorable results. Outside the hut his nose bled insolently, with a will of its own. W. watched the dark drops seep into the ground and disappear. The guide watched, and then he took a thick rope and tied it once around himself and once, a shade too tightly, around W.'s waist. They set off mule-train style. For the first time W. was not following the rocking rhythm of Frau Steinmetz's hips. To his slowed consciousness this in itself bristled with insult. Around his waist was a rope tying him to the African guide. If W. watched his feet, it took him longer to decide where to go. So he kept his eyes up and stumbled behind the guide. Sometimes the rope jerked him rudely ahead.

The wind was strong, and it seemed to blow right through W.'s ears. W. was lonely. Where were his admirers? Tomorrow they would climb the glacier. W. didn't have the strength to untie the rope when the group stopped to rest. The thick knot cut into his ribs when he sat down. The guide told the Steinmetzes, softly, that W. would not participate in the final assault. The others were to rise at 1:30 in the morning, climb the glacier peak, and stand on the summit at sunrise. W. was ordered to stay back and wait for their return at the last hut.

W. was not asleep when the other three slipped off into the darkness. Alone in the cabin he was cast adrift. He imagined he had scaled the glacier face, unaided, and was there, ice pick and flag in hand, when the three emerged from below. The clouds made a halo round his figure. He was smiling and gracious in triumph, with no pain anywhere. His feet had reached some hallowed state beyond pain. Like an experienced drunk W. watched his thoughts stumble and reel and cursed himself. His voice lurched on in the empty cabin. He laughed aloud. Then his nose began to bleed again. The sight of his own blood sobered him. W. dreamt of soaring in a flimsy plane, far above all hikers.

In the middle of his dreams the others came back. After a brief rest they started down again. The descent was rapid. Even Frau Steinmetz was silent now. The three of them held a brief conference to decide the best way of getting W. down the mountain. They took turns supporting him. W. does not remember the descent. For him it never occurred. They placed him in the Land Rover, and the driver gently deposited him at the Moores' doorstep.

The hand of pain caressed his forehead once again. If W. could grab the wrist he knew he'd catch the African cause of it all. Moon-pale fingernails, and the underside as pink and disarming as a blush. The hand that tied the rope around his waist, too tightly. Fingers he'd seen tying knots, turning keys, and incorrectly spelling out his name on blank lines across the page. The skin wrinkled over the knuckles in a misleading smile. And the hands themselves were long-fingered, squat, or stubby. Once or twice he'd seen a diamond or ruby gleam from the back of those hands. But mostly they were unadorned, except with the signs of hard work. W. had been ushered forward by all these hands, crossed palms with some, been held back by one or two. And now these many fingers came to trace the veins in his temple, to stick pins in his ear, and to pinch his toes. And when W. tried to catch them, they danced away beyond his grasp. The doctor gently unwrapped the patient's weak fingers from around his wrist.

On the verandah, where the Moores first welcomed him, there were voices. W.'s two hosts and a third accented voice he did not know. In their protection of him, the Moores had almost become American again. They listened respectfully to the doctor. They paid him. Ellie squinted at the thermometer and shook it down efficiently. Joe asked if W. shouldn't be put in a hospital. The doctor thought it was not that serious. The voices drifted away. W. hoped they had come to some conclusion about his condition. Perhaps the matter could be settled without him. The only sound now was his own breathing.

W. had thought he would emerge from it all transformed. He would come down the mountain on the other side. African? He would be as African as the children, as the white-collared civil servants, as the policemen. He would come down and be one with the wild landscape.

Faces reappeared in the doorway. Ellie waved to him through the grating. They see the beauty of my dreams, W. thought. Even the cook cast a nervous glance over Joe's shoulder. He had already formed his own diagnosis: the visitor's soul was being tormented by his outraged ancestors. The doctor patted his hand, and W. tried to lift himself a few inches off the pillow. They would drink together sometime—some heady local brew whose sanitary properties W. would steel himself to disregard. On his next trip W. would cover himself with red clay, carry a spear, and stride up the mountain barefoot. He'd wear a russet cloak and his toes would grip the earth like talons. He'd lance and stretch his ears and trade his scientific techniques for a communal bond. When he wore clay and beads, he'd be himself for the first time.

Through the barred box window a breeze came. It was the hour before sunset when the mountain made its daily visitation. The clouds which hid the snow cap floated off, as if gently blown away by a giant's breath. The sun was disappearing, the light fell in stripes across the foothills. The shadows were blue. The god, white haired and silent, showed himself to the figures on the plain.

In W.'s room the rectangular grid, the servant's fence, cast its shadow on the ivory wall. W. faced the wrong way to see the mountain, like a picture of itself, emerge from behind the running clouds. His dreams chased their tails inside his head. And in the damp corner his hiking shoes, his knapsack, and his camera waited for his return to health. The Moores and the doctor had stepped outside to catch a glimpse of the mountain before the night settled down. At the first hut, the guide put dehydrated soup into a pan, and another set of climbers rubbed their red ankles.

W.'s legs were like sticks underneath the blanket. The blanket was planed flat over the dip of the canvas cot. There had been no transformation. W. will arise a thinner, weaker man. Then his lungs will fill once more with ordinary air, and his stomach will round out with familiar food. He'll board a jet for home, and the figures on the plain will race on without him. He cannot change. He'll be buried on American soil.

.

The First Secretary

First Secretary Kamau Njoroge Ngugi (CAM-OW EN-CHORE-OH-GHEE EN-GOO-GHEE)—how can you imagine a man without pronouncing his name?—is a small stocky man who has kept his freedom fighters' beard. In the days when he was first being arrested by the colonial government, about twenty-five years ago, the beard was a rebel insignia. Now it's a relic, a patchy growth lightening his face with its curly gray strands. Another souvenir of Kamau's prison days, or perhaps of fighting, is a pronounced limp, amounting almost to the dragging of his right foot. He walks stiffly, with obvious effort, leaning upon a knobheaded walking stock carved from a single mahogany branch.

Kamau is now close to fifty. He's been making news for almost that long, it seems. First, in the days when no Europeans seriously considered African independence, he was a preacher, and then a trade unionist. Then, a few years later he was heard of again as an editor of a Swahili newspaper, again one of the first of its kind. In the fifties he organized a dockworkers' strike which made him an anti-Christ to the British. Christian preacher, party organizer, guerrilla, a member of a mad hatter's government just after the overthrow of the Sultan—he's always been in the center. And now at fifty, after another bloody, three-day coup he's head of state. Kamau's political activities have spanned so many different periods in Zanzibar history it's difficult to understand only one man has been acting throughout.

In all of Kamau's varied careers, though, one characteristic has remained unchanged. Kamau is a speaker, a spell binder, a crowd charmer, and a master of words. People walk for miles brefoot to hear him. They've never been choosy about the subject. They came when he was preaching Christ; they're still coming to hear about socialism. Young bucks in their ankle-length Swahili skirts, barrel-chested dock workers smoking dark cigarettes, older men with a few brown teeth who wear white gowns which drag in the dusty street, women with babies tied on their backs, old women with bent backs and stringy arms—they all turn out for a dash of revolutionary truth.

No Westerners have been let onto the island since Kamau's takeover. Kamau has a reputation for fierceness with reporters, perhaps because he is an old newspaper man himself. And he is known to distrust Americans. But when a New York magazine wrote and asked him about a story, he replied immediately. And I, as the wire service reporter in the nearest capital, was sent to interview him.

I was surprised to be greeted with a delicate, deliberate courtesy. Kamau was punctual, even a few minutes early, for our appointment. His strong handshake, his smile, his direct, amused glance were all disarming. I've seen many African leaders, and Kamau is prepossessing. Not because of his size, his pride, or because of a striking appearance. But he approaches you simply, individually, choosing to disregard everything he knows you know about him.

Kamau is not handsome. His round, kindly face—he is far gentler looking than his pictures—would better suit a country preacher than a self-proclaimed revolutionary. Perhaps this is not the man who just unseated the Revolutionary Council and established himself as head of the latest governing body. Not that violent change would be a novelty for Zanzibar. Zanzibar and her older sister Pemba have sounded like a good idea to pirates and traders for generations. But if Kamau's appearance is singularly ordinary, almost to the point of disguise, his voice would make a stranger turn around. Deep and strong, his voice has a resonance which it is easy to imagine serving the cause of religion. What remains of that one of his nine lives is a melodious intonation, an emotional force behind even straightforward statements, and a musical tone. His voice is alive and warm, as sensual as the man himself in his worn, three-button suit appears not to be. The voice pulls them out of their palm-roofed huts, out from the empty white boxes of interior courtyards where the old and the children sit on their haunches all day and watch the sun play geometrician on the stone floor.

His history? Yes, it's striking, full, dramatic. His life itself is a kind of documentary of the whole island, and he's still young. But others have participated in this series of collapsing events. Others as brave as Kamau were beaten in colonial jails; others were early and had plans.

Recently Kamau announced himself a Marxist. It is reported he toured the island and made speeches promising free primary school education for all children. He talks about land for the landless. But the island's six hundred square miles are not expandable. The city courtyards grow more crowded every year. And the original Revolutionary Council members, Kamau's former colleagues? They are sitting in a barred prison hanging over the sea, on the side of the island where I was not taken.

The tiny Japanese tape recorder I have brought along fascinates Kamau. I show him how to record his voice and replay the tape. He turns his back to me, whispers into the palm-sized microphone, and bends over laughing at the hissing noises that come back. Perhaps it is his smile, and that he smiles often. His teeth are as perfect as a movie star's. His laugh, too, is unexpected. The round preacher's belly shakes, the dark pupils disappear behind hilarious folds of flesh. The cheeks are full and merry, down to the running beard. What about those reports of days of shooting? That Kamau himself never slept those three days, that he, at fifty, led his men to the radio station himself?

The interview took place in a single day. The Ruling Committee issued me a visa for eighteen hours. We talked in the old Zanzibar Hotel, the one place where foreigners are received now. It was obviously inconvenient for Kamau to come to the hotel. But he insisted he had no permanent headquarters, no regular office. We were never alone. The interview was done with tapes, pen, notebook, and film. The Zanzibar Hotel was built by the British when they first came. The furniture is solid oak, square and worn now. Heavy drapes cover windows with lead designs. The stone floor is decorated with a mosaic of blue, gray, and rose. Dark mahogany for the huge, gin-stained bar and the heavy banister, white for the walls and ceiling. They held the trials here in January.

The doorway is a large, magnificently carved example of a vanished art. Flowers and leaves twist and embrace and keep their fluidity in defiance of the forces which have cracked and split the old wood.

Kamau's chauffeur, George Kassim, was present throughout almost all of the interview. A photographer I had brought with me from the mainland came, took his shots, and left. My taxi driver, guide, and watchdog sat on the doorstep. He was a fat Arab who had stepped forward at the airport. Smiling he refused to leave my side. The only English he admitted knowing was the price of his services for the day. He quoted a figure and insisted upon being paid in advance. His trousers were as wide as a skirt at the ankle, and he held them up with a length of rope. A small, white, beaded cap is perched like a bowl on the top of his bare head.

Kamau spoke to George only in Swahili. When I was introduced, George smiled, pulled the cigarette off his lower lip, and held my hand for a moment. I never knew whether or not George understood us. He did not reply when I greeted him in English. I suppose George carried a gun. His huge patched trousers were hooked over his bony hips, and a bandoleer of weapons might have been concealed there. Greasy and ragged, George could have slipped into any section of the city and looked at home. Unlike Kamau who is dark and very African looking, George looked more like an Arab with his long moustache and the lighter, brownish color common to the mixed coastal people. He wore a bandage on his arm which looked as if it had not been changed since the three days of fighting in December.

Interviewer: First Secretary Kamau, sir. How did you first become involved in politics?

Kamau: "Politics"? I don't think there is any such thing. Politics is everything. When I was a boy and learning how to read, what they called "politics" was the news from London published in the *Colonial Times*.

I.: Well, when did you become committed to this course of action? After independence you were associated with the Revolutionary Council. Now you've led the revolt which threw out that government and established the Ruling Committee. Was this something you had planned for a long time?

K.: I could not have been planning it for so long a time because the Revolutionary Council was in power for only a few years. And I was a part of it. I saw that the Council was not fulfilling its promises, that it was not obeying the wishes of the people. Then I made plans. You know on this island, this beautiful island with its cinnamon trees, most of the people who live on this island don't own for themselves a pair of shoes. The Sultan and his families used to wear dresses made out of silks and gold. Now, you newspaper people have called me a Communist and Chinese because I saw that the masses should have shoes before the leaders go driving Mercedes cars and go on boats to sleep. Even some of my fellow Africans think this is communism. For thinking this I am called a rabble-rouser, a revolutionary, all sorts of names which frighten people.

I.: Some refugees who fled during the three days last December have reported that hundreds of people were killed, thrown out on the reef. Was this something that got out of control? Or just accidental?

K.: That's just what I mean. The newspapers write these things without authority. I am one man. If there were hundreds of people killed here, I did not see a single dead one on the street. I was in charge. My lieutenants say what had to be accomplished was accomplished with only a little opposition.

I.: One of the mainland dailies did publish some pictures.

K.: And who can prove they were taken in Zanzibar? Where is the proof? There is none.

I.: So your opinion is that very little blood was shed when your committee took power. Let's go back now and cover some of the biographical details and personal information. [When Kamau smiles, he looks young. Coastal people often have worn down, stained teeth. But Kamau's are like a dentist's son's, vividly white against the matte brown of his face and the black of his beard.]

K.: I notice that Americans are especially surprised by the fact that I did not go for a very long time to school. My father did not want me to go to school.

I.: Did you go to a missionary school?

K.: There are only the church schools in those days, and only two kinds of those. But I don't regret that. I have remained religious.

I.: Yes, you're Christian, aren't you?

K.: You see the missionaries had a very strong effect upon all of us. We pupils thought they knew everything in all the world. The very first things we were taught was the Bible stories. Of course they knew all of those. I used to argue with the teachers. Now, if Adam was the first man, how did Cain go and find himself a wife in Nod? The teacher would get very angry.

I.: But I'm surprised to hear you say you've remained a Christian.

K.: [laughing] Yes, I'm surprised myself! But at least I no longer think that the priests and missionaries know everything. [He is solemn here.] But I myself have remained a believer. Those heroes of the Bible stories can still thrill me more than any others. Oh, I'm no longer a preacher! That was twenty-five years ago. The Ruling Committee is half Moslem and half Christian.

Kamau must be a man of great physical strength, for he sits without changing position. He is crouched low in the deep chair. His hands rest on the top of his cane. His face darkens or relaxes depending upon the question. The tape recorder is on the floor between us. Why, he asks, do I bother with the notebook when it is all on the machine? Oh, I say in reply, that is for the asides...

I.: In these three days when you seized power...

K.: First, we did not "seize" power. When the government on this island republic was no longer serving the interests of the people, myself and some others took it upon ourself to see that the wishes of the people were fulfilled. [No sign of amusement here. He is like a bored schoolmaster.]

I.: Let me put it another way. Why was this particular time chosen as the time when human corruption would end? On December 27th the will of the people was suddenly to be enforced. [George with his back against the wall directly behind Kamau is watching us.] Throwing out the Sultan was itself a giant step forward. Why be so impatient?

K.: Certainly you are right there. But I am fifty years old now. I know human nature. The Council did not want real change. And the people, and I myself, we had used up all of our tolerance for injustice and corruption in those years with the Sultan and the colonial officials. We had not patience left for the faults of our own leaders.

I.: And that made it a propitious time to strike? The party might have eventually disciplined itself and done away with excesses.

K.: [Wearily] Our group would never have tried to halt real reform. They lived in the same palaces and used the same offices that the Sultan and British used to have. They had drivers in uniforms driving them to the office in Mercedes cars.

We are interrupted by Shastri, the photographer I had brought with me from the mainland. His camera and film had been confiscated at the airport, and I had gone on without him. He too had not been able to escape unaccompanied. A taxi driver walked at Shastri's side, holding his camera equipment. Even cagey Shastri would not be losing this tail.

Shastri, like many Indians, likes to be smartly dressed. He wears pointed Italian shoes (the kind that were fashionable in Europe fifteen years ago) and flashy imported "sports" clothes. His puce trousers are creased to a razor's edge, and the ribcage of a much used pocket comb is outlined against his back pocket. His laquered hair falls over his pockmarked forehead in a trembling pompadour.

Shastri enters the cool white shell of the Zanzibar Hotel with his chin up. Both Kamau and I have looked up in time to see him giving American cigarettes to one of the waiters. Shastri apologizes and introduces himself. His manners too are a careful, archaic blend of European forms deduced from French literature. Kamau gravely gets to his feet, leans forward over the cane, and shakes Shastri's hand.

Everything about this young man repells Kamau—the frivolous Western clothes, his swagger, the toothpick he doesn't bother to remove from his teeth. Kamau and I both know why Shastri takes this pose. Kamau himself has spoken eloquently on the subject of injustice to minorities. Still in the physical presence of the defiant Shastri (perhaps it is the odor of spices and hair oil which hangs about him) it is all either of us can do to act naturally.

Kamau's bodyguard, George, feels no such ideological compunctions. He sniffs and then sneers openly at Shastri, who returns the salutation. It is the thought of getting rid of Shastri and his like which spurs on George. Shastri is, however, a first-rate photographer, when he can be bothered to do the job. While Kamau frowns and stares at him, Shastri snaps one, then two more good, up-angle shots of the graybeard. He gets it all in—the slightly popping eyes, the hands flat as gloves on the knob of the cane, the round gold-rimmed glasses. The camera clicks and clicks again. George steps away from the wall. Shastri returns the camera to the case, zips it shut, and hands it over to the taxi driver.

Shastri has caught Kamau in between his set-piece expressions. He was not smiling his well-known white smile, not looking stern or fatherly. His mouth was turned down in an odd expression of full-lipped ambivalence, caused by Shastri or some hidden thought. It will be a revealing photograph. Shastri walks out the door into the white-walled street, without returning George's threatening stare. His guide rolls himself to his feet, nods to Kamau, and follows.

I.: Perhaps you would like to say something about the time before the Revolutionary Council. How long were you established as a group before the overthrow of the Sultan?

K.: That was a very difficult time. Police were on their patrols always. It was very difficult to hold meetings. We got together when we could. Then for some months just before the takeover, we came to realize we had another trouble.

I.: Were these meetings held on any sort of a regular schedule? Did you have one particular spot?

K.: We never met at the same place. The meetings were called just in the last minutes, when we could change the location. [This is obviously a period of his life Kamau is proud of, and he continues with some enthusiasm.]

I.: How many of you attended these meetings?

K.: We knew we were in difficulties when the police came and ambushed us in our house one night. You see we always decided upon the meeting place a few hours in advance. So, they must have had the news from one of us. In those days any group of Africans standing together on the road and talking together was suspected. So we never met together outside. We even avoided one another in the city. There were only eight of us then.

I.: So what became the Revolutionary Council as such did operate before the overthrow of the Sultan. We have to be historians, as well.

K.: We didn't want to make the police's work too easy for them. Messages were run from one to the other. Only at the last minute did we decide upon the final place and time. Sometimes it was at my office on the dock—I was a clerk for a shipping firm there—sometimes in a shed or a storeroom of one of the government buildings. The government buildings were the best places to meet because the guards there were very sleepy. That was how we knew one of us was the informer.

I.: What about the messengers? Or the people who watched you come to the meeting. They could have been the ones to betray you.

K.: [laughing] You see, what happened was that the police came exactly on time! We scheduled the meetings at odd minutes. Oh, I think this one was for fourteen after six. One carelessness on our part, now that I think back on it, was that we all wore watches. And we made a special point of having them set exactly to match. They were very expensive watches, and Africans didn't usually have watches or know how to tell time the European way. So that was a mistake we made, a calling attention to ourselves which was not necessary. On this occasion the police van pulled up at exactly fourteen after six. They were rather stupid in their own way, the police. So there was no doubt but that they had been told of the meeting.

I.: Did you ever think that there might be more than one of you involved, that it was a conspiracy?

K.: It was hard enough to imagine one person betraying the rest. The only reason we escaped arrest was that a boy saw the police park their wagon and get out with guns. He ran to us. We hurried out the other way and managed to get away—with the informer amongst us! You see, then he was trapped. His understanding with the police was that they would let him go free when the rest of us were caught. But when we all ran away he faced a dilemma. He decided to run away with us and hope we would not find out.

I.: Who was this informer? Was it one of the important, early organizers? Someone who came later to the Council?

K.: That whole night we stayed in a room without any light or food or drink until we found out who it was. [Here he was greatly amused again.] The rest of them, they were suspecting me! Because for my job on the dock I knew many police and government people. It would have been easy for me to make the contacts.

George comes up to Kamau, and the two of them stand in the doorway. Kamau bends his head and George whispers into his ear.

Then George goes out. The actual taping of the interview should be finished, I calculate, around two-thirty. Before leaving I hope to have a look around the island, although it is officially closed to all foreigners. There is only one plane on and off the island every day, and it doesn't leave until four. When Kamau returns I ask if I may be taken on a short tour. Is there a jewelry shop where I can buy a souvenir? Kamau's reply is very gracious. Of course, he will instruct the driver himself. The famous gold workers? They're mostly closed down now. They were for the tourists, after all. Now the same workers have more vital jobs, Kamau says, in factories or in the fields. But there is one old man who still has a few things. He settles himself in the armchair, looks at the recorder on the floor between us, and then gazes directly up at me.

K.: Then I remembered something. One of our members had a brother in the police. Many families, especially mixed background families, were split over our cause. Some people still felt an old loyalty to the Sultan, some others didn't mind the British so much. I didn't think too much of this fact when I first heard it. But that night I remembered. [Kamau stopped and looked towards the front door.]

I.: What happened next?

K.: That was the end of the incident.

I.: You mean the man confessed, just like that?

K.: Yes, eventually he admitted everything. And after the business was taken care of, then we found out some other things which should have warned us. You see, we had not been so very clever ourself. This man had been around the city with lots of money. If we had known that earlier it would have made us suspect him. In those days we all gave whatever extra money we had for guns and ammunition.

I.: What did you do with him?

K.: Through several different sources we heard that this man had been seen in the company of one particular police officer. He was the one, all right, without any questions. [He looks up at me laughing again.] And there never were any more of those unwelcome guests coming on time, so we know we got the right man.

I.: Was he tried?

K.: We always saw to it that his widow and children were supported. And the surprising thing was that this man turned out to be one of the most important early organizers. He was the last person I myself would have suspected. [Again the bright laughter.] You see, no one is indispensable, even me!

I.: Is he someone whose name I would recognize?

K.: No, I don't think his name is necessary for the story. This man, our betrayer, was more educated than the rest of us. Most of the others in our group, like myself, had not been past primary school. Several could not read or write at all. But this man, our informer, had been all the way through secondary school. He had travelled abroad. The rest of us relied on him for certain things. He was easy with Europeans and could talk to them like an equal. One of his jobs was to read all of the English newspapers and tell us if they said anything about us. He took minutes in our meetings. In the beginning he was one of the original ones.

I.: So he was one of the original ones.

K.: You see, most of the other educated Africans were very much gradualists. They made public statements denouncing us. Oh, they called us barbarians, and criminals and worse. It's wonderful to hear what they called us then and what they say now. So this particular man for his class was an exception. I always give him credit myself for that. He saw the future when the others of his station wore blindfolds.

Then his personal fortunes turned against him. He was a very handsome man and well-liked by women. He used to work in a dispensary as a pharmacist's assistant. He lost his job after a quarrel with an Asian doctor. After that he could not get such a good job. He became a clerk like me. Then he began to drink so much. And he lost that job. Finally he could not keep up with any job, and he began to live with prostitutes. That's how we heard about all of this extra money.

I.: So he didn't turn against you for ideological reasons.

K.: Finally, it was that he would do anything for money.

I.: Didn't you notice these changes in his behavior?

K.: We always took good care of his children. Kamau does not forget. [Here, it was as if the deserted Hotel lobby was full of detractors.] Kamau did not forget this man's family. Kamau does not cast aside people who have once given their loyalty and their lives. To this day we are feeding his family. His daughter goes to one of the state schools on scholarship.

Kamau's own words seem to have angered him. He stands up heavily, leaning on the cane. The thick stone keeps the inside of the hotel cool, but everyone coming in from the street is damp. I asked Kamau if he would like a beer. He replied he was a teetotaller.

Kamau seemed to be waiting for George's return with anxiety. Or, perhaps the window was just a place to stand. "And your family?" I asked. The beer was lukewarm, unpleasantly close to body temperature.

"We have four sons. All go to school now. But they have all suffered very much for my beliefs. For years they were disallowed in school."

"Is your wife from the island?" I remembered reading something about her in the background material.

Kamau came back and wearily sat down. This time he placed the cane over his knees. "Yes, I married a local girl." He said, "She has suffered too. She is my only wife, and I owe everything to her. When we were children she lived about a mile from my homestead. I used to not like women, except my mother. She is the first one I ever loved." He grinned at me and pointed to the recording machine. "You see, not all of us are 'polygamists.'"

I.: Let's see, where were we? There has been no newspaper published in Zanzibar since the takeover. And no mainland or foreign papers have been allowed on the island, nor have reporters been let in. Only the official government news announcements are heard on the radio every day, once in the morning and once in the evening. Is this a permanent state of affairs?

K.: [vigorously] Your coming today is a good start. We are always glad to welcome honest reporters. But why have people come here to go and print lies about us. Someone like Ali-min [a popular columnist in a left-wing mainland daily] would do us a great deal of good. We will never object to the truth. We only have excluded slanderers. Why should we allow them here?

I.: But as to the actual killings in those days, the crimes of vengeance. It's said that everyone associated with the former Revolutionary Council was slaughtered.

K.: [The walking stick comes down to an upright position.] I think we have covered that ground. There were one or two unfortunate incidents, one involving a well recognized female friend of a former leader. But the people who were fleeing looked over their shoulders and imagined the worst.

I.: I suppose the actual narrative of events for those four days would be hard to reconstruct.

K.: Impossible.

I.: People on the mainland and abroad are eagerly waiting for your plans for bringing development to the island. Internationally, you are looked to for…

K.: [interrupting] First we will remove. The formerly Sultan's palace will be turned into an elementary school, free to all the children of that age in the city. We have already appointed a headmaster. We have changed some of the old street signs, which the Revolutionary Council never got around to doing. The names like Delamere and Victoria which our people could not read or pronounce will be replaced by names of freedom fighters.

Next for reform are the docks and the importing of goods. Zanzibar has always been the first in the exporting of certain products. We need more trade, more traffic, more visitors. You'll tell the world that. But they will have to give us something in return this time.

I.: When would you say you committed your first act of civil disobedience?

K.: Oh, that's a philosophical question! But once I was arrested for my conscience. That was because of some hats, thousands of them which had been dumped at my house by some overly zealous youths. The hats had been collected by some of our young men as a protest against the people's extravagance. Six years in prison is a long time. And all that time I became very determined for two things—to stay alive, which was a very large struggle, and to work for the overthrow of the people who had put me in prison. For ten hours a day we dug trenches in the hot sun, thinking them our graves. And in the night we made plans. The sun, the hard labor digging, the beatings—they only made me more determined.

[Again Kamau seemed amused. It is all a good joke, apparently.] All the time I was in jail, as long as I was not sick, I was plotting and scheming and planning. We weren't allowed books until the very end. We had no paper. So I could only think. And now I want to tell my story. Now there is no one to stop me from telling it.

I.: Do you remember what you read in prison? Were you influenced by any particular thinker.

K.: Oh, that lady writer. Miss Abagail? No, Miss Agatha, Christie. Then, The Adventures of Sherlock Holmes. I liked that very much, although I never met a real English gentleman like Mr. Holmes. Mrs. Warren's Profession. And The Confessions. What was it called? I liked it very much. Oh, yes. Felix Krull. The Confessions of a Confidence Man. The Island of Adventure. They gave us whatever happened to be lying around. Once a guard asked us if there were any particular books we wanted. I asked for some history books, some political books, I also had a copy of famous speeches. Of course I never got the books I asked for.

I.: So it was not in prison that you became influenced by Marx, Lenin and Gandhi.

K.: We read whatever they gave us. Enid Blyton. The Biggles books. I read about forty of those. Marx? Lenin? Our jailors didn't go out and get those for us. Only much later did I read the political thinkers.

I.: So your thinking was not formed by them?

K.: [laughing] No, no. By the time I read them I was so very busy. When I first came abroad I was reading everything I could lay my hands on. I think God interested me more than Marxism, though. I never finished the Marx book. I only read a few chapters. I don't know why everyone calls me Marxist. [Kamau stands. He is impatient with the interview now.]

I.: [talking into the microphone] Perhaps there is one incident, a meeting, an injustice which was the beginning.

K.: But I've told you, I have no career! We never sat down and decided what to do with our lives in those days. I was just here at a certain time. [George is standing in the doorway. Kamau nods at him. George has been joined by another man whom I don't remember seeing before.] But there's no time for this explaining. In the book we will tell all of that. At school the headmaster announced that every boy in Standard One was eight years old, regardless. Some of the boys had already been circumcised. They were men already. [laughing] But officially they were eight years old and there was nothing they could do about it. Now my position is about the same. [George comes and stands behind Kamau.]

I.: [I speak loudly enough into the microphone so that Kamau can easily hear me.] This interview has been with Njoroge Ngugi

Kamau, one of the most autonomous leaders in Africa. The old Sultan is dead; his heirs are in exile. The Revolutionary Council has been unseated, and in its place we have the Ruling Committee headed by Kamau. And yet life in the white courtyards seems much the same. People avoid the sun, hope things will be better for their children, and stay out of the way of police. [I turn off the tape recorder and stand up to shake Kamau's hand.]

"I wanted you to hear the kind of thing that I would wind up with."

"Are you going to tell them all that in your report?" Kamau asks.

"Yes, I want to include some sort of summary to remind people where this is taking place."

"Then I will add some words as well." He picks up the microphone and switches on the machine.

K.: Kamau will see that the people of Zanzibar have shoes to wear and food in their stomachs. The Sultan used to sleep on a golden pillow. Now everyone is saying, why did you throw out the Revolutionary Council? But they were driving the Sultan's cars and sleeping in his beds. One thing Kamau will never do is live in the Sultan's house. I am an ordinary man. There is no philosophy for that, just the truth. Kamau will not forget his promises. And the people of Zanzibar will not forget Kamau. [He puts back the microphone.]

I.: Is that all?

Kamau's eyes are bright. He has profoundly moved himself. We shake hands again, fiercely. I too cannot help but respond to his belief in himself. George hurries out the front door before Kamau. He resembles a bureaucrat already. Kamau crosses the room to speak to my taxi driver, who lifts his soft bulk off of the floor in surprise. The driver listens to Kamau with his hands clasped. Kamau is all smiles at our parting. He laughs out loud at the turkey gobbles of the tape rewinding. I am feeling gay myself, relieved that things have gone well. I promise to send him three copies of the interview when it appears in print. I finish reloading carefully and pack up the machinery.

Outside in front of the huge carved doors we find George with the First Secretary's car, a salt-pitted tan Volkswagon. Two other men, their faces are not easy to see, are sitting in the back seat. George leaves on the motor, which idles high with a hysterical whine, and runs around to open the door. Before he has lowered himself stiffly into the seat Kamau starts talking. He waves the knob of his cane at the pair behind him. George grinds the gears and the flimsy car jerks forward. Kamau salutes me through the window.

When they disappear around the walled corner I am aware for the first time of how hot it is. The white multiplies and bounces back the glare. The short street in front of the Hotel is deserted. Is it the heat? Moslem reclusiveness? A woman with black skirts hurries out of one carved door frame and into the next one. Her head is bent, and she covers her face by holding up a veil with the last two fingers of her hand.

My driver has gone around the corner to fetch his taxi. When he hurries, his baggy trousers flap at his ankles. While he is gone I take the opportunity to shake hands with our silent audience, the waiters. They each accept an American dollar. When the driver returns they are at their positions at the bar. Something to eat? We head down the narrow walled street. The buildings are not all white. Some are brilliant pastels, pink and blue. We stop at an empty square. One side is open to the ocean and a small square of deserted beach. On the bottom floor of one building is the cave of a restaurant. The restaurant is one small room with two round tables and a short counter. An Asian man and a boy of about twelve stand behind the counter. When we approach, we are the only visible customers, the man hurriedly stands up with his hands on the counter. The glass display case shows a lopsided pile of thick pancakes, a dish of nuts, and a bowl of cold tomato sauce. For one pancake and some nuts I hold out a fistful of change. The boy, who is about the age of my youngest daughter, picks out two coins. The driver reaches behind the glass and grabs a handful of nuts. My driver and I take our food and stand by the water. He nods and with a mournful expression accepts half of my pancake. Far out a freighter, or perhaps it is a tanker, interrupts the horizon. The boat doesn't look headed for Zanzibar.

We drive on to another part of the city. For the first time I see people in the street—men in long, dirty white gowns, the women always in black, as if in mourning. Here and there a wooden house breaks the monotony of white and pastel plaster. Children play in the doorways. The driver stops in front of one of a long row of closed shops. He pounds upon the sliding iron door which reaches down to the street. We wait. Then an old man comes around from the back and unlocks the padlock on the pavement. Behind the sliding iron barricade is a store with glass windows.

The shop window is empty of merchandise, but an old display case stands inside. Behind a beaded curtain at the back something acrid is cooking. The owner spits onto the dirt floor and takes some cardboard trays out of a drawer. There are a few pieces of jewelry. A woman peeks around the beaded curtain and speaks to the driver in Swahili. He doesn't bother to reply.

The shopkeeper looks aside while I examine what he has left. There is nothing made of gold, only some imported Indian filigreed silver, what they have in every mainland curio shop. The carved ivory figures, a parade of people following the curve of the tusk, are also from China or India. There seems to be nothing locally made.

Then my eye is stopped by a large signet ring. It is carved from a single block of ivory and has raised calligraphic lettering and what looks like an insignia. The shopkeeper shrugs. The driver bends down, looks closely at the ring, and quotes a price. I hand over the ridiculously small sum to the store owner, and he puts it on top of the glass. At the clink of the money the woman sticks her head around the curtain. I wrap the ring in my handkerchief and put it into my pocket.

It is already time to go to the airport. The sands on the bare beaches are as white and shining as those in the most fashionable resort. We pass the docks. A group of working men in bright wrap skirts are standing together. They are laughing and don't look up as our car sputters past. Farther down on the pier six or seven others are shouldering one another to get under a shower which drains between the boards and into the sea.

A thousand people were reported killed in those three December days. We pass no cemeteries on the way to the airport. The only statue I have seen is in the center of town, and it is of a European in hunting clothes carrying a gun. All along the road to the airport there are beaches, just the sea, coconut palms, and huts made from banana leaf. We pass beyond the city. A boy runs along the side of the road chasing the car. Then he stands and waves, perhaps dreaming of the day when he will ride in such a fine car along the same dusty road.

The airport is empty of passengers. Inside I switch on the recorder. The dozen idle taxi drivers are sitting under the same palm. Their cars are all like the one I rode in, either Czech or Russian, or the Dodges and Hudsons of thirty years ago. A uniformed official solemnly marks my case with chalk. For whom? Then past another uniformed guard and out the locked gate to the edge of the landing field. Is there a toilet? I don't see any sign, and the gate has been locked again behind me. An old man in the white traditional gown sits with a sack between his knees. The sack looks as if it contains all of his possessions, and he as if he had been waiting for hours. Shastri sits as far way as possible from the gate to the terminal. He has his feet propped up on the railing. Several officials mill around. He looks relieved, even pleased to see me. His camera cases are at his feet.

In the distance just a faint whirr, then a green and white checkered plane approaches. It bounces down and stops in front of us. The pilot has a handlebar moustache, like a character in a play. He jumps down from the cockpit, goes through the gate, and disappears into an unmarked door. On his head he wears a soiled white hat with gold braid and stars.

The passengers climb off unassisted as soon as the door with the stairs drops down. There are two Chinese without luggage. A large sack is unloaded from the baggage hold, and one of the Chinese slings it over his shoulder. An African in a London suit steps down carrying a briefcase. He is met by a shorter, fatter African who wears an open shirt. Together they walk past the barricade and past the smiling officials. Although the visitor is immaculately dressed, he also does not seem to have brought a suitcase or a change of clothes.

The refueling is quickly done. The pilot emerges from the unmarked door tucking his shirt into his pants. He climbs into the cockpit and takes his hat off. The plane splutters and coughs. He puts the choke in, and the engine speeds up. My taxi probably required more technical skill.

In the last minutes before boarding we are joined by a young well-dressed African couple. The woman wears a fashionably cut trouser suit, the man a suit jacket. They seem in a hurry. Our machine rises into the air and circles over the shoreline at a few hundred feet. I can see a mother and her child standing by the beach. We rise higher and Zanzibar is behind us, her colors fading. The palm trees turn into arching lines, and then dots. The beaches are white arches, brush strokes, and then a line. The white city with its dirt streets looks surprisingly small, a string of white pebbles circling the blue harbor. The coral surrounds are vast and brightly colored, pink, orange, and gray. The sleepy ocean shows itself made of slow, churning rivers of blue, green, and red. The island becomes a dull brown patch swallowed up in whorls of color. The plane chugs on. Shastri is speaking Swahili to the young African couple, smiling at them, trying to please. The old man is sleeping. I look ahead for the brown smudge of the continental coastline.

My Mothers' Lovers

Come to me, baby. Come into my arms. The large black man opens wide his arms beside the hospital bed. There, he says to the smiling nurse. Just get her onto the sheet. We'll pull her over with the sheet. Haitian? Jamaican? Oh no, he says, laughing. I couldn't want two wives. One is enough for me.

You're her daughter? She's not really my daughter, she has told the Korean resident holding the clipboard. But she lied about her age, too. Said she was fifty-nine, and she's seventy-nine or seventy-eight. I can never remember exactly. The truth is, I am the daughter of her first husband, and he's been dead for thirty years. Yes, I say to the resident with the beautiful thick black hair, I'm her daughter. Write my phone numbers down on the form. All of them. I'll repeat them. I'll come when you call.

Then they are wheeling her to the operating room. She is a small bundle, huddled around her pain.

After the operation, the nurses come and take you by the arm. The doctors don't touch you. They clump together in the hallway and they say they'll speak to you. In a minute.

In the recovery room they have her wired up already and she doesn't open her eyes. There are six others trussed up in the same way. Some are sleeping. One is sitting up and rocking back and forth. The nurses shout at them, shout through the anesthetic, hoping to reach the cringing self. It's all over. You're all right. They shout her name, loudly, several times. You're not alone, they shout. We're not going to leave you alone. It is not an intimate reassurance. If you don't stop thrashing, I'm going to have to tie you down. Fortunately, she is quiet. She knows you're there, the Puerto Rican attendant says.

I'd like to think that when they have her strapped down in the bed, with the pale plastic penis jammed in her mouth, forcing her jaws wide, that this is a rape she is not aware of. This very public violation. All are equally helpless in intensive care. The nervous interns and the experienced, foreign nurses are in command here. They man their stations and the consulting doctors, uneasy away from their Park Avenue offices, make daily forays and retreat rapidly.

You remember your military service. In World War II you volunteered for the Navy and were in intelligence. You'd recognize the atmosphere. This is the closest I have ever been to a military battlefield. The nurse's aide efficiently rolls you over and changes the linens, saying, It's in God's hands. Another accent I can't place. It seems no one here has been born in America. How you hated the Catholic church, with the kind of passionate hatred reserved for kin. The old man opposite is being pumped up again. He must be very rich to have so many doctors. Seven people crouch over his bed, hit his chest and put the bellows in his mouth. When the respirator starts its wheeze again, the doctors and the nurses melt away.

The last of my mother's lovers is a large gentle man who, at no one's bidding or asking, has come to attend at her final illness. He is tall and strong, although not fit, and he makes himself useful with the doctors and nurses. He has hair growing out of his nose and ears, and the attendants assume he is her son, or husband, or brother. They call him by variations on her name, not by his own, unrelated name. After the first week he doesn't bother to correct them. The last of my mother's lovers is one of those rare people who knows things. He is used to taking care of things, to getting the job done without a fuss.

It is clear he loves my mother, although when she was well he was only a friend, no closer than several others. When she was still strong enough to talk, they liked to argue together, about who to blame for Beirut, or the unions. My mother had strong views about politics, and she was an accomplished conversationalist. But in the hospital just before the operation, she is too weak to have opinions. My mother's lover tries to tease her spirit into argument, just as he tries to tempt her poisoned appetite with ice cream sodas and peanut brittle. After years of worrying about getting fat, she slowly turns her head on the pillow and whispers to me: I only weigh ninety pounds, can you believe it? I cannot believe it.

This last lover is perfectly faithful, although he sleeps with another woman, a close friend of my mother's, to whom he happens to be married. This technical act of adultery on his part is of no import. It is a minor indiscretion, not even a betrayal, and overlooked by all parties.

He says, how about a chocolate malt? This is before they take her into the ice chamber from which she will emerge having lost possession of her body. When she was in purgatory, waiting for the operation, he was there too. So, I'll get you a chocolate milk shake, he says. Yesterday, he tells me happily, she drank it all.

She smiles, her eyes even flicker with interest. For a moment, her old chipper self. OK. He runs down to the corner soda fountain and comes back with a paper container overflowing with chocolate ice cream. The chocolate oozes out from under the clear plastic hat and drips on his rain coat and his not very clean black suit. He reaches behind her sparsely covered head and plumps up a second pillow. She pulls the lids down on her eyes, dutifully puts the crooked straw in her mouth and sips a little. Good, she says and sighs. Her head sinks into the pillow. He turns and gives me a big grin.

My mother asks me: Why does he do it? She is dying by centimeters. He comes by every day, or calls. No matter where he is. I don't even know him that well.

Because he loves you, I don't answer.

Who can fathom the sidewinding path of the heart, predict when the snake will silently emerge to seek its unsuspecting quarry, before we realize he has woken and left, again. As we grow older, who can say when the heart's poor serpent will crawl out seeking warmth, except that it will rarely go to the spot we have been watching.

Dr. Death is the man in the white coat. Dr. Death has a paunch and a wad of gum in his cheek because he has given up smoking.

Just before the operation Dr. Death looks at me through bottle-bottomed glasses and says: If you'll excuse me, I'll examine her now. He snaps the curtain shut behind him. She lets him touch her body. Together they conspire to keep the horror of her present condition hidden. He holds the stethoscope against his own chest to warm it before putting it against her skin. Dr. Death is listening, hunched over her ravaged body with its pearly yellow and pink bruises. He gently unties the twisted cotton cord of the hospital gown and looks right at the swollen and gouged chest. Trust me, his gentle fingers say. Trust me, his touch says. I won't let you suffer. It won't be long. She trusted him, and he lied.

We are in England. In the countryside of Kent. Right after the war. That is, World War II. My father has brought his new wife to visit. She is forty-four, I am twelve. It isn't the first time we've met, but it might as well be. We walk to the paddock where I keep my horse, a round-bellied roan named Spearmint. Later I will not use the word paddock because everything connected with England, including my own English accent, I will expunge from my identity. I want my childhood erased, even Spearmint, and I have largely succeeded. But on that day I am in the middle of living it; I cannot cut it out because it hasn't happened yet. I am a sullen teenager. I hate her because my father has married her, and I have swallowed my mother's rage, which will continue to burn undiminished for decades. I am striding across the mud to catch Spearmint because my father has told me she likes to ride. Besides it gets us both out of the house, where everyone is quarrelling.

She follows me across the lawn, and her high-heeled black pumps sink into the mud and manure. I suppose I am hoping she will ride my English pony and fall off. Even though I don't know much, I know that the suit she is wearing is expensive and that it comes from New York. This is something my mother goes on and on about, how thin she is, and how expensive her clothes are. I remember this gray flannel suit with its sharp inverted pleat at the back, ending with an embroidered arrow. I have never seen such a handsome suit. I nod towards the fat, dirty pony, eyeing that narrow skirt. I'll just roll it up, she says, game.

She treats that expensive skirt with no respect, which I respect, hitching it up and shoving the hem into the hand-stitched waistband. She clambers onto the second paddock rail, tosses her cigarette into the mud, and heaves herself stomach down onto Spearmint's mud-caked back. She is a fish flopping on the river's edge, and I am not helping. Then she raises herself up on her arms and with a wrench throws her leg over. With a loud rip the gray flannel skirt splits right up the back. Not a word do I say. Nor does she. I hand her the halter rope, push the lazy Spearmint off balance so he starts to walk. She gives his flank a kick, and the black pump drops from one nylon heel. I am gleeful, but cannot laugh. We both know my father will be furious. I pick the shoe out of a muddy hoofprint and put it back on her outstretched foot. We are silent as Spearmint walks and then trots around the paddock. She has no trouble getting him to do what she wants. Nice pony, she says, sliding off, not looking at the damage to the skirt. She pats his fat roan neck, and the pony turns his head and puts his muzzle in the gray flannel pocket of her jacket, looking for sugar.

In the hospital I have a lot of time to sit around and remember, and a heavy incentive not to think about what is happening in front of my eyes. It is twenty-five years ago this December. I am visiting my mother in California, soon after graduating from college and a few months before my marriage. I can't get used to the wonderfully clement weather, to the blue skies and the green and softly rolling hills. I have come from my new home in Chicago, where an iron gray wind tirelessly patrols the cavernous streets. And the snow is never clean. Not even when it has just fallen. In Chicago the mercury has not crawled past zero for three weeks. I am out in California to spend Christmas with my mother because no one else will. But California, where I was born, is too pretty to be true.

My mother now lives a few blocks from where I went to grammar school before being taken to Europe. She has had over twenty addresses since that time. The appearance of the old neighborhood, however, has changed little since I was in third grade. What were once small cheap stucco houses right next to each other are now small expensive stucco houses right next to each other.

I take a pair of boots to the corner repair shop. Their crepe soles have curled and been chewed up by the ice and gritty snow, and salt has left a white milky ring on the leather. A black man puts down a half-stitched sandal and turns around. He is wearing a tan leather apron stained with the black of his job. He is friendly, in the California way. He was about the age I am now. He asks me where I am staying, hesitates and doesn't let go when I hand him the boots. Oh, he says with the hint of a leer, you are Maisie's daughter. I realize he has had her too. I know it as surely as I know that the sun is shining in Berkeley and a cold wind is blowing in Chicago.

At dinner I mention that I have met the shoeman. Later in the liquored evening she boasts that he was her lover. I say nothing. I feel nothing. That the man is black is no matter, or even that she should pick up lovers who drop her like shoes on the counter. It is something else which sticks in my throat. I can no longer eat at her table. Tomorrow is Christmas. I make excuses, push the food around on my plate because I cannot swallow. All day I sit reading old magazines in a rocking chair by the window, turning my back to the beautiful blue sky. I fly back to Chicago early. I don't think she notices that I haven't eaten anything for two days. Probably she doesn't notice because she is drinking steadily. Three shots of vodka right after breakfast, in the kitchen, and I am not supposed to see.

Back in freezing Chicago, I am starving. No, it is not the fact of the lovers. Or so many of them. It is her own contempt for them, for boyfriends or husbands, her own and other people's. In her dark, all dogs are strays. There is no joy in those adulteries. In so much licentiousness there should be some pleasure, but there is only the worn, corrosive quality of compulsion. Her body, her sexuality is a curse, a hated thing. There is nothing sensual in the wobbly, jellied belly I used to see mounding out of the bedclothes in the morning as I sneaked out, hoping to escape without waking her. Thinking, as I ran up the hill to school through the morning fog, this is the flesh that I sprang from. Often she tells me, insists upon telling me, how all the men ran after her, how many were her lovers. The numbers jar. How many abortions. How many admirers. You don't believe me, she says. Is that why she has to tell me so often? But I do. Just don't tell me about it anymore. I do. Your father loved me, she insists. It's true, I don't any longer believe her. But I do believe that if there was a beauty there, a flame which brought the moths, she was driven to stamp it out.

Now this body alone remains. A body hooked up to hoses, lines which run liquids into her nose and then out the rectum, where the cancer was first found. A clear bag hung high on a hook feeds in a milky liquid and a plastic bag discreetly hidden under the bed— they have finally moved her to a private room—collects the brown and yellow liquids which pass out of the shell. The respirator whines. Every few moments a light goes on, or a buzzer rings and a nurse comes, twiddles the knobs, stares at the oscillating scope. After three weeks of this her body has taken on its own independent identity, and she is barely recognizable. The cadaverous wasted body, where the skin was slack over the bones, has now gone on a drunken rampage. The face, the arms and the hands are distended. Liquid leaks out through the bandages. They wrap her mottled arms in ice.

The nurses have names like Maureen and Rosemary and Eileen. Lace curtain Irish. Shanty Irish, she would probably say. They say, she opened her eyes yesterday. They work eight-hour shifts, replacing bags, watching the machines, packing her hands in ice. They get paid less than what a good carpenter makes, even less than what some teachers earn. Still their weekly bills total in the thousands, and must be paid in cash. I worry that the nurses are Catholic. They are so rosy cheeked and their every visible orifice is extraordinarily clean. They rub the vacant body with oil, turn over the limp trunk with the tubes protruding from either end.

One day I find they have attached earphones to her head. They are running music through her skull. I rip them off. It soothes them, Maureen or Margaret says, the hearing is the last to go.

August 10, 1948

Darling—

I am counting the hours until we are together. Paris is bleak and gray, and the French are no more polite than they ever were. If you were here I wouldn't mind, because we would go to some little restaurant, have a bottle of their good red wine and come back together to my funny little room with its hard, rolled-up pillow. I know you don't believe this, but you are on my mind every hour. Even when I am ostensibly occupied with other things. Business meetings, for example. Money. I came downstairs today hoping to find another letter from you. But the beady-eyed concierge with the black scarf had no blue envelope for me from you today. So I went off downcast to have my coffee alone. I am touching your lips, your cheek, your lovely long-fingered hands. I feel your legs against mine....

In the quiet drawers the long leather gloves are neatly folded. Many have never been worn. Elbow-length white leather, short ones lined with rabbit fur, white cotton gloves with a ridge of dust at the finger seams. When I was sixteen, she said to me, you can't go into New York City without a pair of white gloves, and took hers off and gave them to me. Folded alongside the gloves is the underwear, a silk slip, a pair of underdrawers embroidered with flowers, a matching tan camisole. Body coverings fit for the mistress of a Marquis. I hope she had a lover who treated her like royalty. Curling vines of appliqued silk leaves and trumpet flowers, trailing tendrils of embroidered ribbons. All in elegant beige, at the breast, at the top of the thigh. These are garments to defy the body's perishability. Silk stronger than the skin it caresses, silk whose intimate soft touch lives on after the body of its possessor. These delicate nosegays, stitched by sharp-eyed children in Asian sweatshops, sleep in the drawer now, their job done. This camisole knows nothing of bandages oozing water on a ravaged chest. This smooth beige crotch knows no plastic hoses in the rectum.

The closet door opens. Green suede cowboy boots. High heels in black and violet satin. Very high heels for a woman almost eighty. Low-heeled sensible shoes of maroon leather for walking to work, with a bridle buckle over the arch. They wait, the shoes, the trousers, the empty arms of dresses, the slim hips of hanging skirts, the flat legs of slacks folded over hangers.

I tell myself, don't eat too much or too little. Don't drink at all. Lights out before midnight. Everything regular as a metronome. Don't think before you go to sleep. Hope that you don't dream. If you dream forget the dreams as quickly as possible. Leap out of bed and straight into the shower. Avoid altered states, where the spirit might creep up on the mind. Work, but not so hard that your mind bends around. Don't tell anyone, except in the simplest terms, in the lowest calmest voice, where you are now. Don't encourage questions, or sympathy. Make sure the snake is asleep or firmly locked up behind a closed door. Just try to get through to the other side of this. There will be something else at the other end. Life, some sort of celebration of life. Or at least the remnants of my own life. Not yet. I'm not there yet. It isn't me there swathed up to the chin in a wet sheet, my arms wrapped in ice. Not yet.

She is twenty-one, a senior at university, in 1927 when most women don't go to college. Far away from home, back in her father's home in Kansas, away from Los Angeles where she grew up. Every Thursday she goes horseback riding with her best friend from the sorority, another tall handsome girl. They canter along the trail, taking the small jumps on the path. The cavalry rides here regularly and boards its one hundred horses at the university stables. They meet the officers riding on the path. Now they are letting the horses walk home, the loop of the reins swinging loosely. The horses are stepping along smartly, eager to get back. It is May. She and her friend are majoring in business. That meant, she said fifty years later, you learned a little accounting, a little bookkeeping and some basic economics. I'll never get married, she announces abruptly. The sun is going down and the light hits their backs, from a distance framing their bodies in a sunny nimbus. Never? The sorority sister laughs, holds up her hand, covered by the light pigskin of her riding glove. She spreads her fingers open in front of her face, as if to ward off a blow. There it is, a fat triangular bulge, a diamond stretching the leather. No, you didn't. Laughing, you aren't going to. She gives the startled horse a kick, and the two friends gallop back to the stable, lurching and laughing.

A few years later, she herself is going to be married. She has a big round canary diamond. Quite a beautiful one, she said later. She was back in Los Angeles then, still riding, but now over the soft brown California hills, through the scrub oak. Making everyone laugh because she rode English. His mother said, marry him, please marry him. Yes, she was going to get married and take a trip around the world. She was very fond of the mother. But she had a good job, and somehow a trip around the world seemed like—an interruption. Besides her father didn't approve. She gave back the big yellow diamond. So he took another friend around the world. And those two men were together for the next fifty years. She visited them whenever she went back to Los Angeles. When his lover died the ex-fiancé called her in New York and wept and wept. No one else was alive who had known them so long.

Decades later she is still working. Having worked by now not only in Los Angeles but in San Francisco, Tokyo, Hong Kong and now back in New York again. In Los Angeles and San Francisco and later in Hong Kong, there were lots of friends, many parties. She loves to dance, wears silver shoes with open toes and ankle straps and dances until three in the morning in a hotel ballroom under chandeliers, and then goes to work at seven. Her skirts fan out with the tango, her feet fly, in and out between her partner's legs in an intricate step. There is lots of driving around in convertibles in Los Angeles. Trips up and down the coast, dinner out, lunches in restaurants, martinis. Her father is dead now, one year after her mother. Of grief, she will always say. There is a brother, only one year younger. Like a twin. He is good-looking and likes parties, too. He marries, has three children, and they go to the beach with their aunt, picnic with their aunt on Catalina Island. Later the brother leaves the wife, marries another woman and has five more children. She thinks it wrong. They don't speak. She keeps in touch with the brother's first wife.

My father now enters the picture. Where do they meet? At work, of course. Everyone, or almost everyone, is working in what they call the war effort. My father, a Canadian, is working for the government, on a complicated wartime pricing system, the likes of which this country has not seen since. He has taken a leave from his position as a professor of economics. And from his troublesome family. She too leaves her regular job in the fashion industry and takes a job with the government, working for my father. Leaves Los Angeles, comes to San Francisco. Walks away from all the amusing parties with the movie people. Besides there is gas rationing now, and people aren't driving up and down the coast so much.

They are in love, but the future is clouded. He is serious. So serious. But married. And so handsome. He was the poorest person I ever knew, she said later. Sometimes that was amended to, the tightest person I ever knew. And so handsome. But the wife is angry, very angry. The wife won't let him go. Not that she wants him herself. She doesn't, no she doesn't. Takes a score of lovers to prove she doesn't love him. Proves the opposite. And there are those inconvenient children. Two little girls with permanent frowns and runny noses and underwear which isn't always clean. She doesn't really like children. You don't have to like them just because they are children, she often says.

After the war she and my father will try to adopt an Italian orphan, when there are so many very thin children in Europe with no parents. And my father can have no more children, by his own will. But now she has to worry about these two girls, children she hasn't met. But she knows their names. Late at night in the dark of the inexpensive San Francisco hotel room, she hears the replay of what has been happening at home. Scenes, there are always scenes. Weeping, shouting, threats, accusations. Doors slamming, dishes broken. But when they are together in that drab hotel room, it is so quiet. So peaceful in the chilly dark, as they hold each other. At thirty-nine she was still a virgin when she fell in love with my father.

In the too bright room now, just the gentle wheeze of the respirator, the rushing watery breathing of the machine. Scratch, scratch. It is in a hurry to complete its course, that machine. The nurse comes in on tiptoe. Why tiptoe when there is no one here who can be woken. Maureen or Theresa combs her straggly hair back and clips the nails on her unrecognizable swollen fingers. They say, I just gave her a lovely bath. I touch my lips to her cool, damp forehead. They shout her name and her eyelids flutter. Call her name, Maureen says. She can hear you, Margaret says. Their voices are loud. Don't, I cry, hating them. Let her sleep. For God's sake. The window of her room looks out onto a vacant brick patio. Funny about the scars, how surprised I was to see the straight little cuts above the ears. How could I not have noticed a facelift? She certainly didn't tell me, but I think I know when it was. One of those vacations in Europe. She came back saying, Well, how do I look?

March 2, 1949

Dearest——

Do you realize that this is my first letter to you as my wife. It is a continual source of joy to me to think that we have been married for three whole months now. I often think to myself: She is my wife, now. For me at least these are months which have never been happier, more fulfilling. Because we are finally together. I know that for you there have been some adjustments. That you miss your old job, your old life and your many friends. That my colleagues seem dull and drab. But don't worry, it won't be like this forever. I promise when we go back to New York we will spend some time painting the town. I promise. I'll even let you have more than one drink at the bar before dinner. I am working on mending my ways. Which isn't to say that I think I have been transformed into an easy person to live with, or be married to.

Rome is pitiful now. Every place I go I am reminded that we were here together just last week. But it doesn't make me feel less lonely now. Yesterday a boy approached me on the street. At first I shooed him away. You know how I hate beggars. Then I saw he was selling a pack of cigarettes. My brand, Camels. Anyway, here was this little tyke, with a dirty face and big circles under his eyes. You would have wanted to take him home. I have news for you about that. It no longer looks hopeless. The saddest thing was that all his teeth were rotted. Just a few stumps. I opened the pack of cigarettes at the hotel and inside were twenty homemade cigarettes pasted together from discarded butts. Some still with lipstick on them. The package had probably been thrown away by a soldier. I went back after lunch to look for the boy, to give him some coins, but he was nowhere to be found.

Tomorrow I go to Switzerland to visit Melissa and Jane in their private school in the mountains. I'm not expecting much of a welcome. They have both been well schooled in hating me. I suppose I can't blame them. As you know I was against enrolling them in this school for Hungarian princesses and the children of munitions makers. The headmistress has great pretensions. They are ordinary American girls who should be home in Berkeley starting junior high, not learning how to pour tea for diplomats. But their mother will hear nothing of it. They must marry well, she says, now that they have no father. She forwards me the bills for this ridiculous enterprise. But enough of that.

It must be midnight in New York. I hope you are asleep. I should be home in a month, providing the boat schedules don't change again. In time to celebrate your birthday with you. Outside the moon is shining, as it must be in New York. Perhaps coming through our little apartment window and laying a streak of white across your bed, perhaps kissing your sleeping cheek. In the moonlight it is possible to imagine the great avenues of Rome once again full of triumphant parades. I wish you were here to curl up next to me on this very narrow bed, which seems to be stuffed with hand grenades left over from the battlefields. And of course the freezing bathroom is down the hall...Good night, my darling...

Funny, he doesn't look like an angel, the last of my mother's lovers. This rather paunchy, middle-aged man. The black suit is decidedly droopy. It sags in the crotch. The jacket hangs limply from the shoulders, and no evidence of wings beneath the cloth can be seen. No wings popping out at the ankle, just wrinkled black socks falling down not very smartly above the plain scuffed shoes.

She always appreciated a well-dressed man. You'd have thought they would have sent one of those to comfort her. He's hiding, this angel. He's disguising himself in that tacky dark coat, posing as an ordinary, unassuming fool so that the devil won't notice him. He doesn't want to be too beautiful. The face is long, saggy, often with a stubble at the end of the day. Actually, he looks a little like my father. And his hair. No golden curls. Around the baldness he doesn't apologize for are a few lank, black ringlets. Absurd, really. His eyes give him away. In the eyes it can be seen that he knows everything, understands everything, that he is indeed an angel. He has discovered the devil's own work here, and he, the angel, has come to vanquish the evil one. Of course he must come in disguise. The devil is everywhere here, often invoking the name of God. The angel's gentle eyes let me know he is here to help the meek and the helpless. We whisper quietly together in the dark, turning our backs on the nurses, plan how to outwit them, tomorrow's battle, and the next day's and the next day's.

January 4, 1956

Darling—

You wouldn't recognize London. The bombed-out buildings have almost all been rebuilt. Those dreary shopkeepers in the white aprons now have fat rosy cheeks, and there is no more of that rationing you hated. Even with prosperity, however, the British are no better looking.

I'm sorry you got stuck with the cleaning-up after New Year's. It was a terrific party. I hope Melissa helped you, although I know you wouldn't ask her, as you should. She certainly enjoyed the party. Before I left I wrote a check for Jane's tuition, so don't pay any bills until I return. Especially not to that good-looking gardener. I wonder how your board meeting went. Did they elect you president? They've been getting your substantial administrative skills for free.

You must be in bed now. Tomorrow I know you have an appointment with the tax people. Just explain that I am out of the country and will bring in the records when I return. I have great confidence in your ability to convince our former employer, the United States government, that we haven't done anything illegal. This comes with all of my love, as sleepiness overtakes me…

The nurses keep her covered up to the chin. That way they think I won't notice what they've all done to her. I see where the second surgery has cut into her thigh. Well, they said, if she ever does recover. Not to have a leg. But the toes never moved again, have turned dark blue. Occasionally her eyelids flutter and even almost open. I don't think you ever thought she was going to recover, Doctor Death.

The nurses sneak antibiotics into the IV against my explicit instructions, which the doctor assures me are being followed. When Theresa or Maureen go for coffee I look in her chart for the No Code. When they catch me reading the chart, they take it away, saying it's confidential.

December 6, 1959

Dearest—

I'm not going to make these trips any longer without you. They will have to find a way to send you or else I won't go. And I know you didn't marry me to sit home alone. One good thing about Mexico is that the sun is shining. How wonderful the sun felt on my face when I walked out of the hotel. It reminded me of California. Remember those mornings in San Francisco when I used to walk you to work, before we were married? The altitude has hit me hard this time. And my arm still hurts.

Good night my dearest, I'll be home soon....

It is a gray day, but there won't be snow. Yesterday it was
sleeting so the family is grateful there is no sleet today. Something
cruel about the sleet, the way it bites into even the firmest cheek.
And there are several young faces in the cemetery today, including
the bright cheek of the young minister who will read the
Presbyterian prayers and make it all official. The sky today is a
somber gray and blue, the colors of a military uniform. She would
have appreciated this display of nature's subtlety. The gray is not
harsh, the blue is pale, as if watered down by tears, or projected
from the great distance of heaven. In spite of the Eastern cold the
clouds look uncharacteristically soft at the edges, as welcoming as
a fresh bed to the traveller. The family too has been projected from
great distances, brought to stand around the modest hole in the
ground which is temporarily covered with a piece of bright green
artificial grass. Next to the green the square black marble urn sits
on a small stand, upright like the person whose ashes it contains.
She is to be buried next to my father who was buried at his own
insistence in a simple wooden coffin, long before anyone thought
that request would have to be honored.

As we wait the sharp heels of our dress shoes sink into the
mud. How to proceed. The handsome young grave digger
hurries over and asks if we want him to drain the water out of the
hole for the few minutes of the ceremony. The family discreetly
marches a few feet away through the mud, groups by the railing
of another family's plot, turns its collective back. When we return
the little bright square of astroturf has been lifted away, and the
black and white marble urn squats in the bottom of the wet hole,
keeping its shining dignity in spite of the streaks of mud slapped
across its face.

One of the girls starts to cry and the minister, who isn't much
older than a college girl herself, begins to read the passage from the
scripture. She is a stranger, but at least a Scot. The prayers and
poems have been placed between the covers of a somber black
leather binder. The minister is wearing a prim black coat with a
double row of brass buttons. Just an ordinary cloth coat from a
department store. But her eyes are piercing blue and there is
nothing funereal about her presence. She turns her face to the gray

and blue sky and reads, and with bowed heads we listen to to what we don't believe.

All this talk of Heaven, she said. If only I could believe it. I'd like to think you go to some sort of a happy hunting ground with lots of flowers. I'd like to believe that, but I just can't. But she would have liked the gentle mien of this no-nonsense young minister, with her crisp handshake and Canadian accent. Then the flowers, daisies, roses, yellow and red ones, all thrown into the hole. The flowers cover the mud-streaked face of the marble box.

Later, a niece from California, her brother's daughter from his first wife, reproaches me quietly over the telephone: She was raised a Catholic, you know.

He Was a Big Boy, Still Is

— Come in. Come in. No. I'm just glad I was here. That's all. No. It doesn't matter about the other appointment, I just wanted to be here when you came. Some forms have to be signed.

— No. No. It's not inconvenient. I was just working. That's all.

— What a pretty hat. You don't see hats with real feathers on them much anymore. Bird of paradise? Lots of women wore them in the twenties. That bird's extinct now.

— Oh, no. I didn't mean that hat looked old. It's beautiful. Really. The colors. They're beautiful. Such a long tail.

— I understand. Of course, you didn't come here to talk about your hat. Yes, I am his lawyer. No, really. I am. Yes, I know, you have to leave at twelve. Well, that's fine. OK. Look. Your son. Jackson. Here's the score.

— No. That's just a phrase.

— Yes. I saw him yesterday.

— He did seem a little better. He was still in the ward. But he spoke a little. He wouldn't answer any questions.

— Why would they want to kill him?

— Oh, the electric chair. You mean, if he were convicted. Well, we're a long way from being there yet. Besides we don't have the electric chair anymore. Not in this state.

— It's a different sort of thing. They kill you differently. Anyway, they want him alive now. He hasn't even been tried yet. They definitely want him alive at this point.

— The State. So that they can prove their case against him. Sure. That's why they put him in the hospital. So he couldn't try to kill himself again.

— They can't just execute him. They want to keep him alive now, so they can kill him later? Well, there are lots of problems with the prosecution's case.

— You know. With what they have to prove. They haven't proved he killed anyone yet.

— Like on TV? Not really. You see they have to prove that Jackson, your son, murdered a particular person on a particular day. And they haven't got his head.

— The victim's head.
So you see they haven't got a real murder yet.
Anyway, that's their problem.
Look. I know you're in a hurry. But it's important.
Jackson, your son. Is he married?

— Well, what do *you* call him?

— Oh, it's the other way, then. George Washington Jackson. What *do* you call him? What name does he prefer? They're not about to let him out anytime soon.

— What about when you're not mad at him?

— Georgie? Well, for the moment I'll stick to Jackson. All his records say Jackson George Washington.

— Yes, he really is hard to talk to. I know. I have the bruises to show for it, don't I? Ha-ha.

— Well, he's in jail already, isn't he? He's on suicide watch. He's in Ad Seg. Twenty-three hours a day. But it's really a prison. I mean, he couldn't walk out of there, could he?

— Look, if you have to go, let's at least get those forms done. Then you won't have made a trip for nothing. OK?

— With all the crazies? He's just there for observation now. I'm trying to make sure that the doctors are not giving him more drugs. After he attacked me they put him on Haldol. But I can't really do much for him until someone signs his papers.

— No, not those kind of drugs. The ones the doctors give you.

— Yes, the ones that make you crazier when you're crazy.

— You haven't got time to go see him? OK, what about his sister? I wasn't afraid. Ha-ha. But look what happened to me!

— Yes, there are guards there. How old is she?

— Well, it might be a bit of a shock for her. All those men locked up.

— Oh, she's been inside herself. What for?

— She could probably get that expunged. If it's been five years. Might be worth her while.

— That just means erased. Taken off her record. So that every time she was picked up it wouldn't show up on the computer.

— No, I can't really do it for her. It's just filling out some forms. She can do it herself. Can she read?

— Cruel? Yes, I know, filling out those forms can be cruel. You forgot your reading glasses? Well, maybe I could help her if she came by. Then she could do the forms.

— Maybe—I'm awfully busy. Mostly with Jackson's murder case.

— She could come at lunch time? OK. I'll put it down. Twelve o'clock. What's her name?

— No, we don't do divorces either. No, the public defender is just criminal... That's our jurisdiction.

— Just means I can't do it for you. Legal Aid are the folks who do that. Now let's go through this means test—to prove how poor you are. I know, another silly form. There is lots of that around here. You know what they say. If the State went any slower they'd have to change the calendar. Ha-ha.

— Yes, if Georgie had a real lawyer he wouldn't have to fill out any of these forms. I know. But then there'd be the bills, wouldn't there. Don't forget that! You'd be paying.

— Up front? Most of them want their money up front. Yes, I suppose they do. About how much up front?

— Pricey, and in cash. Hmm. Anyway *we* have to do this form. Otherwise I can't help him. Is he married? I don't know. Now, he doesn't own a house. No, don't laugh. Or a car.

— Why else would he steal one? People who own cars don't usually steal them. You'd be surprised. To get a better one. Or for someone else.

— Why? You know. If he was part of a car theft gang. Now let's move on. Jewelry?

— Yes, they ask about jewelry on the form. You can lie, of course. Lots of people do. It takes years for them to catch up with you. And they only do on real estate. You know, if you own a home. That's when they get you. They take a lien out on the property when it's sold. Don't worry about it...unless you own a house...

— Really? Yes, I'm sure about the divorce. I can't help you there. We don't do divorces.

— That diamond ring? Is that an "Item of substantial value"? I'm sorry. I just assumed it was fake. Besides it isn't his, is it? It's yours.

— Your husband gave it to you? Well, he can't be all bad, then.

— Oh, he can, can he?

— How do you know what it's worth.

— Oh, they told you that at Tiffany's. Well, I'd believe them. They ought to know. Nice piece of change. Any other assets? You know, cash in the bank?

— Well, I don't believe in banks either. Charge you a bloody twenty bucks when your check bounces...Darn right they're crooks.

— Oh, you mean those kind of crooks. Bank robbers. It might get stolen. But it might get stolen at home, too. We know that, don't we?

— Stocks? Bonds?

— Ha-ha. Certainly if I had them I wouldn't be sitting here. Just sign. I know it's almost 12:00. But if we could cover a couple of more things. I wouldn't want you to have to come all this way again.

— Hang on. It will help me later. Let's start with childhood injuries. Especially head injuries or illness. Any time when he was growing up when he...well, behaved peculiarly. Got into trouble at school? Acted up?

— Yeah. That's the kind of thing.

— What kind of an operation?

— Even if you can't remember the name. Try and describe the kind of operation.

— Done at the State school. Uh-huh.
Sounds like a lobotomy. Hang on a sec. I just want to catch that.
Do you know the year? Just approximately.

— OK. The year you lived in Baltimore with your husband when
he was working in the shipyards. When Jackson was living with
his grandmother. OK. That's when it must have been...

— That's close enough. It was an operation on the brain. You're
sure about that.

— The name isn't important. They did a lot of those operations
back then.

— No, there wasn't anything in his medical report. But then he
probably wouldn't have told the doctor about it. Or me. Course
he hasn't told anyone anything, has he? Not even his name.

— Why was his grandmother afraid of him?

— Go on.

— Did she ever recover?

— Did she ever speak again. Was she ever able to tell anyone what
happened? Maybe it *was* an accident.

— And no charges were brought.

— Just sent him to the school where the operation was...

— I understand. He was a big boy, still is.

— Even at 14 he was six feet? He must weigh 250 now. You did
sign the papers then?

— There were lots of papers? Yes. There usually are. But your
recollection is you did sign something. Uh-huh. Of course.
Seemed like a good idea. A blessing. Someone else signed for
you?

— But you agreed to the operation. Hang on. Let me make a note about that. If you would just slow down then my notes will be more accurate. More useful later on.
Now, how was he different after the operation? This is very important.

— What do you mean skipping?

— Oh, *slipping*. OK. Slipping in what way?

— Yes, I'm quite sure I can't do your divorce.

— An annulment? I don't really know anything about annulments. Is your husband dead, then?
I don't think you can get an annulment because he just hasn't been around for a while.

— Too ornery to die. Yes, we all know about that. Well, if we could get back to the slipping. How was he not the same afterwards?

— What do you mean different voices?

— Which one of these people might be more likely to commit a crime? To get into a fight?

— Not Georgie.

— No, I won't tell him you told me about his grandmother.

— Yes, I'm sure he does have quite a temper. Remember, I've got bruises to show for it. Ha-ha.

— Like his old man. Hmm. No it doesn't sound like an annulment is the answer when you lived together fifteen years and have three children. Let's just finish up. I know, it's after 12:00. I eat lunch too.

— Yes, tomorrow with your daughter.

— How old was he when he went in the Army?

— His grandmother thought it was a good idea? A lot of people thought it made a man out of you. Unfortunately there was a war on.

— Well, if you really think he's dead you could try to get him declared dead. But it has to be something like seven years. I can't remember. It often does seem like that those who most deserve to, don't die. Well, that's justice for you, or God's will.

— No, I didn't mean to bring up religion. It's just, well… noteworthy. If you have any proof of the fact that he might be dead you could try it.
Look, do you have my phone number here? Before you go. Be sure and take that.

— You can call collect. I'll accept the charge if I'm here. Just sign.

— Legal Aid is the place to try. They're right down the street.

— They're probably open now. Maybe if you just scooted right over there you could get someone to help you with that divorce. Or maybe they know about annulments. Shall I try the office for you? Here's the number. Shall I call now and ask? Why not?

Technician

I

Tommy Angelino had been out of work for over two months when, on an otherwise ordinary hot and muggy summer day, the first Sunday in August, his father slipped the folded morning newspaper between Tommy's bent head and his plate of bacon, potatoes, eggs and muffin. The kitchen where Tommy and his father George were sitting, kitty-cornered at the square red and white table with its silvery chrome trim, was blooming with yellow sunlight. Outside the window a cardinal, a streak of red against the unrelieved gray concrete of the back yard, perched on the cement birdbath and ruffled his pleated wings. Behind them the living room and the dining room windows were dark, the shades and heavy curtains drawn against the heat wave which had kept the temperature and humidity up, above ninety-five all week all over the east. The Angelinos small wooden house in Trenton with its velvet sofa and chairs and triple drapes smelled slightly sour, as if a feverish sleeper had tossed and turned all night, pulling the air in the house around him like a damp sheet.

In his eagerness to get Tommy's attention George pierced the bright, bulging yolk of Tommy's egg with the folded corner of the newspaper. Then, making matters worse, he apologetically grabbed Tommy's arm, causing Tommy to bite down painfully on his fork, all before Tommy was properly awake. Before his pale blue eyes were open. Tommy wasn't strikingly handsome, or even good-looking. But his pale blue eyes were almond shaped—pretty, too pretty for a guy, his fiancée Arlette said. Tommy shook his head and continued swirling his fork with potato and egg on the end around the plate. Even though he was only in his mid-twenties, Tommy worried about eating too many eggs. But Gloria his mom still made him eggs, bacon and fried potatoes for breakfast on Sunday. And now that he was living at home again, the sweet curling smell of frying bacon drifting up to the third floor got Tommy out of bed on Sundays. His dad didn't mean any harm. But still! At times like this Tommy longed to have his own place.

In May a narrow, colored slip of paper no longer than a pencil had unexpectedly been included with Tommy's bi-weekly pay-check. At first Tommy thought it was one of those cheery solicitations for a donation to the Red Cross or to the society for crippled or homeless animals. The slim pink message had flown out of his pay envelope and helicoptered onto the black tarmac of the parking lot, and Tommy almost didn't bother to pick it up. His back always twinged when he bent over, from an old high school athletic injury. Then when he stood up with a groan and casually read the typed message, Tommy felt as if he had received a body blow to the stomach: "We regret to inform you that as of May 30, 1983 your services will no longer be required by the Hogarth Pharmaceutical Company."

Services? Tommy worked as a clerk in the stockroom. It was his job to keep track of all the packages going in and out of the dispensary. He'd heard about the job through a friend of his Uncle Mike's. Now he was fired? Didn't he deserve more than a little pink printed slip? It was as if his doctor, friendly, white-haired Doctor Smyth, who had given Tommy all his shots since he'd had whooping cough in first grade, had unexpectedly told Tommy he had only six months to live.

"It's only a job," his friend Anthony said when Tommy stopped by his house that same evening for a beer.

"Right, Ants," Tommy agreed vigorously, as he opened the sweating refrigerator door to get himself a second one. But in his heart he didn't believe it. It felt like a death sentence. Tommy had only held three real jobs, unless you counted delivering liquor over the Christmas vacation.

But in another way he wasn't surprised. He knew he should have gone to college. But he didn't like any of the people from the high school who went to the community college, and all the courses were boring. Besides he could always go later, couldn't he? And he didn't want to ask Gloria and George for the money. He was still young enough to think that he'd be healthy forever. Everyone else was, well, settled. But he, Tommy, just seemed to wander from one thing to another. Even at Hogarth Tommy felt as if he was still pretending to be a grown-up with a real job.

He got dressed up in the morning in his clean white shirt, and he wore a tie sometimes too. But it wasn't really him. And they didn't even care if he wore a tie at Hogarth so why did he bother. It was as if someone else parked the car and then stood clumped together with the others shaking out a Styrofoam cup from the clear plastic sleeve beside the coffee pot. Because real work was something harder, something grander. So he was still waiting, even when he had a job. Waiting for something to happen. And what was going to happen to a kid twenty-two years old from Trenton with no college and no marketable skills. What happened was that he got fired from the one job he was lucky enough to get through some family friend.

Even Anthony, Tommy's closest friend, seemed to have settled down, working in his father's business. And in high school if there was one thing that Ants was sure of, it was that he'd never work for his father. Never. Now, three days a week Ants worked behind the counter with his uncle, his aunt, his father, and two sisters and a cousin, at the Polish butcher shop in the Trenton Farmers' Market. Half of the customers hardly spoke English. Anthony and his sisters and cousins knew enough Polish to talk to the ladies with braids of white hair curled around their small, neat heads.

The butcher shop made enough to support two huge families comfortably, including the many relatives who, for one reason or another, were incapable of working. The customers, who stood on tiptoe three deep to peer over the counter at Anthony, wore cotton wash dresses or serviceable work trousers and handed Anthony fresh new twenty dollar bills. The business supported everyone, even the old men who somehow never learned English and were lost when their wives died until the family found a widow or spinster for them. Then there were the boys—sometimes these boys were twenty-eight or twenty-nine—who got themselves in trouble with the police and had to be pried out of jail by fast-talking and pricey Jewish lawyers. The girls were less trouble, although they sometimes married men who beat them and pulled their hair out in clumps. Or worse, weren't Catholic. But if they got married, at least they were off the family rolls.

Ants complained bitterly that his father and uncle handed out hundreds in cash to the relatives—or worse to friends who were down on their luck—while they begrudgingly doled out tens and twenties to him. Tommy agreed vigorously, that it was unfair. But he secretly wished his family could give him a job. There were never any paychecks issued at the Polish butcher's. A deep distrust of all governments and tax collectors placed a premium on cash transactions. The sign above the register said, In God We Trust, All Others Pay Cash. And they meant it.

No wonder that the shop coined money. The little Eastern European ladies, their pale pink scalps showed between yellowish-white strands of thin, tired braids, paid more than seven dollars an ounce for dried mushrooms shipped directly from the forests near Cracow. One thing was clear. That generation was not replaced. The younger women with their blond-haired kids bought cider and apples and the trinket jewelry, but the forests outside Cracow meant nothing to them. The store stocked imported lingonberries, their deep purple color regal enough for a queen's velvet cape, dark seeded mustard which gleamed like burnished brass, and bright cherry syrup in a bottle with a goose neck. At Christmas Anthony's father took over two hundred orders for their own cured ham. The West Side ladies from Princeton even came down at Christmas for one of those sweet hams. In the old days they sent the servants or the chauffeur. Now they came themselves. Just as if they didn't live in America, week in and week out their faithful customers came to buy blood sausage, thick black bread trucked down from Canada on Wednesday nights, and fresh horseradish root with threads like hairs sticking out from its gnarled trunk.

When he got fired, the second person Tommy told was his girl, Arlette. Well, she was really his fiancée. Whenever Arlette introduced Tommy to one of her relatives—they were all short, quick moving, and with beautiful sleek brown hair, just like Arlette—she said, "This is my fiancé, Tommy Angelino." And she'd hold her left arm in such a way everyone's eyes just swooped right down to that fourth finger at the word fiancé.

Tommy thought the whole business of being engaged was stupid. He didn't buy her a diamond, even though Arlette mentioned more than once that her aunt's husband was a jeweler in Philadelphia and a small diamond, she didn't care about a big one, didn't even cost that much. Well, Tommy wasn't going to buy a diamond, from Arlette's relatives or anyone else. But he did give her a ring, a little ruby set in white gold, for her twenty-first birthday last year. Tommy insisted it wasn't an engagement ring, but Arlette immediately slipped the little ruby ring right on her left ring finger where it stayed.

When Tommy told Arlette he'd been fired, she started to cry. So Tommy had to put his arm around her and hold her, "Don't worry." But almost three months later Tommy was no longer sure something would turn up. And now when Arlette asked him about a job, he stomped out of the room and shouted at the icebox for not closing. Then Arlette didn't ask him any more questions.

These days Tommy's father was home too, on disability. So the two men rattled around the house getting on each other's nerves. They even managed to annoy Tommy's mother, Gloria, who was as even tempered as a sunny day in June. Tommy complained to his mother that his Dad sat in his bathrobe all day in front of the television, forecasting doom, not only for the immediate members of their relatively small Italian family, but for the rest of what he called civilization as well.

George dragged Tommy down three flights of stairs to watch a shaky news clip showing a collapsed fireman being administered oxygen on the sidewalk. Nothing seemed to cheer up George more than goodness gone wrong. That the person who thought he was doing the right thing turned out to cause harm. The policeman who was chasing a fleeing two-bit drug seller when his heavy foot slipped on the accelerator, running his car up on the sidewalk and breaking the back of a woman loading groceries into her car. "That brought them up short," George would say gleefully, as if he himself had been responsible for bringing the poor foolish good-doer up short. No justice, he would croak cheerfully at Tommy with his teeth out.

To his mother Tommy complained bitterly that George had the TV blasting all day—he was hard of hearing—making Tommy a prisoner in his attic room, which was stifling in August. While

George whispered to Gloria as they lay beside one another right beneath Tommy's room, that if he George were able-bodied and single and in his twenties in Trenton in 1983 he'd surely have found another job by now. He wouldn't lie on his back listening to some expensive tape recorder, waiting for work to come to him. We didn't have all that expensive junk to play with either, he explained to Gloria, as if he thought she had suddenly arrived on earth from another planet.

Gloria sighed and rolled over in the sticky night. "That air conditioner must be broken, again," Gloria answered, and they both listened to the uneven gasps of the machine jammed into the scarred window frame.

Before his sickness. Well, it wasn't really a sickness. Before his injury George—he'd been christened Georgio by his Italian grandmother. Before this happened, before his accident, George had never missed a day of work or spent a day in bed. When Georgio's father had come to pay court to Tommy's grandmother they rode the trolley from Camden to Trenton, without any fear in the evening, and then the two of them sat on a stone bench eating ices in the cool peaceful shadows of the old city graveyard. There overarching, stippled sycamore and weeping cherry trees shaded both the tombstones of George Washington's soldiers and the graves of babies who died of whooping cough or diphtheria in the nineteenth century, to be memorialized by tiny carved stone rosebuds trailing waving granite ribbons.

The overgrown weeds in that same Trenton graveyard were now littered with broken half-pint bottles, obscene worms of slimy white rubber, and the syringes and needles of addicts. The broken-down cast-iron fence had given up on keeping out the drunks, prostitutes and dope pushers. The carved stone bench had long since fallen over and been buried by the undauntable dandelions. The tilted slate tombstones were sharply chipped and edged now. But as if in compensation for all the indignities they had suffered, their leaning faces were streaked a beautifully variegated black and purple from decades of soot-filled rain.

If Tommy had heard it once, he'd heard it a hundred, no a thousand times. How Georgio's father had never gone to school because his mother needed an operation. Just when he was a precocious boy of six teaching himself to read English with old

newspapers he fished from the trash cans, brushing off the grease
stains and the coal ashes. Don't forget the grease stains, Dad,
Tommy said, actually laughing out loud to himself. As he lay in his
child's bed with the slightly sour sheets kicked back, Tommy could
fill in his mother's lines too. In those days, children took care of
their parents. And, I know, Mom, respected them. Well, his mother
replied, now there was no respect—for the living or the dead.

Another persistent theme was how neither Georgio nor his
father—and recently even Gloria was included in this part of the
litany—had ever had his opportunities. What opportunities,
Tommy wanted to know. To fight it out with the black kids who
brandished knives and sometimes guns in the bathrooms at
Trenton High? So that Tommy learned never to go to the bathroom
from morning until afternoon. Tommy never told Gloria that
because she would have made him transfer immediately to Sacred
Heart. That was what education was today. Where were all those
wonderful opportunities? True, he'd learned to read and write.
Tommy even had taken a couple of courses at the community
college. But that was hardly an opportunity, or even an education.
What were they talking about, anyway? It was a jungle out there.
When he finally found the placement officer at the college in his
office on the fourth try, Tommy couldn't even get out of him a copy
of the companies who listed jobs. In the office, they demanded
proof of his current enrollment at the school. And of course he
didn't have any. So Tommy left the office without getting any help.

But Tommy didn't feel like laughing three months after he was
fired when he still didn't have a job or any prospect of a job. Every
morning Gloria asked him if he was going to go by and check the
bulletin at the unemployment office. It made Tommy mad to stand
in line with all of the other dopes who didn't have jobs. So he just
stopped coming down to breakfast so that she couldn't ask him
until dinner time, when instead of asking directly she asked him
what he had done that day. If Gloria told him once, she told him
fifty times to call some friend, or relative, or relative of a friend, to
whom she had just happened to mention that her son Tommy was
looking for a job. Tommy got the impression that all of Trenton was
consumed with helping him find a job and talked about nothing
else. And there was a recession too. Even if it wasn't a depression.
Of course the government didn't call it that. But what else could

you call ten million unemployed? And they always jimmied the statistics, so you knew it was really more. But mostly Tommy knew he was one of them. One of the thousands reported on the news, one of the 6.0 percent was him.

Tommy had to give up the apartment he had been sharing with two high school friends. Three of them had gone away and then ended up back in Trenton, the place they couldn't wait to get out of as soon as they graduated from high school. At graduation they all vowed they never would ever come back to New Jersey. They'd be in Alaska, or Hawaii, or maybe California. But here they all were, back in Trenton five years later. Then Tommy's best friend Anthony practically lived in the apartment too because his mother wouldn't let him bring his Jewish girlfriend to the house. Not only wasn't she Catholic, but worse than that she was German. Ants had always had lots of girlfriends, even though he wasn't all that good-looking. Usually he was sleeping with three or four women at the same time.

When Tommy was fired, his Mom and Dad said, of course he could have his old attic room back on the third floor. And Ants moved into his old apartment. But his old childhood room seemed cramped. Not that their clapboard bachelor apartment was so big, but he didn't have to tiptoe around in it. Back at home the attic fan ran all night with a loud, syncopated tick, in a losing battle against the steam bath of New Jersey in August, right next to his ear. At least he felt at home surrounded by his old baseball trophies. His uniform and equipment still stood ready, the toes of his cleated shoes curled up as if he had just stepped out of them. He lay sweating in the bed of his youth, staring at the all too familiar crisscross of electric lines and telephone wires framed by his dormer window and told himself soon summer would be over.

Still, a fellow shouldn't live with his mother and his father when he's 23 years old. Tommy had spent a couple years away from home. He'd hitchhiked on small planes across country. Half the time the student pilots took him up for the hours. When Tommy told his mother what a great time he'd had, she just shook her head. But she did sometimes wonder when he was going to grow up.

On Saturday night Gloria still waited up for Tommy to come in, sitting in her robe in front of the orange and green blur of the television screen. When he complained that he was 23 years old, thank you, she scurried into bed at the sound of his car. But Tommy heard her softly close the bathroom door when he tiptoed up the stairs. The television's demonic after-light, a tiny gleaming eye in the center of the warm, darkening screen, told Tommy Gloria had just left the room as he groped his way between the light-shadowed mounds of the living room chairs shrouded in their white throw covers.

When Tommy didn't come home Saturday night at all, Gloria wouldn't speak to him or look at him until the middle of Sunday midday dinner. Even in August on Sunday a white embroidered cloth was put on the table and the family assembled in the middle of the day to eat pasta, and sometimes veal and sausage, and almost always soup, and usually pie and ice cream for dessert, because Sunday evening was the one night Gloria didn't cook. And ever since Tommy could remember, his bachelor Uncle Mike, Gloria's baby brother, joined them at the rosewood table for Sunday dinner.

On this Sunday morning George simply looked at Tommy and shrugged as Gloria slammed the screen door on her way out to the garage. She was going to church alone again. But this morning George was not interested in Gloria's mood. George had circled the advertisement in the Trenton Times with a blue laundry marker. Now he pointed to it again, jabbing the paper noisily with his finger, thick and square as a carpenter's chisel, while Tommy watched his mother's stiff shoulders, her upper body first framed and then draped with the rectangular webbed matte of the mesh screen, as she stepped down through the succession of shrinking, darkening images of herself on her way to say an extra set of prayers for Tommy's salvation.

"Read it," George said, excitedly. "It says 'laboratory or medical experience.'" George grasped the paper in his thick, trembling fingers and rattled it under Tommy's nose. Since his accident George's voice had lost its timbre. His entire body had shrunk in on itself. Tommy was glad to see him take an interest in something.

"Okay. Okay. But let me finish my breakfast!" Tommy, who wasn't fussy, did wish that his father would get dressed instead of spending all day in his not very clean blue terry cloth bathrobe. There was something repellent about the slack, blue-veined, pale flesh of George's calves. Couldn't his father put his pants on? Since today was Sunday at least George would get dressed for Sunday dinner. But he could get dressed during the week, too, Tommy said to himself, not really wanting to criticize. Instead of slopping around in those mothy maroon slippers all day.

Tommy forgot his mouth was full of egg and muffin. "Is being fired from a drug company previous medical experience?" he asked his father, laughing.

"Of course it is," George answered, full of certainty. "It's experience. You worked there." George looked around the sunny, daisy-colored kitchen as if summoning the shiny kitchen canisters for support, or as if he forgot Gloria had left. "You ran that stock-room for over a year!" It was true. Hogarth had seemed to like him at first. His father sat up on the white plastic kitchen chair with certainty, and it was as if his blue robe with the grimy lapels had been turned into a snappy three-piece business suit. Tommy smiled at his father's exaggeration, but George was in no mood to be dismissed. He stared at Tommy sternly. It was time to get down to business. The whole summer had gone by, and he had nothing. OK, OK, Tommy said.

That night George complained to Gloria that Tommy had no spunk, that was all, the kid had no confidence in himself. "Been babied all his life," George said grumpily, as if he were confessing it to himself.

Gloria flicked on the radio beside the bed. On some topics there was no point in arguing. It was worse than discussing politics. During these Sunday dinners George and Gloria's baby brother, Tommy's Uncle Mike, who was a former police officer, would get into fierce discussions about politics and crime. Before his illness George would jump up from the table and stomp around the dining room, making the china cups and saucers in the corner cupboard tremble. They both agreed, heatedly, that the city, not to say the country, was going to the dogs. It was a good thing the law makers finally realized it and had got around to doing something about crime. At least they had reenacted the death penalty, although Uncle Mike said they never executed people for years. If at all.

Tommy sat silently or left the room during these discussions. His high school civics teacher, an earnest curly haired woman in her thirties, who was far too pretty to be an old maid school teacher, had taken his high school class through a two-week unit on crime, the prisons and the justice system. They even went to see a murder trial in court, all the kids shuffling and giggling as they trooped in and sat in the front pew to stare at the backs of the two lawyers, one in a blue suit and one in a gray suit, bent over so many papers on those big tables, while the judge, dressed in a comical black robe, frowned down at all of them from his elevated perch. The lawyers jumped up, waved their arms, turned heel on the jury, and then crouched over their wrinkled yellow legal pads. The defendant, a thin young man who looked uncomfortable in his suit, sat without moving or changing expression throughout.

The class saw a film about drug abuse and went on a tour of the Mercer County jail. There Tommy actually saw someone he went to school with sitting on a plastic bench and smoking a cigarette, in a bare cell with not much in it but a cot and a stainless steel toilet with no seat. The fellow—to Tommy he'd always be Little Billy who couldn't connect the bat and ball—stared right back at Tommy through the bars. Maybe it was a mistake, Tommy thought later. Why didn't I wave hello? But Little Billy didn't acknowledge Tommy's existence either. Still, the little blue pig eyes were unmistakably the same. Tommy was sure. Now those pink childish cheeks were covered with blond stubble and the little blue pig eyes were steely and squinty, instead of puzzled. But the blond-haired man with his sleeves defiantly rolled up to show a blue and black tattoo of a woman in a hula skirt was the same pale-haired kid who Tommy struck out and struck out again in the playground.

"Those benefits," George's voice was earnest. He dipped the triangle of his buttered toast up and down in his coffee now that Gloria was gone. "Once you're on the State payroll." His trembling hand almost knocked over the coffee. "All those benefits," George gestured vaguely around the empty kitchen. "They would have helped me, I'll tell you that."

Whenever George mentioned the violations his body had recently suffered, Tommy felt so sorry. That this should happen to his own father. But the sorrow expressed itself as nausea. "You're right, Dad. You're right." Tommy shook his head to get the cobwebs out. He tried to catch his father's enthusiasm. Wasn't that the least he could do for his old man who was, after all, only trying to help him. Tommy laid down his eggy fork and peered at the ad his father had pushed under his nose, turning the paper over absentmindedly when he finished, as if he expected to find more

information on the other side of the page. The square advertisement, banded in black by the other columns, did not list a phone
number or department. Just a three-digit box number for written
replies before September 1, 1983.

New Position, Paramedical Technician.
Previous medical or laboratory experience desirable but not
required. Must be willing to go through six-month training
period. High school diploma, some college, preferably
science courses. Generous benefit package. New Jersey State
retirement, disability, and health insurance program
participation available after probationary period.

Poor George. No wonder he had benefits and insurance policies
on his mind. He had been at home on partial disability for over six
months. That was all he was entitled to after fifteen years of
working as a guard for First Jersey Savings. The family had some
savings, but the cash balances dwindled with a frightening,
centripetal speed, a precious liquid being swirled down the drain
with a disconcerting momentum, slipping through their fingers
quicker than soapy water in the kitchen sink. After all, you couldn't
not pay the doctors, could you? Gloria had started to hint that
Tommy might help pay for the groceries.

There was a lot of talk about insurance. Tommy had never
thought about insurance until a kid working with him on liquor
deliveries fell out of a truck and broke his neck. They'd been
talking and joking together only a few moments before. The
company couldn't even notify the family because it turned out his
IDs were all forged. For three months the kid had been answering
to a name that wasn't his. A nice-looking kid too, tall and blonde
with a neat diagonal scar across his tan belly. There was some sort
of regulation that prevented the company from just cremating the
body, getting rid of it, so his strangely peaceful and unmarred
body stayed in the funeral parlor for a week. And Tommy, as the
least important employee in the store, was sent over every day to
inquire about whether or not it had been claimed. The company
kept the insurance money in a special bank account for a year, in
case someone from the family ever came forward to claim it. But
nobody ever did.

Last March, when George and his partner at the bank were jumped at six a.m. in the parking lot as they went to clean out the night deposit boxes, Tommy's education in these matters began. Two kids knocked down Tommy's father, who broke his leg and three ribs in the fall, and then demanded the vault keys. Then, when George was lying on the ground in a muddy puddle, curled up in pain, they gratuitously smacked him in the face with a baseball bat, knocking out five teeth and cracking his skull. What most amazed George, though, was that these two black kids beat up his black partner with the same enthusiasm as they attacked him. And even though he got a whole new set of teeth out of the company, George spent three weeks in the hospital with tubes running in and out of him. For another six weeks, he had to drink his food through a plastic straw while waiting for his jaw full of wire to heal.

George still needed a cane five months later. The kids didn't even get away with anything but the forty dollars George and his partner together had in their wallets. The kids panicked when George fell down and screamed with pain and dropped the deposit bag as they ran away. But even if they'd been smarter crooks, they would have gotten very little. First Jersey Savings had several years ago taken the vault keys from the guards, anticipating just such an incident. The kids would have gotten only what was in the overnight bags, and all of that was insured. The banks long ago decided they would make sure the guards weren't able to open up any of the big safes. As George said, the security people anticipated a holdup such as this would occur sooner or later.

"We were just window-dressing." George said, sputtering through his new teeth. "Sitting ducks." That the company expected it, had set them up for it in a way, made George madder than anything. Only the illiterate teenagers didn't know that this kind of bank holdup was as outmoded as a stagecoach heist. They were as much dupes of the situation as George and his partner, or so it seemed to Tommy. And if it hadn't been for his father lying there in so much pain, Tommy would have laughed and laughed.

At least they had the death penalty now. A few months before George had his teeth knocked out and his head split open the State legislature had passed a law putting the death penalty back in place. Tommy happened to be driving past the State House on the hot July day the new law was passed. The TV crews stood among the tall ceremonial columns on the Capitol steps. With their headsets like space helmets, and their shoulders draped with cameras and wires, the TV people seemed to be messengers from another world, or perhaps just New York, as they turned the cameras on the clump of legislators and the Governor, who was reading from a statement.

The news commentators were immediately recognizable by their bright colored, stylish clothes, by their composure and their make-up. The interviewers seemed impervious to the midday July heat. The lawmakers were sweating and squinting under the camera lights, smiling just a little when the soft gray, foam covered microphone was held in front of their lips like an ice cream cone.

Tommy saw the story on the news that same night. He recognized the skinny black woman in the bright red dress for whom the camera and sound crew left an empty circle as she talked directly into the snout of the camera lens before turning and offering the microphone and her profile to the law makers.

She asked a short, square senator, whose ambitious face glistened in the heat, when the penalty would go into effect and what would be the method of execution. The sweat poured down his face, the drops falling from his jaw like water dripping from a leaking tap. When the Senator answered his glance was cunningly off-center, a little to the right of the camera. No, they didn't intend to bring back the electric chair, known familiarly as Old Sparky. After all, the Senator said, the victims have rights too. Yes, lethal injection would be the method. It seemed the most humane, didn't it? And he raised his eyebrows slightly as if to pass on the question to the audience several hours away and on the other side of the screen.

Looking at the shiny coins of golden butterfat floating on the top of George's coffee, Tommy realized George's trauma, especially the exhausting, painful weeks in the hospital, just lying there and praying to recover his former strength, had aged his father all too measurably. He had lost weight, a good thing everyone said, but his spirits had shrunk two sizes along with his waist. George now fell asleep in front of the television every evening after dinner, even if a movie with his favorite actor, Gary Cooper, was playing. Tommy saw Gloria turn away and hide her eyes when George stumbled over the names of friends who had been part of the family for decades. There was a ten-year age difference between them, but this was the first time Tommy was aware of it. George who loved to play poker and smoke cigars, now sat for eight hours in his shabby robe—he wouldn't wear the new plaid one Gloria brought to the hospital— facing the plastic gray-blue television. From the bowels of the dark and empty living room he could be heard to sigh and mumble in reply to the eerie pulsating lights on the screen, flickering like a signal from a distant planet. But this Sunday morning George was awake, alert. Like his old self. And Tommy was glad to see it, even if the old man was getting on his case.

"What about your Red Cross training?" he asked Tommy shrewdly. When George didn't shave his chin moved up and down like a soft ball, only covered with prickly gray hairs, like the chin of an old dog. The way his cheeks sagged over his nearly empty gums added to the appearance of grizzled, canine certitude.

True enough! Tommy had eight weeks of Red Cross training in life saving (and a certificate with a gold seal) from the two summers when he worked as a lifeguard at the swimming pool. Before he injured his back Tommy had also worked one night a week as a volunteer for the First Aid and Rescue Squad. The baseball team supplied a fourth man to the Rescue Squad regularly one or two nights a week. In exchange the Rescue Squad collected money from the emergency room residents for team shirts emblazoned with a blue felt hawk's head and the team members' names. The money collected by the Rescue Squad also paid for an end of the season bash at the best Italian bar in Trenton.

Until Tommy freakishly injured his back—he dislocated his shoulder while pitching a curve ball—he enjoyed working with the Rescue Squad. The regular guys were men in their thirties or early forties who appreciated a pair of young strong arms to help carry the leaden weight of a stricken patient. Tommy learned the smell of excrement was the smell of death, as the body releases its earthly burden at the departure of the spirit.

Most of the time the guys sat drinking coffee in the hospital cafeteria or hung around behind the emergency room reception desk with the nurses. There weren't that many people who needed rescuing. They were fat, friendly men who liked taking charge, liked helping people in trouble. The residents in the emergency room taught Tommy how to give injections, the correct twist for a tourniquet, how to pump up the gray armband of the blood pressure kit and then listen to the thump of the heart through a stethoscope. Tommy learned how much power the doctors had and how they talked about the patients when they made a mistake, or weren't sure of something. He learned how to gently lift a man onto a gurney or a stretcher without inflicting pain and to quell his terror as the patient gasped at the oxygen while careening down the middle of the road, the beating red light of the ambulance splashing drunkenly over the cars clumped along the edge of the road like cowering animals.

"Full benefits," George reminded him, "means family coverage." He nodded his head sagely, a toothless, smiling sphinx. He was right of course. Tommy's girlfriend Arlette had been working as a legal secretary since high school. Now she wanted to quit, get married and go to community college part-time. Arlette said if she didn't go to college now, probably she would never go. Maybe she was right about that. George craftily folded his toast over his bacon to make an envelope and then crammed it all into his mouth at once, since Gloria wasn't there. In spite of all of the expensive dental work paid for by the bank, George preferred to eat without his new teeth. Sometimes he wouldn't put his plate in until supper. If Gloria caught him with his teeth out she ran up and got them and made him put them in. She said it was like going around with your pants unzipped. Tommy thought George liked to eat without his plate because he could cram more into his mouth that way, although since the accident even his love of food had been diminished.

"And I wouldn't even have to move to Florida," Tommy said. He pushed aside the newspaper and pinched the last rubbery bite of egg into the stippled corner of his toast. George had been suggesting that Tommy go to Florida to work for an old Army buddy who, in George's words, had made a killing in dead bodies. George's buddy was the only licensed undertaker in a burgeoning neighborhood near the space center.

Tommy's evasive responses to this repeated suggestion became increasingly less confident as the glorious bright days of June turned into the dragging heat of July and August, and his unemployment insurance ran out. The truth was that with only a high school diploma there wasn't much to choose from for a guy who couldn't or wouldn't stand behind a counter all day selling something, or work pitching food in a steaming kitchen, or do day labor in construction, which was only a seasonal job anyway.

"The unions have every damn job sewn up," George said when Tommy complained one Friday that all the jobs listed at the unemployment office were for twenty hours a week at minimum wage, to do things like clean the drains and sewers in the city. Work they couldn't even make the prisoners do. When the city ordered the prisoners to clean out the sewers after a storm, some smart aleck civil rights lawyer got a court order to stop it. No wonder Trenton was broke. One week Tommy worked at slightly better than minimum wage as a delivery boy for a liquor store, but he had to quit when his back acted up. He was replaced by a Hispanic teenager who was on the lam from immigration and couldn't read or write English, but whose arms and back were strong.

Further surgery might have improved Tommy's condition, but he remembered all too vividly from years ago waking up in a cold sweat in the operating room just as the doctor was about to set his shoulder. He was all trussed up and tied to the table, like a piece of meat, surrounded by glass and chrome. People were staring at him over white surgical masks. The doctor, a bald, yellow-faced man dressed in dark green, wrinkled scrubs, was surprised to have a wide-awake patient lurching off the table in the operating room an hour after the anesthetic. With seigniorial authority he gestured to a tall, redheaded nurse who was standing and unwrapping the shining, sterilized instruments. The nurse—Tommy would never forget her—came towards him with her green eyes wide open over the sexless white mask. She walked briskly over and stood in front of Tommy who was trying to free his legs.

"Put your arms around my neck, honey," she said, holding out her own freckled arms invitingly. Tommy groggily draped his arms around her neck, and as he sank into her bosom and inhaled her wonderful female smell the last thing he felt was a gentle punch, as if from an air gun, at the base of his spine as the needle entered. For the next two weeks he lay flat on his back unable to move anything but his eyes because of a spinal headache. The pretty green-eyed nurse came to visit him regularly and ended up telling poor immobile Tommy about her problems with her boyfriend, a married doctor, as she changed his sheets and manipulated the tubes and bottles which fed liquids in and out of his immobilized body.

Tommy reminded his father, "The manager at Hogarth might write me a recommendation or even take me back when this slump

is over." Now that his eyes were open and he had some coffee in
him, Tommy could get himself going. "I was the only one in the
stockroom who could make the damned inventory come out
right." And it was true. No one else could get all of those little
colored slips to balance. But then, if he was so valuable at Hogarth
why did they fire him?

Later George confided to Gloria, "He's living in a dream world,
thinking Hogarth is going to take him back."

To her family and friends Gloria explained Tommy's situation
by saying: "He was the last one hired and the youngest, so he was
the first fired." To Tommy she said: "If they'd known you had a
family to support, they never would have fired you. They thought
you were a kid who didn't need a job."

Tommy sensed there was some truth to his mother's words.
Hadn't the supervisor at Hogarth apologized when Tommy pointed
out that he was the only reliable worker in the stockroom. The other
clerk, a black guy, didn't do anything. Or hardly anything.

The supervisor, a kindly, fat man, who smoked and wheezed as
he talked, tried to explain. "It's unfair, Tommy. I know it's unfair.
But try to understand, it's nothing against you personally." He
took the cigarette out of his mouth, coughed, spit, looked around
and continued. "The Hogarth Chemical Company has nothing
against you personally. Someone has to go."

"What about him?" Tommy gestured in the direction of the
other clerk, who was heading off to lunch. You're afraid to fire him,
Tommy thought to himself.

The supervisor shook his head, but didn't meet Tommy's eye.
"Management," it sounded to Tommy like the Kremlin, "is
impersonal." Tommy didn't want the guy to get upset and cough
some more. He was embarrassed to see a man his father's age hang
his head and lie and apologize because of some stupid front-office
policy. So Tommy just stomped out of the storeroom and went to
collect his final paycheck.

"OK, Dad, you win," Tommy said. That same week Arlette
typed up a pristine letter of application for Tommy during her
lunch hour. For three years she had been working in a small law
office, for the nicest group of people, even if they were lawyers. But
George was right, she wanted Tommy to get a real job so they could
be married. She had been a fiancée long enough. All her friends

were having baby showers and after every one she found an excuse to quarrel with Tommy. These fights always ended with Arlette's tears seeping through Tommy's collar and then dripping down his back. Besides Tommy wanted to get married too. Didn't they both want the same thing?

One of the older secretaries wrote those sentences about Tommy's medical experience. She made it sound like he was practically a doctor, but someone had just neglected to award him the degree. But there were no outright lies. When you added it all up, Tommy had done lots of things which had some relation to medicine. This secretary lined up all the other information about his schooling and other jobs so the piece of paper looked like a real résumé. Tommy's life so far now filled three-quarters of a clean white page, and he was only twenty-three. Even the weekend job delivering beer had been retitled, Retail Transportation Assistant.

When Arlette brought the letter and résumé over to Gloria's house she was breathless, her olive skin dark against the butter yellow of her square-necked sun dress. A blush escaped from under the harsh slash of powdered pink on her face. This was going to do it. Arlette was convinced. Full of hope she pushed under Tommy's nose the perfectly typed application, with its résumé and bright white envelope with a flag stamp primly attached with a shiny paper clip, just like a letter an executive would sign. Tommy carefully aligned his small, blue signature in the space above his typed name, as if he were easing a brand new car into his own garage. Even his name now looked businesslike. Arlette had stuck in his middle initial which Tommy didn't ordinarily use. How did you know what it was, he asked her.

Arlette took the pen from him, smiled at her future mother-in-law, and blew on Tommy's small signature. Then Gloria laughed because Tommy had signed his name with a ball point pen. When she blushed Tommy didn't at all mind the idea of getting married. He pulled Arlette down on his lap. She quickly folded the letter away in her purse, snapping shut the gilt clasp with her strong fingers. Those long, red lacquer-tipped fingers gave marvelous, deep back rubs, pulling the pain out from recesses between the vertebrae.

Tommy walked his fingers down the ridged, stepping stones of her bare back. It would be all right with him to move up the wedding date if he got a job. He didn't really want to move to a new state. If he got the job he could move out of his old attic room to his own place, where he wouldn't know that his mother was waiting for him. It was time for him to leave home, no doubt about that. Every time Tommy mentioned going to Florida Arlette started to cry, saying she knew he'd never come back to Trenton and marry her if he left again.

So Tommy started to say he was going to move to Florida, just to tease. He was going to call his father's old buddy next week, or tomorrow. He'd heard it was really pretty down there. He didn't want some crummy office job in Trenton. There were lots of things to do in that town in Florida, which had a college nearby with lots of pretty girls. Until Arlette caught on and threw one of Gloria's needlepoint cushions at him across the room, sending skimming and then crashing to the floor a translucent bone-white saucer, decorated with a wreath of roses, which had been consigned to be an ashtray years ago when its matching rose-ringed cup had splintered into a dozen pieces under George's elbow.

II

Gloria told Tommy to allow at least an extra half hour to find a parking place in the middle of Trenton when he went for the interview. The Capitol police swooped down like vultures to ticket and tow near the State House. "I'm going to play your birthday and the date today," Gloria said after breakfast, as she put the cereal bowls with their swirls of milky residue in the dishwasher. Gloria was on her way to her job as a bookkeeper in a laundry where everyone played the numbers: their house numbers, their birthday or their sweetheart's birthday, their anniversaries, or any other number which had momentary significance. The numbers racket had been taken over by the State, and the illegal bookies had been replaced by a newly grown tentacle of government bureaucracy.

A few years ago Tommy and Ants used to hang out in the Italian bars in West Trenton, but now Tommy got lost in the one-way streets. The government had taken over the city. He had to go back to the train station—that was new too—and start over again, as if making his way out from the maze of a spider's web. The buildings he might have recognized were boarded-up or in the process of being torn down. There had been little reason for Tommy to go to Trenton recently, and he wasn't used to the city's daytime physiognomy: the pudgy, white-faced civil servants hurrying back from lunch at one-fifteen, the young legislative assistants in brief tailored jackets and short, pleated skirts which flipped smartly around their knees as their high heels tapped down the sidewalk. These energetic young women were always clutching a newspaper, or a sheaf of bills, each boasting its own number in heavy block letters. Where were they hurrying to?

Then, the contrasting leisurely pace of the lobbyists and the silver-haired legislators who never missed a pair of sleek, stockinged legs scissoring by. These were men who had been trading in power since the time of Caesar, while the fresh-faced aides waiting outside the Assembly meeting room and continually counting the votes were eternally young. The white world of state government, its lawmakers housed in those heavy sand-colored buildings by the river, filled the town with bustle and importance until the curtain rang down on the civil service day. Then the Capitol's pale white or steel structures, shining icy castles in the setting sun, were emptied out, left as enormous, dry, hollow combs until the hive's activity began the next working day.

Tommy had no sense of this world of bureaucracy, except to see that there was no place to park and everyone else in the world had a job. On this bright September day the sidewalks were filled with meandering office workers catching the last rays of summer. Trenton actually looked like an inhabited city, not like a shell abandoned at nightfall. Aside from his year in the stockroom of the Hogarth Pharmaceutical Company, Tommy's other jobs had all been jobs where he knew, and they knew, that he was only going to stay a few weeks. So what if he hated being a messenger boy, or being an hourly at the post office over Christmas. So did everyone else.

After high school he had wanted to go to Alaska; a friend told him there were bears there. But when he couldn't sleep at night away from home, even after a whole six pack, he came back. And now, here it was September four years later, and some of his high school classmates were going to graduate from college this year. And here he was stuck in a rut. Tommy could no longer fool himself. He had no job, no prospect of a job until this interview, and it didn't look like

Hogarth was going to take him back. He'd left three messages with the Supervisor who no longer returned his calls.

Tommy crawled along looking for a parking place on the narrow, potholed streets lined with sagging buildings which hid behind the skirts of the marble Capitol. If he could just tide himself over this bare spot, then maybe he could go to Alaska, or California. The clear blue backdrop of this fall day was kind even to these shabby nineteenth-century tenements. A few hopeful tufts of green poked up between the cracks in the sidewalk. But there were no parking spots. Finally, Tommy just dumped his mother's ten-year-old car in a bus stop. When he slammed the door behind him Tommy noticed that his mother's car was the oldest car on this dismal street, except for the unidentifiable carcass of a machine which now had neither wheels nor engine. And this was a slum, wasn't it?

An old black man sat on a stoop drinking out of a bottle in a paper bag. Where did the people who lived here get the money for cars? Tommy had heard Mike talk about pimps and drug dealers who changed out of their designer suits into ragged pants and frayed T-shirts when they went to collect their welfare or unemployment checks, putting on an appropriately stooped and deflated posture as they stood in line for their government handout.

Before dinner last Sunday Tommy's Uncle Mike, Gloria's younger brother, who used to be a cop, also told stories of rickety old wooden buildings, like the ones on this street two blocks from the Capitol, which were stacked high with cash and guns. Hundreds of hundred dollar bills jammed into boxes or garbage bags. And that the people who lived in these buildings drove nothing but the latest Mercedes and Jaguars.

"I admire their taste," laughed Mike, who traded in his Caddy for a new model every year himself. This past Sunday Mike surprised everyone by announcing that finally two guys had been arrested and charged in the assault against George and his partner. Gloria came out of the kitchen and stood in the doorway, holding her flour-covered hands away from her hips as if they didn't belong to her body.

"You'll have to go and make an identification," Mike said to George. "Do a lineup."

"One of them had a mask on," George said nervously.

"So, just say you recognize him anyway." Mike was speaking to Gloria now. "Look, by the time they're brought in for a lineup you can be sure they have plenty of circumstantial. Besides, there are all those appeals. They go over every bent blade of grass."

George nodded, without taking his eyes away from the screen. "I think I'd recognize them anyway. The guy who hit me had a funny smell to him."

Tommy had been talking to Arlette in the kitchen. "You aren't going to get close enough to smell him," he heard Mike say as he walked back into the living room.

"Anyway, they usually confess, don't they?" George asked. On TV the criminals usually confessed. Or they were so guilty they didn't need to confess, it was clear without saying anything they were guilty as sin.

Mike shrugged. The three of them turned back to the ball game. The bases were loaded, and it was an out. Gloria shouted a question from the kitchen where the water was running, but the three men either didn't hear or chose not to listen. The tiny figures in the white suits against the greenish background of the artificial turf had recaptured their attention. "Look at that. He never even saw it!" Tommy said when the pitcher curled himself into a ball and threw a perfect strike.

The bright September sun made Tommy squint as he climbed out from his mother's old car. A uniformed traffic cop, an old man who could hardly walk, told him the coffee-colored building next to the State House was the address on his letter. As Tommy passed, an old black gardener paid him no heed as he combed the earth between the chrysanthemums in the shadowed circular bed before the building.

The entrance hall had a marble floor and grand, if dusty Doric columns, positioned at the top of three long steps running the length of the lobby. Perhaps this was the original exterior. Behind these squat columns, the facade of an older structure, a dingy glass front display case, held tattered banners and flags, the once bright embroidery of fallen armies now hanging limply from their gilt-tipped poles. Fallen down in the cases were the hand-written white cards identifying the local battle where these flags had once been standards. With its somber pink and black marble, the shining brass of the elevator door and the darkened gilt behind glass, the entrance hall might have been a Roman temple or an Egyptian tomb. This was a public building which introduced itself seriously, but perhaps because it was nearer the parking lot, almost everyone came through the side entrance.

The white-haired lady behind the newsstand and candy counter had her rounded back to the empty marble foyer when Tommy pushed through the old-fashioned revolving door. She turned abruptly when Tommy came up in his hurried way and asked for directions. But her eyes were sewn shut, and her face was tilted up but without recognition, when Tommy held the letter out and asked his question. A hand-lettered message taped under the glass above the peanut clusters said the booth was operated by the blind. No bills over a dollar could be accepted.

A young black man holding a white mop upside down and wearing a white turban which was not a lot cleaner wasn't much more helpful. "It's in the basement," he said, looking up at the ceiling and not at the floor he was supposed to be washing or at the piece of paper Tommy held under his nose. The large brass arrows on the clock above the elevator pointed to eleven. At least he wasn't late yet.

The careful pressing Gloria had given Tommy's only summer suit had melted away. He must have put on a few pounds since he had worn it in June at his cousin's wedding. Tommy promised himself he would get back in shape, as he stood sweating in the sinking elevator which halted in the sub-basement with a bounce. The elevator cracked its square metal smile and deposited Tommy into a dun-colored concrete corridor.

The grayish floor was polished to a high sheen from decades of shoe leather and grit. A series of closed doors lined both sides of the corridor, which ended in shadows in both directions. There was not a soul to be seen. Here and there the wooden doors with glass tops were lit from within with a golden light. On the corrugated glass tops of some doors gilt lettering announced "Third Appellate Division—Records" or "Office of the Deputy Assistant Clerk, First Supreme Court." The rest room had the same heavy wooden door with glass the color of dirty snow and gilt letters edged with green, spelling MEN.

When Tommy found B-1309—he had turned in the right direction by chance—it had no gilt letters. You could see translucent outlines of where the golden letters had been scraped off.

The words in onion-like transparency were almost legible. "St rage—Suprem -J diciary" A white index card taped above the brass door handle had Room B-1309 typed in small ordinary type, with uneven spacing.

Since he was now a few minutes late, Tommy knocked and then immediately tried the door. Gloria said punctuality was the politeness of kings. The door was locked. From inside Tommy heard the scrape, scrape of metal chair casters over the uncarpeted gray-green concrete. Then the metal lock slid back invisibly. The door opened on a dark rectangular room whose only furniture was a standard, government-issue gray metal desk and two chairs. A chair with a torn green plastic seat and an old-fashioned square wooden chair faced each other across the desk whose gray-green spongy top showed several gouges. When Tommy sat down the wooden chair rocked diagonally on its round metal heels. Built into the wall was a gray metal bookcase, its shelves empty except for a forgotten stack of reports, with the date 1968–9 written in a shaky script across the unbound spine. A narrow window high above the desk did not shed enough light to read by. Two fluorescent tubes dangled from the ceiling.

The desk was empty except for Arlette's letter, which Tommy recognized by his own small blue signature, and the interviewer's black plastic briefcase with the State seal blurrily stamped on its face in gilt. The sleazy, matte briefcase lay aslant on the desk top, as if it had been jettisoned by an owner who was on a life-and-death mission elsewhere. The haphazard angle of the briefcase on the desk top was at odds with the rectangularity of the other cold and steely objects in the boxy room. Tommy's white letter of application was another patch of bright contrast, its crisp vellum folds trembling like the wings of a browsing summer butterfly. The letter might have floated in from the window to light for a moment on the dented, grimy surface of the government-issue desk.

Except for Tommy's unsteady wooden chair, this interior had a leaden immutability. The wooden chair added a clickety-clack after-comment to Tommy's eager questions. The uneven legs teeter-tottered when Tommy lurched forward in an effort to follow his mother's advice, to speak up and make himself heard, to look alert and make a good impression. But his collar was choking him, and Tommy was damp and uncomfortable. He didn't feel he was making a good impression.

His own voice seemed to be coming from a great distance, from the end of that long lightless corridor. The cool of the dark basement had simply made him clammy. Besides it was hard to sound intelligent or even interested when answering all those questions about his health. Why were they so interested in his childhood diseases? What about his unfortunately abbreviated education. Finally, they did get to what the interviewer referred to as his job history. Tommy decided to be honest about that. He said he'd been laid off, but that he might be rehired by the pharmaceutical company. I ran the whole stockroom, he said with a burst of energy and an interior salute to Gloria.

The interviewer was a small, tidy man who wore an economical gray three-piece suit, a gleaming white nylon shirt, a sea-green tie, and thick horn-rimmed glasses whose extreme correction made the eyes behind small and inaccessible. Somehow Tommy never did get his name. Plicket? Truncett? Something with the cross bar of a T at the end? Never mind. The interviewer rarely looked up from the form he was filling out, and he seemed to expect little, and certainly not personal attention, from Tommy. Only short answers to his very direct questions. At first the man's voice was so thin and gray, coming from inside the modest drum of his tightly vested chest, that Tommy had to keep saying, "What's that?" and "Pardon me, Sir,"—embarrassed that he hadn't quite caught the interviewer's name and couldn't address him properly. All the while Tommy was leaning forward so that the wooden chair clickety-clacked after his interjections like false teeth.

The interviewer wrote down Tommy's simple answers on a white and black xeroxed form which had Tommy's name printed in pencil at the top. Tommy had no way of knowing whether he was the first, the tenth, or the hundredth person to be considered for the advertised position. When the interviewer asked about his police record, Tommy hesitated for just a minute. He had been arrested with Ants for joy riding in high school. They took Ants' uncle's car, and damned if he didn't call the police. Then one other time Tommy had been arrested with a whole party of kids on the shore and booked for smoking pot. Tommy thought both of these probably weren't on any record, but he told the interviewer about the joyriding incident anyway. Explained it. Said he and his best friend borrowed a relative's car. That way, if it came up. And as for the marijuana incident, he had given an absent friend's name and address to the police in Asbury Park anyhow.

When Tommy inquired about his chances, the man raised his head and stared at Tommy through his thick, concealing lenses and only said: "Of course there have been a number of inappropriate applications." Tommy stared back with his mouth open. What could be meant by that? "Your profile and qualifications are more in line with what we had in mind." Later when Tommy told Gloria that, she agreed it was encouraging. That sounded positive, didn't it? The interviewer said little else, however, and he clearly didn't like answering questions.

The job was in a State correctional institution. It involved some training, and there would be variety in the work. When Tommy asked about salary, the gray man looked up in a little book and then quoted Tommy a range of figures. Even Gloria was agreeably surprised. It was much more than what he had been making at Hogarth. Of course the salary quoted was an annual figure, and at Hogarth he was paid twice a month. But by the time you counted the free health insurance—maybe that was why they asked so many questions about his medical history—and the other benefits, like retirement, it was more than two times Tommy's former wage.

Tommy noticed that the interviewer had filled up only about half of the page with his pale, neat writing. Tommy was asked to sign the sheet at the bottom where the date was. They didn't seem to want Tommy's stamp on anything else. At the end of the interview the man threw Arlette's beautifully typed letter into the empty mouth of the gray metal wastebasket, which seemed a shame to Tommy, although he guessed they had everything they needed, his name, date and social security number now, as well as his phone number.

"Come back two weeks from today, same time," the interviewer said. He ripped off the sheet with Tommy's identifying information and those faint penciled notes and put the piece of paper in a folder. For a brief moment Tommy thought to himself: He's going to offer me the job right now! But the interviewer just continued as if talking to himself. "Of course a stable background is required. Some testing. There are educational requirements."

What sort of education? This had always been Tommy's fear, that not going to college would catch up with him.

"But in your case the practical experience will count for a great deal." The interviewer wasn't very specific about the kind of education, although he had listened intently when Tommy described his work with the rescue squad. "There will be three of you," the gray man continued, clipping the gilt clasp shut on his plastic briefcase. "I think you understand the situation. The need for confidentiality. The waiting period."

Tommy didn't understand any of it. What need for confidentiality? Because it was something to do with prisons. Maybe they were worried that he had a record. Those opaque glasses gave out as little information as the wrinkled gray glass on the top of the office door. "We'll provide all of the technical training you'll need, of course," the interviewer said.

Tommy could hear someone moving around outside the door. The interviewer flipped back his paper-white shirt cuff to check the time. "Well, then?" He held out his hand with a ghostly smile. When he stood up he was surprisingly small and compact, as if he himself could have been folded away in the black plastic briefcase. He briefly touched Tommy's hand to terminate the interview before scurrying to unlock the door. Tommy hadn't realized the door had been locked behind him. When the door was snapped open, Tommy hurtled through immediately. On the other side, so close Tommy thought he might have been listening at the keyhole, was the next candidate, a stout, balding man in a tan suit, holding in both hands a straw hat with a striped blue and red band. He turned the hat in front of his puffy belly as if he were winding up a rope. Farther down the corridor a tall, lanky black man in a blue jump suit, he looked about Tommy's age, watched Tommy and smoked as he leaned against the wall with one foot up. Tommy wondered if he was waiting for an interview too. As Tommy turned to go back towards the elevator, he watched the black man grind his cigarette butt into the smooth concrete floor.

III

"I'm the hangman, then," Tommy said to himself two weeks later, as he rose in the gray and gold steel coffin of the elevator with its heavy ornamental brass door. Today the legislature was in session. The marble entrance of the State House sent back a smart click, click from the busy heels of lawyers, secretaries, lobbyists and clerks. Outside the October sky was bright and the air crisp, the clouds white as a sheet of new foolscap. Funny, Tommy had always thought of the hangman as a big, burly chested fellow with a black hood over his head. Just two slits for the eyes. But no, it was going to be himself, Tommy Angelino, a regular guy, a nice guy who never hurt anybody. Didn't the high school baseball team elect him captain? That proved everybody liked him, didn't it? Gloria used to complain the house had been taken over by his laughing friends, although she actually liked them. Now he wasn't going to be allowed to tell anyone, not even his friends, or his old teammates, or his mother, or his fiancée, what he had been hired to do. His real job title—Execution Technician—would not appear anywhere on his personnel file or on his payroll record. Instead, an imaginary job description and title, First Assistant Deputy Correctional Agent, had been created to cover up what he had been hired to do.

There was a probationary period for the job. There would be three of them. Three hangmen altogether. Of course they didn't use the term hangman. Three Execution Technicians, the gray man told Tommy. Or First Assistant Deputy Correctional Agents. And they weren't hangmen. They didn't string people up in America in the 1980s. The three Execution Technicians would be the ones who would administer the lethal injection. And why three? So that none of them would know who actually caused the death.

"Otherwise it might be on your conscience," Tommy interjected abruptly, teetering forward again on the uneven stubby legs of the wooden chair. The interviewer's small mouth twitched, quickly, like a rabbit's nose. He explained the job title and description again, emphasizing once more the need for confidentiality, speaking slowly, as if he thought Tommy was too stupid to have gotten it the first time. Tommy got the impression he'd be fired if he told anyone what he had really been hired to do.

The Execution Technicians were going to sit behind a curtain. What kind of a curtain, Tommy wondered. A heavy, ivory colored curtain like the one in Gloria's dining room? A slimy blue plastic curtain like the one in the pitted shower in his old bachelor apartment?

"Isn't there someone who knows?" Tommy asked.

The voice from behind the thick glasses was patient, with just a slight edge of sarcasm. It hesitated, as if it considered not answering. "The warden knows," the gray voice finally replied.

"Why the warden? Besides, the guy who sets up the...thing ...the apparatus....whatever it's called. He'll know which tube has the...stuff. The injection. I mean, someone has to load it." Tommy stopped himself. The interviewer was silent. He sat immobile, gray and papery. Tommy couldn't see his eyes.

"And what about the witnesses? The description. You know, the description of the thing. It said there would be six witnesses."

"No," the gray-green interviewer replied. The color of his suit blended in perfectly with the dull green desk top. He was not going to address any of Tommy's questions. "They never see you. No one sees you. The witnesses are just...Well, just part of the public participation."

"What...?" Tommy had been going to say. "What if I mess up?" But he thought better of it. He decided the gray man didn't want to hear about that. His job was to hire someone. Once that was done his responsibility was over. Besides someone had probably thought of what to do if he messed up or made a mistake. And how could he mess up? It was pressing a plunger. It didn't take any brains to do that.

"A certified IV technician and a physician will be present," the rabbit's mouth said. "To resuscitate, if necessary."

"Resuscitate?" Tommy exclaimed, tipping forward rapidly to a loud clatter. "What's the point of that?" He felt like laughing out loud. Later Tommy reproached himself. No sooner had he got a job, and a good job too, than he was saying stupid things. Making his new boss regret having hired him.

"Well," the rabbit was almost apologetic. "In case there is a last minute pardon. Or a reprieve."

Tommy clamped his mouth shut and nodded. Here he was on the verge of losing the job before he actually had it. Tommy pushed himself out through the revolving door and into the waning October sun. But he guessed he hadn't done anything that bad because the gray man told him to report to work at the prison the next Monday. So he did have the job after all.

George nodded vigorously, his chin bobbing up and down and taking the phone receiver with it. Uncle Mike wanted all the details. "Full benefits, including maternity." Gloria hung her head over his shoulder, waiting to fill in if George left out something. "Two times his former salary. Plus disability, dental, and even retirement." George continued laughing. When he laughed Tommy saw he had his teeth out again in the middle of the day. Gloria ran upstairs to get them, shaking her head at Tommy as she passed him on her way.

"Right in Trenton, isn't it?" George asked. Tommy nodded. And George nodded again into the telephone. "No, Mike, it wasn't six months." George shook his head. "No, only since June." Tommy shook his head. He had been fired in May. "I know that's a long time to be unemployed. But it's not six months." George smiled. Tommy shook his head again. "Mike, there's a recession out there. Oh, I know it's not the thirties, but..."

Tommy first tried out the cover story on his mother. He'd be working as a Corrections Agent in the records department of the prison, or the correctional facility, he explained. He told his mother his official title, First Assistant Deputy Correctional Agent. Probably they'd shift him around some, he explained to his mother. He'd be getting some training. She was preparing dinner in the kitchen, so at least she wasn't looking him in the eye. Tommy looked around the counter. No asparagus? he asked. Tommy loved fresh asparagus.

Sometimes he'd be in the mail room, sometimes in the administration. Gloria smiled and smiled, as if she couldn't believe his good luck. She didn't ask any questions. She just went on peeling the vegetables for Tommy's favorite Sunday dinner: roast pork, pan browned potatoes, carrots, onions and fresh horseradish and sour cream. Gloria's eyes were streaming from cutting the onions. Don't pay any attention, she said, wiping her tears on her apron.

Tommy was leaning against the sink and staring out the window into the asphalt-covered back yard so that he could avoid looking into Gloria's tear-streaked face. Even though he knew it was the onions, seeing his mother cry made him feel like crying too. In the small square concrete back yard the metal picnic table was draped in plastic, although winter was not near. They had hardly eaten there at all this summer. The chairs lay helplessly upended, their thin elderly legs in the air. Gloria popped a carrot into her mouth, blew her nose and said, "So you'll get married, then."

Arlette was coming momentarily. In the background Tommy could hear George still shouting to Mike over the phone, but it was no longer about Tommy's new job. A subpoena had been delivered to the house by a man with a badge of some sort, but not a police officer. George thought he was being arrested. Mike was explaining that he was just being called to court as a witness. George covered his other ear with his hand and nodded.

"Arlette's older than you were when you got married," Tommy said to his weeping mother. A blue jay took a cheeky perch on one of the metal chair legs. Tommy rapped on the window, but the bird just stared back at him through the window and ruffled its feathers.

"What's all the medical experience for?" Gloria broke a peeled carrot and held out half to Tommy. Tommy had hoped they were finished with the subject of his job. Oh, that. Well, he was supposed to be a backup for the prison doctor on minor things. To go in for one of the medical nurses when the doctor was busy. You know, write down complaints and things. He would be giving out pills. Who knew, even maybe giving injections. Of course, anything life-threatening a real doctor had to do.

Gloria was spooning pan drippings over the onions. She pushed a strand of hair out of her eyes. "I don't think he's getting any better," she said, nodding her head towards the voice coming from the living room.

Then Arlette came bounding into the kitchen, crashing against the table and almost toppling it. Arlette usually sported large bruises from bumping into low lying objects. She was short-sighted, but wouldn't wear glasses or try contact lenses. She could sweet talk her way out of it, she said, if a cop stopped her and asked about the restriction on her driver's license. It was contrary to her nature to slow down or accommodate to obstacles. Now, here she was in the kitchen, almost knocking over Gloria who stood behind the table with a spoonful of drippings in one hand, and crashing into Tommy from behind. Her arms and legs were flying, her voice was high, shrill and exciting. With her presence the kitchen was suddenly full of people. The globe of tear-stained apprehension between Tommy and Gloria was shattered into a thousand specks of light.

"It was my letter, my beautiful letter." When Arlette laughed, she was so young, so pretty, everyone around her had to smile. "It was. It was," she insisted, jumping up and down.

"No. No." Gloria said, straightening up and wiping her hands. "It was because I played his birthday the day of the interview." Gloria put her hands on Arlette's shoulders to hold her still long enough to kiss her. "Then I played it backwards."

Tommy laughed, too. "Don't forget, I'll be on probation for six months," he warned. He watched these two women toss their happiness between them. He guessed he would do anything for either one of them. Gloria dribbled dripping and herbs over the roast, as she danced from side to side. Then she squeezed a lemon from high. The chops were held neatly to the bone with string tied in bows by the butcher. "Did you get that at Ants' place in the market?" Tommy asked. Gloria nodded. "I keep saying I'll go to the supermarket, which is cheaper, but I end up back there."

Arlette bent over and plucked out a darkened onion skin as the pan slid back into the oven. Tommy propelled Arlette backwards into the living room. "God, you can eat all the time." Arlette was all spiky arms and legs and barely weighed one hundred pounds, although she regularly ate him under the table, including pizza, fried onion rings and fudge ripple ice cream together, any one of which would give him indigestion. As the door swung closed behind them Tommy heard Gloria run the water to rinse her hands in the sink and start singing to herself as she made bubbles splashing the water over the pans in the sink.

Tommy wanted to put off the wedding until after January, but Arlette had her heart set on getting married over Christmas. A friend of the family had offered them a banquet hall on the Sunday between Christmas and New Year's at the ordinary, not the holiday rates. Even Gloria thought that was too good to turn down. George still wasn't fully recovered, but at least his medical expenses were leveling off. And for the moment he was well enough to enjoy his son's wedding, so why not go ahead?

I haven't even been working a month, Tommy wanted to object. "Oh, I guess it doesn't make any difference," he said instead, giving in to his mother. He suspected Arlette, who grinned, had put his mother up to asking him.

When the date was set, Gloria was as excited as Arlette. Gloria hand-embroidered a set of sheets, table linens, and hand towels. Every night she sat sewing bright blue and yellow cross stitches on the white cloth. She even stopped telling George to put his teeth in.

The little pastel crosses flew across the material, and soon there was a whole bouquet of embroidered flowers, with ribbons trailing across Gloria's lap.

Arlette's mother, her father died some years ago, gave the couple a pull-out sofa. Another cousin had by sheerest luck heard about a tiny house a few blocks from the prison where Tommy would be working eventually. The house was just a couple of miles from Gloria's, close to Arlette's favorite Italian ice cream store, near the river and the railroad tracks, in what was still an old Italian neighborhood. The house had one tiny bedroom, a small square living room and a narrow kitchen with a window which looked out onto its own minute patch of grass and the arching branches of the neighbor's magnolia tree, which carried heavily scented purple tulip flowers for a few days in the spring. In winter its bare arms rested emptily on the tar paper roof of the neighbor's garage.

The house was like a play house. It had been fashioned by a carpenter who worked at the prison as a place to live in alone after he retired, but he didn't survive to take advantage of his own compact design. The family was happy to rent to a young couple. Arlette's office gave her a kitchen shower. Between the coffee grinder, toaster oven, and pans from the lawyers and secretaries, Gloria's linens, and the ceramic table lamps and end tables Arlette found in Gloria's basement, the young people were ready to set up housekeeping in their miniature home without spending any of their own money.

Even though it was in the middle of the Christmas rush, when everyone was tired, the wedding was happy, with a bottomless supply of pink sparkling wine, a five-tier wedding cake crammed with candied fruit and a fluted border of sugar roses. On its highest layer, the circle which contained all of Arlette's dreams, a black-haired bride in a gown of spun sugar and a groom in a licorice top hat stood beneath an arch of real roses. Tommy and Arlette twirled around and around the hall full of streamers and flowers. Arlette said her cheeks were so tired from smiling they ached for a week. Tommy danced with every woman and girl in the room, and with Arlette as often as he could in between.

In the middle of the wedding party Uncle Mike came and slapped Tommy's back hard, saying, "Well, my boy." He really did call Tommy "my boy." Probably because he had no children of his own to tease him about talking like that. For a wedding present he had given the young people his car, a year-old Cadillac. Quite a gift, George pointed out. Tommy wanted to say more than thank you, but he couldn't find any other words. So he just pounded Uncle Mike on the back, and said, Thank you. Thank you. Here all of a sudden he was a man with a car, a house, a job, and a wife, instead of being an unemployed dropout.

"What next? What next?" Mike asked. Tommy looked over his shoulder and saw Arlette laughing with her head thrown back. Tommy loved his uncle, but that slap had hit him in the wrong place on his shoulder so he just grinned and bobbed his head, bending over to mask the pain. Fortunately, Uncle Mike didn't seem to expect an answer, he just grinned and stared at Tommy and said again, "Well? What next?" Tommy was too tired to think of anything new to say, he just hugged his Uncle and thanked him again.

Arlette couldn't wait to quit work. Tommy wondered what she would do all day without a job. She did miss the camaraderie in the office. She even missed the lawyers. Her own boss hadn't been too bad. A former prosecutor who expected to be a judge someday, at least his head was on straight. No coddling of criminals in that office. As if she sensed his worry, at the end of every day Arlette told Tommy in detail about how she spent her time, looking for a bathroom rug, having lunch with the still unmarried and now frankly envious girls from her high school who felt trapped as clerks and secretaries in the State government.

Arlette never asked Tommy what he did all day. What he did was serious, and important, and permanent. Actually Tommy didn't care much what she did during the day as long as every night she was waiting for him to come home. After dinner they hurried into the boxlike bedroom which barely held their new queen-sized bed and made love and fell asleep in each other's arms. Then Tommy woke the next morning and waited for the night all day the next day.

Arlette turned the tiny house into a home for two surprised people who had never had more than a room to call their own. Gloria said it first, Tommy overheard her. He's very happy, she said. He's really very happy. And it was true. To think that only a few months ago Tommy had actually considered moving to

Florida. Who would want to live there? To think he considered going to work for that old friend of his father's, the mortician. Had even thought, in more than a passing way, it would be fun to be single in Florida near that community college. How foolish and youthful that all seemed now. He was a married man, with a home, a job and a car.

Tommy left the house promptly at 8:45 each morning. At 7:30 Arlette fixed him a hot breakfast of oatmeal, bacon and eggs, or waffles or french toast—which she ate as well. At this rate he'd look like the other paunchy guards in a matter of months. When Tommy didn't exercise, the flab came and draped itself in layers all over him, like a shroud. Then Tommy went off to the little room he had been assigned temporarily in the basement of one of the anonymous State office buildings. There he had his own desk, chair, a bookcase and nothing to put in it and a phone. The Supervisor explained that during the probationary period it had been decided to house him away from the prison. Later, the Supervisor explained, when he was in training at the prison, he would have an office, or at least a cubicle, there. But now his presence among the other prison officers would just raise questions, since there was nothing for him to do yet. He had been hired, but no one was sure what to do with him. Someone was working out the details.

"How come you're in the State House all the time?" Gloria asked suspiciously. "What are you doing?" Gloria sensed that paperwork would not be what Tommy was going to be doing. She sometimes called Tommy from the dry cleaning plant where she worked when the shift was changing, while she was waiting for her ride home. It was true Tommy had no specific duties. Twice a day the mail cart would rattle past his closed, opaque door and occasionally a pink interoffice envelope, a bright paper tongue, was stuck out at him through the square mail slot in the door. Those interoffice envelopes contained blurry mimeographs of the new State policy on smoking in offices or notifications of a change in the tax reporting of social security. The messages from the head of administrative services, or his deputy assistant, were sent spiraling into the green metal wastebasket beside his desk. Most of the time Tommy sat in the office and read magazines and news-papers. At least he could skip the want ads.

"It's awfully quiet there," Gloria said. He could barely hear her over the crashing and clanking at the dry cleaning plant. "Don't you work with anybody? Where's your boss?"

Tommy heard the hiss of steam behind her question. Perhaps because she couldn't hear him very well Gloria seemed satisfied when Tommy explained that he was only temporarily alone. Really, he had a lot to do or a lot he was about to have to do. He'd have responsibilities. Gloria didn't seem to hear the lie when Tommy said he would be working at a clinic for drug addicts at the prison. In the meantime he had to do some reading in preparation.

"I don't know," Gloria said, over the hiss of steam and the ringing of the cash register. "Working for all those prisoners..."

I won't be working for them, Tommy started to answer. But before Gloria could finish her ride came. Wasn't it almost true, what Tommy had told her? It would be different when he moved to the prison. There would be more for him to do then. There would be others there. Including the two others who had the same job.

IV

"No questions then?" the man in gray asked, pausing before he stamped PERMANENT on a pale yellow folder which now had Tommy's name typed on the tab. The gray man carried a rubber stamp and the stamping pad in the same black plastic fold-over briefcase with the gilt state seal. The interview marked the end of the four-month probationary period. The State even made him have a physical. Well, Gloria said, at least they got you to go to the doctor. It was true. Tommy distrusted doctors. Feared them. Their high rates. And what about all those unnecessary operations? Tommy thought of a hundred such questions the day of his examination. But the doctor who gave him his physical was a doddering old man with front teeth missing from his watery smile and a thick brush of black bristly hair growing out of both ears. He never once looked Tommy in the eye, as he told Tommy to turn around, lie down, bend over, pull apart his cheeks and open his mouth.

Tommy shook his head, looking out the small slit of a window above the Supervisor's head. No questions. Everything seemed settled. It was less than six months ago that he had come to the same room for his interview. It felt like six years. It was four o'clock and had started to snow—big, heavy, soft clumps hitting the small, dirty window and then sliding down the pane to melt into the cracks around the lead frame. It was late January and six inches was predicted. Tommy wanted to get started for home before the roads became covered with a shiny skin of ice. He wanted to drive Arlette to the store. She was afraid to drive in bad weather.

The gray rabbit man was explaining that probably nothing would happen for at least a year or perhaps even two. "Not-withstanding," the Supervisor explained, "it's important to have all the personnel in place.... For legal reasons." Tommy's file had grown to the point where it had at least a dozen pieces of paper in it. None of them bore his signature.

Tommy nodded, as if he understood. The big star-shaped snowflakes were plopping against the window like insects hitting an electric exterminator. "For legal reasons," the Supervisor continued. "Everything must be done exactly according to the regulations."

If Tommy didn't leave soon, he'd surely be stuck on the road, with trucks bearing down on the back of his neck. Or he himself would be trapped, gripping the wheel and swearing, behind a timid driver with no snow tires. What about the other two, he wanted to ask. My partners, where are they? Tommy watched a dazzling curtain of snow form on the outside of the grimy window. He just wanted to go home.

Before the Supervisor stamped PERMANENT on his file, Tommy had to take another written test. The Supervisor's nose twitched. "The psychologists..." he said, pushing a paper and pencil under Tommy's nose. Was he smiling? "I had to persuade them you weren't too young." No, it wasn't a smile after all. Just a flicker, or perhaps just an involuntary twitch.

"Do you agree in a general way with the precept 'an eye for an eye, a tooth for a tooth'?"

Tommy checked "Most of the time." "Always" might be regarded as too extreme. "Never" was clearly the wrong answer. Somehow "Occasionally" didn't quite describe how Tommy felt about vengeance. Vengeance? It was a word out of the Bible. Not a word Tommy used everyday. He wasn't particularly mad at anybody. But when he thought of someone harming Arlette. Or the unnamed, unborn baby which might be inside of her. He didn't think words then. He just felt his face get hot and his feet moved around on the floor if he was sitting down. And his hands itched. But to do what? To do what?

As for the question: "Do you believe the courts and the criminal justice system are usually fair and just?" Tommy just checked "Most of the time." But when the piece of paper asked if he ever got drunk or smoked marijuana Tommy couldn't figure out what to say. It wasn't believable that anyone who was in high school in the late 1970s had never smoked marijuana. So Tommy checked "Occasionally" and then wrote in the margin, "But not now!"

He did not know how to make up answers to the personal questions. Of course he was married without children, for the moment. His parents were both living. He didn't have any hobbies. Chewing the pencil and staring over the empty desk at the man in gray, Tommy wanted to lie and say that he played backgammon, or at least the guitar. Baseball! He loved to play baseball. But he hadn't played for several years. He checked sports. Staying in bed with Arlette on weekends when he could persuade her that whatever impelled her to get out of bed and get dressed could wait. No space for that. Couldn't put that down. Who would know whether or not he really played backgammon, Tommy thought, as he folded over the answer sheet and handed it to the Supervisor. Tommy sort of knew how it was played. He'd watched Gloria and her friends play one summer, when the family uncharacteristically rented a bungalow at the shore. Funny, he hadn't seen Gloria or any of her friends play the game since that summer, which must have been a decade ago, at least.

It turned out no one would ever have known about Tommy's white lie because the Supervisor, he was wearing the same suit, the color of gray-green newsprint smudge, quickly took Tommy's sheet, checked over his entries against a xeroxed code sheet he removed from the plastic briefcase, made some checks and zeros next to his answers and came up with a score of twenty-six. The Supervisor wrote the final number down on a separate piece of paper with only the date, January 29, 1984, the number 26, and Tommy's name on it. Then he tore up Tommy's test sheet and dropped it in the wastebasket. So Tommy could have put down backgammon, or the guitar, or tennis, and no one would have known the difference. No one would have cared. Passing the test seemed to be another one of those official milestones, like being made permanent, or being hired, an event which didn't really exist anywhere. But someone somewhere on some piece of paper said it had to be done. And someone made it happen. So he did what he had to do to do it. It was another official thing which the State did with its invisible bureaucracy, behind its own back. And now he was Permanent. Now he was in place. He had passed the test. Silly as it was. The Supervisor smiled at him. Somehow it had come about. He really had the job. The title was attached to his name on a folder. He was the one who was going to do it. But not now. Not yet. Later. Later, he'd have to do something. Perhaps. Now he just had the job and the title.

As the winter settled in Tommy actually was busy. They did give him an office in the prison itself. He was interviewed at length by a consulting psychiatrist who had worked for the prison for many years. The psychiatrist, a humorless man with a short European beard, also never wrote anything down, although Tommy supposed that the confidential file with his name and title on it was growing larger somewhere inside the dark interior of a locked drawer. Tommy sensed that somehow all of these people lied about what they did too, the Supervisor, the prison doctor, the psychiatrist. They were probably like him, people who couldn't get jobs anywhere else.

All of those regulations and procedures in connection with the new penalty. There were twenty pages of administrative directives printed up on blue recycled paper, most of which didn't apply to his job of Execution Technician. What the Execution Technician did, really, was just press a button, or a lever. Tommy hadn't seen the machine yet. As if someone else was doing it. The laughable part was that Tommy had more technical expertise than he needed for the job. He was overqualified. The regulations seemed to be designed to divide up the job of killing the prisoner into tiny separate and distinct steps. It was like watching a child who didn't want to eat cut his meat into smaller and smaller pieces, until finally it wasn't recognizable and looked chewed, and no one noticed the child had fed the bits to the dog under the table.

Tommy's part was not the last step or even the most important one. There were the doctors whose job it was to stand by to resuscitate against the prisoner's will, and to certify death. There were the people who took away the prisoner's body and disposed of the possessions. The State had decided it would not pay more than $25 to embalm the person who was to be executed. Who decided that? The budget guys or the embalming people? Tommy tried to grasp all of the parts played, as well as his own. But his imagination balked when it came to visualizing the moment, the actual moment when the poison, the poisoned sleep medicine traveled along to deliver the fatal blow. Tommy assumed it was like being put to sleep before an operation, except that the equipment was more elaborate. But then he read somewhere it wasn't like that after all, that the person was strapped down, and squirmed or wriggled, or prayed and sang, or shouted curses, and the body convulsed. The thought made Tommy break out in a sweat. What if he got sick right in the middle of it? In spite of all the preparation.

The regulations were written in language which was opaque, impossible to penetrate. Twenty words were used to say something which could be plainly said in three. The cold words cascaded over the blue pages, falling from numbered paragraph to numbered paragraph, like icy foamy water running down a steep, stony gully. The person who was to be executed was called "the condemned," lower case. The condemned had to have a physical and psychological test upon entry. Just like me, Tommy thought. The condemned was allowed to place daily phone calls, but could only be visited by family members or clergy from the community who presented proper clerical credentials, whatever those might be. Calls and visits by the attorney of record were allowed to the Capital Sentencing Unit (hereafter referred to as the CSU). There were capital letters for the death house, but not for its inhabitants. The tone was one of unwavering certainty, as if the regulations were issued directly from the mouth of an all-knowing being.

The regulations addressed the question of the pre-execution sedative, the permitted requests for the last meal (no alcohol), and how many hours of recreation the condemned was permitted. The condemned could only have a few things in his cell, but his cell was bigger than the ordinary cells. There was a separate phone line installed for the sole purpose of receiving news of a last-minute stay of the execution or a commutation. There was even a special code so that the Superintendent of the prison would know the call was authentic. No incoming call on the special line reserved for the Governor would be deemed authentic unless preceded by the special code. Everyone in the line of command had to learn a special code.

After the execution, the condemned was renamed "the deceased" and a final set of decimal-numbered paragraphs concerned the disposal of the physical body and its owner's former possessions. One of the last things the prisoner did before being executed was fill out a form indicating what he wanted done with his wallet, pictures and his outside clothes. They did seem to have thought of everything. Several people must have worked it all out, probably at a committee meeting, or more likely several meetings. Although the regulations were anonymous, they were said to originate from the Standards Development Unit (the SDU). But it didn't say the SDU would answer questions. Tommy wondered if that was where the little gray man with the rabbit mouth worked. There didn't seem to be anyone whose job it was to answer questions.

Tommy was one of the least important members of the team. There was a whole Operational Staff. Like the CSU and the SDU, they had their own set of capital letters. Two real doctors (they were part of the OS) had to be present to certify death, but only one was to be on the prison staff. A nurse and a certified IV therapist, whatever that was, were also required to be present.

The regulations also spelled out the secrecy procedures. The identity of the person actually inflicting the lethal injection was to be unknown even to the person himself. The regulations were very explicit about that. "Procedures shall be designed to insure that the identity of those persons shall be confidential, and that the identity of the person actually inflicting the lethal substance is unknown even to the person himself." That was clear enough, wasn't it, even if it took a lot of words to say it. But they kept repeating that all through the training sessions. No one will know, the psychiatrist assured Tommy. No one will know who did it.

The actual room where the deed was to take place was called the Execution Suite, which made Tommy guffaw because it sounded like a place at a Holiday Inn. Everyone around him frowned. The Execution Suite had to be equipped with a cardiac monitor and life-support equipment and medication to revive the condemned in case there was a last-minute stay or reprieve. All of the fuss and bother about a stay or a reprieve, and how likely was that, after all. And yet another special and private telephone was installed in the Execution Suite in case of an emergency. Tommy had heard of midnight commutations. The Governor couldn't live with the decision, so he issued a last-minute pardon, if he had the power to do it. Sometimes the Governor couldn't commute. So then who would use the special telephone and issue the reprieve? Tommy guessed that's why that phone was there. In fact there was a provision for three phones on the line, sequenced to receive the final call.

The technical training began with three brief sessions with one of the prison doctors. A middle-aged Japanese American, the doctor seemed to want to get it all over as quickly as possible. With crisp efficiency the doctor explained the medical, or rather the quasi-medical equipment to Tommy. After all, medical equipment was supposed to save lives, and this equipment had the opposite purpose, didn't it. So should it be called medical equipment? Actually, it was all really very simple, just a feeder line into a single intravenous line. The only medical complication was caused by the unusual length of the feeder line. It could get twisted or tangled.

The three Execution Technicians and the warden and two doctors and someone called the Health Services Coordinator were required to sit in a vestibule behind a curtain, several yards behind the head of the condemned. That was the reason why the tubes and valves and hook-ups were a bit tricky. Some self-appointed inventor had designed the machine; the prison doctors had no particular aptitude or enthusiasm for the job. There was a rumor one had even quit over it. The bullet-proof wall separating them was thick. All the lines had to be threaded through this wall. Did someone think that a drugged man strapped down on a stretcher could start a shootout? Perhaps they were worried about disruptions from the other observers. Then the equipment was designed so that all three of them could simultaneously activate the injection. At the signal all three leads were to fill up at the same time, one with a lethal dose of poison, two with a harmless saline solution. The apparatus was actually rather crude, not much more complicated, and probably less efficient, than the guillotine or the hangman's drop.

Tommy couldn't understand why the condemned had to be given a sedative first. Especially since he was required to be conscious. It didn't seem to make much sense to give someone a tranquilizer, forcibly if necessary, and then insist he be awake for what came next. Especially when what came next was his own execution. Couldn't he sleep that one out?

The Nisei doctor had been working for the prison for thirty years—since he graduated from the Harvard Medical School in the early fifties, at a time when Japanese-American doctors were not exactly welcome in many American hospitals. The doctor had a tic in his smooth, hairless cheek, where a dimple might have once been. Tommy wondered if the tic had developed with the job. During the training sessions Tommy had the feeling this wasn't the worst assignment this doctor had ever had. What about all those doctors who said they wouldn't take part in executions? Wasn't that why his position was created? So the doctor wouldn't have to be defrocked? Still, Tommy supposed the prison doctor would be the one giving the sedative, as well as certifying death. Tommy wondered who mixed the lethal medicine. During the training session the doctor didn't wear any prison ID. Nor did he wear the little plastic name card with his picture that Tommy and all of the other employees were required to wear when they entered the prison walls. Nor did his green hospital coat have a name stitched on the pocket. The doctor said his name hurriedly when he introduced himself at the beginning of the session. Something beginning with a T and with lots of A's and S's in between. That was as much as Tommy got. And Tommy never did have another chance to catch it.

Tommy read and reread the pages of blue regulations, which had arrived on his desk in an envelope marked CONFIDENTIAL. Although the regulations specified every detail, every moment for the procedure, something critical seemed to be missing, in spite of the specificity of the new titles, the names for all of the places and people involved. It was like the script for a play where all the players on stage were going to be hidden behind cardboard cut-outs.

There was a monthly meeting with the Health Care Supervisor (HCS) for everyone connected with what was referred to as the implementation. Tommy did have a few questions. What about the final meal? The regulations provided that the condemned could request the food of his choice at the last regularly scheduled dinner not less than eight hours before the scheduled execution. Well, it said no alcohol or beer or wine was permitted. But the food of his choice was to be provided subject to reasonable availability and cost. Tommy wanted to know what reasonable availability and cost meant. What about steak? Lobster? What about asparagus, if it was out of season. And did that regulation mean that all executions had to be at two in the morning? If the last meal was at the prison dinner hour, that was five o'clock.

The Health Care Supervisor frowned. So the last meal was lunch, or even breakfast? Of course not. Well, then there would be another meal after the last meal. It wasn't the last meal after all. Tommy also wanted to know why the regulations always referred to the condemned as "he"? Weren't there some women who were going to the CSU? The Health Care Supervisor pointed out that the regulations provided for a licensed gynecologist to examine a female condemned, and the implementation would be postponed if the condemned were pregnant. That meant the condemned could be "she," didn't it? The HCS couldn't deny the logic of that.

The HCS was a fat, kindly man who wore a frown with his uniform. He reminded Tommy of his old boss at Hogarth, the man who was embarrassed to be the one to have to explain to Tommy why they were firing him. It seemed to Tommy that he was putting the HCS on the hot seat in exactly the same way. He didn't mean to. It was just that he had all of these questions. The system seemed to be riddled with nice guys who were stuck with explaining how an impersonal abstract policy, which sounded perfectly reasonable as long as it was all in the abstract, was going to affect a very unabstract, alive, real person, maybe even someone like you or me. And someone had to do it.

Why were two representatives from the television networks allowed in to witness the implementation if they couldn't film the event. What was the point of that? The HCS frowned at Tommy and blew smoke out of his nose like a comic book dragon. He promised to check that one out with the Superintendent himself and get back to Tommy about it at the meeting next month. As if to see Tommy more clearly, he removed the cigarette from his mouth, peeling a small piece of paper from his lips as he stared at Tommy from under his frown.

The rabbit man turned out to be a kind of general administrator, although Tommy never did get straight what his title was or what he supervised. He dropped by Tommy's office every other week; moving quickly with little abrupt gestures, he would appear unannounced at Tommy's desk. Tommy's office was halfway down a corridor leading to one of the maximum security, administrative segregation units. Not the death bloc, but the regular administrative segregation section, where they put ordinary prisoners for protection or punishment. Tommy's office was a subdivided square room with one tiny barred window looking out onto the parking lot. There was a yellowed roll-up shade over the window. When Tommy couldn't stand to look at the parking lot any longer, he pulled down the shade. The shade was in the habit of snapping up abruptly. With a sharp report, like a gunshot. And even though Tommy knew what it was, he jumped every time. Tommy felt as if he were crawling out from a burrow when he came out from that office. When the Supervisor came to visit, he sat bolt upright with his hands on his knees in the wooden chair which was the only piece of furniture except for Tommy's regulation gray desk and chair. Once Arlette had suggested he bring in a framed picture of flowers for his office. She didn't have another place for it, and someone had given it to them. Tommy couldn't stop laughing at the idea.

"Looks like snow again," the Supervisor said, not looking out the window which had its shade down, but staring around the room at the hodgepodge of junk Tommy had collected. Usually he didn't say much more than that. Just waited for Tommy to ask something. At first Tommy had lots of questions. But there never were any answers, at least not any answers which made sense. Not from the rabbit man, or the HCS with the frown, or the Superintendent or anyone else. The man whose eyes were hidden, the man with the mouth which twitched like a rabbit's nose, mainly wanted to be sure that Tommy was regularly reporting to work. He posed, and then answered for himself, hypothetical questions about the pension plan, the health benefits, and all those coded deductions in Tommy's paychecks. He mentioned employee counseling. They had no conversations.

One day the Supervisor paused by the messy pile of newspapers on Tommy's desk. He read out a large, black headline announcing a verdict in the latest murder trial in Gloucester county. "I wouldn't bother with that too much," the Supervisor said, taking off his thick glasses and reaching for the neatly folded handkerchief in his breast pocket. It was the closest the Supervisor had ever come to directly mentioning the reason why Tommy was hired. Now that his thick glasses were off Tommy saw his eyes for the first time. They were not small and slitty as Tommy imagined, but large, wide open and pale blue, almost the color of Tommy's own. The Supervisor ignored Tommy's frankly curious stare—perhaps he couldn't see it—and turned his blank, pink face towards the empty dingy wall behind Tommy's head, all the while holding his thick glasses between thumb and forefinger and methodically rotating the lens clockwise inside the pristine white square of handkerchief.

In spite of the Supervisor's warning Tommy did read everything he could get his hands on about murder. When a killer was sentenced to death, or executed in another state, Tommy eagerly looked for the reports of the murderer's last words of remorse, or prayer, or lack of them, before he went to join his victims. When Tommy was hired, after the death penalty had been in effect almost two years, there were still only three people on death row. The same three who had been sentenced just after Tommy had been hired were alone on death row for several months. It was as if there had been an initial flurry of activity, to show it could be done, and then everyone in the system was afraid to do it again.

Benjamin Jones was a twenty-year-old black man from Florida—the State's first death row convict wasn't even from New Jersey—who had been sentenced as a juvenile five years ago in Georgia for his role in the robbery of a gas station. His partner allegedly—Tommy snorted when they said allegedly—shot the attendant. Anyway, that was now the official version of the events since the co-defendant, whether or not he had been the shooter, had already been executed in Georgia. Jones, however, was released and drifted up to New Jersey where he committed two forthright felony murders during a spree of robberies and burglaries after forty-eight hours on coke and alcohol. The victims he was tried for were murdered in their living room. Since he denied both murders, he was convicted on the basis of circumstantial evidence. In his case, the fact that he was found driving around in one of the victim's cars while trying to forge a signature on her credit card proved persuasive to the jury, especially in the face of his surly silence. Killing more than one person at the same time was the basis for the death penalty.

The second man, Darby Ross, was a slight white man in his mid-thirties with a wispy, elfin beard. His pale face reminded Tommy of someone, but Tommy couldn't catch who it was. The memory would flicker across his consciousness, a shadow, and then be gone. Someone on an opposing team from his baseball days? The little runny-nosed boy who sat behind him in fifth grade? Darby had been linked to the murder of fifteen young girls, young women who were picked up on the boardwalk or lured into his car from supermarket parking lots. Darby taped his arm in a sling and pretended to need help. All the women were sadistically tortured and raped in a satanic, drug-heightened ritual before being murdered. The evidence was circumstantial, and there was lots of it. One odd circumstance was half the victims were black, and half were white. The circumstances were all similar. For the moment he had only been convicted of murder for two of the white teenagers who disappeared in Atlantic City. Charges were pending against him in other counties. As far as Tommy was concerned, either one of the two would have been suitable candidates for his newly acquired skills.

Gregory Griselli, the third man, was a diminutive druggist in his forties who had paid someone to kill his wife. He hadn't even been a suspect at first, he wept so convincingly at the funeral, but the actual strangler gave a very convincing confession which included details of Gregory coming to meet him at a garage on a particular night with several thousand dollars in grocery bags. Everyone wondered why Griselli couldn't just find some way of poisoning her using the stock in his pharmacy. Gregory refused to speak to anyone after his sentence was imposed. The court appointed a public defender appellate lawyer for him against his wishes. Gregory let the private lawyers who were so eager to represent him at trial go hang for their fees after he was convicted. He didn't take the stand to contradict the evidence against him, although he had no criminal record. But he didn't think that the evidence made him guilty. Tommy felt sorry for his kids, two boys eight and ten, who had to look at their father and know he killed their mother. They changed their names and went to live with the maternal grandparents.

Once as he trotted down the slippery cement corridor of the prison Tommy saw walking towards him the heavy-set, older man, the man holding the straw boater, who had been waiting outside in the corridor on that hot day in August when Tommy went for his interview. Neither Tommy nor the older man, he had a pleasant face with thinning hair on top, exchanged any sign of recognition. He looked like a man who had seen some reversals in his life. Tommy wondered what kind of job he had before, and whether the Supervisor wondered if he was too old for the job.

At Sunday dinners with Gloria, George and Uncle Mike, Tommy found himself talking excitedly about the latest murder trial. Last Sunday Arlette looked up from the corner of the living room where she and Gloria were sifting through the wedding proofs. "Oh, I wish he wouldn't talk about that all the time," Arlette whispered to Gloria. "The cops should just kill them, and save the taxpayers the trouble."

"Now, that's really good of both of you," Gloria said, holding up a shot of Arlette pursing her brilliant red mouth over the dark wedding cake Tommy was feeding her, so that she seemed to be kissing his fingers. "Don't pay any attention," Gloria whispered, as she wrote "enlarge" on the back of the proof. To Tommy she said, half-laughing, "Leave that stuff at the office. You're upsetting your wife, and she's in a delicate condition."

George and Uncle Mike listened to Tommy, not the way Tommy's friend Anthony might have listened, but they listened. Every week the newspapers and the television had a new one. The crimes came so fast and furiously it was hard to remember the murders from just a few months ago. The trials of Darby and Benjamin, dragged on for weeks, monopolizing most of the front and back of the local papers every day. The pictures of the crime scene, blood, disarray, signs of violence, but no person there. Only the back of a uniformed policeman or emergency medical assistant. It was like looking at your own death scene. Then no sooner did the public finish clucking over the victims' fates, than the stories turned to the murderer's unfortunate family history.

Benjamin took the stand to describe how he'd been beaten with a golf club by his stepfather and then left to fend for himself at age eleven. He didn't attend school after fifth grade, and he never did learn to read. His mother was ranting crazy. Then he went on to say his family was just like all others. They had the same problems that all families had. This after two days of expert testimony that his treatment in childhood would have made a gerbil pathological. The jury regretfully sentenced him to death. They saw no hope. Then silence. Probably many newspaper readers thought he had been executed already.

No sooner had Darby and Benjamin and Griselli been sentenced to die, but Arthur Davenport from Bridgetown shot his wife in the head and then strangled four of his five children, one right after another, as they huddled in the corner weeping. The fifth child ran outside and saw more than any child should witness. The father planned to kill himself, but didn't, collapsed weeping instead, and asked the State to do the job.

"Ah," Mike said. "He'll get off. Even if they give it to him. It'll be overturned. For some damned reason you've never heard of. I tell you what I'd do," Mike picked up one of Gloria's white napkins, held it lengthwise and turned it into the coil of a rope. Then he wrapped the napkin around his hands and twisted. "Bastards."

"No you wouldn't," Tommy protested. "If you really had the chance." He didn't know why he said that.

"You're both giving me a stomachache," Gloria said, and went into the kitchen.

Arthur Davenport, the man from Bridgetown, was an accountant. He hired a fancy lawyer from New York City who, it was rumored, had sold the rights to a book about the case for half a million dollars. The defense was temporary insanity—he heard voices, the doctors said. But it took the jury less than three hours to find Davenport guilty on four counts of capital murder and one count of manslaughter. Since the wife had been holding the baby when she was shot, and the baby was first dropped on its head, the jury found manslaughter for the death of the baby. Another half a day, and the jury sentenced him to death, although the doctor who testified he was crazy was very sincere and took no fee. Tommy was impressed, but probably that was a negative with the jury. So Davenport joined Darby, Griselli and Benjamin on death row to make four, three white men, one black man, and the victims, black and white, men and women and children.

"Well," Tommy said to Ants, "that's one they'll never get overturned. He said right out he killed all of them. Never denied it."

Anthony nodded. He was singularly uninterested in this particular case, or in Tommy's other horror stories.

"Look," Tommy insisted. A pleading note crept into his voice. "That guy is as sane as..."

Ants laughed. "As you, maybe! Come on... It's all crazy!" And Ants walked out of the room, leaving Tommy alone with his unfinished sentence.

The local prosecutor was finally moving along the case against the two kids charged with the assault upon George and his partner. Even though it was over a year later, George was still limping when he went to the prosecutor's office to go over his statement one more time.

"One wore a mask," George said to Tommy. "At the lineup I wasn't sure. But my partner picked him right out. It must be the right ones." Turned out the two punks—neither of them had ever worked a day in his life—were out on bail and waiting trial on an almost identical robbery in another town when George and his partner were attacked. They didn't get much from that robbery either. Nor had they learned anything from being in jail. The judge let them out because they were supposed to be in school, and because no one had been seriously hurt. But one of the other men went on disability because he was afraid to come back to work. George kept asking Mike what he thought would happen this time.

"Don't tell your Dad," Uncle Mike said in a whisper when Tommy asked the same question, "but the case will plead out. They'll probably get time served." Apparently the evidence wasn't considered particularly strong, in spite of the identification by both George and his partner and some marked bills. The two kids claimed to be elsewhere, home asleep in their beds like good boys.

"Punks," Mike said. "Besides, the prosecutor took one look at your dad and saw that he'd be a terrible witness." According to Mike the prosecutor could tell George would be shaky on the stand, that he would waver on the identification. The kids themselves would not be witnesses. They both had arrests and a couple of convictions, although neither one was twenty-one yet.

"But why?" Tommy asked again. How could anyone not believe and trust his father, or at least feel sorry for him. The more Tommy read about lawyers, the picky little rules, the court formalities, and most of all about how long everything took, the less sense any of it made. The prosecutors would hang a desperate man who stole a loaf of bread to feed his starving children, and the defense attorneys would ask the jury to recommend the most rabid mass murderer for outpatient psychiatric counseling. The judges fell asleep on the bench, or didn't understand the arguments, and the police shot twelve-year-old kids in the back when they ran down the city alleys. Meanwhile those on bail or on parole, or awaiting trial, went on crime sprees as if violence was about to go out of style. And that didn't seem too likely. Or maybe it was just their last chance. Reading the daily newspapers could make a law-abiding citizen want to round up his own neighborhood lynch mob. Finally, Tommy just concentrated upon the crimes themselves—weren't they horrible enough to justify any kind of punishment? Who cared how the defendants got to the execution suite, or when they had their last meal, or what it cost.

Alone in his little cinder-block office with its limited view of the facility parking lot, Tommy nodded in agreement when he read that a state legislator said death by injection was too good for someone who tortured and murdered fifteen women. Who cared about some technical question on jury selection which no one, not even the lawyers, seemed to understand anyway. So what if the fifteen-year-old he was actually convicted of murdering had been arrested with marijuana a couple of years ago. Tommy knew how phony that could be. Did that mean it was all right to kill her? And like that, too. There ought to be something you could do to a guy who did that. Killing him was too good for him.

The stunned parents were interviewed mercilessly on television by a reporter who looked not much older than their dead daughter. The father stared into the camera with large, blank eyes and said their daughter had run away from home, and they hadn't heard anything from her in over a year. The mother couldn't speak. Her voice had disappeared into the empty space where her heart once was. She periodically bobbed her head as if she agreed with whatever her husband or anyone else said. A school psychologist was quoted as saying the victim had been withdrawn in school, skipping classes to hang out in the video game parlors. The psychologist suspected problems at home. Hard to persuade kids these days that it's worth their while to learn to write their names, let alone learn to read, was the psychologist's unasked-for opinion. The girl's body had been dumped in the pine barrens. She was identified by her slightly overlapping front teeth.

The merciless reporters interviewed the girl's dentist too. His bulgy eyes filled up with tears when he talked about her back molars. The prosecutor's office had lost the autopsy report on another one of the victims, and the parents had insisted upon a cremation, so they didn't bother prosecuting that one. At least those parents didn't have to be interviewed over and over.

Darby himself loved to give interviews. He adored the press. He managed to outsmart the prison phone security system, getting calls out to the reporters about once a week. Darby was eloquent on the subject of the injustices of the present criminal justice system in comparison to the majesty of the promises in the Bill of Rights. He vowed to fight his appeals until all his unconstitutional convictions were put aside. He never indicated remorse, or admitted any role in the killings of the women, even when eye witnesses came out of the woodwork to testify against him. As far as he was concerned, it was a case of mistaken identification. The wrong man had been convicted.

While all of this was going on Benjamin, who had an IQ of 80, had discovered that a weeping black Jesus stared back at him from the stippled gray cinder block of his cell every night promptly at five, just before his dinner was pushed through the slot. Strangely, Jesus used the same brand of barely coherent speech which was Benjamin's own signature. The weeping Jesus absolved Benjamin for his sins with communications so ungrammatical only Benjamin could understand them.

Benjamin now said that he deserved to die and was willing to die because God had forgiven him. His three government lawyers devoted themselves even more vigorously to the fight to save his life over his objection, arguing among other things that Benjamin was obviously incompetent to make the decision to die now, although a court had already decided he was mentally capable of committing murder and deserved the State's highest punishment. The lawyers argued it was immoral for the State to execute someone so crazy he didn't understand what was happening to him. Besides the point of the death penalty was that the person who got it had no say about when it would happen. The State decided for you. That was the point. You didn't control your own death.

In the meantime in a southern county the jury had been out four days on a case involving a young man who was a straight A student in high school, the son of a stock broker, who strangled his pregnant girlfriend, or fiancée, and dumped her body in the town reservoir. At trial he took the stand and protested his innocence, but there were rumors a confession had been suppressed. He had an alibi, but some of her things, a numbered rugby jersey, her make-up kit, had been found in his red sports car, a birthday present from his Dad. He admitted they had been together and in the car, but he said it was the day before. Then it was said he had been selling speed and the girlfriend was going to tell the school authorities, or his father. Her best friend had seen the two of them in his car on the day determined to be the day of the murder. When the prosecutor held up the rugby shirt, the witness said, yes, the victim had been wearing it. She cried on the stand. Tommy didn't understand why people didn't want to talk about these things.

Gloria was passing a breast of roast chicken to Tommy and barely listening when Tommy asked her if she thought the stock broker's son did it. "What...?" She looked at Tommy and her puzzled expression was glazed with a golden, slightly greasy sweat.

"I do," Arlette interjected hotly. "How could he? She was pregnant with their child. He deserves whatever he gets. "

Tommy impatiently started to tell the whole story again, the witness, the alibi, the numbered rugby shirt.

Gloria interrupted him. "I don't know...about this job." She put the platter down and looked at Tommy with disconcerting directness. "It's all so wrong. And no one stops it." Hearing her voice trail off like that, Tommy was reminded of the time right after graduation, when he just stayed in his room all day. Gloria used to climb the three flights of stairs to his attic room and then just stare, first at him—lying on the bed with his headset on—then at the clothes, records, tapes, and athletic equipment strewn all over. She'd open her mouth, take a deep breath, and then either say something completely matter of fact, like telling him the time, or go back downstairs without a word. Then one morning Tommy just got out of bed and left home.

"I just don't know, except that it's upsetting your wife..." Gloria said now, wiping her hands on her napkin. "Those awful people. Something has to be done. " She handed Tommy the butter in its covered silver dish and tilted her head towards George. "It isn't right," she said. Tommy, balancing the slippery butter dish in his hand, winced as he looked at his father, eating slowly with his head down, seemingly not hearing the conversation. He did not meet his mother's questioning gaze.

V

It is Friday, the 13th of April. In 1984 there are three Fridays the thirteenth, and this is the second. Tommy is up at six in the morning, as usual. He cannot sleep past six in the morning these days, no matter what time he goes to bed at night. Arlette is three months pregnant and snoring lightly, her lips trembling with the exhalation of each breath. At least I know she's alive, Tommy thinks gratefully. Recently he has been waking up in the middle of the night terrified that something has happened to Arlette. Wide awake he simply lies rigid next to her waiting for the sweet music of her breathing. Now Tommy curls against her and hopes to catch her sleep. Her mouth is open, the red threads of yesterday's lipstick fluttering with each breath.

Since the pregnancy Tommy has taken to getting up first. He goes to the kitchen, puts the water on to boil and drops a piece of whole wheat toast in the toaster's gaping mouth. He smiles to himself, thinking of Ants and his other roommate kidding him about how hopeless he was in the kitchen. Ants, not surprisingly, was an excellent cook. If Arlette immediately eats a piece of dry toast, while propped up on one elbow on the flowered pillow, while sipping a cup of hot tea, while staring gratefully and groggily at Tommy, if she can get down the toast and a couple of swallows of tea, before putting her bare feet flat on the carpet, then she is less likely to vomit for an hour in the bathroom. Tommy never anticipated the violence of pregnancy, and every time she lurches out of bed retching and runs to the bathroom, it is a fierce surprise. Of course he knew where babies came from. And even he had heard about morning sickness. But to see his own Arlette gagging as she got out of bed in the morning because a baby had seized control of her body was another matter altogether.

While Tommy waits for the kettle to boil, makes himself a cup of instant coffee, all he takes for breakfast these days, gingerly he approaches the morning headlines. An unemployed janitor beat to death an emergency room nurse as she left the hospital at two in the morning. The twenty-two-year old nurse had been working overtime to save the life of a suicidal teenager overdosed on her mother's sleeping pills. The apprehended man had bundled up her bloodstained clothes and dumped them in the garbage in front of his rooming house, where the smell of blood was noticed by the landlord as he put the cans out on the curb.

The nurse was a local girl, a few classes behind Tommy in the high school. The newspaper printed her picture from the high school year book on the front page. The portrait of the hopeful graduate, her hair softly curled around her neck, the whole head and bare shoulders set off by the black velvet photographer's drape, cannot be reconciled with the newspaper's graphic, almost gleeful, description of the acts committed upon her head and body prior to death. The photographer's black velvet wrap is echoed in a black border around the picture. Tommy's hands start to shake. Arlette knew the woman, even had an English class with her. Arlette must not see this picture, especially early in the morning. He will call Gloria from work and make sure that she doesn't mention anything.

The springs creak and Tommy hears Arlette padding solidly to the bathroom. He lays the paper face down on the kitchen table. Arlette comes into the kitchen wearing a furry yellow robe with a pink tulip embroidered on the collar. The robe was a present from her office. Every time she talks to one of the secretaries she mentions how often that she wears it, and if she is wearing it right now. Tommy wants her to hurry back to bed now so that he can bring her breakfast. Arlette is smiling which means she hasn't been sick. Tommy pulls her down onto his lap and kisses her sleep stiff hair and slightly sour neck. Her spicy smell prickles his nose. Tommy takes a deep breath and holds it, as if he were inhaling the fragrance of a rose. Arlette leans back, yawns and closes her eyes, and Tommy slides the paper under his chair. He slips his hands inside the fuzzy robe and spreads his fingers over the little round bump on the top of her flat stomach. So far only Arlette has felt anything, although Tommy comes and puts his hand on her stomach, reaching under her dress if they are alone, when he sees her attention drift inward. He has not yet felt the quickening of his child.

"Too early for him to be up," Arlette says, curling her feet beneath her on Tommy's lap. She assumes she will have a boy because that is what most of the relatives want. She's grown prettier with the pregnancy. Not like some women, Tommy thinks proudly, who get mottled and lumpy with the hormonal changes. Her olive skin has darkened, especially around the eyes, but it is translucent, delicate. It is as if her complexion has moved over three hues in the color spectrum. Now Arlette looks Moroccan or Cuban, instead of what she is, a dark southern Italian. By the end of the pregnancy she will have huge, blue-black shadows under her eyes. Tiny waving lines, like the inky tracery of a river system seen from the air, have appeared on the sandy inside of her thighs.

Arlette, who could not sit still for a three-hour movie, now sometimes sleeps until Tommy comes home. Arlette who used to be busier than all the bees, who went to work and then stayed up half the night talking or dancing, now just waited for him to come home. Occasionally she goes out to do an errand, but mostly she just waits until it is time to start their dinner. He was the reason for this altered state, and it only makes sense when he is there. Tommy also felt his existence in suspension while away from her. It was not that they were so close, in fact they talk little these days. It was that they had turned into one person, with another person growing somewhere inside them. Those few times when they quarreled, it was like having an argument with yourself or getting mad at yourself. And the quarrels were so half-hearted neither one bothered to finish them. What were they about, after all?

Now that Tommy had been moved inside the prison walls no one seemed to care whether he stayed in his office, as long as he clocked in at the beginning of the working day and was conspicuously present between four and five in the afternoon before punching out. Calls from the Superintendent or visits from the Supervisor came either at nine-thirty or at four in the afternoon. Since the center of his working day was uninterrupted, Tommy started going to court. At first he asked permission, then since no one seemed to care, he just went. There were trials every day, and almost every week a murder trial was in process. Soon Tommy was one of the courthouse regulars along with the stooped pensioners who couldn't stand to stay at home, the reporters with their notebooks, the sketch artists, and the occasional high school class which traipsed in on a civics assignment.

The courthouse corridor regulars always knew how far along the latest rape trial was, when the victim would take the stand, and when a capital murder was scheduled for penalty phase, when you could watch the jury deciding life or death. Penalty phase was usually the only time the defendants stood up and spoke for themselves. The rape cases drew bigger audiences than the murders, perhaps because the surviving victim was there to see, often displaying her scars. The shame of living on afterwards, of telling a husband or boyfriend, of having to recount the acts imposed in foreign, legal language, sometimes the victims seemed to choke again on the deeds, or the words. The suffering was still alive to be witnessed.

Tommy strained to hear what the lawyers said to the judge. Sometimes the lawyers huddled on one side of the bench, with the judge standing over the raised platform with his head bent over, and they all conferred in hushed voices, the incantations of a cabal. In these secret conferences the lawyers and the judge spoke over the blinking court reporter, her head bent forward like a daffodil, straddling the spindle-legged transcribing machine as if it were a rocking horse. The defendants, incongruous in suits and ties, sat with their backs to the audience, letting their lawyers plead for mercy. Tommy didn't understand what the lawyers were doing. The judge sent the jury out of the room during these discussions, and Tommy knew, he just knew the lawyers were lying most of the time. Both sides were lying. And the judge was lying too. They were lying as surely as the defendant was lying by wearing a brand new three piece suit, when his normal clothing was the grimy leather jacket covered with the victim's blood which the prosecutor held up for the jury to see.

Tommy saw three days of the trial of Johnson Dennis Johnson who was being tried for the murder, rape and kidnapping of Dolores Evan, fourteen, his landlord's stepdaughter. Two witnesses testified that Johnson was seen with her in his car on the last night she was alive, three days before her body was found in what the newspapers referred to as a wooded area, but was really a decorative band of shrubs at the border of the interstate. It took the jury two days to find Johnson guilty of murder, mostly on the evidence of pictures of his face with scratches on it soon after the murder, and hair and fiber samples taken from his car.

Johnson's mother and his nineteen-year-old sister, the family had emigrated from the Dominican Republic ten years ago, testified that he had been in the house watching television with them at the time that the pathologist estimated the murder took place. Perhaps it was that the mother and sister remembered a little too clearly what programs were on the television that night, exactly what episode, what the characters did, as if they had been told to watch a rerun. Or as if they had been studying the TV guide.

At penalty phase Johnson told the jury not to spare his life if they believed he did the terrible things done to that girl. Because then I ought to die. And if you think I'm capable of that now, think what I'll be like after thirty years in prison. So just have it over and done with. The jury was out for five days.

There was only physical evidence, circumstantial evidence. The court watchers agreed that there were few features of Johnson's life that made it worth saving. Johnson, a frail young man, sat quietly throughout, seemingly impervious to the presence in the front row of the devastated woman who was the victim's mother. As Tommy remarked to the retired gym teacher, "It's hard to imagine him doing all that, isn't it?"

The school teacher pulled her hand-knit cardigan around her shoulders. "To raise a child for that," she said, shaking her head.

A man with a ribbon of scar which ran down his cheek and into his shirt collar, closed his tobacco stained fingers. "I know what I would have done if I'd been in that jury room."

The school teacher nodded in agreement. "Send him back where he came from."

The jurors were opaque. Tommy watched the large black woman who was the foreperson in Johnson's case. Her eyes went from the judge to the lawyers to the defendant, without a blink or change in expression. Next to her a young man with a scraggly beard, he looked like a college student, was having difficulty keeping awake. As the trial progressed the juror next to him, a pleasant looking, older woman would nudge him awake, or cough, just as he was dropping off. A woman who looked about six-months pregnant was also having trouble keeping awake through the testimony on fibers, wounds and time of death. By the end of the trial you could tell who had become friends, who disliked whom, after the long hours when they were locked in together deliberating.

The defense psychiatrist put several people into a trance with his testimony about the defendant's head injuries which were supposed to have something to do with his mental capacity. Why were those scans and information about temporal lobes even relevant? What did cranium damage have to do with a fourteen-year-old being dragged into a car and then beaten to death with a hammer? By the time the trial was over the word *murder* would probably induce a yawn from every one of the fourteen jurors.

They listened as a defense social worker from New York testified that Johnson had been sexually abused. Then they listened equally respectfully to a teacher who said that Johnson beat up younger students and was known to carry brass knuckles. Johnson occasionally leaned over to ask his lawyers a question.

Throughout the trial Johnson's mother sat in the first row, a little black lady of indeterminate age. Her gray hair lay in ribs which looked ironed onto her head. Johnson was her last child before she'd had her innards out, as she put it. The defense psychiatrist said that all of Johnson's aggressive behavior was because he hated her. How could anyone hate a skinny black lady who fed her children by cleaning office buildings at night? When the prosecutor cross-examined her, she said, "Yes sir," to every question. And when the defense attorney asked her questions, she said, "Yes sir," to him too, even though that answer was now the exact opposite to what she had said previously. Johnson's mother also said that everything was in the Lord's hands now. She had done the best she could. When she was on the stand, Johnson's mother looked at him as if he was a bad boy who needed a licking. She didn't seem particularly mad at him.

The prosecution psychiatrist had enough anger for everyone in the courtroom. He called Johnson a sociopath, an emotionally stunted human being, someone who had never done a kind or considerate or courteous thing that anyone could remember, that he was worse than an animal. The defense psychiatrist emphasized his bleak childhood, the beatings and sexual abuse by the stepfather, which Johnson's mother couldn't remember, but she said might have happened, since she was away from home working most nights, and the fact that Johnson left school in fourth grade because he was termed incorrigible. Johnson's mother seemed offended by this recharacterization of his childhood. Johnson had tested very high on some intelligence tests although he barely passed from one grade to the next. The defense psychiatrist said that terms like sociopath had been discredited in the profession, and they didn't mean anything. The prosecution replied, discredited or not, a sociopath was what the jury saw before them. The jury didn't seem to understand or care very much about the debate in the professional literature. The defense attorney said his client was like a sick, dumb animal, but not evil. And Tommy thought, we know what we do with sick, dumb animals: Put them out of their misery. Put them to sleep.

Tommy missed the final day of the penalty phase because a meeting had been called by the Health Care Supervisor. When he came back the jury had been sent home after returning a verdict of death. The next morning Tommy read that Johnson laughed and laughed for hours back in his cell. The jurors said in post-verdict interviews that most of them favored death from the first day, but one juror held out for five days.

Tommy wished he could talk to Ants about these things. He even wanted to tell Ants—first swearing him to secrecy, which they used to do for girls, or cars, or money—about the true nature of his job. But Anthony was undergoing his own metamorphosis. He had fallen in love. With Julia, the daughter of a wealthy tax lawyer from Princeton. Ants was in no mood to listen. Anthony's mother called Tommy to tell him how bad it was. "Slumming," was the word Anthony's mother used, spitting out her disgust. "She's just slumming with a Pollack from Trenton." Tommy was shocked, that Ants' mother would say that about her own son.

Whatever the girl's intentions Ants hardly came around anymore. He let his hair grow, rode a motorcycle, and was a foreigner when he peeled around the corner onto Tommy and Arlette's quiet street. Arlette just stared and stared at Julia who came without lipstick and seemed to have no interest in clothes, although her very pale jeans sported a designer label. The fascination was mutual. Julia couldn't take her eyes off of Arlette's distended stomach and bloated face. They were after all the same age. From her pregnancy torpor Arlette looked at Julia's pink and white complexion with envy. Even in blue jeans, there was nothing haphazard about this young woman. Her hair was the color of white honey, with pale flecks in it.

Arlette told Tommy with an edge to her voice that such color didn't happen by itself. When Julia spoke, her voice was low and firm, each syllable clear as a school bell.

Tommy thought she had a figure to knock your eyes out. But she had a lot of silly ideas and plenty to say for herself, unasked. She had ideas about the United Nations and the President and foreign policy. And crime and lawyers, too. Listening to this confident voice emerging from such a pretty mouth, Tommy could see why Ants was in love with her. She felt sorry for prisoners, whose lives might have been straightened out by a child guidance counselor. Tommy certainly didn't believe that, and he contradicted her hotly. But it upset both Ants and Arlette when they argued. Ants had only known her for a year. Was a year of being in love a reason not to see your best friend? But Ants just didn't seem to want to come spend Saturday with Tommy, doing what they used to do, anything or nothing.

During the few hours when Arlette is not ministering to her pregnant body's incessant demands for food or sleep, she and Tommy are silent together, communicating with gestures. Tommy senses he can't reach her. It is as if she has disappeared deep inside herself, as if her whole self has wrapped itself around the creature growing inside of her. She hears what Tommy says, but she is only listening to the tiny being growing inside of her. Tommy stares at her puffy face and rounded belly with its bouncing cheerful mound of pubic hair and is happy if she is not feeling nauseous or exhausted.

Recently Arlette has become afraid to be alone in the house at night. In the evening they curl up under the comforter and watch movies on their tiny television. Arlette refuses to see anything with blood or violence. Her favorites are the melodramas, and she cries and laughs, even when she has seen the film before. It is as if the pregnancy—something they started together—has thrown up a wall between them and around them. The pregnancy, a simple bodily function, has transported Arlette's spirit into a realm where Tommy cannot follow. Tommy stands at the gate waiting for her to return. When he is not with her he feels fiercely protective. He restrains himself from calling home in the middle of the day. And when they venture outside Tommy positions himself to shield the round bump where the baby is swimming in wait.

The county prosecutor hadn't even bothered to inform George and his partner that the case against their two assailants had been concluded. Tommy heard by chance that the kids were scheduled for sentencing. George got dressed in a suit and tie, and he and Tommy sat for hours waiting for the case to be called. George asked his partner if he wanted to come, but he was already back at work. "You're better off forgetting all that," he told George. "You'll never get satisfaction there."

Finally, after listening to the incomprehensible legalese, when George had just told Tommy he was ready to go home, the judge announced their case. The defendants both had aliases, and they had both entered pleas to aggravated assault. The audience in the courtroom was very grave when the two boys, they seemed shockingly young, were escorted into the court with an armed guard in shackles. A woman in the front row, Tommy assumed it was one of the mothers, buried her head in a blue Kleenex. Before the judge pronounced sentence, he delivered a lecture about the importance of setting an example. The two boys stood with their heads bowed and said nothing. But the fact was the kids would be out on the street again in six months.

As they filed out of the courtroom, their chains clanking, George caught the eye of the taller one. "Did you see that?" George's voice was shaking. "He recognized me."

"How do you know?" Tommy asked, leaning forward. George's voice carried over the coming and goings of defendants and lawyers.

The uniformed bailiff frowned and leaned over to silence George with a tap on the shoulder. The next case had started. A new group of defendants and lawyers stood up below the judge who stifled a yawn.

"I don't want to hear about it," Gloria said when they came home. It made her sick to her stomach to think of those kids getting out. "And you..." she said accusingly to Tommy. "The taxpayers pay you to take care of the..." Then, under her breath she said "...bastards."

Tommy was so surprised to hear his mother say "bastards" that the unformed accusation against himself didn't register. Besides Tommy's two cousins were at the house and they wanted to talk football.

"I can't believe your mother said 'bastards,'" Arlette said. Arlette spends hours on the phone talking to Gloria. Once Gloria hinted that her son could have done better than to marry a neighborhood girl with no college, but now Arlette is the daughter she never had. At first Gloria didn't want Tommy to know, but Arlette got it out of her. Gloria had gone to the doctor. It wasn't certain yet. They were still doing tests.

Tests? What kind of tests, Tommy asked. But Arlette just said they were doing tests—female tests. Tommy could tell when Arlette was talking to Gloria about medical things because she'd pull the phone receiver around the corner, go into the tiny closet and close the door. She talked from among the raincoats and jackets while only the curled blue phone cord emerged from inside the closet. Neither of them would tell Tommy anything.

When Arlette had these long, secret telephone conversations with Gloria, Tommy walked out onto their small back porch and stared at the metal door of the garage. The inside was jammed with half-empty paint cans, splintered lumber, and a broken power mower. Its dull tar-paper roof became a source of glory during the week when the purple magnolia tree bloomed and its flowers were draped across it.

Mr. Russo next door often greeted Tommy by asking Tommy if he had a nice day. Tommy remembered the gentle purple and white tulip blossoms carelessly releasing their faint perfume into the cluttered yard. Tommy couldn't remember if it had been a nice day or not. He'd been inside all day, first at the office, then at the courthouse. The summer fragrance of the river reminded Tommy of how much he hated being indoors all day.

Tommy was surprised Arlette didn't seem to miss her job. Bending over with laughter, until he had to laugh too, Arlette used to tell Tommy and Gloria how the secretaries called and pretended to be a collection agency when they wanted the clients to pay their legal bills, and the outrageous lies they told to cover up for the lawyers when they couldn't be found. No, Arlette didn't seem to miss any of it. Arlette who was always grabbing your hand and pulling it, saying look at that, now didn't seem to need anybody or want to do anything. Arlette who jumped up a half dozen times during dinner, until an exasperated Gloria would command her to sit still, was now happy to stare lazily at the television all evening, eating rocky road ice cream from the carton Tommy had picked up for her on the way home. Arlette said the ice cream tasted bad when it was kept in the freezer for even a single day, so Tommy brought home a fresh pint every day.

Tommy thought it tasted fine when he finished off the rest of it at two in the morning as he sat in the semi-dark living room in front of the television with the sound off. In the middle of the night Tommy's dreams frequently startle him. He sits up with his teeth clenched and his neck in a vise, after drifting off to sleep curled against Arlette's side, his arms thrown across her stomach. At midnight his eyes snap open, the lids rolling up as tight as the sprung window shade in his office.

In his dreams, Darby merged with Dr. Smyth, his friendly, white-haired physician. Or Anthony was a prisoner at the CSU, trying to call Tommy over to his cell when they both knew Tommy couldn't talk to prisoners while he was on duty. Once in his dreams Julia came to him. Then Tommy was put in the embarrassing position of telling Anthony to be quiet, of hiding their friendship, of pretending they didn't recognize each other. In the dream Anthony hardly spoke any English, was no more comprehensible than Benjamin, and Tommy was always laboriously keeping the CSU daily log. Frequently what he was writing was incomprehensible, even to himself, as strange as Chinese ideographs. Or Tommy was swimming away from the CSU, towards his coffin-like office, or down the gray-green basement corridor to room B1309, where in his dreams the rabbit had his permanent den under water.

These dreams caused Tommy to leave the sighing, sleep-sour body of his pregnant wife. He padded the few yards into the boxy living room. There he stared away his nightmares by watching a screen filled with silent, flickering figures of a manageable dimension, who then blended with and blotted out the images in his dreams and the replay of the day's events in his mind's eye.

VI

The fat priest, he wasn't much older than Tommy, walked down the aisle in front of the casket, swinging the smoldering incense, chanting the prayers, loudly. Almost embarrassingly loudly, Tommy thought. Tommy stood beside the first pew of the small Catholic church with Gloria, Arlette, now obviously and awkwardly pregnant, and George, who wore a rented black suit under protest. Gloria threw up her hands and begged Tommy to talk to him. It had been—just like that—Gloria told everyone. No sickness. No warning. Uncle Mike had just dropped dead of a heart attack. Not really dropped dead. But fallen over. In his car, on the street. He was found by one of his old buddies on the force who responded to an anonymous caller who noticed a new Cadillac stalled in the middle of the street with the driver slumped over the wheel. The policeman approached with his gun drawn, and then put it away sadly. When a uniformed officer arrived at Gloria's door at four o'clock on Saturday, Gloria's voice rose and rose, calling George. She thought, it must be Tommy. Something had happened to Tommy or Arlette. George was struck dumb. It was another unanticipated body blow.

The funeral came at the end of three days of people. People at Gloria's house. People sitting on folding chairs at the funeral home. People eating, people drinking, people smoking, and people laughing. Gloria cried and cried, until she had no more tears, then she was transported back to an earlier time, and Tommy was shocked to hear her laughter, curiously transformed into a mirthless sound. That was the strangest part. It was a party. Neighbors and cousins who hadn't seen one another in years caught up with each other's lives. For the first time in his memory Tommy felt he was not in the forefront of his mother's consciousness. She had gone somewhere else to grieve, back to the time before he was born.

Members of the force who had retired or moved came to talk about the changes—none of them good—which had taken place since the new chief took over. These police officers loved each other and Mike. They all flirted with Gloria and one seemed to be an old flame. Men Tommy didn't know came and threw their arms around him. When Tommy said he worked in the prison, these men nodded. At least you aren't a lawyer, one said. Maybe they thought he was a lawyer because he was wearing his wedding suit, the one dark suit he owned. One thing was clear, they all regarded him as the man in the house now.

The women embraced him and searched his face tearfully. Uncle Mike had never married, and he used to say Gloria and George and Tommy were his only family, but it turned out he had several lady friends. They all knew who Tommy was and about Arlette and the baby. Tommy embraced their unfamiliar bodies mechanically, without quite getting their names. Funny, Mike never mentioning any of them.

The little Trenton church had new stained-glass windows. Tommy hadn't been inside the church for years in spite of, or perhaps because of, Gloria's protestations. Tommy remembered the church as dark, but now celebrating his uncle's death the church was flooded with light. The blues and reds and yellows of the new stained-glass pictures were bright as cartoon colors. Surrounding them the plaster was white, as shiny and white as the priest's surplice. Two altar boys, one blond and one dark, swung the incense behind the priest. They were more angelic than the blunt-featured women with heavy gauze-covered arms who were pictured as guarding heaven.

Gloria picked out an expensive casket, a heavy silver-gray model, which bore a stylistic resemblance to Mike's Cadillac, Tommy thought. George said it was ridiculous to spend thousands of dollars on a box which was going in the ground. Gloria said, fine, she'd spend her own savings for it. Tommy had never heard them fight, and he didn't know Gloria had her own money. Then it turned out that Mike had a policeman's burial policy which paid for the casket, the funeral and everything. The heavy casket sat up high on its rubber-wheeled cart, covered with a white silk cloth with a gold embroidered cross throughout the ceremony. The white and gold cloth dropped ceremoniously to the floor in heavy folds, like drapery on a graveyard statue, when it was pulled off.

Flowers were banked at both sides of the altar. Most prominent was a large blue and white wreath in the shape of a policeman's badge with Mike's number, ten ten, in blue carnations at the center. Throughout the chanting, the raising and lowering of the chalice, the taking of the wafer on the tongue, the drinking of the blood, the wiping away of the human touch with a white satin cloth, Tommy kept glancing over at the blue and white badge made out of flowers. The wreath was propped on an easel, so that it was level with the altar. So that was what being a cop came down to, a corny wreath at your funeral with your number on it.

Tommy and the other five pall bearers lifted the silver and gray casket on their shoulders and placed it gently on the red extended tongue of carpet from the hearse, then stood silently as it was withdrawn. Tommy shivered as the coffin slid onto the red carpet. The shield of flowers followed in its own separate limousine, ahead of the family.

In June of 1984 the newspapers seemed to carry more than the usual quantum of greed, misery and suffering. The averted faces of American boy soldiers, their shoulders weighed down with expensive weaponry, stared blankly out of the front page from the camera flattened backdrop of jungle. They looked like bewildered, reluctant killers who wished they were watching the war on television.

At home the most recent murder involved a young Hispanic, Enrico Ruiz, who kidnapped a couple of white teenagers parked near a lake. Raped the girl, shot the boyfriend in the head, then shot the girl in the back and left her for dead. She survived to make the identification, but was paralyzed for life. The jury didn't take long. In four hours they came back with a unanimous verdict: guilty. Another two hours, and they voted for death, with no mitigation. The murderer was eighteen at his trial. It wasn't clear how much he understood about the goings-on in the courtroom. His attorney and some civil liberties organization were quoted in the morning newspapers as saying that one of the principal issues on appeal would be whether the law permitted the execution of someone who was a juvenile at the time of the crime. His lawyer was quoted as saying after the verdict, "he's just a kid."

"A kid?" Tommy blurted it out loud in the kitchen. "You can't call someone who does that a kid."

"Tommy?" Arlette's voice was distant, feminine. Tommy was waiting for the water to boil again so he could bring her tea and toast. "What's the matter?"

"Nothing. Nothing." Those lawyers! They ought to go on trial instead of the killers. Tommy burned his tongue on his coffee and then banged his mug down on the kitchen table, splashing hot liquid on his hand as well.

There had been some spotting in the sixth month, and Arlette had been ordered to stay in bed. Tommy walked into the bedroom, waving his arms and carrying the newspaper. Arlette looked so pasty Tommy forgot what he was saying. He opened the window and plumped up a pillow behind her back. She gave him a watery smile. Her belly was stretched now, although the rest of her body was still thin. She was only comfortable lying half on her side with a pillow under one knee. The doctor was concerned about blood clots too. Arlette, who had never been sick a day in her life, turned out to be fragile in pregnancy. Sometimes she cried and said she always wanted ten children, but she didn't think she could stand to go through this even one more time. Who would have expected this? She had always been healthy as a horse.

By any objective standard Arlette now looks terrible, but every blemish and distention is heartbreakingly dear to Tommy. He lies next to her, and the warmth radiates from her belly into his groin and up to his chest. Now when he laces his fingers over her belly Tommy feels the poke of a tiny elbow or the bump of a heel. When they lie next to one another they watch the ripples circumnavigate her navel. Only a few more weeks now. Gloria has the days until the due date marked off in red on the kitchen calendar, and Tommy secretly goes and counts them. When Tommy feels so angry he thinks his head is about to blow off, he thinks of the feathery signals from his baby, turning beneath his fingers in its watery sleep.

All month the prison had been in an uproar. Johnson has suffered a religious conversion. He was baptized during a contact visit with his Spiritual Advisor, a man who wore a long gold embroidered robe. Before the guards realized what was going on the Minister, he called himself God's One and Only True Minion, had taken a paper cup full of water from the children's drinking fountain in the visiting room and poured it over Johnson's head. Now Johnson decided he didn't want to appeal his death sentence. He confessed to the murder. He said he was ready to die and go directly to heaven, as God's Only Minister told him he would. The gates of heaven would be wide open and waiting for him. He wanted to talk to God himself about all his crimes as soon as possible and get everything settled once and for all. His lawyers' desperate pleas for his silence were blissfully ignored, nor were the lawyers successful in blocking the publication of these statements.

God's One and Only True Minion was his only counsel now, and his defense attorneys could do little more than wring their hands as they attempted to get a court order to cut off his communications with the outside. How did the reporters get through to him with so little trouble, the lawyers wondered, when visitors to the death house were supposedly strictly scrutinized.

None of these technicalities bothered Johnson who publicly entrusted his immortality to God's One and Only True Minion. He needed no other intermediaries in this world or the next, not the court which he preferred not to have protect him, not lawyers who said they were acting on his behalf, not any other ordinary counselor. He fired his public defenders who promptly took the matter to court, where a special hearing was held. The court appointed other lawyers to represent him against his wishes. Johnson said he didn't mind being the first, in fact he preferred it. God couldn't miss him coming in, if he were first. Let the little children learn not to fear death from his example.

Two weeks later he went on a hunger strike. The Super-intendent called in Tommy and the Nisei doctor and told them they might have to attach and monitor the IV's if the court upheld the decision to force-feed the prisoner. In the meantime TV crews and newspaper reporters waited outside the prison gates every day and asked everyone who came in and out about Johnson's condition, as if Johnson was the most important person in the place. The reporters regularly intercepted the Chief Warden on his way to work in the morning, and he used the opportunity to mention deficiencies in correctional budgets. God's One and Only True Minion was a tall white man who wore a fez and a majestic beard. Sometimes when he waited in the corridor during the count, prisoners could be heard to catcall, "Hey, white boy." The way he swooped in and out twice a day, every time causing consternation among the guards assigned to pat and frisk all visitors, might well convince anyone he had the ear of the Lord. Those voluminous flowing robes could have concealed anything, as well as a large man. The prison always assigned special guards to take him aside to be frisked, and everyone always came out of the little cubicle smiling.

The prison officials racked their brains for an excuse to keep him out, but the Spiritual Advisor did lay claim to a congregation of sorts, a ragtag band who lived in tents in a field without electricity or running water while they waited for the Second Coming. The regulations were vague about the definition of clergy, but they clearly envisioned visits by ministers. The Attorney General advised the Superintendent there might be a legal problem if the Spiritual Advisor were categorically barred when other, more conventional church people were admitted. None of this made sense to Tommy. The lawyers made everything worse and then fought with one another. Every fight, every snag required a court appearance and new papers to be filed.

After every visit from God's One and Only True Minion Johnson repeated his vow to starve himself into heaven as rapidly as possible, if the authorities refused to carry out his wish for the more humane method of execution. God's One and Only True Minion spoke in riddles from his painted van which was given a special space in the prison parking lot. His words seemed to add up to saying that Johnson was now in a position of moral superiority to the victims, who had simply had the misfortune to be murdered. The long, bearded face of the Spiritual Advisor began to appear regularly in the newspapers as part of the stories about the hunger strike. His following grew. All the spaces for tents in the open field were filled. The surrounding householders worried about sanitary conditions. Several community meetings were held, but nothing was done. The tent community was technically in compliance with the arguably inadequate health regulations. Johnson refused to meet with the lawyers assigned by the court, but motions and arguments on his behalf were carried on anyway. The usual array of organizations lined up in predictable postures on both sides.

Then when the public was getting tired of the Spiritual Advisor's beatific gaze and the details of the menus Johnson refused, Darby had a gall bladder attack. He sued to have his own doctor brought in after claiming that the prison doctor was a sadist who examined him with out-of-date equipment, before incorrectly diagnosing his condition as indigestion. An out-of-state pro bono lawyer filed a million dollar damage claim against the doctor, the Superintendent, the Commissioner of the Prisons, and the Governor, all in their personal capacity. The big numbers nudged Johnson and God's One and Only True Minion right off the crime pages.

Darby was almost as gifted at public relations as God's One and Only True Minion. He had a knack for getting reporters to print his complaints about his health and prison conditions. Who would have thought anyone cared about either? He made fun of the institutional rules, the guards, and the Superintendent. He even made jokes at his own expense. Two publishers offered him a book contract for his autobiography. He filed suit against his first defense trial attorney who had signed a book contract himself for Darby's life story and an account of the trial. Darby claimed he was too upset to know what he was signing when the lawyer produced a consent form with his signature. Darby gave out the unlisted phone number on the wing, and Darby's opinions on copyright and the ethics of publishers as well as lawyers were featured in the Sunday newspaper. It took the prison officials two weeks to get the number changed again, and for another week the calls for Darby from reporters were rerouted to a nursing home where they were sporadically answered by a sentient person. Everyone seemed to have forgotten that two months ago Darby had been convicted of two murders of defenseless young women, and it was likely he would be convicted of more.

At least the guys at the CSU knew who they were. They were the guys who the state was going to kill. Their deaths belonged to the public. They were celebrities. They could say anything, and anything could be said about them. They were going to die so they could be treated as if they were dead already. Everyone liked to read about them. They passed the time in different ways. Davenport, the accountant who had killed his wife and children, was obsessed with numerology. At the slightest hint of interest from anyone he would bring out complicated charts and magic number squares, showing how a set of prime numbers always summed to the same number, a magic number, across, diagonally, up or down. Didn't it prove the existence of a rational order?

Sometimes Tommy was assigned to check in the visitors. The regulations required that all headgear be removed before entering the visitors' lounge. A single embrace was allowed at the beginning and end of the visit. Otherwise no bodily contact was permitted during the visit, except hand-holding. Anyone who might be a girlfriend had to be turned into a wife. Guards asked for marriage licenses. Men who had dismembered women and beaten them insensible now sat on plastic chairs and held hands with their women, like teenagers.

The regulations governed when to eat, when to go to work, when to have a phone call, when to have a shower. And death row had more rules, more special treatment. Men who never restrained themselves, who shot and killed on an impulse, had every aspect of their life monitored by a camera and the rules on blue paper. The language of the regulations was the language of no man or woman. It was language with all traces of emotion bleached out. Sentences used the passive voice, and whenever a particularly gruesome or distasteful act was described, such as killing a prisoner, or the removal of a dead body, a stream of multisyllabic words poured over the page. The act of killing became the implementation of the warrant appointing the execution date. The pushing of the button for killing became the carrying out of the instructions pursuant to the administrative plan manual subdivision (a) of the subsection concerned with carrying out the dated execution warrant. Tommy's mind fogged over when he read the regulations. His mind was on a carousel passing the same streamered sentences time and time again, watching the painted phrases going up and down. Were they doing it, or weren't they? Who did it? And would he do it?

"That fellow Darby," George said. "He has the gift of gab." Then George started to laugh. "Come on, mama," he said to Gloria. George got up from the table, held his arms above his head and snapped his fingers, while swaying and moving his feet slowly in a circle. It was not like any dancing Tommy had seen before. "I'm not dead yet." His clothes hung on him, and he was carelessly shaven. His movements were disjointed, as if his extremities had been thrown at his trunk and stuck there.

Gloria shook her head, but she smiled. Then Tommy got up and imitated his father's dancing. Gloria laughed at Tommy, and said, "Look how fat you've gotten!" And Tommy stuck out what was now a beer belly. "I'm pregnant," he said and threw his mother a kiss.

"At least Mom laughed," Tommy said to Arlette when he got home.

Since Arlette couldn't leave the house without permission from the doctor, Tommy now went out for food, bringing back leaky silver-paper packages which left a spicy smell in the car's innards for days.

Arlette finished off her chicken wing and chewed the end of the bone. Tommy was rubbing her ankles. The TV was running behind Tommy's back. Arlette pointed to a figure on the screen with a greasy finger. "That woman won five million dollars in a lottery." Tommy handed her a Kleenex, and Arlette wiped her hands. The woman who won the lottery and her husband were holding hands. No, they wouldn't do anything special with the money. Sell their trailer and move into a mansion? Why? That was their home. Get new teeth, the woman said giggling, pulling her husband's arm up with her hand and covering her mouth.

The news switched to a clump of African children, their spiked arms and legs stripped of flesh and dusty black, like the sharp remnants of trees after a forest fire. When the camera zoomed closer their eyes seemed all whites except for a well of hunger at their center, which seemed to take in the whole house, white starched curtains, greasy food containers, and the sleepy overfed couple on the couch. Tommy put his head down, and Arlette changed the channel. Tommy heard a familiar voice. The Superintendent was answering a reporter's questions about Johnson's hunger strike. How long could he hold out, an offstage voice asked. The Superintendent looked straight at Tommy from the screen and answered gravely.

"There's your boss!" Arlette said. "He looks funny."

The Superintendent said that starvation was a painful way to die, but since Johnson had a constitutional right to refuse medical treatment the prison would not give him pain killers against his will. But yes, they were considering forced feeding through a tube. No, that was not medical treatment. A final decision had not yet been made, and probably a court order would be required.

"Oh, God," Tommy said. He reached over Arlette's stomach for the monitor. That probably means me, he said to himself. I hope they don't call me in.

Arlette put down her plate with its small, shiny bones picked clean and curled onto her side. She pulled Tommy's head to her and stroked his hair. They had been practicing breathing, and Tommy easily synchronized his own breath to the rise and fall of her breasts. Inhaling the sweet combination of barbeque sauce, chicken fat, baby powder, and cologne, Tommy dozed off as Arlette turned off the sound.

When there was a security crisis or a holiday, Tommy was called to substitute for the regular guards who had put in long, overtime hours. He filled in at the prison mail room. For four hours a day he slit open letters to inmates, looking for cash, drugs, razor blades, or pornographic pictures. The inmates decorated their cells with poster-sized pictures of naked women, some in bondage, some with swollen breasts and buttocks. The women serenely unfolded their sexual organs. There had been a motion to take down such pictures after a church group toured the prison. Darby issued a statement when a court found the proposed order unconstitutional.

Tommy wasn't supposed to read the letters to prisoners, but he did. Many were unintelligible, with childishly drawn capital letters and misspelled words. Mostly, they were just messages, messages with a pained urgency. A mother wrote about her surgery. Four weeks in the hospital but now, thank God, she could get down to the cellar. Hot denials from girlfriends which picked right up from the slam down hang up of last week's phone call. Solicitations offering legal assistance. Pleas from those who couldn't make it to visit. The baby was sick, and its mother didn't know a doctor. She didn't make it to the welfare office to pick up the check. I had to go to work, and I was too tired to do anything else. The pennies were squealing from being pinched so hard. It was enough to make a man yearn to be out on the street where he could at least steal a car.

Some prisoners conducted several passionate epistolary romances simultaneously from behind bars. Others met a woman, convinced her she was in love, and got married, and all while they were locked up within the prison walls. A marriage sometimes warranted a single conjugal visit, but sometimes it didn't.

In the visitors' lounge desultory teenagers chewed gum and twirled the red, plug-in phones by their coiled cords. Were these kids in tight jeans and high heels wives? Baby sisters? Girlfriends? If they weren't prancing around the plastic floor or pawing the ground, they were lying down flat out on the red benches, blowing smoke at the ceiling. Then in a small stall, a cylindrical phone booth, they would plug in their red telephone and shout to their friend, father, brother, or husband, gesticulating to the upper half of him visible through the barrier.

Tommy began to slip away from the office more often. Johnson had begun taking water and some food. Things were temporarily calm. If the rabbit man was not there, no one else cared what he did. When he was there the rabbit man didn't notice or comment upon his absences. Tommy would arrive first thing in the morning, make a couple of phone calls to register his presence, then disappear for four or five hours. He either sat in court, or went to the basement where he played checkers on a rippling black and red portable board with a guard who had worked there so long he could tell a supervisor's footstep half a corridor away, in plenty of time to roll up and stash the board, slip the checkers into his pants pockets, and light a cigarette. This guard had been at the prison for so long he knew how to get everything done. The other guards and even the inmates asked him for advice. "We're nothing but a cap and pair of pants to them," this guard was fond of saying. It wasn't clear whether "them" was the prisoners or the bosses, but Tommy found himself agreeing to both versions.

The guards hated courts, judges and lawyers. They talked about the appeals going on and on forever. They said, by the time the feds get around to the new death sentences we'll all be retired. And it was true, wasn't it? The courts seemed to have endless amounts of time for these death cases, but a civil case couldn't get a hearing. The appeals dragged on for years, with the costs multiplying exponentially, as the legal system chased its own tail. Still, Tommy was relieved it was all taking so long. Then it wasn't Tommy's problem, was it? He didn't make the decision. It was his job to run law books from Darby's cell back and forth to the library. It was Tommy's job to write in the daily log book for the CSU every time he brought a book of cases for Darby or delivered a holy message for Benjamin. His entries included the time and place: "delivered law books (three)" or "No. 6 shouting, 10 p.m. to 10:45 p.m. January 31. Others yelled at him to shut up."

The rest of the prison activities revolved around the count. Three times a day all prisoners had to be counted and located. The count took over an hour three times a day, and no one, guard or prisoner, could move from one wing to another while the count was being called out over the loudspeaker. If there was a discrepancy in the totals for a wing or section, all the names for that wing were read out over the loudspeaker and the prisoners answered individually by their names and numbers.

The prison was old, except for the death house which had been refurbished and included the latest technical innovations in security. In the rest of the prison the walls, the windows, and the offices were dirty and surpassingly ugly. No one was to be gratified by being here. There was not a colorful picture, nor a graceful curve anywhere. The doors were opened by an old computer buried in a central control room.

The guards, most of whom had barely graduated from high school, were like the astronauts trapped in a space craft, at the mercy of the people far away. They were powerless to change the trajectory of their ship or open the doors. The control panel was crude, wooden with big red and green lights. It looked as if it had been hammered together on weekends in the prison shop, and it probably had been. Buzzers went off as the men stared out through a thick plastic bullet-proof barrier. God help the guard who was taken hostage, since everyone else would be huddled in here. If the prison went up in a riot, the control room operators would be encased in a bubble, pushing buttons and sounding alarms, hoping the electricity would not be cut.

The death house was the most modern, even luxurious, part of the place. It had been rebuilt as soon as the penalty was reenacted, with shiny chrome plumbing and thick plastic and metal doors and computerized locks. The count was simple here, everyone was always in his cell. For the death house inmates there was no sitting in booths and shouting into telephone receivers. Members of their families, their teams of defense lawyers, and the clergy visited in a new, clean and separate room.

Darby had no visitors except his many lawyers. His step-mother never came from California for the trial and had been quoted as saying that she hoped the State would execute him because there never had been anything good about him. He refused to see the Catholic priest, who he called a turned-collar publicity seeker. Darby had been granted special permission to bring in a computer, and a death penalty fanatic donated the money for online library access. At night he wrote long memos to his ever-changing cadre of lawyers. Occasionally he wrote letters and drafted petitions for the others.

As for Johnson, his mother and sister visited regularly. Now that the hunger strike had stopped they came with a celebratory air. Darby wrote a legal-sounding petition for Benjamin to have his own minister present at his execution. After all, the rules provided for it, didn't they? Didn't they come right out and say in the regulations that if a condemned person made a request in writing a clergyman of his choice could be present at the event. The clergyman would be allowed to sit with the witnesses, six adults chosen from the public by the Superintendent, and the eight representatives of the news media. Tommy read it himself in the regulations.

Tommy spent three days a week in the death wing. One of his jobs was to answer their questions about the regulations. Of course he wasn't a lawyer, and some of the prisoners knew more about the law than he did. But he tried. The regulations seemed clear enough on their face. They all had copies. But questions arose nonetheless. Another part of his job was to keep the log of the death house. He wrote down who came and went, who sent letters, who was working out in his cell with barbells, and who didn't eat their dinner. Over the course of months some of the inmates had become friendly, and he held brief shouted conversations with them which were listened to by everyone else.

Every Thursday Tommy had to monitor the death row prisoners taking their mandated showers. He stood in his clothes at the edge of the curtainless communal shower and watched as Darby, curiously slight but pot-bellied, vigorously soaped his flopping genitals, lathered the straggly hair under his arms, while occasionally glancing over his shoulder at Tommy. As if to ask, hey, you never seen a naked man before? Griselli sang hymns as he soaped his stomach and groin. Davenport was silent and straight, letting the water fall like rain over his body.

Benjamin stood under the steady stream with his back to Tommy and asked only to have the water turned on as hot as possible. Tommy was afraid that he would burn himself, but as hot as possible was not scalding hot, although the steam billowed out into the unit. The prison never let the water get above 100 degrees. Benjamin always turned his front away from Tommy. He was as modest as a school girl. He reached around behind him for the towel Tommy held out and immediately wrapped it around his waist.

Tommy complained to the Supervisor that he shouldn't have to stand there holding the towel, like some locker room attendant. We can't issue them the towels, the Supervisor said simply. They could strangle themselves. But Tommy still didn't like it, standing there holding the towel like a servant. Sometimes he left it on the back of the chair outside the shower and when the inmate was finished he stepped back to get it. It was absolutely contrary to the regulations to ever turn your back on an inmate. Once Tommy felt a chill of fear, and he was certain someone was eyeing his back. Tommy didn't follow all the rules to the letter, anyway. How could you? Only a robot or a fool could completely conform to all the rules. They were made up by people who sat in offices somewhere, not people who had been here.

Because the building took three times longer to refurbish than was expected and cost five times more than estimated, an arbitrary number of cells were set aside late in the construction calendar. There were so many special provisions for prisoners sentenced to death the Unit cost many times more than the other cellblocks. Already the CSU was far too small. The men had to be kept apart from one another, after all they had been found unfit to remain in society. But they had to have a place where they could meet in privacy and confidence with their lawyers. Their lawyers were all enormously suspicious of anyone overhearing their conversations. As if all the appeals weren't hopeless anyway. Tommy locked the lawyers in with the clients and peered through the long thin observation window every fifteen minutes, as required by the regulations. Usually the inmate would be nodding while the lawyer talked. Sometimes the lawyer would be writing and nodding, and the prisoner would be talking. Sometimes they both sat without speaking. Tommy had a grudging respect for a few of the lawyers, especially the ones who represented the crazy ones. He thought they earned their money.

What about the women? That was something Tommy always wondered about. He knew they didn't let the women prisoners in with the men, except in that one place where only men over fifty-five could go. Where were they going to put the woman who burned her three children to death in a fire she set in her own home, standing outside while she listened to them scream. The mother said she was saving them from suffering in a cruel world. She told a reporter she thought the children were about to be sexually abused by her estranged husband. He had just been granted custody after she had been found to be mentally unstable. There was apparently some factual basis for both conclusions. She herself knew suffering; she had regularly been beaten by the same husband. Now he was going to take away her children. Where were they going to put her, if the jury decided she was sane enough to be sentenced to death. Arlette said she couldn't stand to see the woman's picture or to hear anything about the case.

When Tommy drove at night through the capital—some blocks were as devastated as a war zone—he saw the dudes in black leather coming out of their lairs to claim the city. The gleaming metal and glass office buildings of official authority were deserted shells at six o'clock, their white fluorescent lights blazing for the cleaning crews who went from cubicle to office, pushing askew the gray furniture, slipping open desk drawers, taking the bits of forgotten change, a sweater, or stamps. The faceless cleaning people regularly took the apple or candy bar left on a desk top. Occasionally they made off with a jacket or a pair of shoes. These men and women in iron-gray uniforms who came with large plastic bins on rubber wheels left no traces of themselves, no sign they had been there. Until, perhaps after several days, an attorney missed a silver pen, or his spare suit was gone, the one kept in the claptrap temporary closet for an unexpected call to court. Or a typist missed her souvenir coin from Caesar's Palace. Where did all the lifted bits and pieces go, and who ate the food? Did all those relics from the daytime inhabitants drift from one household to another, flotsam in the swirl of daily life until they came to rest in a child's hand, or a mother's kitchen.

Tommy hated driving through the city, although this summer evening as he came home from a night shift a soft warm summer rain blessed the scene indiscriminately. The filthy streets, the now straggly trees starved for fresh air, the crumbling, boarded-up buildings near the train station, once the tenements and then the family homes of immigrants who came to work in the pottery factories. Now a different pack of kids dragged the pot-holed streets in their souped-up cars—looking for a sale, or a buy, or a pickup, or a trick. But never for work. They never looked for work. No one seemed to just work for a living anymore.

Before his accident Tommy's father had worked every day in his life. No one gave George anything, not even a job. Gloria, too. She went to her Uncle's dry cleaning shop every morning, did the books in a cluttered cubicle, surrounded by a clatter and the steam of the huge cleaning machines. All around her women like herself ran up hems, replaced tattered linings, and laughed at the irreverent jokes of the young girls, most of them right out of high school, who stood at the cash register. These gum-chewing sassy girls dumped the dirty clothes in a bag, grumbled as they tracked down the missing shirts, and swore they weren't going to work anymore when they got married, or won the lottery. Well, Gloria and the other women didn't think they were going to work forever either. They took this job, or another one just like it, just temporarily. To pay off the Christmas bills, or to pay the doctor, or because a husband was drunk, or laid up, or in the army, or had run off, or died. Someone had to carry on. Then they just kept working for years and years after that unpaid Christmas. They too had thought that when they got married and had kids, of course they'd quit working. But it didn't work out that way. They stayed on, developed varicose veins from standing behind the counter, just like their mothers and aunts who had worked their whole lives, too. Where were all those women who didn't work, it must be somewhere else, in another place.

Someone was putting gas in those noisy cars. The clothes the unemployed wore were sharper than anything hanging in Tommy's closet. They go to jail and then complain they had to steal cars or TVs to feed themselves. Back on the street on poverty bail in forty-eight hours, the crooks would be in their satin and leather riding around in new cars. A lie. It's a lie, Tommy said out loud to himself, as he drove past the desecrated cemetery opposite the railroad station.

Tommy avoided eye contact with the guys in the car next to him who were checking out his car at the stoplight. One held a huge silver radio on his lap, blasting rock music onto the shining street loud enough to awaken the soldiers from the Battle of Trenton. The driver was hanging out the window and shouting to a fat girl—she couldn't have been more than thirteen—leaning against the cast-iron fence of the graveyard. A few wispy fruit trees struggled to survive, and from out of a bed of broken colored glass and used sanitary napkins, the purple leaves of a plum tree displayed their perfect beauty. Tommy ignored the man in the passenger seat who wore a tight blue turban made from a mesh stocking. Around his wrist was a bracelet of scars and his biceps were decorated with inky black tatoos of snakes and women.

Glad to be home, Tommy stuffed Mike's big car into the only parking space left on his small street. Gloria and George, who never took vacations, had gone for an extended stay with some cousins at the shore, and Tommy felt more than ever that he and Arlette lived on a desert island. In Chambersburg the houses marched to the edge of the sidewalk with no green frill of lawn. The awnings were bolted up, as if in permanent eye-opening surprise. Some houses had tiny concrete front porches, sheltered from the sun and rain by a plastic overhang crimped into the kind of bumpy waves which had been fashionable as hairstyles thirty years ago. Tommy and Arlette were the only young people on the block.

The awnings cast green shadows on the gray concrete. Crossing that green shadow before his door, Tommy felt the day's questions slip away. He didn't care if some prisoner starved himself or whether Darby sold his life story three times over. He slipped open the door and wrapped the stillness around himself. Arlette was sleeping, and her sleeping cast a spell of dreaming over the house. From the kitchen faint voices, first a man talking rapidly, then a women laughing. Tommy's skin crawled, but it was just the portable TV perched akimbo on the windowsill. The kitchen smelled of apples and cinnamon. Arlette lay on top of the unmade bed in her loose dress with her arms over her head. There were dark circles around her closed eyes.

Tommy shut the bedroom door and sat at the plastic kitchen table, where the black face of the oven stared back at him unblinkingly. He took a beer from the refrigerator without getting up and put his head down on the table, his hand soothed by the cool, wet bottle. No more questions tonight.

VII

The Health Care Supervisor called a special meeting of all the death house personnel in early August to explain the status of Benjamin's and Johnson's case. Johnson's death sentence had been reversed, and the judge had imposed a life sentence, finding that the hold-out juror had been coerced. He would be transferred from the death house. Tommy wondered if anyone would pay attention to any hunger strike which took place off of death row.

Everyone had read the newspapers and was wondering if Benjamin would be allowed consent to execution and reject all appeals. The Superintendent had said unequivocally that executions were not issued on demand. And no one would be executed until all court appeals were completed and all due process complied with. The Superintendent frowned as he said this. Other officials were heard to comment that it would save the State some money to get it over with. In addition to Tommy, at the meeting there was the Nisei doctor, a custodian assigned to the special post-execution cleanup, or disposal duties, a registered nurse, a certified IV technician, one of the dieticians from the prison kitchen, the clerk who was responsible for clearing the authorized visitors and witnesses, and the guard assigned to monitor the special telephone line from the Governor's office. There were also two or three others Tommy didn't recognize.

The guard was a portly, serene black man with a limp who walked with the rolling gait of a sailor. He gave the impression of having seen a lot of strange things come and go in his lifetime, and of having long ago stopped trying to figure them out. He listened and listened and never said a word or asked a question. He was also the only person in the room who went out of his way to be polite. Perhaps this assignment was a way to give him light duty until retirement. The regular guards took punishing abuse from the inmates, both black and white. With the new long sentences some prisoners were looking at fifty years before they would see a parole officer. The atmosphere inside had become poisonous.

The Health Care Supervisor explained that it was possible that the operational staff would be called upon to perform their duties earlier than expected. Everyone had expected the appeals process to take four or five years. The other states where executions were in progress were several years ahead. But apparently the appeals were now speeding up. The Legislature and the Governor were considering cutting off some avenues of judicial review. The courts were hurrying along the cases. The United States Supreme Court had lost patience, and the other federal courts were falling into line.

Tommy sat next to the registered nurse, a heavy, sullen black woman. Motionless behind the small, student desk in the education wing, she seemed to pay no attention to what the Supervisor was saying. She smoked throughout the meeting and flicked the ashes on the floor at Tommy's feet. Tommy found himself becoming annoyed at the casual way she threw down the cigarette butts next to his feet. After the meeting, he stopped her in the corridor under the pretext of asking something about her job. With her big breasts and square blue-black face, the nurse was not the type of woman Tommy would ordinarily have found attractive. But he pressed his body up against her in the empty prison corridor, looking around furtively to make sure no office doors were open and no legs appeared down the hall.

The nurse looked up at him with large dark eyes, first surprised, then with hatred. She rubbed herself against him painfully and then turned and sauntered away down the corridor, showing him her thick back and broad behind. Tommy didn't even know her name, but he remained in a state of excitement all day. When he came home he shouted at Arlette, even though she had gotten out of bed especially to prepare him a favorite dinner: pork chops, fresh corn, and sliced beefsteak tomatoes interlocked with rings of red Bermuda onion. She had even cooked Tommy a lemon meringue pie. Today was an active day for her.

Tommy forgot what it was like to be unemployed, not to have anywhere to go in the morning. The rhythm of work made the weeks fly. Tommy liked coming to work, and he no longer thought about Alaska. He didn't even miss his old friend Ants anymore. Preparations for the rehearsal had begun. The Health Care Supervisor wanted to do a dry run of the procedures. Not that anything was imminent. But just to be prepared. To make sure all the personnel were in place and everyone knew what to do. Mostly, it was waiting. Waiting for someone else to make a decision. Waiting for the last turn-down from the last court. Waiting for the phone call from the Governor which would not come, waiting for the condemned to be wheeled in, waiting for the signal to give the injection. The whole process was nothing more than one big wait. Tommy was being paid thousands of dollars to wait to do an act which would take a few seconds, at most. Killing took so little time, especially in comparison to saving life. It was a lot easier. The pages of regulations, the special staff with their functions described in high-flying, obfuscating language, the supposedly elaborate equipment and the specially designated facilities were a bureaucratic smoke screen. What was to be done was really very simple. It was the pretense that it was something other than simple which was complicated and hard to understand. Why bother? Why not just say what it was?

As if the institution wasn't in enough of a tizzy, the sentencing of Enrico Ruiz, the Hispanic who raped and murdered two teenagers, was causing additional confusion. The Department of Prisons said they couldn't put him on death row because a regulation said that a person under twenty-one could not be confined with adult inmates. But another regulation required all persons sentenced to death to be confined together in that special section of the prison set aside for them. The others sentenced to death were necessarily adults, weren't they? There were rumors that the legislature was about to declare that they never intended to sentence juveniles to death anyhow. It was an oversight on their part not to spell that out earlier. The Department temporarily held Ruiz in an isolated wing of a juvenile detention center while waiting for the judicial authorities to solve this conundrum. Another trouble was brewing over the woman who set her house on fire and killed her children. She was sentenced to death.

New problems had arisen with Benjamin who continued to assert that he wished to die and meet his God. Benjamin now said that although he would willingly go first, he would refuse the sedative which was required prior to administration of the lethal injection. He preferred, he said, to face final judgment with his senses fully alert. It would be a joyous moment. Besides, he said in a letter typed by Darby and smuggled out to the local newspaper, since the lethal injection itself was not painful, what was the reason for the sedative? Benjamin, who had been labeled as mildly retarded at sentencing, suddenly made a lot of sense. Maybe the uncanny Spiritual Advisor with the fez was really drafting the letters or dictating to Darby.

Darby championed Benjamin's constitutional right to stop all legal action on his behalf. "He ought to be able to sign himself out of here," Darby said in his colorful way. "Save the State the cost of the appeals and make room for someone else." Since the death house was filled almost to capacity, some other part of the building would have to be remodeled at considerable expense unless someone went out feet first. "Besides," Darby quipped, "people ought to be able to free themselves from the lawyers at death's door, if nowhere else." It was hard to argue with that.

Benjamin's face had become beatific. His behavior was also beyond reproach, by any human standard. He was always gentle and gracious, even to the guards who sometimes taunted him and whispered blasphemous words as they walked by his cell. For the first time in his life, he seemed happy. It was as if he had found what he was born for. When the reporters interviewed his mother, she cried and cried. At first the TV people were fascinated by this uninhibited display of grief. Or frustration. Or bewilderment. Or confusion. But they soon became bored with her tears, whatever their source, and with her repeated, trembling assurances that it was all in the hands of the Lord, although she and her son believed in widely disparate gods. Once more the legislators, both those for and against the death penalty, were the object of media attention. After all, it was August and hot and most of the people in the state who ordinarily made the news were on holiday in places where it was cool and there were no telephones.

The politicians had a lot to say about who deserved to die. They were the only ones who knew the answers. The Superintendent and the cops seemed humble and humanitarian by comparison. There was a temporary lull in the death penalty news when a judge was indicted for bribery. The circumstances, the judge claimed he simply found five thousand dollars in cash in his top desk drawer after going to the men's room, briefly captured the public's imagination. The judge insisted upon giving long interviews and saying that he had done no wrong. He had no idea where the money, all in hundred dollar bills, had come from. "I know my rights," the judge said loudly looking straight into the camera. "There's a frame-up. I'll fight this all the way to the Supreme Court." His defense attorney could do little but point out that the judge certainly ought to know his rights. A small band on the State House steps, there were more reporters than members of the public, clapped with enthusiasm when the judge appeared after his arraignment. He was released without bond.

At last when he and Gloria had returned from vacation, George had gone back to work. Or it seemed he had gone back to work. The bank as an act of charity assigned him an inside job where he was required to do nothing but sit in the basement and watch a flickering row of television monitors. He just had to sit in front of the gray screens all day. But even though the task was simple, or really no task at all, George often seemed confused. He claimed he couldn't watch all twelve screens at once, although they showed only four or five different locations within the bank. He had difficulty recognizing individual faces on the blurry black and white screen. He couldn't tell the authorized employees from intruders. Several times he set off the alarm system unadvisedly, calling in the security people to apprehend a clerk, or a vault custodian, who was walking quickly and appeared to George to be making a getaway. Twice he called security on the same young black trainee who, George claimed, was skulking out of the basement with his coat on, when the employee was just going home. Gloria told Tommy she was afraid he'd never be himself again.

Gloria now focused all of her attention on the arrival of the baby. She called Tommy at his office to ask if she could pick up something for dinner for them. She often dropped by in the evening with a magazine for Arlette to make the time go quicker, or Gloria would shampoo and curl her hair. Then the two women would sit on Tommy's bed and Arlette would paint Gloria's toes.

Now Tommy could honestly say he was too busy to talk to his mother when she called him at the office. He stomped his feet under the desk and told Gloria that he could hear his boss coming and he had to hang up. Once Gloria called when the nurse was in the office and Tommy had locked the door. They were drinking some rum Tommy brought in. "Who's that with you?" Gloria asked, when she heard the woman's low laugh. "Who are you talking to?"

Tommy said that it was probably better if she didn't call him anymore at the office. "I'll see you Sunday, Ma," he said. "Did you play my number today?" Certainly Gloria was the only person who ever asked what he did at work.

Tommy rarely saw Anthony who had moved into an apartment with Julia, over the hysterical objections of her father. Ants was planning to go get a job, even it was only at minimum wage, in the town where Julia was going to college. Anthony still worked three days a week at the Polish butcher shop, but neither his father nor his uncle spoke to him. They paid him his wages in cash without a word. The only person who would talk to him at the family butcher shop was Ginny, his seventeen-year-old cousin who worked with him behind the counter three days a week. She was more in love with him than ever since he let his hair grow and started riding around on the motorcycle.

Ants asked Tommy for tips on how to find a job in a new city. Tommy had to laugh. "Remember me?" he felt like saying, "I was unemployed for six months." But instead, he told Ants, "Just keep showing up at the unemployment office. In a college town, there will be work."

Anthony nodded grimly and asked Tommy if he could come and stay for a few days while Julia went home to get her clothes ready for college. He also asked if he could take Tommy's only dark suit.

Johnson had resumed his hunger strike. A ruling came down to force-feed him. Now a law suit was started challenging the legality of the forced feeding. He had to recover his strength. Since he wasn't now under a sentence of death, no one had much interest in whether he wanted to live or die. Johnson himself was characteristically philosophical about the new ruling. He believed he would be sentenced to death again, at some other legal proceeding, even though the imposition of the life sentence could not be appealed. He said he wouldn't resist the forced feeding, even though he knew the process was painful, torturous even. He was quoted as saying that he was sure the State would soon see the error of its ways and stop feeding him and keeping him alive against his will.

The Spiritual Advisor said he was going to pray for the Supreme Court to be enlightened by the Divine Spirit and lift the order. One of Johnson's advisers thought his direct appeal should be reinstated because his repentance and change of heart were matters relevant to sentence. He was a different person now. The jury which sentenced him to death should be reconvened so that it could now consider sparing the life of the man he now was.

Darby got the paper to print what he would like for his last meal. He sensed that the hunger strike was losing interest. He wanted to test the kitchen. Steak, it would be un-American not to order steak, fried onions, mushrooms, Belgian endive salad and rum raisin ice cream. The Attorney General would have to issue a special interpretation of the regulations for the Belgian endive and the rum raisin ice cream. The endive had to be brought from a specialty food store in Manhattan, and the rum raisin violated the provision against alcohol.

An outraged mother wrote saying that she didn't see why the taxpayers paid for T-bone steaks and fancy ice cream for condemned murderers when hungry school children were only served canned beans and catsup as a vegetable. She didn't know or care what Belgian endive was, but she guessed it cost a mite more than the one tablespoon, or rather a little plastic package, of ordinary Hunt's tomato catsup which was what her son was given to eat as a vegetable in his lunch at school, courtesy of the State. A religiously oriented citizen replied by asking in the Letters column if the outraged mother had forgotten the quality of mercy. He hoped that she and her children would live long and be able to afford steak, and perhaps she would have the privilege one day of tasting Belgian endive, a pale white and green vegetable similar to lettuce but with a more delicate flavor. The writer of the letter applauded Darby's choice. Had she forgotten the prisoner would probably never eat again.

Tommy had given up on trying to keep straight all of the legal maneuvering. The death penalty kept the lawyers busier than a hundred bankruptcies. The government paid and paid, and that meant the taxpayers paid for it all. All the shenanigans and hours and hours of court time and enough printed paper to slay a forest and fill up several libraries.

Tommy was waiting now. Perhaps there would be a stay, perhaps there would be further appeals. There might be some as yet unheard of challenge to the process. But sooner or later the operation would go ahead. Whether it was Johnson, or Darby, or Enrico, or someone who hadn't yet been sentenced. Too many preparations had been made. Too many people were waiting for it to happen. Too many people had thought they had thought it through and made commitments on paper. The equipment and personnel were all in place.

The Operational Staff had gone through several complete rehearsals, laughing a little about the fact that they wouldn't be laughing if this was the real thing. Picking up the special phone and listening to it buzz, for the first time Tommy saw his two counterparts. They greeted one another matter of factly behind the curtain without exchanging names. One was the older man Tommy had seen in the corridor when, it seemed like years ago, he came for his first interview. The third was a small Spanish fellow Tommy's age whose face was mapped with purple burn scars.

The three of them sat in a row on stools behind the curtain, which turned out to be a plain brown muslin curtain, not a plastic one. When they saw the Health Care Supervisor raise his hand, they simultaneously pressed the three little handles which released clear fluid into three identical lines. This time the liquid in the lines spilled out of a plastic bottle on the flat, empty gurney covered by a blank white sheet. It was as if the machinery had had an embarrassing accident on the bed linen.

The doctor, the registered nurse and the certified IV technician watched the fluid flow and checked to see that all three lines were going. Everyone was quiet. Everyone was deliberate. No one caught anyone else's eye. The eight chairs for the radio, television and newspaper people were empty, but in place, as were the chairs for the public witnesses. Even though it was just a rehearsal. Tommy found going through the procedures was a relief. They had spent so much time talking about it, to do it was easier. It wasn't hard at all. Everything was clear; even though nothing made any sense. At each stage someone told Tommy what he was supposed to do. He hoped his tube would be the one to carry the lethal injection, whether it was Darby, or Benjamin, or someone who he hadn't met yet. It was just like giving an anesthetic, wasn't it? He had no questions left.